RIVAL CÆSARS

A Romance of
Ambition, Love, and War

The warp and the woof—they are woven by me,
But the shadows and coloring rest, mortal with thee—
'Tis thine to cast o'er them, the glory or gloom—
The sunlight of morning or hues of the tomb.[1]

Two things greater
Than all things are,
And the first is love,
And the second is war.[2]

---

1   Mary Gardiner "The Dying Year" *The Knickerbocker* (January 1845) Vol.XXV No.1.
2   Rudyard Kipling "The Ballad of the King's Jest" *Macmillan's Magazine* (February 1890).

Illustration from the original edition, signed by Walter J. Enright (1879–1969). A Chicago native, he attended the Chicago Art Institute. Enright became a professional cartoonist in New York City, where his work was published in the *New York American* and the *New York World*. He illustrated a number of books and was published in *The Century Magazine, Redbook, Collier's, Scribner, McClure's,* and *Life.*

RAGNAR REDBEARD

Rival Caesars

*A Romance of
Ambition, Love, and War*
by
Arthur Desmond & Will H. Dilg
writing as
DESMOND DILG

Preface and annotations by
KEVIN I. SLAUGHTER

Introduction by
DARRELL W. CONDER

UNDERWORLD AMUSEMENTS
Baltimore

"Publisher's Preface" and annotations ©2020 Kevin I. Slaughter.
"This Is Book II" ©2007 Darrell W. Conder.
Title lettering by Paul Slagle. www.PaulSlagle.com
Managing editor, design/typesetting by Kevin I. Slaughter.
Copyediting by Daniel Acheampong.
Special thanks to Trevor Blake, Chip Smith, Justin Thomas
and Mark A. Sullivan (LXX).

Paperback ISBN: 978-1-943687-21-3
REV:X·X·MMXX

More information on Ragnar Redbeard at the Union of Egoists project.
www.UnionOfEgoists.com

Thanks to Sidney E. Parker, the first modern Redbeard scholar.
www.SidParker.com

Published by Underworld Amusements.
www.UnderworldAmusements.com

Dedicated to the memory of the late Perry A. Hull[1] of Chicago

A man of valiant and limitless ambitions, cut down in the heyday of a brilliant and successful career; a man in whom the hereditary joy of struggle was instinctively strong, who daily delighted in returning blow for blow; one to whom the godlike pleasures of victory were as the breath of life; a "man among men" who was at all times a terror to his enemies and whose Homeric fidelity to friends and associates was as effective and unswerving as it was romantic and royal.

—THE AUTHOR.

---

1   Perry A. Hull (1850–1902) was born in Ohio and became a prominent trial attorney in Chicago after moving there in 1871. He was appointed the Master in Chancery for the Circuit Court of Cook County and was a member of the Republican Cook County Central Committee. He founded the Chicago-Texas Oil Syndicate and died on a business trip in Beaumont, TX.

CONTENTS

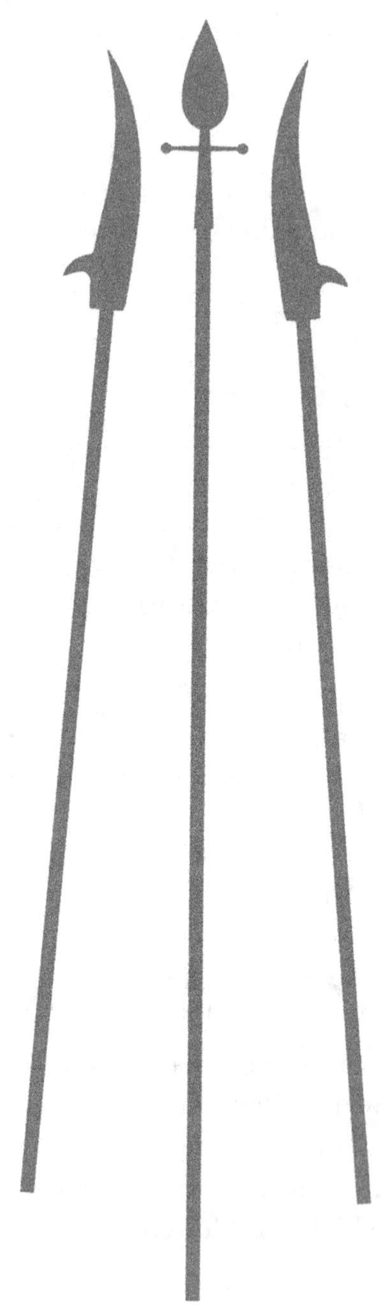

PUBLISHER'S PREFACE
Kevin I. Slaughter

I had no intention of writing anything other than back-cover copy for this release. Things changed, however, during the editing process, when I made a connection *definitively* linking *this* book—*Rival Cæsars*, officially attributed to "Desmond Dilg"— to Arthur Desmond.

If you are reading these words, you are probably already aware that Arthur Desmond wrote under the name "Ragnar Redbeard" (among other pseudonyms), most famously in penning the perennially controversial underground classic *Might is Right*. In the introductory text that follows this eleventh-hour publisher's preface, Darrell Conder provides compelling anecdotal evidence that Arthur Desmond's hand also lies behind the authorial voice of Desmond Dilg, but my subsequent discovery, as you'll see, ups the ante. By any reasonable account, I think it cinches it.

I suppose I might have simply appended Conder's introduction with a notation or postscript alerting readers to the dispositive evidence I am now teasing, but that seemed inappropriate somehow, especially considering that I've lost contact with the guy. So I am presenting it here—in due course. First, I thought I may as well pad out these opening festivities with a few words concerning the enduring legacy of the present volume's *infamous* author (he did have a co-author, who also wrote a fishing book), some remarks on the first man to rediscover said author's identity, and, finally, a bit of information about the aforementioned author of our introduction.

One thing that needs to be understood is that it has always been public knowledge in Australia and New Zealand that Arthur Desmond was Ragnar Redbeard. The two names were mentioned one after the other in newspapers reprinting Redbeard's bombastic poetry, and the connection was unambiguous in the published recollections of Desmond's erstwhile revolutionary comrades. It has been mentioned in articles ranging from the 1920s to the present day without interruption. His move to America and intentional obfuscation of his identity using numerous new pseudonyms assured this knowledge would be lost to the world outside of trans-Tasman scholarship. With such poor international communication on the history of this radical, the Desmond-Redbeard conjunction gave way to an elusive authorship mystery that would hold for roughly half a century and would be doggedly kept obscure for decades more, even against the best intentions of the few researchers who discovered the link. It's a curious situation, I know, but there you have it.[1]

I started working towards a new edition of *Might is Right* many years ago and, for a long time, struggled to find a way to make the work *distinct* from the growing number of editions that varied greatly in both quality and textual fidelity. The project floundered because I refused to release a book that didn't significantly improve upon what had been published before. It was only when I began collaborating with author and archivist Trevor Blake that a solution came into focus. In short, we decided to tear the book apart, every edition of it, and then *reassemble* it with a

---

1   The third volume in the Underworld Amusements series of Redbeard books will feature some of the "lost evidence" in the introduction, along with a great deal of "lost work" by the "revolutionary poet."

plethora of annotations. This labor-intensive task would then be supplemented with the most comprehensive Ragnar Redbeard bibliography ever compiled and, for the first time, appended with an exhaustive index. Substantive work on a version of the book thus conceived began in 2015. The resulting block of deadwood, titled *Might is Right: The Authoritative Edition* (hereinafter *AMiR*), was finally published on Walpurgisnacht of 2019.

Of course, my initial encounter with the text of *Might is Right* came many years before I would entertain—and then realize—the notion of publishing a premium edition. I cut my teeth on the 1983 Loompanics Unlimited edition, edited by Mike Hoy and L.A. Rollins. That respectably produced book featured an introduction by British egoist Sidney E. Parker (and, incidentally, came out the same year Rebel Press put out their edition of Max Stirner's *The Ego and Its Own*, also with an introduction by Parker). Parker's introductory essay, "Ragnar Redbeard and the Right of Might," was originally published in Mark A. Sullivan's New York-based individualist-anarchist (and gay-liberationist) journal *The Storm*, which ran from 1973 to 1988. It's fascinating to revisit now because Parker was *just shy* of definitively being able to say that Arthur Desmond was Ragnar Redbeard. It wasn't until some time after the publication of his widely read essay that Parker, delving more deeply, would emerge with incontrovertible proof that Desmond was indeed Redbeard. Unfortunately, his subsequent findings were buried in a letter to the editor that ran in a single issue of *The Storm* and went largely unnoticed.

During the years of production of *AMiR*, Trevor and I were in regular contact with Darrell W. Conder, the man who edited the first and only other scholarly edition of *Might is Right*.[1] Conder is an interesting character. He grew up in and was eventually employed by a Christian sect known as the Worldwide Church of God. In 1995, he wrote a book entitled *Mystery Babylon the Great: The Mother of Harlots and Abominations of the Earth*.

---

1   Darrell W. Conder, *Might is Right or Survival of the Fitest* (Springfield: Dil Pickle Press 2005).

While that book was apparently well received among the narrow audience of Conder's church brethren, he would be excommunicated after writing a follow-up book called *Mystery Babylon and the Lost Ten Tribes in the End Time* the following year. By Conder's account, his second book was deemed too heretical for the obscure Christian sect he was involved in (he recalls being branded a "modern-day anti-Christ" by his fellow religionists).

Conder grew to revel in his new role as a Church of God apostate, eventually becoming more disillusioned with Christianity and religion in general. He identified as an agnostic when he discovered Redbeard's infamous tome and seemingly became a convert to a religion of *Might is Right*. It was in his 2006 edition of *Might is Right* that he almost gave the impression that Arthur Desmond may *not* have been Ragnar Redbeard after all. As with Sidney Parker before, subsequent research led Conder to discover incontrovertible proof that Desmond was Redbeard, but his revised findings were again consigned to obscurity, in this case being published in a PDF file only available on CD by mail order.[1] Hardly anyone would see it. It was during the production of *AMiR* that Conder granted us permission to publish material from his important but absurdly obscure biographical research. Not long after that, we lost touch with him. I hope he is doing well and that the lapse in communication will be resolved in time.

In any event, I am pleased to finally make Conder's relevant research widely available in this new edition of *Rival Cæsars*. More fortuitously, I am now able to use some of his other unpublished work—along with my own research—to uncover a cipher with reference to the remaining authorial mystery. If we are now convinced by irrefutable evidence that Arthur Desmond was Ragnar Redbeard, can we likewise move beyond speculation to prove the claim that Arthur Desmond was also, at least in part, Desmond Dilg?

The first proof is not as strong as the second I will present,

---

1 Darrell W. Conder, *I Beheld Desmond as Lightning Fall - to Chicago!* (Port Townsend: eLudic Domain, 2007).

but it is more evidence on the scale. I will begin by noting that the opening quote in Chapter X of *Rival Cæsars* can be found in *The Lays of Ancient Rome* by Thomas Babington Macaulay; this book was also quoted in *Might is Right* (see *AMiR* 4.3:10).

With this in mind, I will now point the curious reader to relevant passages, the significance of which will be explained. The first point of interest comes up in Chapter III, where a magical incantation in an unknown tongue is evoked: "Tuhituhi tene tehemana Ko Na-r Thur ar." The second is in Chapter IV, where it is revealed that "Konar Thurar" was known as the "recorder" and was the first scribe of the secret cult, responsible for having written down the secrets and ceremonies some 800 years prior to the events of the story.

Okay, I realize that few readers will be in a position to discern how such otherwise baffling bits of fantasy might bear on the question of authorship, so let me walk you through it. The first line is a phrase in the Māori language of *te reo*. It turns out that in 1885, a decade before *Rival Cæsars* was published, Desmond had written, in longhand, an entire manifesto in this language. This manifesto included, *inter alia*, translated portions of Henry George's work *Progress and Poverty*.

If we begin with the reasonable conjecture that Desmond was probably singular among Chicago writers of the time in being able to write in a language that was (and remains) exotic in the United States, the proof I've been teasing will now be revealed. In *te reo*, this type of invocation is known as a *karakia*, and the poetic and magical nature of this kind of ceremonial incantation means that literal translations aren't always possible. After consulting multiple Māori translators, the best understanding is that phrase is a sort of pidgin *te reo,* with the third word, "tehemana," being a transliteration of an English word. As for "Ko Na-r Thur ar," or "Konar Thurar," a slightly decoded variation of the name would read as "Arthur Konar."

When translated in context, one could read the incantation as

"AS WRITTEN BY ARTHUR KONAR DESMOND."

The likelihood that someone other than Arthur Desmond would write in *te reo* and very slightly scramble his real name is, I submit, infinitesimal. It makes no sense otherwise!

From what little information is to be found, it appears that Arthur Desmond sold *Rival Cæsars* almost exclusively through his Thurland & Thurland book concern. It seems, however, that some quantity made it across the pond to John Basil Barnhill, the Illinois native who was the editor of the early British egoist/Nietzschean journal *The Eagle and The Serpent (1898-1902)*. Barnhill was using the pseudonym John Erwin McCall. The British Library has noted that in their copy, "a slip bearing the imprint of 'J. E. McCall, London' is pasted on the titlepage."

Rival Cæsars has remained incredibly rare and elusive since it was first published. When I started working on this new edition, it had been out of print since its original publication in 1903. I resolved that it would be released as part of a series of Redbeard books comprising a complete collection of known and heretofore unknown writings by Desmond. If any doubts remained as to the book's authorship, I am confident these can now be laid to rest.

THIS IS BOOK II
Darrell W. Conder

When Arthur Desmond, a.k.a. Ragnar Redbeard, finished writing his infamous book *Survival of the Fittest* in 1896, he ended it with the words "END OF BOOK I," to which a postscript was added: "P.S. Book II will be issued when circumstances demand it." In 1903, when Desmond reprinted his book under the revised title of *Might is Right*, that postscript was included, as it was in all "Redbeard"-era printings.

Since no "Book II" appeared in Desmond's lifetime, it is generally thought that he never wrote a sequel to *Might is Right*. However, on October 11, 1902, Arthur Desmond sent a lengthy book to the U.S. Copyright Office with the equally lengthy title of *Rival Cæsars: A Romance of Ambition, Love, and War. Being the Tale of a Vice-President, a Major General, and Three Brilliant and Beautiful Women*, which he co-wrote with famed Chicagoan Will H. Dilg under the pseudonym of Desmond Dilg.

In 1903, *Rival Cæsars* was released to the public through Desmond's own Thurland & Thurland Printers and Publishers of Chicago, Richard Thurland being the name by which Arthur Desmond was then concealing his identity.[1]

Although it is written as a novel, *Rival Cæsars* is unique for several reasons. First is Desmond's fabulous claim that the book was composed from an unknown stash of private letters, deeds, personal memoranda, half-written memories, copies of secret

---

[1] Darrell W. Conder, *I Beheld Desmond as Lightning Fall - to Chicago!* (Port Townsend: eLudic Domain, 2007).

political negotiations, old love letters, etc., discovered "among
the secret archives of a plundered monastery on the island of
Cuba." However, Arthur Desmond's dubious claims and ques-
tionable methods of notoriety are not the focus of this introduction. The real question centers on the relationship of *Rival
Cæsars* to Desmond's revolutionary book *Might is Right*.

When *Rival Cæsars* is read as a companion to *Might is Right*,
the astute Ragnar Redbeard fan will immediately notice what
the casual reader will not: *Rival Cæsars* was not just another
printer's pulp-mill byproduct. Indeed, this point is made crystal
clear in Desmond's introduction:

> The views and opinions of the great mass of living men
> (and women) are still bubbling over with illusion and
> conventional fallacy. They delight to steep their souls
> in parroted fables and accept the fashionable historians
> as unimpeachable messengers from Heaven. The fact
> that "History is a series of lies agreed upon" (which was
> Napoleon Bonaparte's mature opinion) never seems to
> even dawn upon them.
>
> Thus, romances have ever been written, and shall
> continue to be written, to relate the true things that no-
> body believes.
>
> **Therefore, the readers of this book are expected to
> think between the lines. Nay, they are commanded so
> to do.**[1]
>
> Let them also remember that if the whole truth relat-
> ing to any great man could be published, the tale would
> be counted as incredible, abnormal, fabulous.
>
> For even as the light of the sun exceedeth that of the
> moon, so doth the wonders of solid fact exceed by far
> those of mere invention.

Keeping in mind the blatant revolutionary message of *Might
is Right*, Desmond's demand that readers glean a message from

---

1   Emphasis added.

                                    RIVAL CÆSARS

"between the lines" of *Rival Cæsars* reveals a book with a hidden agenda. Even more telling is Desmond's invitation, printed on the overleaf of the title page, for readers "to correspond with the author." To spell it out for those less familiar with Ragnar Redbeard and his radical philosophies, both *Might is Right* and *Rival Cæsars* are serious works intent on sending a message to Desmond's reading public—or, more to the point, a message to "men of iron" with the ambition to go forth and capture their share of wealth and fame.

Going back to his days as an agitator on the streets of Sydney to his flight to Chicago and beyond, those who have done their homework and truly understand "Ragnar Redbeard" will see that *Rival Cæsars is* "Book II" of *Might is Right*.

Whereas *Might is Right* had been written to spark "all real men" into action and revolt, *Rival Cæsars* was the not-too-subtly-disguised battle plan. It was Arthur Desmond's call to arms.

With the details of Desmond's life carefully scrutinized, it becomes obvious that *Might is Right* was an awakening call and that *Rival Cæsars* was his plan of action for those who could read between the lines. The latter book was nothing short of Arthur Desmond's call to any stout-hearted American to rally behind an American Cæsar to claim their share of riches, glory, and fame in the vein of Cæsar, Napoleon, and Cecil Rhodes!

For those not well versed in Arthur Desmond's past activities, these observations may sound a bit overboard. It doesn't take much digging into Arthur Desmond's past to see where he could have come up with the idea of writing a "novel" as an advertising ploy to garner support for a cause; Desmond's friend William Lane had used the same tactic when he was drumming up support for his "New Australia" colony. Lane generated both the necessary funding and the commitment of some five hundred "colonists" through the publication of his novel *The Working Man's Paradise*. The book had been a

resounding success for William Lane's plan, and an obser-
vant Arthur Desmond, standing on the sidelines and watching Lane and his disciples sail off for South America, surely
paid heed! A similar effort was undertaken by another of
Desmond's friends, Samuel A. Rosa, who produced a somewhat successful book about open revolution, which Desmond
advertised in his last Australian journal, *The Standard Bearer/
Hard Kash*:

> We have received from S.A. Rosa (a prominent Sydney
> orator of striking natural ability) a copy of his latest
> literary work, *The Coming Terror*. It is a political ro-
> mance, graphically written. The plot of the story is
> laid in Sydney, and the leading idea is that of a popular
> hero who becomes Dictator and uses Law and Order
> to smash up the great robber rings. The first chapter
> opens with a dramatic and terrible scene—a raging,
> blood-drunken mob looting the Great Austria Bank.
> The crowd fight each other for the gold—the gold that
> had been made out of their slavery and starvation. The
> book ought to be read, especially by all interested in
> bringing about a social renaissance. S.A. Rosa is a man
> whose ability is not appreciated at its proper value, but
> his time will come."[1]

Let us recall the information imparted by Arthur Desmond's
Australian friend John Arthur Andrews[2] about someone who
was surely Desmond and his disappointment at not leading a
revolution in the streets of Sydney:

> One man, who was more inclined to view an insur-
> rection as desirable than as a last resort, was sadly
> disappointed. It appeared that he had ruined himself

---

[1]   *The Standard Bearer*, "Hard Kash", Chap. III, December 17, 1893, p. 1.
[2]   John Arthur Andrews (1865–1903), Sydney anarchist, published a series of
retrospective articles about the Active Service Brigade in *Tocsin* during May 1900. This is
excerpted from May 17, 1900, Number IV, "The Verge of Revolution—1890–1894."

financially to place an armed force ready for action. Later on, about the time when the Active Service Brigade was commencing its operations, the same man thought that in the excitement thus being occasioned, it would be easy to start a revolution, and so it would have been. He laid a plan before me, by which some hundreds of thousands of pounds could have been undoubtedly secured for the "sinews of war," but I advised decidedly against it. Had I known as much about the circumstances as I knew later on, I could not honestly have said that the scheme was likely to fail; however, I doubted some parts of it at that time, and he attached some weight to my opinion. Personally, I did not want to see even a successful revolt if it could be done without, as I was convinced that the only result would be to place power in the hands of designing demagogues, who would be worse enemies to liberty than the capitalists or the Dibbs government, but that was not the point just then. A few months afterwards, he quitted Australia in disgust and, according to one report, went to South Africa to enlist under Cecil Rhodes, who was then intent on founding a new republic.

The subject of *Rival Cæsars* centers on the story of Vice President of the United States Aaron Burr and Secretary of the Treasury Alexander Hamilton and the circumstances leading up to their famous 1804 duel, in which Hamilton was killed. The Burr-Hamilton duel is significant.

Those who know both *Might is Right*'s message and their history will understand why Desmond selected the story of Hamilton and Burr for *Rival Cæsars*. First, Desmond was writing for an American audience, hence the need for a significant American tale. Second, Desmond had an agenda, hence the need for a hero with the kind of self-serving courage called for in *Might is Right*. Most important, Desmond needed an American hero who had achieved both fame and fortune with revolutionary heroics. For this role, there was no better example than Aaron Burr, who actually led an armed insurrection against the United States government. Even though the venture failed, with Burr being put on trial for high treason by orders of President Thomas Jefferson (under whom Burr had served as vice president), in every way Aaron Burr fitted the hero for "Book II" of *Might is Right*.

Contemporaries described Aaron Burr as a man who had "an ardent love of military glory," with Alexander Hamilton ominously calling him the "Catiline of America," which was a reference to Lucius Sergius Catilina (108 BC–62 BC), known in English as Catiline.

Catiline was the first-century-BC Roman best remembered for the "Catiline conspiracy," which was his attempt to overthrow the Roman Republic, particularly the power of the aristocratic Senate. Besides the slaughter of the Roman Senate, Catiline's plans included burning large sections of Rome. When his conspiracy unraveled, Catiline was denounced by the great Cicero. In turn, Catiline violently responded that he would put out his own fire with the general destruction of everything around him. In the end, Catiline died in battle at the front of his troops.

It is no coincidence that Desmond once called himself "Catiline" when signing a poetic piece he had written calling for the purification of the world by fire, and it was no coincidence that Desmond chose an American "Catiline" for the hero of *Rival Cæsars*:

THE FLAMES OF FREEDOM

In every age and cause and clime,
The mightiest weapon of war and time,
For battling down the lords of crime,
                    Is fire,
                    Fire,
                    Victorious fire.

It shatters armies
With its flashes,
Whelming empires
In thunder crashes.

By fire perished Babylon,
Nineveh, Thebes, and Rome.
Fire burnt down Jerusalem
And flamed Diana's dome,
The glow of blazing Carthage
Lit up the Punic foam,
And fire swept Troy and Sodom
To their everlasting home.
                    Manifest destiny!
                    Must is must—
                    Ashes to ashes,
                    Dust to dust.
Trembling, flickering, leaping higher,
Blood and iron, days of ire,
Wrathful, vengeful, higher, higher,
Beauteous, sun-born, cleansing fire.
                    Belshazzar's hall it made his tomb,
                    It flung Napoleon to his doom.

Verily, verily, verily!
The days of the Judgment is nigh—
O! Goddess of Liberty, hearken!
You are holding your torch too high!
Lower it,
Lower it,
Lower it,
Lower it before I die.
Temples to ashes,
DEBT to dust,
Fire consumeth
Things accursed.

CATILINE
London, 1899

You are requested to make at least five legible copies of this and pass them to good men in different places. Be sure and put upon each one of them this request, and sign no name whatever.[1]

As the above date demonstrates, near the time he was conceiving *Rival Cæsars*, Arthur Desmond contemptuously viewed the old order as hopelessly corrupt and took every opportunity to exhort his readers to bring it down by any means possible—including the ultimate purification by fire. Such examples should tell any thinking person that by the turn of the twentieth century, everything in Desmond's life was geared towards promoting himself at the head of a new world order, since he saw himself superior to the herds laboring around him. So obvious was Desmond's ambition that those who knew him seemed to either admire the man as a new Cæsar or loathe him as a dangerous revolutionary, which was why one contemporary

---

1   George G. Reeve, writing in the August 6, 1921, issue of *Ross's Monthly*, tells of one of Desmond's poems, which he signed as "Catiline", and notes that "[it] glorified in the use of fire as a force for purification of the world." This author obtained a copy of the poem from the Mitchell Library, Dwyer Papers, which is used in this reproduction.

Chicagoan contemptuously remarked that Arthur Desmond was a man suffering from "delusions of grandeur."[1]

Although he is now often denigrated as a traitor, Vice President Aaron Burr should be judged by the times in which he lived, as with all historic personages.

Within years of the Revolution, America had reverted to a sea of corruption as self-serving politicians made the new republic but a carbon copy of King George III's government, which they had so recently fought to overthrow. Indeed, there is more than ample evidence to support the charge that the Revolutionary War was engineered simply to further enrich the elite families of the Thirteen Colonies, which means that many of the men Americans now hail as heroes of the Republic were, in reality, greedy frauds. But such is the stuff of romanticized "history," no matter who, what, when, or where!

This inconvenient background is why many of the early "Founding Fathers" considered the Constitution "a botched document," and why virtually none thought the American people worthy of their rights as citizens. Alexander Hamilton wrote, "For my part, I am not much attached to the majesty of the multitude. I consider them in general as very ill-qualified to judge for themselves what government will best suit their peculiar situations." Such attitudes explain why, at the slightest provocation, one heard talk of secession in the newly formed American states. In fact, many of the Revolution's greatest minds thought things would disintegrate to the point that only a dictatorship could save the new United States of America, which was the observation of Gouverneur Morris, who went so far as to call for a Cromwell or a Bonaparte to arise.

For Aaron Burr and other "patriots" (such as Hamilton), to consider revolution a practical remedy for seemingly

---

1   Ralph Chaplin, *Wobbly: The Rough-And-Tumble Story of an American Radical* (Chicago: University Of Chicago Press, 1948) p. 316.

irreconcilable political disagreements was quite logical, especially since they had all recently fought and won a treasonous rebellion against their lawful government, i.e., King George III. But to underscore that the leaders of the Revolution were interested only in their own welfare, and not the welfare of the "common man," one need only to turn to the letters and other documents of the time, such as this letter from Harrison Gray Otis of Massachusetts to Alexander Hamilton: "[Aaron] Burr loves nothing but himself, thinks of nothing but his own aggrandizement, and will be content with nothing short of permanent power in his own hands." He wrote to Gouverneur Morris that Burr had "no principle public or private, could be bound by no agreement, will listen to no monitor but his ambition ... He is sanguine enough to hope for everything, daring enough to attempt everything, wicked enough to scruple nothing."[1] (In other words, Aaron Burr was the very embodiment of Redbeard's "might is right" philosophy!)

The extent of Aaron Burr's conspiratorial plans is made plain in this August 6, 1804, letter from British Ambassador to the U.S. Anthony Merry to British Foreign Secretary Dudley Ryder, 1st Earl of Harrowby:

> My Lord, I have just received an offer from Mr. Burr, the actual vice president of the United States...to lend his assistance to His Majesty's Government in any Manner in which they may think fit to employ him, particularly in endeavouring to effect a Separation of the Western Part of the United States from that which lies between the Atlantick [sic] and the Mountains, in its whole Extent....
>
> It is therefore only necessary for me to add that if, after what is generally known of the Profligacy of Mr. Burr's Character, His Majesty's Ministers should think proper to listen to his offer, his present Situation in this Country where he is now cast off as much by the

1   *op.cit.* p. 96.

democratic as by the Federal Party, and where he still preserves Connections with some People of Influence, added to his great Ambition and Spirit of Revenge against the present Administration [Thomas Jefferson], may possibly induce him to exert the Talents and Activity which he possesses with Fidelity to his Employers.[1]

Likely inspired by Napoleon's stunning victories throughout Europe, as were so many others of that time and afterward (including a yet-to-be-born Englishman named Arthur Desmond), Aaron Burr envisioned himself at the head of an American empire, to be achieved by first conquering Texas and then Mexico. Burr knew that the enormous quantities of gold to be had in South America, combined with Mexican ports, would allow him to build a navy that could dominate the Gulf of Mexico and the Caribbean. This kind of a power base would enable Burr to grow powerful enough to eventually challenge the U.S. government itself; potentially, he could become the de facto emperor of the Americas. Such dreams were not beyond those who had the power and daring, as Ragnar Redbeard rightly observed.

There is no need to recount the whole Burr conspiracy, how he planned to rob his foe, President Thomas Jefferson, of his only true presidential achievement—the Louisiana Purchase—and how the whole thing unraveled by the treachery of his "friend" and fellow conspirator—and the commander of the U.S. Army—Brigadier General James Wilkinson; the point is that Aaron Burr was Arthur Desmond's role model, which he made clear in *Rival Cæsars*. But more to the point, Desmond's writings and his subsequent activities clearly indicate a plan in motion, very much along the lines of the Burr conspiracy, with a bit of William Lane's "New Australia" dream thrown in! In other words, Arthur Desmond was publishing a blueprint disguised as a novel, along the lines of William Lane's *The Working Man's Paradise* and Sam Rosa's *The Coming Terror*, to generate support and as a recruiting tool.

1   *op.cit.* p. 352.

What were Arthur Desmond's revolutionary plans? Were they aimed at overthrowing the U.S. government? This author thinks that Desmond was attempting to revive Aaron Burr's plan and had his sights on the invasion and conquest of Mexico to set up a personal empire, much like his contemporary hero Sir Cecil Rhodes had done on the African continent. This is why the last chapter of *Rival Cæsars* is simply composed of an old 1806 song called *The Plains of Mexico.*[1]

Arthur Desmond's preoccupation with the conquest of Mexico stretches back into his Australian adventures, which undoubtedly is why Desmond's friend and former Australian prime minister William "Billy" Hughes "slyly" insinuated that Desmond may have been Mexican president General Victoriano Huerta, who had seized the reins of the Mexican government in 1913, noting that the two men looked a lot alike![2] Hughes knew better of course, but voicing such an observation surely indicates that those who knew Arthur Desmond during his Australian days knew him well enough to have believed rumors that he played some kind of role in the Mexican Revolution. Such rumors opened the door to some wild speculation, such as the suggestion that Ragnar Redbeard was really the famous Ambrose Bierce, the one-time editor of the *Cosmopolitan*, and that he, having traveled down to Mexico to join the infamous Pancho Villa, was stood against a wall and shot during the Madero revolt.[3]

From his revolutionary days in Sydney right through to his last defiant days in Chicago, Arthur Desmond was a consistent foe of "democracies" and weak, spineless men. He spent a large part of his life demanding that "all true men" should take what was rightfully theirs by any means possible. That same career

---

[1]   As noted in the body of the novel, and typical of Desmond, the poem is actually a novel and uncredited reworking of an existing poem titled "The Michigan Emigrant's Song."—KIS

[2]   George G. Reeve, "Ragnar Redbeard," *Ross's Monthly,* August 6, 1921.

[3]   *ibid.*

also reveals a man who saw himself superior to the herds laboring around him, which was the central theme of *Might is Right*. Again, in the pages of *Might is Right*, Desmond carefully and logically sent forth the call for "all true men" to attain conquest, glory, and the spoils of war. It was their nature; it was their right. He specifically targeted Central and South America by reason of "human mongrelism". As an example, he pointed out that a half-breed was then president of Mexico, referring to Porfirio Diaz, who was mostly of Indian descent. The pages of *Might is Right* were nothing short of a call to arms for all real men to throw caution to the wind and conquer such squalid places and, in the process, achieve fabulous wealth and personal glory. In *Rival Cæsars,* the feasibility of conquest was forcibly argued in the "romantic" tale of Aaron Burr, the example being calculated to reassure any interested American that such dreams were not treasonous, which Desmond tops off by demanding that they read between the lines and then by inviting them to correspond with the author.

Certainly, history is clear that Mexico was ripe for the taking during the years Desmond wrote *Might is Right* and *Rival Cæsars*. It would, in fact, fall to the revolutionary Francisco Madero some seven years later, who was then overthrown by Gen. Victoriano Huerta, who was overthrown by Venustiano Carranza, who was overthrown by Adolfo de la Huerta, etc. This means that one must seriously consider that Arthur Desmond might well have succeeded in duplicating the actions of his hero, the international pirate Cecil Rhodes, had he been able to raise the necessary army, supplies, and capital. Obviously, such a plan never got further than the printing presses of Chicago, despite Desmond's personal invitation for readers to correspond with the author.[1] Indeed, Arthur "Ragnar Redbeard" Desmond must have felt more than a tinge of envy and personal defeat as he sat in Chicago and followed the progress of the successful 1910 Mexican Revolution. Such was the fizzle with which the

---

1 This type of invitation was typical of Desmond, who, in most of his publications, had invited readers to personally correspond with him.

grandiose dreams of Ragnar Redbeard ended.

Whether or not anyone actually read and understood between the lines and corresponded with the author is unknown. Probably not, as the surviving evidence in the years after *Rival Cæsars* publication shows that Arthur Desmond continued as one of the teeming mass of Chicagoans sweating out a living in the trades. However, *Rival Cæsars* is important to this study because the book's text provides solid evidence that it was written by the author of *Might is Right.* The writing style and contents of both books are unmistakably Redbeardian. For example, we read Desmond's praise of Oliver Cromwell, Napoleon, and Julius Cæsar in *Rival Cæsars* and find the same in *Might is Right*, we find Desmond's favorable reference to Darwinism in *Rival Cæsars* as in *Might is Right*,[1] and we see the same archaic language (including "Redbeard's" favorite word, "mayhap") scattered about both books. Also, just as important are the poetic verses scattered throughout both books, which was Arthur Desmond's trademark.

So important are the contents and writing style of *Rival Cæsars* to the evidence that Desmond and "Redbeard" were one and the same, and to also back this author's assertion that Desmond was using the book as a recruiting tool for revolution, that we shall here feature a number of excerpts from *Rival Cæsars*, which are usually in the form of conversation between the book's various characters:

> Money is perhaps the mightiest of all weapons in the hands of daring and fearless men. It is, I believe, more regal than kings and parliaments.... I could shake the world if I had money.... the want of money is the root of all evil....

---

1   In the opening pages of *Rival Cæsars* Desmond writes: "Here and there grew widespreading shade trees, upon the lower branches of which the small boy swung by his hands, exactly as his ancestors did, the primordial monkey in the primordial forest."

But what is 'evil'? That is the question.

Listen to your own untrammeled soul and answer: Why should a man deliberately encircle his mind with needless prison walls? No man can reach highest excellence who puts limits to his own thought. Let us be bold in thought, my friend, if we are to be bold in deed.

Eagles are we! ... The freest birds under the sun—and the boldest. The limits of their soaring is as the strength of their pinions...

But the eagles battle with one another in their limitless and lofty flight... That is so... And why should they not? What are their talons for? Is not the world a world of beak and claw?

In the beginning, nature made man a contending animal. Are we not all Greeks and Trojans? We must therefore make up our minds for a life of continual battle. We must fight, I say, morning, noon, and night, if need be, against an entire world.

He who would do great things must avoid women, you know, as much as possible, shunning all that tends to weakness and effeminacy. The love of woman makes man too fearful of consequences....Women have ever been the stumbling block and betrayers of ambition. They sit by the wayside to lure men into ineffectiveness. Woman's love for man is intensely selfish. They want him all to themselves. They tremble with terror if he whom they love dares to risk himself. They want to make sure of him, not so much for his sake but for their own....

Thus [Lord] Chesterfield writes, "Women are children of a larger growth. For solid reasoning or good sense I never knew one that had it. Sensible men must regard them without idolatry."

Weakness is to compromise, to hesitate, to be half-hearted. Are not the great names of ancient and modern times the names of haughty and aggressive personalities who carried their loves and convictions to "extremes," that is to say, to logical and clean-cut conclusions? Mediocrity is safe, no doubt it is, but it is very commonplace and of a drab color. Mediocrity is for men of the secondary, the bloodless type.... "He who would be famous must go forth and risk his hide and hair." ... War, for example, is an "extreme," and yet it is now and ever has been the first fountain of wealth and honor. Not for nothing has the highest need of praise been granted to the successful soldier.

The lamb must ever be food for the lion and the wolf. What else were lambs made for?

As long as there is human rivalry and love, there must be war. Indeed, so long as two men desire the same territory or the same woman, there must be bloodshed and hatred, jealousy, and war.

Good or bad, I propose to be something great. I was never born to be a camp follower. The world as yet needs its conquerors, and I will be one of them. Ah, how grand to be absolute master and lord it over millions.

Perhaps you have a rival who would kill you for jealousy.

Nevertheless, take heart and be bold. What is to be will be. If the open grave is there, you can't escape it. You can't evade destiny. Don't be intimidated by a foreboding of future trouble. Be bold, I say, be bold. This is my advice to every man in love. The universe itself bends in homage before him who loves and wars and is strong.

The joy of absolute and unlimited victory, the grandest and most god-like of all joys, swelled up fiercely within him. Lifting the now clean, shiny blade to his lips (his eyes with triumph red), he kissed the naked steel softly, saying, as a clap of thunder burst directly overhead, "Good blade! Mighty overcomer! Trusty friend! I salute thee! Verily thou art my savior, my deliverer, my iron redeemer! Glorious steel, ruler of earth and ocean, thou wast never a backbiter yet! In the hour of need, thou didst not desert me!"

This world is tilting ground for mighty individuals and mighty races of men to strive and triumph, reign and possess—if they can.

Two superb warriors were they, two hurtling egos, two great elemental powers personified, two rival theories of empire. Armed, they stood and calmly gazed into one another's souls at ten paces. How grand, how splendid they looked, those two bold, strong men, weapons in hands, haughty, terrible, world-defiant, appealing to eternal nature's iron code. "Where the white skull-bone of the dead horse lay, two brothers fought at dawn of day; 'neath the cedar tree that swayed above, they strove and bled for power and love."

Upon the shoulders of the living, the coffin of the dead
is slowly, reverently raised and borne into the Holy Hall.
By the altar of the crucified Jew, on the great black catafalque in the center aisle, it rests between two columns...

Sound, sound the trumpet, blow the fife
    To all the listening world proclaim
One crowded hour of glorious strife
    Is worth an age without a name.

Even if we didn't have all the other evidence connecting
Arthur Desmond to Ragnar Redbeard, those who have studied
"Redbeardian" philosophy will see in *Rival Cæsars* an unmistak-
able continuation of Desmond's *"Might is Right"* philosophy.

As for the release of *Rival Cæsars*, the only note of the book by
the press is this brief mention in the June 4, 1903, *Chicago Daily
Tribune*:

Dilg's *Rival Cæsars.*

Desmond Dilg of this city has written a romance around
the Burr–Hamilton imbroglio. This has been a favorite
theme with novelists lately, but none of them has treated the matter exactly as has Mr. Dilg. According to him,
both these men and many other prominent characters of
the early days were members of a secret order—the Iron
Cross—and the death of Hamilton was a sentence of
which Burr was really the executor. Many famous men
are brought into the story, which contains many stirring
scenes. While not making out Burr as actual hero, the
tale is by no means favorable to Hamilton, who is painted in dark colors. The book is called *Rival Cæsars*, and it

is published by Thurland & Thurland, Chicago.

There are no surviving printing and sales records for *Rival Cæsars*. However, it seems to have enjoyed some measure of success, essentially being embraced by an unsuspecting reading public as a novel. Because very few copies have survived the 100-plus years since its printing, when an example comes onto the market, it is quickly snapped up regardless of cost. Will H. Dilg went on to bigger and better things after concluding his business venture with Arthur Desmond. In addition to his Izaak Walton League duties, Dilg devoted his spare time to writing fishing stories for various magazines and achieved some infamy when the details of his divorce scandals were widely reported in the *Chicago Daily Tribune* (in 1914 and 1925, Dilg twice divorced the same woman). On March 17, 1927, Will H. Dilg was in Washington, D.C., seeking to "interest President Calvin Coolidge in establishing a department of conservation to carry on the work championed by the Waltonians," when he succumbed to cancer.[1]

There is no evidence that Will H. Dilg and Arthur Desmond continued a business association or even a friendship following the publication of *Rival Cæsars*.

---

[1]   *Chicago Daily Tribune,* March 29, 1927, p. 15: "W. H. DILG, IZAAK WALTON LEAGUE FOUNDER, IS DEAD".

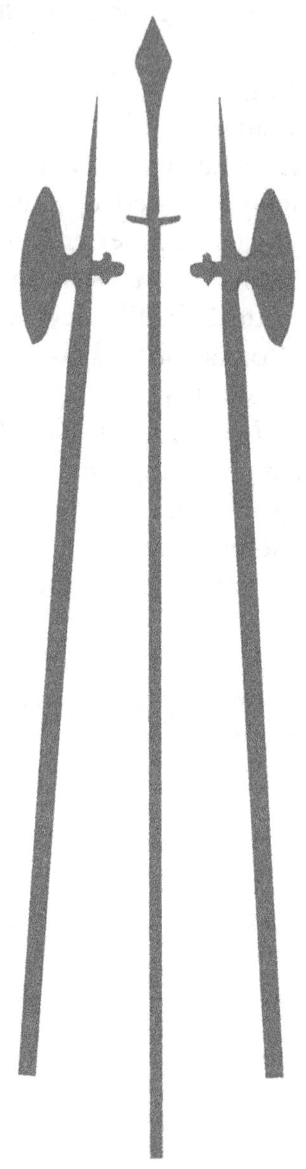

INTRODUCTORY NOTE
Desmond Dilg

From original documents preserved from utter destruction in a very remarkable manner, this book has been written.

The discovery of these documents (withered and tattered and mouldy with age and damp) is in itself a strange and tragic story. Some day, it shall be related.

Sufficient however for the present to say that these papers were found by an American scout among the secreted archives of a plundered monastery on the island of Cuba.

For over two years, the contents of three small boxes (clamped with iron and eaten by ants) containing private letters, deeds, personal memoranda, half-written memoirs, parchments, copies of secret political negotiations, suppressed pamphlets and treaties, love letters, old newspaper cuttings, and books have been placed in the possession of the writer that he might relate, in regular sequence, this true tale of love and jealousy, ambition, intrigue, and war—a tale quite as remarkable and romantic as anything to be found in the classic literatures of ancient or of feudal times.

It is understood, however, that many of the facts and happenings bearing on the actual record of the two principal characters are intentionally veiled or wholly omitted.

Notwithstanding the alleged tolerance of our times, the day has certainly not arrived when famous but unfortunate historical personages can be actually placed upon the stage with all their manifold faults and failings, as well as their idealisms and successful deeds.

The views and opinions of the great mass of living men (and women) are still bubbling over with illusion and conventional fallacy. They delight to steep their souls in parroted fables and accept the fashionable historians as unimpeachable messengers from heaven. The fact that "History is a series of lies agreed upon" (which was Napoleon Bonaparte's mature opinion) never seems to even dawn upon them.

Thus, romances have ever been written, and shall continue to be written, to relate the true things that nobody believes.

Therefore, the readers of this book are expected to think between the lines. Nay, they are commanded so to do.

Let them also remember that if the whole truth relating to any great man could be published, the tale would be counted as incredible, abnormal, fabulous.

For even as the light of the sun exceedeth that of the moon, so doth the wonders of solid fact exceed by far those of mere invention.

Rival Caesars

*A Romance of
Ambition, Love, and War*

Being the Tale of a Vice President,
a Major General, and Three
Brilliant and Beautiful Women

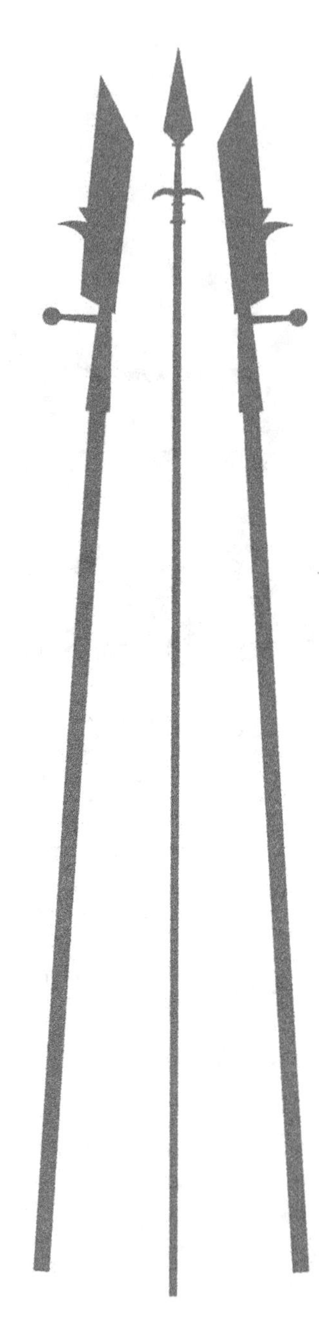

Chapter I

THE BLOOD COMPACT

"An' trust me on my troth
If thou keep faith with me,
My dearest friend, as my own heart,
Right welcome shalt thou be."[1]

'Twas the early morning of a beautiful summer day. Two handsome young men, dressed in the height of fashion and conversing earnestly, walked rapidly into the old town along Broadway.

They were returning from a duel. As if well accustomed to the locality, they turned sharply round a corner and entered Wall Street.

Rapiers hung by their sides with glittering hilts and shining scabbards. Their hair profusely powdered and combed back over prominent brows, hung down behind in the shape of queues over well-fitting, silver-buttoned, velvet coats.

They wore stylish ruffles, slashed scarlet vests, knee breeches, garters, silken hose, and broad silver buckles flashed in the sunlight upon their low red-heeled shoes.

Judging by their dress, general appearance, and distinctly aristocratic deportment, they were men of good family and superior standing. There was an indefinite "something" about them, that undefinable "something" that denotes men intended by birth and nature for the exercise of power and high command. Both were of medium height and seemed "for dignity composed and high exploit."

One bore his arm with care as if it had been hurt. He had dark-grey eyes, a frank, generous, cheerful countenance, an aq-

1   Thomas Percy "Ballad of George Barnwell," *Reliques of Ancient English Poetry Consisting of Old Heroic Ballads, Songs, and Other Pieces, of Our Earlier Poets, Together with Some Few of Later Date, and a Copious Glossary* (Templeman, 1840).

uiline nose, a powerful chin, a high forehead, light-colored hair, and a mouth at once indicative of great eloquence and business capacity. A curious, sphinx-like repose rested upon his features, a repose that seemed as it were to penetrate without effort into the very heart of things. His general manner betokened pride and self-confidence with a strong dash of caution.

The other man was more compactly built and remarkably handsome. His limbs were in perfect proportion, he walked with a gait of unconscious pride, and his cameo-like beauty of feature was very striking. His hands were of extreme delicacy, yet with long, powerful fingers. He had a not-large head with projecting brows, a swarthy sun-tanned complexion, small shell-like ears, dark curly hair, eagle nose, and black, orb-like, Oriental eye yes that seemed, when he talked, to emit sparks.

His look was that of an eagle in its flight: dauntless, graceful, calculating, and remorseless. Decidedly an extraordinary—a very extraordinary—individual.

As these two young men turned the corner, a finely caparisoned family chaise, drawn by two beautiful, small, white stallions and driven by a coal-black slave, trotted jauntily by. In it sat two fashionably attired young ladies, accompanied by a jovial old gentleman. All smiled graciously upon the two pedestrians, who lifted their hats and bowed profoundly in return, with true Chesterfieldian grace of manner, while the old gentleman waved his hand in a courtly old-fashioned style, full of friendliness, as the carriage swept past.

"O, Catherine," whispered the darkest of the two ladies, a lovely damozel of about eighteen, "who is that divinely dark young man with Aleck? He looks just like the magic prince in the last story book that Cousin Clinton sent over from London. I've never seen him before. And doesn't he walk elegantly? Who is he?"

"O, he is a Puritan collegian from Princeton on a visit," answered Catherine. "They say he is a grandson of the great Jonathan Edwards, whom we hear so much about on Sundays. His mother was a celebrated Puritan beauty. I forget his name, but I met him at the Livingstons. Tell you what we'll do: we'll ask Aleck to bring him over next Thursday to Judge Livingston's at Elizabethtown. There is to be a great birthday party, and everybody is invited."

At this, the first fair speaker clapped her hands delightedly, saying, "I'm so pleased. I like him already. He is just charming. I do believe I'll fall in love with him."

At this impetuous outburst, Catherine admonished her, saying, "You ought to be more reserved, Betsy. It is not proper for a young girl to express such open admiration for a man, more especially one she has never seen before."

"You jealous old dear. I believe you're in love with this Sir Puritan yourself."

At this outburst, Catherine blushed crimson, while the old gentleman laughed outright.

In the year 1775, New York was a beautiful little half-Dutch town of 20,000 inhabitants.

It was ruled over (and almost entirely owned) by less than half a dozen colonial families, which included the Livingstons, the Clintons, the Mortises, and the De Lanceys.

The cobblestone streets were crooked and narrow. Here and there grew wide-spreading shade trees, upon the lower branches of which a small boy swung by his hands, exactly as his ancestor did, the primordial monkey in the primordial forest.

The houses were prim and whitewashed, with plain oak doors and brass knockers. Along the streets were rows of empty lots, littered with rubbish, also wide unfenced common lands, green with grass and parklike with trees, upon which cows, horses, sheep, and goats grazed placidly, with jangling bells lashed securely around their necks by thongs of plaited green hide.

There was a row of gloomy old cannons where the Battery now stands. Wooden wharves built on piles, rafted down from Colonel Schuyler's estate, jutted into the harbor. Fastened to these wharves by heavy twisted hawsers were numbers of heavy old-fashioned, square-rigged trading craft with high poops and blue figureheads. Also moored nearby, were tall trans-Atlantic clippers, smellful emigrant ships, fore-and-aft smuggling schooners, coasting brigs, revenue cutters, long, low, heavily armed privateers from the Spanish Main, greasy, wide-ribbed, bulging whalers from Baffin's Bay, heavy warships from Plymouth Hoe, and quick-sailing slavers from the Congo coast.

After passing the Livingston carriage, the two young men turned up a narrow court, above the entrance of which hung a creaking lamp. Climbing a flight of stone steps, the front man knocked at the heavy door in a peculiar way. The janitor, in semi-military uniform, evidently an old soldier, opened it to them. Brushing past him, they walked rapidly up a flight of oaken stairs and entered a large room overlooking the harbor.

At one end of this room was a wide, old-fashioned fireplace. The tables, chairs, shelves, and hooks on the walls were crowded and littered with papers, books, hats, canes, guns, swords, overcoats, and the general bric-a-brac of an 18th century bachelor's apartment. Upon the walls hung pictures of famous battles, famous generals, and famous local beauties.

On the mantel stood a bronze statuette of Cromwell at Naseby, leading his Ironsides against his king, and another of Cæsar crossing the Rubicon to make war upon his government.

Between the legs of Cæsar's horse lay two books: one, the *Holy Bible*; the other, *The Prince* by Niccolo Machiavelli

Upon one end of a large table in the center of the room lay a great heap of law books, and on the other end, a substantial breakfast for two stood ready and inviting.

On entering, each man helped himself to a gobletful of French wine from a sideboard and then proceeded to where a basin of water stood in a small alcove. The taller of the two removed his coat, rolled up the sleeves of his shirt, and began to carefully wash the dry blood from his swollen arm.

His friend assisted him to unwrap the hardened bandage tied tightly below the elbow. When the bandage had been well-saturated with water, it was gradually unwound, exposing a deep, ugly gash from which the blood slowly oozed. After washing the wound, they rubbed it over with some salve and neatly bound it up again with a new linen bandage.

"I regret," spoke the wounded man, that, this affair was not fought with pistols. The bullet is the thing. I challenged him, and, of course, he had the choice of weapons. This placed me at a great disadvantage, as you saw. I am not, like you, a first-class swordsman. My forte is not the rapier but the pistol. With it, I am well-practiced, taking quick aim and firing first. These naval officers are seldom good pistol shots. He had the advantage over me in this affair, but I have the satisfaction at least of having left my brand on him."

"Of course," answered the other "I quite agree with you. I prefer the bullet myself to the sword. It is not that, however, I am concerned about but this. This duel must be kept secret as far as possible. It will not do to have it talked about too much. The public situation is becoming explosive. Serious trouble is brewing between the people and the king, and should either of us get the reputation of being noticeably antagonistic to the king's officers, the fact would do us much present injury. As your second, therefore, I advise hushing the matter up. What do you think?"

"I agree with you," answered the wounded man. "We should not be too precipitate in openly taking sides until we see how things are going to shape. My sympathies are all, as you know, with the colonists, but I have no particular desire to become a mere solitary martyr. I do not wish to run my neck into a halter without some prospect of adequate backing."

Both men then seated themselves at the table and proceeded to eat heartily.

"Now," said the unwounded man, "let us forget the duel for an hour or so while we talk confidentially. I have been waiting long for a convenient opportunity to discuss important business with you. There is no better time than the present. Afterwards, as I go down to the ferry, I can call at the old doctors and send him up to dress your wounded arm."

The wounded man looked at the speaker inquiringly. The latter continued talking while his face lit up with enthusiasm.

"A grander duel than that between individuals is imminent: a civil war, a revolution. This you yourself must already have observed. Revolution must come. It is inevitable. No negotiations can stop it. The cry for independence is ever growing stronger, and both sides have gone too far to now back down. The rapacity of the king and his hidebound ministry is preparing a situation brimful of battle and also of vast possibilities for young men like you and I. How pleasing is it to feel that we may be living in an age of great and heroic doings?

"I believe that fame, honor, and wealth are soon to be won, and won easily, by men who are prepared to stake their lives, who are ready to risk their necks, to advance their fortunes. The tide of popular passion is every hour swelling higher, and we—I say, you and I—must float ourselves into power and position upon its topmost crest. Shall it be said of us in after years that we studied the history of the rise and fall of empires, republics, revolutions, and Cæsars for naught? Shall men say of us that we missed our opportunity?"

"What you say," answered the wounded man, "is almost exactly what I myself have been thinking for a long time. Revolt is in the air. The farmers are becoming desperate, the merchants sullen, the mechanics riotous, and many of the wealthy old Colonial families are ready to join in and back the movement with money.

"I know for a fact that the Schuylers, Livingstons, and Clintons are ready to follow Hancock's and the Adams' example.

"There is also every possibility, and every probability, of European intervention on our behalf. France is burning to revenge the loss of Canada and her western posts. She can effectually aid us because of her fleet. Holland and Spain are also likely to lend assistance indirectly.

"I agree with you that in the impending conflict, fame, power and wealth may be rapidly won by new men possessed of masterful brains and stout hearts. The popular agitators (mostly mere writers and talkers) who have led the discontented multitude successfully up to the present time are men of somewhat inferior standing, though some few of them possess remarkable energy and even genius.

"Talkers and writers are very seldom deed-doers; nevertheless, they have their part to play. They cannot be entirely dispensed with, not as yet anyhow. They are now at a crisis in their agitation. They have stirred up the Great Deep but are wholly incapable of directing popular energy into practical channels.

"These men have scarcely given a thought to the darker and deeper problems of statecraft nor the results that spring automatically, as it were, from triumphant insurrection.

"Now, if the rebellion is left in their hands alone, it must degenerate into a mere war of words and thus become discredited. These fluent agitators, as I said before, are not fighting men, though the instinct towards strife is strong upon them. Let it, therefore, be our business to turn them into warriors, they and their followers. Let us transform their arguments into drawn swords and concrete deeds.

"This is OUR chance, I say. The people want reinforcements from the propertied and educated classes, and you want fame, position, wealth. They require men of a higher type to assist in winning over the landed interests of the South and the great mercantile and trading interests of the seaports.

"You and I have given special study to statesmanship, to law, to finance, and to war. We know how to speak and write. The study of the great classics has cleansed our minds of all the sickly fog and discouraging drivel of modern Gallic philosophy. We have learnt that power and government are still to be controlled as of yore by this."

Here the speaker tapped the hilt of his sword significantly, and continued:

"But neither of us are wealthy, and if we are ever to do anything of value to ourselves or to others, we must get money to operate with. Money is perhaps the mightiest of all weapons in the hands of daring and fearless men. It is, I believe, more regal than kings and parliaments. Now, how do you propose that we shall surmount this difficulty, the matter of preliminary finance? Want of money is what bothers me. I could shake the world if I had money."

"Ah, my friend," interjected the unwounded man, "the want of money is the root of all evil."

Whereupon the other smiled and continued:

"But what is 'evil'? That is the question. Money may be used both for evil and for good. And then a man must secure his own position before he can benefit others.

"Of course, I know, that both of us have a talent for war, and thus, as all things are possible in war, all things are possible to you and me.

"Success in war generally solves the money problem for the

 RIVAL CÆSARS

winner. If successful in war, it is feasible for us to gain not only wealth but power and fame, including the love and admiration of women and the gratitude of our delighted countrymen for ages yet to come. Indeed, if war breaks out, it will do so in the very nick of time for you and me."

"Yes," said the unwounded man. "The bringing about of a new shuffle may end an ill game. Anyhow, war is the only occupation fit for a gentleman."

To which his wounded friend replied, "I agree with you. I scorn the grovelling ambitions of clerks and suburban beings. What is more beautiful than to have one's name live forever, linked with the heroes of all the ages?"

"I don't care much," answered the unwounded young man, toying maliciously with a bundle of his friend's tailor's bills, I.O.Us, and *billet-douxs,* "for the hurrahs of the herd after I am dead. Posthumous fame has no attractions for me, none whatever. What care I for the opinions of posterity? But I do care for success in my own lifetime. After my bones are rotten, what does it matter whether millions of semi-brainless beings curse or bless my memory? It is equally one to me whether they hang my bones in chains, like they did the bones of Cromwell, or build a pyramid of stone over my mouldering coffin.

"Today only do I regard. Today I know. Today is mine. Today I wish to be something. Tomorrow is a supposition, a problem that I am not particularly interested in solving. Let tomorrow fight its own battles."

"Yet you are very ambitious," answered the wounded man. "I never met a man more so. Yours is the Cæsarian temperament. The spirit of ambition within you knows no bounds."

"And why should it know bounds?" replied his friend. "Listen to your own untrammeled soul and answer: Why should a man deliberately encircle his mind with needless prison walls? No man can reach highest excellence who puts limits to his own thought. Let us be bold in thought, my friend, if we are to be bold in deed."

"Verily, you and I are birds of a feather," replied he of the bandaged arm, with an expression of delight.

"Well said! Eagles are we!" answered he of the flashing black eyes enthusiastically. "The freest birds under the sun—and the boldest. The limits of their soaring is as the strength of their pinions."

"But the eagles battle with one another in their limitless and lofty flight," said the wounded man in a tone of prophetic interrogation.

"That is so," was the ready reply. "And why should they not? What are their talons for? Is not the world a world of beak and claw?"

"When we have winged our way to the highest empyrean, however, I hope we shall not draw off and swoop at each other," said the wounded man, with an expansive and very expressive smile.

"I hope so too. That is the very point," was the reply. "Let us twain mount and soar together. There is quarry to spare for both. Let us agree in advance not to turn our beaks and claws against each other in the hour of success."

"It is well for us to talk like this," said he of the bandaged arm. "We thus learn to know one another's real thoughts. It is good to be frank sometimes."

"I agree with you," answered his friend. "It is good to have someone to whom we can unveil our real thoughts now and then. It is not well for Adam to be alone mentally any more than sexually. Somehow, I have been unaccountably attracted towards you. I have a strange premonition that your destiny and mine are in some inscrutable way woven together. Indeed, I am sure of it."

"You are a fatalist," said he of the light-colored hair in an inquiring tone.

"In some sense I am, but I do not so class myself. I believe one's fate is not wholly in one's own hands, however. There are great unknown laws of being that urge and drive a man on without him having the slightest power to prevent the climax, whatever it happens to be. Believe me, there is a truth hidden in the idea of destiny.

"But to return to our subject. You know that my friend Mathias Ogden is a splendid young fellow, but he does not understand me. I cannot tell him half of what I know or feel. On the other hand, I see that your brain is actually seething with the selfsame thought that is in mine. Therefore, I have been attracted to you ever since that day of the riot in the fields. I read all about it and of your wild Horation harangue to the mob. Since then, I have been irresistibly drawn nearer you. I've said to myself, *That's the man to do it: he understands.* Indeed, I traveled down here specially to make your acquaintance and get in touch with the other leaders of the revolt.

"For two months now, I have studied you and your published pamphlets, and I know you have been regarding me with critical self-questioning. We have drank together, fought together, and aided each other with friendliness in many an intrigue.

"My practical proposal now is, therefore, that we carry our friendship further and cement it into permanency by an oath of brotherhood, according to the old custom. Let us formally determine to assist one another all through life and especially through the days of turmoil and war that are assuredly nigh. Let us be sworn brothers as against all others, as it were two against millions. Let us turn passing events to our own advantage. Out of conditions as they exist, let us carve our fortunes and realize our ambitions.

"In the beginning, nature made man a contending animal. Are we not all Greeks or Trojans? We must, therefore, make up our minds for a life of continual battle. We must fight, I say, morning, noon, and night, if need be, against an entire world.

"My proposal stands, therefore, that you and I, here and now, swear and pledge our word of honor to a life-long alliance, brotherhood, and friendship. What do you think?"

To this, the man with the wound replied with deliberation:

"Your proposition is excellent and will serve us both. I also have considered the advisability of suggesting something similar myself. I can clearly see that you and I can aid each of success in life most wonderfully and in numberless ways. We are verily birds of a feather.

"In the event of war, neither of us shall be long without a commission. Then a word spoken at the right moment, in the right ears, may make a man or mar him. Military ability often fails to meet its just reward, especially if its friends at headquarters are inactive or have not for themselves achieved positions of responsibility, influence, and power. You see the point?

"The personal alliance that you propose should, in my opinion, not be too noticeable. Perhaps it might be better if kept entirely secret. Under certain circumstances, two friends can aid one another most effectively if their mutual friendship remains generally unknown. They might even quarrel a little now and again, for form's sake, pretending enmity for the ultimate advantage of both. We must, however, endeavor to be distinctly practical, not following fanciful daydreams and will-o'-the-wisps. I also have been drawn towards you, but I am inclined to think you over-enthusiastic.

"You are also, I fancy, somewhat too fond of 'petticoats' to make a quick success in the cold-blooded business of war, politics, and statecraft. He who would do great things must avoid women, you know, as much as possible, shunning all that tends to weakness and effeminacy. The love of woman makes man too fearful of consequences. Now will your all-too-evident failings

 RIVAL CÆSARS

in this regard spoil your efficiency? That is the question. You must understand what I mean, for you've read Plutarch, Livy, and Sallust, and you know what was the ruin of Marc Antony.

"Women have ever been the stumbling block and betrayers of ambition. They sit by the wayside to lure men into ineffectiveness. Woman's love for man is intensely selfish. They want him all to themselves. They tremble with terror if he whom they love dares to risk himself. They want to make sure of him, not so much for his sake but for their own."

"I do not think," replied the unwounded man, his black eyes gleaming and sparkling like balls of polished steel, "that I shall fall from the blandishments of the feminine. I love women, as all men do, but am determined they shall never enslave me. I feel too strongly that life is a grand call-to-action to permit myself to be dragged down into nothingness by mere sensual enjoyment.

"Then again, if as you say, I am inclined to be over-enthusiastic and impressionable, you are inclined to be over-cautious. That is, of course, your heritage from old Caledonia.

"Then you ought to know that I am a devotee of Lord Chesterfield's. This renders me immune to the wiles feminine. Thus Chesterfield writes, 'Women are children of a larger growth. For solid reasoning or good sense I never knew one that had it. Sensible men must regard them without idolatry.'

"I am also sure that Miss Schuyler did not smile upon you today for nothing when we passed the Livingston carriage, and there are others I wot of besides this beauteous dark-eyed Miss Betsy."

To which the man with the wound replied, "Ah, my dear boy, you are altogether on the wrong trail. Miss Betsy is very attractive, but it is not she who has captured my heart."

"Who, then, is the fair one?"

"She is a Mrs. Prevost, an attractive young widow with whom I am enamored, madly in love. Indeed, my passion for this most charming of women can only perish when I perish. Some day, I will introduce you to her. My happiness is at her mercy. She is a divine woman, I do assure you, and a perfect lady.

"As for Chesterfield, don't trust overmuch to him. I've read his 'Letters' myself, but the love of woman has a way of carrying a man beyond himself as it were, beyond all reasoning, beyond all bounds, beyond all philosophy. When a man is really in love, he is liable to go far and do almost anything. Love is really a sort of madness that sweeps over men and women, like a tempest, and drives them together, no matter what obstacles intervene."

"I can see you are hopelessly smitten," said the unwounded man, laughing. "I shall be most happy some day to behold this paragon of womankind."

"However," replied the wounded one, "this eternal woman question can afford to stand aside for awhile. In affairs of the heart, you and I are even as others, not without weaknesses and faults. Nevertheless, our very failings may possibly act as brakes upon our idealisms and thus, perhaps, save both of us from going to extremes."

"Perhaps you are right," was the reply. "But talking of extremes, why should we not go to extremes if we desire to play a part in the great world drama?

"As I understand human nature, to 'go to extremes' is ever symptomatic of genius and greatness. Weakness is to compromise, to hesitate, to be half-hearted. Are not the great names of ancient and modern times the names of haughty and aggressive personalities who carried their loves and convictions to 'extremes,' that is to say, to logical and clean-cut conclusions?

"Mediocrity is safe, no doubt it is, but it is very commonplace and of a drab color. Mediocrity is for men of the secondary, the bloodless type. I do not believe it is in your make-up, and I am sure it is not in mine. Both of us, I am satisfied, feel the solid truth that is in the old saw: 'He who would be famous must go forth and risk his hide and hair.'

"War, for example, is an 'extreme,' and yet it is now and ever has been the first fountain of wealth and honor. Not for nothing has the highest meed of praise been granted to the successful soldier."

"But did you never think that a time might possibly arrive when wars shall cease from of the Earth, the lion lay down with the lamb, the tiger eat straw like a cow, and so forth, as those old Hebrew prophets pathetically affirm?" said the wounded man said with a suggestive smile.

"Never can that be," replied the other emphatically. "Men were made for contending. The love of strife is in their very nature. It is born in them. All the higher and nobler families of men are warrior families and vice versa. Unfitness for war is unfitness for existence. History and our own eyes tell us this. What coward nation, for example, has either rights or privileges? A peaceful, acquiescent disposition in any man or nation is the great inefficiency. The lamb must ever be food for the lion and the wolf. What else were lambs made for?

"However, it is quite possible for an age of cankering tranquility to settle down on the world for a time, but, after all, it will only be as a passing interlude between lurid whirl-blasts of conquest and carnage.

"As long as there is human rivalry and love, there must be war. Indeed, so long as two men desire the same territory or the same woman, there must be bloodshed and hatred, jealousy and war. Even your friendship and mine would scarcely stand such a strain, as I've outlined.

"But to get back to business, the matter of a sworn compact between us," said the wounded man, "I am agreeable to join you in this. The advantages of it are clear to me. Let us face the world together, shoulder to shoulder. And let us reduce the compact to writing and swear in the good old way of the brotherhood to which we already belong. Here is pen and ink and paper. You write first and sign. Then I will copy word for word what you write and also sign. Then you shall keep my signature and I yours, Word it after the penal obligation and model of the Burning Scroll."

The speaker then drew his sword from the scabbard and leaned it point upwards against an open tome of Blackstone.

His friend proceeded to write, and this is what he wrote:

To . . . . ,
    I, A . . . .   B . . . . , without reservation or equivocation, in the presence of this cup of blood and the Iron Sign of Ing, do hereby and here-on, solemnly and sincerely, pledge myself, until life be no more, to uphold your name, defend your fame, and promote your material welfare at all times and upon all occasions, in sickness or in sorrow, in failure or distress, in power or in glory.

"Furthermore, I do faithfully swear to stand by you in every danger (whether you be right or wrong) and never to divulge your secrets, nor aid your foes nor consciously do you any injury whatsoever nor believe or repeat any evil report about you, your wife, your children, or your family.

"Furthermore, I formally swear on my word of honor, and seal said oath with my very heart's blood, should I ever break this, my solemn obligation as a brother in blood of the Holy Ing, that you, A . . . . H . . . . , are then at liberty to regard me as no longer your sworn friend but your sworn enemy and denounce me as a perjured wretch before the iron altar of the Ing and, thereafter, pursue me to the grave and beyond it with unrelenting hostility to the end of the end. *Mortuum Bellum.*

"Signed and sealed, in the presence of the above A . . . . H . . . . , from the veins of my heart, this . . . . . day of . . . . . . , 1775.
                    A . . . .   B . . . .

The writer then cleaned the pen carefully and, drawing a small pocket knife from his fob, made a quick, deep incision through the skin of his left arm, according to the old formula still in constant use.

Dipping the pen into the rich, red blood that ran from the puncture he carefully signed his name in bold, regular round-hand.

Then he took his sword, pushed it through the written paper, and handed the paper over the table to the wounded man, making at the same time the sign of fellowship with his left hand and saying, "E la moot."

Thereupon, the wounded one took the ink and writing material across the table and copied the document, word for word. Then he wrote his own name in the blood that oozed through the bandage of his wounded arm and went through the same ceremony (including the sign), repeating the penal word "E la moot."

The pen was then re-dipped in the blood of both men and ceremoniously dropped into a goblet of wine that stood on the center of the table.

Whereupon each man arose, took up his sword in his left hand, and rested the flat of it on the other's left shoulder. Then they drank the goblet of wine mixed with blood between them, repeating this toast one after the other and word for word:

> "An' trust me on my troth:
> If thou keep faith with me,
> My dearest friend, as my own heart,
> Right welcome shalt thou be."

Putting down the drained wine goblet, they then raised their naked swords aloft and grasping each other by the right hand, swore the ancient, symbolical oath of Thurar—the oath without words.

As the wounded man sat down again, he said, looking keenly across the table:

"As brethren of the blood, we are now bound to each other by the strongest bond that human hand and brain can bind. Henceforth, we are not two but one. Ten thousand brains shall plot and plan to destroy one or both should this ancient and binding pledge ever be broken or betrayed by one or the other.

"Now I would suggest, as my arm is still somewhat painful, that we postpone further action until next Thursday evening at Judge Livingstons.

"In the meantime, we can think over the names of all those whom we might invite to join us. They should all be gentlemen and men of influence. We can possibly form a private revolutionary lodge of the Iron Cross, with you and I (unknown to the others, perhaps) as the real moving spirits. I think we can reckon upon Brockholst, Livingston, Rodgers, Mason, Clinton, Troup, Fish, Tilghman, Ewing, Van Ness, and young Roosevelt."

"Agreed," answered the other enthusiastically as he rose to go. "We can and must combine to 'do things,' but not with too many. We must chance our lives, I tell you, if we are ever to be successful and famous. If we fail, the fate of all failures shall, of course, be ours, but if we win, we literally win a kingdom. My good old grandfather wrote *The Power of the Will* as his life's work. I will write *The Will to Power* as mine.

"Good or bad, I propose to be something great. I was never born to be a camp-follower. The world as yet needs its conquerors, and I will be one of them.

"Ah, how grand to be absolute master and lord it over millions. Already I dream, yes,

> "I dream of a beautiful queen,
> Afloat on the Hudson's tide
> With warriors in golden sheen
> And Cæsar by her side."

"Yes," replied the wounded man, laughing heartily. "Your enthusiasm is quite infectious. Without doubt, the world is yet to Cæsar. He is the conqueror. It is still 'Hail all hail' for the spoils of power and victory. Whoso would win great stakes must still play the iron game with iron nerve. You are right.

"Nothing changes but the hands on the dial. Human history is but a record of what is about to occur. It happens once more what happened of yore. The glory and the failures of the past are all prophesies of the future.

"Exiles and outlaws, for example, founded the City of the Seven Hills. Exiles and outlaws—men driven from Europe—founded these Thirteen Colonies, whose stupendous future shall yet surpass (in good and in evil) all that is recorded of republican and imperial Rome.

"There is before us and our posterity a glory, a power, and a grandeur greater than that of anything the mind of Plutarch's men could even conceive.

"Like you, I also have my daydreams, my castles in the air.

> "I dream of an empire as great
> And prouder than Rome of old,
> With its temples and towers of Fate,
> Its Eagles of war and gold."

Then the two bosom friends walked down the stairs to the front door and cordially bade each other goodbye, the unwounded man saying, "Well, we will meet again next Thursday night at Judge Livingston's"

"Yes, and in the meantime, let us think over whom we are to invite to join us. It is of great importance that we should select only trustworthy men."

"As I pass the doctor's house, I will call and send him up to dress your wound," said the unwounded man.

"Thank you, my dear friend," answered the other.

Thereupon, he of the bandaged arm, fair hair, and pink complexion walked musingly upstairs to his room. Seating himself by the table whereon the oath of brotherhood was written, he picked up the pen with which the signatures had been made, looked at it cynically, saying half aloud,

"BUT I WILL BE THE CÆSAR,
    MR. AARON BURR."

Almost at the same instant of time, the other man—he of the deep dark, dazzling eyes (walking rapidly toward Broadway) —was thinking and saying to himself,

"BUT I WILL BE THE CÆSAR,
    MR. ALEXANDER HAMILTON."

Chapter II

THE EIGHT-DAY CLOCK

*"O, there's nothing half so sweet in life,
As love's young dream."*[1]

*"There Galahad sat with manly grace,
The kindly grandeur on his face,
There Merolt of the Iron Mace
And love-lorn Tristram there."*[2]

A week after the events related in the last chapter, a birthday party was given at Judge Livingston's.

Aaron Burr and Alexander Hamilton were both present, together with a number of other young men about town. By far, the larger proportion of them had arrived early, attended by their lady relatives.

The evening passed most enjoyably with music and dancing and the usual love-glances, inseparable from all such gatherings.

The birthday celebration, however, was being used for a double purpose. Under the outward show of social pleasure and family entertainment, a revolutionary lodge was to be formed: a lodge that afterwards played the chief role in all the memorable events leading up to and connected with the War of Independence.

The disguise of the social gathering was adopted at the shrewd suggestion of Chancellor Livingston, he who afterwards swore in General Washington as first president of the United States.

In 1775, the secret agents of the king's government were

---

1   Frederick Marryat *Jacob Faithful* (Philadelphia: E. L. Carey & A. Hart, 1834).
2   From "The Bridal of Triermain" from *Scott's Poetical Works* by Walter Scott (Milner and Sowerby, 1852). The second line was originally "Yet maiden meekness in his face".

employed in large numbers to shadow prominent businessmen known or suspected of dissatisfaction to the government.

As the hours rolled on, the male element gradually disappeared from the dance hall and supper room, leaving the women to themselves. Burr and Hamilton, however, stayed until the very last—as if with design.

Now, women find little pleasure in the society of women, and, therefore, the disappearance of the men caused a certain element of dullness to come over the assembly.

Betsy Schuyler, daughter of Colonel (afterwards General) Schuyler, sat disconsolately upon a low, cushioned stool while the two Miss Rannesslaers, her cousins, were holding a gossiping conversation nearby with Miss Morton and Miss Leah Roosevelt, all of whom were members of New York's leading merchant families.

Betsy looked around, and then, it suddenly dawned upon her that there was not a man left in the room except Judge Van Horn, an old friend of her father's. He was busy expounding the intricacies of a new dance of the Sir Roger de Coverly type to Miss Alexander, the daughter of Lord Stirling.

Now Miss Betsy was filled with an irresistible spirit of curiosity. Whatever happened to be hidden from her, that she straightway desired to fathom with passionate eagerness.

"Where have they gone? What is the matter?" she whispered to her sister Catherine. "Mr. Burr and Mr. Hamilton were both here just now. Why, we've not a solitary soul to dance with, no, not one."

"I saw them go. They all stepped out one by one," said Catherine. I saw Aleck beckon the Magic Prince, and they went off together through the side door. I see you are deeply interested in Mr. Burr, Betsy."

"Yes," said Betsy frankly, and her large, good-natured eyes lighted up. "I like him and Mr. Hamilton too, but where have they gone to, I wonder? It seems so strange that they should all disappear so suddenly, every one of them."

"I suppose," replied Catherine, "it is something about those horrid politics, the king, the riots, and the taxes."

"When the men leave us, everything becomes dead and dull. There is no company if there is no MAN. And then the men are so dreadfully selfish. How I wish I was a man," said Betsy. Then she began to lilt in an undertone—and her voice was sweet and very pleasing:

> "All, all is dull about the house,
>   the world is drab and gray
> There's no more luck about the house,
>   when the men are gone away."[1]

"I like those dear, delightful old melodies. Betsy, they are so pleasing and naive and so truthful and so simple too. Anyone can understand them. But the clever new songs seem so false and strained and hollow and dreadfully pretentious."

"Songs should be simple and pathetic and make one feel generous and noble thoughts."

"O, I wish I could write songs, Betsy."

"So do I," answered Betsy, "you are so true and loving a sister, I am sure you could not but write charming and beautiful lyrics."

Suddenly, Betsy arose, saying vehemently while tossing out her lustrous, wavy hair, "Catherine, I wish I was a man."

At that, Catherine held up her hands in amazement, saying, "You mad girl, you! What do you wish that for?"

"Why, I'd gird on my father's pistols," answered Betsy, laughing, "and ride away to the wars on Jupiter." (Jupiter was her favorite saddle horse.)

---

1   Jean Adam "There's Nae Luck About the House" (circa 1750): "For there's nae luck about the house. /There's nae luck at a' / There's little pleasure in the house. / When our gudeman's awa.'"

"Why, what put that crazy notion into your head?"

"I always thought it, Catherine, but didn't know how to say it before."

"Then how did you learn?" inquired Catherine. "Your head is full of wild things."

"Why, I just read a poem about it this morning in an old London magazine. It's fine, Catherine. I know you'll like it too. It is called 'If I were a man.'"

"Let me see it," urged Catherine, with increasing curiosity.

Betsy fumbled in the folds of her dress and pulled out a small square fragment of smoky-colored paper. Upon it, the following two verses were printed in old-fashioned type (wherein every *f* was an *s*):

> Far off from this fair false dower—
> This glamour of mart and stage—
> I would fly to the plains of power
> And the conqueror's scarlet page.
>
> And there, as in days supernal,
> I would battle my life away,
> For the warrior lives eternal,
> But the dreamer dies in a day.[1]
>
> Lady Helen

"But the warriors don't live any more, Betsy," said Catherine, after reading the poem. "They are all dead and buried in books, you know. Now, by the way, I heard your Magic Prince declare this very afternoon (in conversation with father) 'The reason there are no great poets and writers now is because there are no great deeds or heroes to write about. The world is becoming

---

1   An inversion or satire of John Boyle O'Reilly "The Cry of the Dreamer." "No, no! from the street's rude bustle,/From the trophies of mart and stage,/I would fly to the woods' low rustle/And the meadows' kindly page./Let me dream as of old by the river,/And be loved for the dream alway;/For a dreamer lives forever,/And a toiler dies in a day."

                                                        RIVAL CÆSARS

tame and sad and dreary.'"

"And what did Papa reply to that?"

"Papa thought there were some heroes still but that their greatness is somewhat obscured by popular illusions or their activity strangled by untoward circumstances."

"Mr. Burr contended, however, that there is no field of activity for great men without the coming of great wars, great struggles, and great revolutions, also that the true hero could not be obscured nor his genius strangled."

"Father again replied that in the colonization of America there is still a superb arena for the display of aggressive heroism. The field of action is ever the same. 'America today,' said he, 'is even as Europe was in the days of King Arthur and Beowulf—it is just being opened up. Therefore, the heroic age has not passed away.'"

"'Perhaps,' replied Mr. Burr, 'but where are the heroes?'"

"Which do you think right, Catherine? I know you delight to read those dear old stories of how our forefathers loved and fought and died."

"I think the Magic Prince was nearest right, but father was certainly not wrong. There must be great afflictions and sorrows and forlorn hopes to bring out the best that is in men. Tranquility and fatness makes life awfully dreary, Betsy. It is the overcoming of dangers and difficulties that makes heroes."

"Catherine, do you know what I think?"

"No."

"I think Mr. Burr and Mr. Hamilton are going to be real live heroes. You see, they are not like other young men, no, not a bit. All the others whom we know are so dreadfully commonplace," urged Betsy with girlish enthusiasm. "They haven't an idea in them, and then, they make love so ridiculously too, simpering like girls and so timid."

"You are right, Betsy, Mr. Hamilton and Mr. Burr are not

like other men, and, what is more, I suspect we are going to have a big war soon. There is a whole lot of plotting going on and talk of rebellion. Mother says the house is full of powder and shot."

"Then I am certain they will become famous," said Betsy. "They will do great deeds, both of them, I am sure, They will lead regiments and ride boldly, just as it is in the history books and the pictures, and the common people will cheer them, and the flags will fly so gaily, and the drums will roll so grandly. O, it will be so fine, Catherine, won't it? And we will wave our 'kerchiefs to them from the balconies as they ride past, prancing proudly in triumph. How jolly it will all be! O, my, I wish it would come."

"But they will get killed or perhaps wounded," said the more thoughtful Catherine. "The king has many soldiers."

"Then I would cry my eyes out and lay flowers on their graves, or nurse them back to health, and I would never speak to a king's soldier again, no, never."

To which Catherine replied:

"I am also tired of merely reading in books about the 'great lover,' 'great hero,' 'the great prince.' I long to see him in the flesh and blood, even as you do."

"Yes, I know you do, Catherine, you are always dreaming of great old days when men were as true in love as they were bold in war: when they went out to carry off the one maiden of their choice against all opposition and dared to do valiant things against wicked kings. O, how I wish I was living in those dreadfully romantic old times. It would be grand—delightful! Wouldn't it be fine to marry a great man, Catherine, and be like a princess?"

"Yes, it would, Betsy. But where is the great man? Where is the Prince Charming? The conquering hero?"

"O, he'll come," answered Betsy, laughing joyously.

"But what if he doesn't come?"

"O, he'll come; I know he'll come. I'm sure of it. He's here now, I think, but we won't know him for sure till after the great deeds are done."

"Betsy, I don't know what to make of you. He may not come till we are too old."

"O, don't talk so dreadfully, Catherine. The world is so beautiful yet."

"Betsy," answered Catherine, as with a sudden inspiration, "I do believe you are right. Those grand old times will return. Something tells me."

"O, how I wish they would," said Betsy. "Then no more mere reading and singing about knights and warriors and valiant kings-of-men but living right alongside of them and loving them and assisting them and suffering for them too. Yes, I do wish a great struggle would come, Catherine. I want to find me a man and a king, and I know you do too. I will never marry one who is not brave and bold and famous and successful."

"Betsy, you're an awful little pagan, you don't hide your feelings a bit. You should be more reticent, Betsy. Besides, if no war comes, how can you know your hero?"

"Why should I be more reticent, Catherine? I am only talking to you, and nobody is listening."

"It's not the fashion, Betsy, that's all I know. But like you, I also wish that my husband should be manly and bold, strong and great. I don't like those sleek, namby-pamby sort of men who've no daring in them. A woman should be good and true and a man should be strong, bold, and full of spirit."

"I'll tell you what we'll do," said Betsy jokingly. "You and I shall marry Mr. Burr and Mr. Hamilton between us. I know you like them both as much as I do, but you don't say it, you dear deceiver, you!"

"Now, for goodness sake, be quiet, Betsy," said Catherine, blushing furiously.

Whereupon Betsy arose, saying, "I think I'll go out and see

where the men have gone to. It's as solemn as a funeral in here since they all went away."

"O, don't, pray don't," answered Catherine impetuously. "Father would be very angry with you for doing such a thing. You've often heard him say that well-bred ladies should never inquire or hunt too much after the affairs of men, nor attempt to discover men's secrets; 'Men know and have to mix up in things women should avoid,' he says over and over again."

"Nevertheless, I am going," said Betsy willfully. "I can't stand those Van Ranneslaer girls. They won't talk, except when you squeeze them. They're just like dolls, and the room is as dull as a church when the Reverend Salem Smidt preaches."

Now the men had gone out by a side door opening on a long dark corridor, and Miss Betsy followed.

Perceiving a small swinging oil lamp hanging at one end of the passageway, she walked softly on tiptoe towards it, her head full of mischief and bubbling over with curiosity. A sort of strange instinct seemed to hurry her on.

As she approached nearer to the light, however, a feeling of sudden apprehension, a shadowy sense of foreboding, fell upon her, for she beheld in the half-shadow beyond the light what appeared to be the seated figure of a weirdly strange, strong old man with a long, white beard and a shining double-edged dagger lying across his knees.

I wonder, she thought, *who he is, and what he is doing there. I never saw him before, and yet, I know everything and everybody in this house, for I played here when a little girl. When in New York, it has always been my home. The curious old man by the door of the basement! What does it mean?*

Just then, through the door alongside of which sat the old man, came a dull, muffled sound, as of the shuffling of many feet and the falling on the floor inside of some heavy body.

Whereupon the old man with the naked dagger arose from

his seat and gave two distinct knocks upon the upper panel of the door with the iron hilt of his weapon. The knocks sounded bodeful of evil to Betsy.

Immediately, the shuffling inside ceased. All again was silent as the grave, except of the distant sound of what appeared to be the steady strokes of a hammer on a coffin and a solitary voice intoning a prayer or incantation.

O, thought Betsy, as her heart beat wildly, *I know what it is now. It is a secret society, and all the men are in there, and the dance of tonight was only an excuse for them gathering together here to avoid arousing the suspicion of the government.*

Then a thought full of strategy came into her quick, teeming brain.

I'll go down the old hidden passage in the wall and look in. That will be fine. I'll see it all.

Whereupon, she turned and fled up the corridor.

However, her presence had been detected by the suspicious old man, who was evidently acting as outer door guard. He immediately passed in a report through the hidden speaking tube that a "something" dressed in white had swept rapidly up the passage. At the same time, he opened a cupboard in the wall and turned what appeared to be a large iron crank five times.

Meanwhile, Betsy passed the drawing room door and climbed the stairs to her own room. There she rapidly made some alterations in her dress, and climbing another flight of stairs, she entered a half-dark lumber room with a deep recess in the wall near the sunken fireplace. Betsy went into the recess and removed from the wall a set of shelves containing old books, manuscripts, Indian curiosities etc., revealing an opening in the stonework about two feet square.

Crushing herself through this opening, she found herself on the rungs of a rusty iron ladder let into the stone and leading upward at an inclined plane.

Gathering her skirts tight about her, she moved swiftly through the dust and cobwebs as if perfectly familiar with the place. Often had she been through it in her childhood days.

Presently, she stood on what appeared to be a landing. Opening without hesitation a door on the left, she entered another dark passage. Down it she went to the end. Then lifting a trap door by a big iron ring, she descended another flight of stone steps and found herself in a small, dark alcove.

Through the north wall of the alcove, a curiously blended red light shone. It was the light from the lodge room shining through the glass panel of a large, old-fashioned eight-day clock. Betsy approached it stealthily.

The clock was over ten feet tall and fastened by iron bolts to the wall. Behind the clock and inside the alcove where Betsy stood, were a number of cog wheels and iron levers, all forming part of some curious old-fashioned machine.

Betsy, with girlish activity, climbed over this mechanism and stepped into the interior of the clock, alongside of the great iron weights and swinging bronze pendulum.

She moved cautiously so as not to disturb the swing of the pendulum. As she stepped in, however, a very slight change took place in the mechanism. The old rusty cogs seemed to move behind Betsy in the dark, without her observing them. Chains fastened to the rear wall began to slowly tighten.

Betsy climbed up inside the clock to where the light shone in. Here she found the coloring matter (frosted on the glass) had been, on the lower corner, carefully scraped off as if by some one bent on the same purpose of curiosity as herself.

Betsy balanced her body steadily and looked long and earnestly into the lodge room. In pure delight with herself, thus she thought: *Now I can see everything. There they are, every one of them. But I wonder what they do. I wonder what their secrets are.*

Just then, by command of the Supreme One, Aaron Burr repeated aloud the omnific word of the Great Ing.

Then the members of the lodge marched around the hall with right arms bare to the shoulder and saluted the symbol of the Ing with their swords, upon which there was blood.

O, this is delightful, thought Betsy. *This is quite an adventure. It is just like the magic story book—even the Magic Prince is in it too—and all in real life. How often I have heard old Judge Van Horn say, "Romance is a fool compared to fact." And here I*

am, hidden inside the old clock, and there my brothers, within the weird secret lodge, together with my father, my cousins, the Magic Prince, and Aleck. But those awful lamps—with the light shining through the eye sockets in the grinning skulls—they are horrible! They make my flesh creep! And all the men have got their swords drawn and wine glasses in their hands, and there is blood upon _____ , and their throats are bare. And what is that laying on the stone floor by the great hole in the flags? It makes me shudder.

Here Betsy trembled violently, for she perceived what appeared to be the bodies of three men, wrapped in red cloth, laying at the foot of the iron altar of the Ing, upon which stood the three amens, the Iron Cross, the bowl of red-liquid, and the Flaming Scroll.

Betsy continued to reflect:

I wonder what it means. Are those things on the floor dead men, or what are they? What is the blood for? What is the fire for? And the curious bright sword (like brass) sticking upright in the coffin? And the long coil of rope? And the yellow flag with the coiled snake? And the great red spear?

O, my, I'm getting frightened. I wish now I had not done this. I feel like a spy, like a very criminal.

Presently, Hamilton began to speak, and a sense of enchantment and calm swept hypnotically over her as she continued to listen to his very pleasing voice.

Then came the terrific ritual and the awful oath of the revolutionary brotherhood, also the secret signs, the grips and words, the explanation of the reversible symbols, the interpretation of the Flaming Scroll, the Sap of the Iron Ing, the naked blades, the klinking of the glasses, the drinking of the _____ and other things not to be mentioned to the ears of the non-instructed.

All of which Betsy heard and saw distinctly and treasured up in a very retentive memory to her dying day.

It was only to be expected that the terrific and ancient ritual (the ritual that tamed the fierce souls of Gothic kings and Scythian conquerors) would have a somewhat cooling effect upon this impulsive Albany maiden.

But Betsy was not an ordinary young woman. About her, there was something daring and romantic, tragic and ambitious. She was never satisfied with the humdrum. She longed to be more than her associates. In fact, she was not "content with her lot." She felt there was something wanting in her life, though she did not know what it was. Almost unconsciously, down deep in her heart, she was searching for that undefinable partner of her being, without whose discovery no woman is complete. In fact, the "old, old story" was stirring in her soul.

Now, Miss Betsy was also a furious little rebel, and she therefore listened to the short speeches of Hamilton and Burr with beating heart and unlimited approval.

When Burr concluded she thought:

O, this is really lovely. I wouldn't have missed it for anything. Mr. Burr is a real hero. I could hug him and Mr. Hamilton too. Why, they're all heroes, yes, every one of them. Are they not plotting in secret to overthrow an evil king? How noble they look, so young, so brave, so valiant, so strong, sword in hand, swearing allegiance to their country's cause and vengeance on the wicked oppressor. O, I love them. I'd like to kiss every one of them. How Catherine would like to be here! I do declare, the heroes have really come alive again.

There they are, right before me. Why, now I see it all. Is not valor and ambition stamped on their brows?

And then their speeches: how very unusual and yet how divinely beautiful and full of manliness.1 Indeed they speak like gods. How unlike the tiresome sentimentalism of that old fogey, the kings-college professor, whom my uncle brings home to dinner sometimes.

And then Mr. Burr with his glorious black eyes, how grand he is! What an air of natural distinction and pride there is about him! How beautiful to look upon! He is a veritable hero. I know he is a hero, I know, I know!

Aleck Hamilton I like too, but the "Magic Prince," he charms my very soul and fills me with dreams. How extraordinary and radiant he is, like an inspired prophet or a knight of old going forth to lead his people in the wars: Aye, and when he lifts his sword to take that fearful oath, he does it with all the gesture and grace of a king.

During all this time, the mechanism around and behind Betsy was moving quietly towards her. However, in the excitement at what she saw, she had failed to observe that the machinery had imprisoned her as in a trap.

Presently, she felt a pressure on her back and tried to turn round and escape but could not.

Straightway, much to Betsy's confusion, a strange clanging noise arose within the clock. The clanging sounded like the crowing of a cock.

The sound had a magical effect on the members of the lodge. At the second crow, the lights went out, and dead silence reigned in the lodge room. Betsy, trembling with fear, wished

---

1 ≠   Readers desirous of obtaining printed copies of the most extraordinary and remarkable speeches—speeches not hitherto known to exist—are hereby invited to communicate by letter with the author, in care of publishers. The original manuscripts now lying before us are the handwriting of Aaron Burr's only daughter and dated "St. Ingo, Island of Cuba, 1814," In the year 1812. Theodosia Burr sailed from Charleston with her father's private papers, in an armed privateer, bound for New York. Though never again publicly heard of in the United States, she nevertheless lived until the year 1861. But that is another story hereafter to be told.

herself a thousand miles away. Meantime, the mechanism continued to work, and the pressure on Miss Betsy's back became more insistent.

Then from out the darkness came the voice of the master of the lodge, her own father, saying, "An alarm from the Evil One." To your steel, my brothers! To your steel! The hour is now!"

The cock continued to crow vociferously. Then the trampling of many feet approached the clock in the darkness. Miss Betsy was in a cold sweat from fear of the unknown.

On the iron altar within the lodge, the master's iron hammer rang angrily three times.

KLANG!

KLANG!

KLANG!

Chapter III.

THE SECRET SOCIETY

The gentle Gawain, Pelinore,
Percival, Sir Kay the Keen,
And Lancelot, that evermore
Looked stol'n-wise on the Queen.[1]
—The Death of Arthur.

Now, in order that the reader may have a clear, consecutive, and proper comprehension of the happenings both within and without the secret lodge, it is essential to go back upon our story somewhat.

We must return, therefore, to the festive hall before the disappearance of the men and long before Miss Betsy set out upon her venturous quest.

"Betsy, you dreadful little flirt. You are acting scandalously. There is Aleck, Hamilton over yonder, looking as if he was about to be hung, and this is actually the fourth time tonight you have danced with his dark-eyed friend, the mysterious Mr. Burr the 'Magic Prince,' as you call him." Thus said Catherine Schuyler to her sister Elizabeth, who straightway replied:

"There now, you fault-finding dear. Why, you yourself danced thrice with Mr. Troup, while Moncrieffe (who is I know in love with you) sulked sadly and then in desperation danced with the two Clinton girls.

"As for the Magic Prince, he quite beglamoured me with his courteous and bewitching ways. When he talks to me, I feel like a princess, and he just makes me do anything he wants. And

1 *The Bridal of Triermain, or the Vale of St. John* by Sir Walter Scott 1st Baronet, 1813.

73

then his eyes, they're just too, too awful. O, Catherine, they pierce into one's soul, and his voice, when he speaks, it is just like the tones of some wonderful fairy bell."

"I see you are in love with him, Betsy, but how about Aleck?" said Catherine.

"You can have him, Catherine, I know you like him," answered Betsy. "But I have neglected him shamefully. Go over and talk to him and try to make him happy. Poor, dear Aleck. I like him too; he is such a good companion. But then he is so dreadfully sentimental and so full of flowery compliments."

Whereupon Miss Betsy moved rapidly over to Hamilton's side and began talking to him in a happy-go-lucky, good-natured, bantering way.

Now, the Livingstons at the time of these happenings were one of the wealthiest families in New York. The founders of the family were of that hard, level-headed Scotch-Irish strain (renowned for its valor and partisanship)—a strain that has given to America so many celebrated politicians, fluent orators, and dashing warriors.

In the Colonial days, when only property-holders could vote or hold office, their influence was immense. They were very prolific, and their ramifications and affiliations with other of the old ruling families were quite phenomenal. They had countless cousins, sisters, aunts. Indeed, the Livingstons were more than a family: they were a tribe. Being staunch Presbyterians, all their instincts were entirely anti-royalist, and their great wealth (in rents and trade) proved of immense assistance to the revolutionary propaganda.

Judge Livingston was wont to say, "When evil men bear sway, the place of honor is in the ranks of revolt!"

Little wonder, therefore, that all his sons took an active part in the War of Independence and thereafter became prominent and successful political and mercantile chiefs.

The family was closely connected with General Phillip Schuyler's family, also with the Van Ranselaers, Moncrieffes and Clintons. Thus, the gathering of the evening was somewhat in the nature of a family reunion. Not more than three persons present were unrelated. It was, as it were, a rally of the clans.

Now, Betsy Schuyler had hazel eyes and dark hair and a fresh, clear, healthy complexion. Her slender profile was very bewitching, her bust fully developed, and her manner bubbling over with human friendliness, joy-of-life, and animal spirits.

A low-cut dress, adorned around the edges with French lace, exposed her snowy shoulders and breast. Upon a pillar-like neck, her well-formed head was firmly poised. She possessed a bright, happy, joyous smile, and over her high, square forehead, a thick mass of lustrous hair was coquettishly combed back and fastened behind in a fashion peculiar to the time.

Catherine, her sister, though about the same age, was more staid in manner, more mature and womanly, with a kind-hearted, good-natured, and somewhat studious expression. She was utterly without guile and deeply in love with Alexander Hamilton, though she felt in her heart that he was rather attracted towards her more beautiful and very vivacious sister.

Betsy was frank and full of fun, everlastingly teasing or tormenting somebody, always laughing and romping, a regular little tomboy, yet, withal, well-bred and ladylike.

She was extremely fond of music. The tones of the string band in the dance room seemed to shake her very soul with excitement.

It was curious to observe, however, that when she talked to Aaron Burr, her whole demeanor changed. She became more subdued, she blushed, stammered, a wistful expression came over her face, and her half-hidden bosom heaved with rapider pulsations.

One could plainly perceive that she was deeply in love with Burr, although she had not known him more than two hours. Even a tyro in the arts of Cupid could not fail to observe that Burr was first favorite. Hamilton saw it with some pique, but not overly resentful feelings.

Burr, being a splendid judge of character, understood Miss Betsy thoroughly. He paid her, therefore, every attention, as it was his nature to do. Her very evident liking for him flattered his vanity, though his heart remained wholly unmoved.

Hamilton, on the other hand, admired Miss Betsy, and though he did not passionately love her, it was in his mind to woo and win her.

His admiration for her was wholly of the judgment. He saw her many charms and attraction and, therefore, had concluded in his own mind to make her his wife if he could. He therefore never missed an opportunity to be by her side, and she thus had become accustomed to his attentions, compliments, and moods.

Betsy looked upon him as a pleasant, handsome, and witty companion and an accomplished, well-bred partner in the ball-room. It fed her womanly pride and instinct to know that the "able young collegian" whom everybody praised so much and who "could talk like an angel and write like a prince" delighted to be her own special gallant, laying siege to her maiden heart.

Indeed, if the more fascinating Burr had not appeared upon the scene at this particular time, it is very probable Betsy would have married Hamilton within the year.

Her parents both spoke of him as a "promising young man," destined mayhap to fill a great role, and she well knew that quite a number of other fair maidens and heiresses in New York were 'setting their caps' at him, including her own sister Catherine.

"Mr. Hamilton," said Betsy as they met, "you look quite gloomy and out of sorts, as if your heart had grown old with some deep sorrow. What is the matter with you? Why didn't you come and ask one to dance as you used to do? You know I have been waiting for you all the evening."

"I thought," he replied with a bantering smile, "that you appeared so charmed with the society and attentions of my mesmeric friend from Princeton, I did not consider it prudent to intrude. Mr. Burr is a real 'gay Lothario.' He shines among the ladies. There, he's in his element."

"Now, Mr. Hamilton, don't be so ill-natured," said Betsy coaxingly. "You know I never forget old friends."

"Well, never mind, Miss Schuyler," he answered laughingly. "Shall I have the honor and pleasure of dancing with you now?'

"Ha, ha, you jealous man," she laughed in mocking banter as they moved glidingly through the figure of the old-fashioned gavotte. "I hope you don't kill Mr. Burr and hang up his gory head on an iron hook on the 'keep' of your 'donjon castle.' That's the way it goes in the storybooks, you know, is it not? If you do, Mr. Hamilton, then it will be for me to jump into your castle-moat and drown, whereupon you'll go away to the wars and never smile again."

Thus she bantered him from time to time as they danced gaily in the grand old stately way of our fathers. He felt young, strong, and happy, for he knew that all the world was yet before him.

"You are getting positively dramatic, Miss Betsy," he said to her in his most impressive tones. "Nevertheless, I may be really going to the wars before long."

"And will Mr. Burr go too?" answered Betsy impulsively. Then she thought of the mistake she had made, and as a tear

moistened her eye, she continued, "I hope you don't get wounded or killed, Mr. Hamilton: that would be too dreadful."

"I must take my chances, Miss Betsy, with the rest. Men must
fight, you know. It is in their nature."

"War is dreadful, Mr. Hamilton," said Betsy mechanically
(because she had heard others say the same thing so often before).

After enjoying themselves another hour with the ladies, Hamilton and Burr approached one another as if by pre-arrangement.
Then they walked out of the dance hall by a side door and found
themselves in a long dark corridor, at the end of which a flickering oil-lamp made the surrounding darkness barely visible.

"Hamilton," whispered Burr, "are they all here?"

"Every one of them, and all are bold men, true, freeborn, and
of good standing, just as commanded in the ritual."

"Are they all Brethren of the second degree?"

"Yes, every man of them. Some of them have been obligated
for years."

"Do they know the object of the gathering?" inquired Burr.

"Yes, they are all enthusiastic for immediate action and eager
for adventure. They are the right stuff for a revolution. Not a
man among them has ever had his spirit broken."

"Who do you think we should select as our chief, Hamilton?"

"I suggest Colonel Schuyler. First, because he is wealthy and
closely connected in business with all the leading men of New
York. Second, because he is our personal friend, thus he is likely
in many matters to be influenced by our purpose. Third, because
he is a mature man of sound practical judgment, a past master
of the Iron Cross, knows the 'unwritten' code by heart, and is
respected and known to nearly everybody of any consequence.

He is the wealthiest man in the city.

"But in addition to that," continued Hamilton, smiling frankly at Burr and noting the effect of his words, "I want to marry his daughter, Betsy—if you do not."

The insinuation implied by Hamilton's words was thoroughly understood by Burr, who, without pretending to notice them, replied warily:

"I don't wonder at your weakness for the beautiful Miss Betsy. She is a most charming girl, and so is her sister. I see you have an eye for female loveliness, Hamilton. I congratulate you upon your choice. She is an heiress too, I hear. Her father, I believe, is one of the largest patroon landowners in Albany and Saratoga. I can assure you, Hamilton, if you want to marry her, no opposition shall come from me. I am not your friend in name only. Even if I loved her (which I don't), I would not say or do anything to prevent your success. I am a man of honor, Hamilton, and when I swear friendship to a man, I mean it.

And, as you have invited her father to be our most excellent chief, I see no objection to him, though, personally, I had a strong predilection for Judge Livingston. When I came to New York to find out how things really were, I brought with me several letters of introduction to the Livingstons, who, as you know, are related (by marriage) to my mother's family, the Edwards."

"Yes," answered Hamilton; "you told me of it before. Livingston is a thorough-going man of the 'right color,' but so, also, is Schuyler. Between them they have all the hidden strings in their hands (as far as New York is concerned), and they are also in constant correspondence with the revolutionists in Boston and down South. I fancy also that Livingston is one of the Supreme Seven, whose identity is the standing mystery of our order."

"You mean the high court of the Iron Cross ?"

"Yes."

Burr and Hamilton, thus conversing, walked slowly down

the dark corridor to where a glimmering oil lamp swung overhead at the far end.

Here they found a white-bearded but powerful old man, seated on a chair alongside of a heavy iron-studded oaken door. In his hand, he held a long, broad-bladed, double-edged dagger with a square hilt of solid steel.

As the two young men approached him from out of the dark and came under the glow of the lamp, he stood up and spake unto them in tones that conveyed both command and threat. As he spake, an iron door slid out of the wall behind them, and, moving noiselessly across the corridor, it closed them in most effectually.

"Who goes there?" the old man said as he brought his shining weapon to the "point."

"A companion," replied Burr.

"A companion," repeated Hamilton.

"Advance, companions two, and give the first Sign of Om," spake the man on guard.

Whereupon they stepped forward, each at the same instant making a peculiar movement of the left hand (ending at the left ear), and placing the right foot directly in front of the left.

Whereupon the Old Man lowered his ugly-looking weapon, saying, "Pass, brethren. The sign is right. The line is right. All is right. Go forward and fear not. Knock and it shall be opened unto you."

Hamilton walked on to the door and gave five peculiar knocks at irregular intervals, which were answered from the inside by a rubbing on the panel. Whereupon the great oaken door rolled back into the wall, and Burr and Hamilton entered.

Just inside stood another guard or sentinel. He held in his hand a peculiar instrument with a sharp edge and shaped like a horse shoe, He also made a sign to them as they passed him, which they returned.

Then the door closed, seemingly of its own volition, and a heavy red curtain rolled automatically across it. Upon the curtain was embroidered a gashed hand and the words

**Tuhituhi tene tehemana
Ko Na-r Thur ar.**

The room or hall was oblong in shape, with a stone fireplace geometrically in the center and raised dais at the north end. Its low roof was upheld by square stone pillars and the walls were white-washed. It was dimly lit by long wax candles, and a large old-fashioned eight-day clock ticked steadily against the southern wall.

Upon the dais were seven black armchairs and around the room were a number of wooden benches or seats. At the northeast corner was what appeared to be a tomb or mausoleum built of wooden blocks and painted to look like granite. The floor was of stone flags, one of which swung easily open on a pivot (if trod upon), displaying a dark yawning chasm down below, from which a peculiar light shone. Attached to the roof were strange instruments and several sets of falling curtains, each curtain of a different color. The curtains hung on hooks and links made of white bone, and upon each curtain was painted emblematic scenes from the Oral Legend and the Flaming Scroll,

Twenty-one men were present, mostly young men, all dressed in the then height of fashion. The stamp of superior station, assured standing, and even of culture was observable on the faces of many. (The reader is here expected to remember that the American Revolution was led and organized entirely by men of independent position, indeed the wealthiest men of their day.)

Vivaciously, they chatted together in groups, some sitting, some walking, some standing. The dangers of the times, the distracted state of the country, the trend of passing events, and the various personal charms and attractions of the ladies (left behind in the ballroom) were the principal subjects under discussion or dispute.

However, as soon as Hamilton and Burr strode in, the buzz of voices gradually subsided, for everybody expectantly recognized in them the master spirits of the gathering.

For a week past, Burr and Hamilton had been quietly, yet successfully, 'sounding' their most trustworthy acquaintances with regard to the formation of another private revolutionary lodge of the Iron Cross. Nearly every man approached consented to join.

The first business transacted upon this particular evening was the election of a presiding officer. Colonel Phillip Schuyler (nominated by Burr and seconded by Hamilton) was unanimously appointed to the position, formally chosen to be "master of the hammer." He was thereupon installed by the united brethren in due style. Each brother signified his allegiance to "the wielder of the weapon" by a sign and a symbolic word.

Colonel Schuyler then seated himself in the left-hand chair upon the dais. Over his head on the wall hung the original rebel standard of the Thirteen Colonies. It consisted of bright orange silk with a hissing black rattlesnake coiled in the center. The snake had thirteen rattles, its head being raised menacingly as if to strike. Painted underneath the serpent was the extremely suggestive and eloquent motto

"DON'T TREAD ON ME."

Four of the brethren then went over to a half-hidden alcove in the eastern wall, where they lifted up an oblong heavy object, carried it out, and ceremoniously placed it in front of the Master of the hammer. Over this heavy object hung a black pall, afterwards hooked up to the low ceiling in the form of a square.

Upon raising the cover, a common but very heavy pine coffin, painted black, was disclosed. On one side of the coffin, curious characters were traced, apparently in some cryptic sign language, and on the other side, these words in plain English:

?

Then, with flint and steel, a small fire of dry resinous wood was lit in the exact middle of the hall—by Judge Livingston.

As the bright red flame flared up, a pungent but very pleasing odor pervaded the air.

On top of the coffin, two yellow tapers were placed, one at each end, and upon the center lay an open book alongside a glass bowl of red liquid like unto blood. Also sticking through the coffin was a broad shining sword with a plain square hilt.

The open book had iron leaves and raised gold characters thereon, and from it streamed forth a curious radiance, which in the semi-darkness appeared to illuminate the space immediately around with a sort of magical, semi-religious glow.

When, subsequently, the central fire became from time to time obscured during the course of the impressive and weird ceremonial, a similar mysterious light shone like a halo or aura from the broad gleaming blade of the uplifted sword.

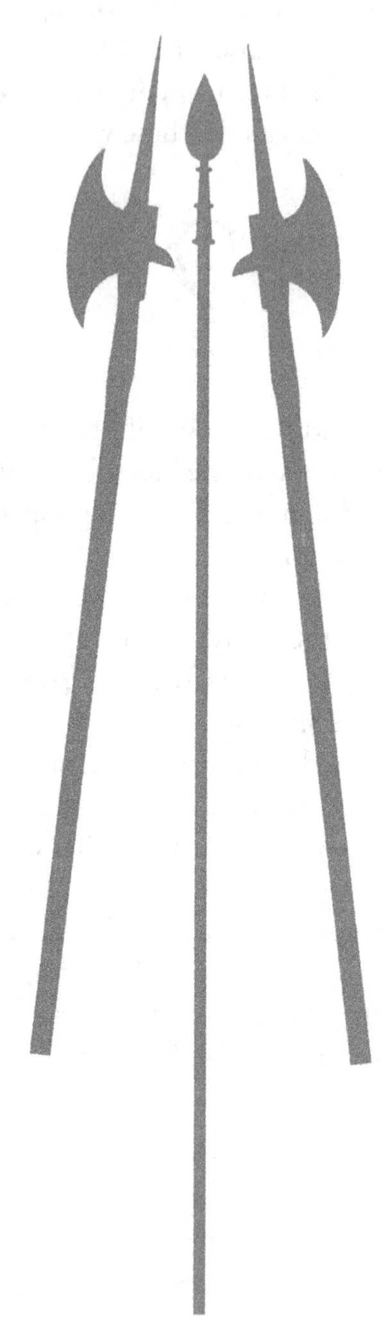

Chapter IV

"THE INITIATION OF BETSY"

*"My brothers, My brothers,
Come speak to me true,
What now shall we do?
What now shall we do?"[1]*

For sufficient reasons it has been decided to omit the short pithy speeches that the brethren made in the arcanum of the secret lodge. According to the custom of the order, every member had to openly express an opinion whenever business of importance came up.

There were present on this occasion John Swartwout, Robert Troup, Henry Lee, Henry Bayard, Phillip Freneau, Tench Tilghman, Isaac Roosevelt, besides Burr, Hamilton, Schuyler, Livingston, and many others.

Hamilton's address bristled with practical suggestions for stirring up the multitude: Roosevelt spoke of finance and the possibility of a big loan from King Louis of France to fight King George of England; Colonel Schuyler spoke of Indian tactics, bush warfare and the ease with which disciplined armies might be paralyzed by systematic guerrilla strategy—Judge Livingston spoke of what he had already done to precipitate a crisis in N. Y.; Robert Troup spoke upon the possible dangers of mobocracy hereafter; John Swartwout urged the necessity of safeguarding title deeds after the British power had been broken; Tench Tilghman spoke of the necessity of actively promoting each other's material prosperity; and Aaron Burr concluded by urging the justice of active resistance to a tyrannical government, affirming

---

1   Acts 2:37 "Now when they heard this, they were pricked in their heart, and said unto Peter and to the rest of the apostles, Men and brethren, what shall we do?"

that men of property should never hesitate to defend their possessions by force of arms against all attack, whether made by
kings, mobs, or governors.

Now, the most striking thing about all these speeches when
read today is that in no sense do they conform to the current
conventional ideal that our revolutionary forefathers were intense "equality lovers." Rather do they go to show that the men
who forcibly changed our form of government 125 years ago
were intense patricians in all their sympathies, in all their theories, and in all their final purpose. Hence many things.1

"Burr speaks with startling boldness," said Judge Livingston
to Phillip Schuyler. "He is a strong, strange young fellow with
an almost heathen clearness of vision, and his voice rings in
one's ears like a clarion of battle."

"You are right," replied Schuyler, "and he will go far. But I
fancy he hasn't told us all he thinks. There are fathomless recesses in that man's mind. There is an elemental 'something' in him."

"However, I believe he is thoroughly sincere," said Livingston, "and at bottom a resolute and noble spirit, but I wonder
where he obtained those strong, intense, clear-cut, level-headed thoughts, and at so young an age too. Everything about him
conveys the idea of force, character, originality, and indomitable will."

"He is the son of the Reverend Aaron Burr, president of
Princeton College," replied Schuyler, "and has probably studied books in the recesses of the college library that average men
have never even heard of."

"What do you think of young Hamilton?" inquired Livingston.

"I have a good opinion of him also. He possesses natural elo-

---

1 ≠   The responsible leaders of the revolution were all wealthy men. Today, they would
be called millionaires. Hancock & Adams were the two richest men In Mass., Washington &
Jefferson the two richest in Virginia, Livingston & Schuyler, were two of the most opulent in New
York, and Morris of Philadelphia and Bayard of Baltimore were rich men. A longer list could be
given, but this is sufficient.

                                         RIVAL CÆSARS

quence of a high order, probably derived from the French blood that I believe runs in his veins. I think his is a saner brain than Burr's, however."

"Colonel Schuyler, I think both these young men are distinct acquisitions," said Livingston. "They are college-bred, full of spirit and ambition. They are noble in bearing and noble in speech. Indeed, I think they are the very men we require to bridle incendiary demagogues and, at the same time, overthrow the printed and spoken arguments of such aggressive royalists as Dr. Cooper, Chief Justice DeLancey, and the Rivington Press. Livingston, as Burr says, we must be just as ready to defend our liberties and property from the greed of a mobocracy as from the greed of a tyrant.

"I have just been thinking the very same thought," replied Livingston. "Burr and Hamilton are the very men we want."

"Now what do you say to take them up between us? You and I have done well in this world already, and we can thus well afford to push these two young men's fortunes. Clinton may also agree to lend a hand. I am aware that neither Burr nor Hamilton are over well-supplied with ready cash, and without cash, they cannot do much."

"I have already half-adopted Hamilton, myself. He is a great favorite in my family," said Philip Schuyler smiling.

"And so he is in mine," replied Livingston. "But, personally, I have a strong predilection for Burr. He comes well recommended from the North with strong letters of introduction to friends of mine in New York. After tonight, I shall surely take him in hand. I shall see to it that his brain is not mullified for want of financial means. It is money that talks, Schuyler. Want of gold is a great hindrance to a man."

"Verily," answered the colonel, smiling. "Money is king, the king of kings."

"No doubt of that," said Livingston. "It can perform miracles. It can hire heroes. It can organize armies. It can conquer tyrants, aye, and tame the madness of the maddest majority."

"Yes," said Schuyler. "It can do nearly anything. As my friend Dr. Franklin saith, "it can postpone death, cure disease, release the captive, bring sight to the blind, clothe the naked, feed the hungry, destroy the despot, win the love of women, and procure all reasonable earthly happiness to any man who is not too entirely told. In course of time, perhaps, it may even resurrect the dead, create life, and storm the very gates of heaven, for money is force, and force is the essence of the universe."

"Ah," replied Judge Livingston, smiling jocularly. "No wonder the astute children of Israel set up the golden calf and boldly worshiped it in the Asiatic desert. No wonder, for truly there is a supernatural magic in gold—a something half-divine."

As the buzz of conversation increased throughout the hall, Hamilton again stood up and suggested that the ceremony of forming the new lodge and the election of permanent officers be proceeded with in accordance with the unwritten traditions of the order.

"It is growing late," he said, "and we have much routine business before us."

"Yes," interjected Burr, "and the ladies in the drawing room must be wondering what has become of us all."

"You're always thinking of the ladies, Burr," replied Hamilton with a smile full of banter and hidden meaning.

Colonel Schuyler struck one blow on the Iron Altar of the Ing and said, "Brethren I demand your attention to open and dedicate this new lodge of the Iron Cross." Whereupon, all arose, drew their swords, and held them point upwards.

"What is our first duty upon assembling?" said the Master.

"To see that none are present but sworn and tried brethren," answered Burr from the south end of the hall (where he was stationed in his official capacity as deputy-grand-Seig).

"Take heed, brethren, is there anyone here unknown or doubtful or suspected?"

"All are good men and true," answered Burr. "Brethren, aid me to form the Iron Circle," spoke the colonel.

Whereupon, every man stepped forward into the center of the hall, holding his naked sword in the right hand. Then, placing each man his left hand upon his neighbor's shoulder, they form in a circle. At a word from the Master, every sword was uplifted and its tip immersed in the blood on the altar, remaining there fully 60 seconds, during which time the Master slowly, solemnly intoned part of the ritual and invocation of the order, which of course cannot be divulged.

The swords were then withdrawn and (while the Master recited another portion of the ritual) clanged together in the form of an arch of steel above the smoking flame that also stood upon the altar, while the blood from off the blades dripped hissing into the brazier.

Colonel Schuyler then stepped into the middle of the circle with an illuminated manuscript in his hand and called upon the brethren to repeat after him, word for word, the ancient and solemn oath of the degree (which they did). First, however, be pointed out to them the figure or letters traced on both sides of the unopened coffin and said they represented the chart or original authorization issued by the Supreme Grand Lodge of Dalkarlheim, founded exactly 800 years ago by Iron Skeggi, the unvanquished Jarl, and thereafter handed down in secret (from fear of the Oriental Conquest) through Konar Thurar the "recorder."

After further impressive ceremonial (which it is unlawful to even mention), every brother formally wiped the blood from of his sword and returned to his seat.

Then the master of the hammer reascended the dais and, turning round with the uplifted sign, said:

"Let us now close this lodge of the Iron Cross in the usual form and chant the parting ode." Each man then filled his long drinking goblet (made of horn) from a large leather bottle of red wine and sang together, while clinking drinking cup to drinking cup:

"Oh, spirit of our Iron Creed,
So stern and strong and high
Help us in this hour of need—
The foe is drawing nigh.
Aid us to free our fatherland
And in its glories share.
Behold thy sign—the naked brand!
Behold the cross we bear!
O, Power—"

Suddenly, in the midst of the solemn anthem, the cock crowed lustily inside of the eight-day clock.

The mechanism had discovered Betsy. Consternation was on every face. Each man's thought was of "spies."

Immediately, the chant ceased, and the master's hammer sounded angrily on the iron altar, and he spake in a hoarse menacing tone, saying, "An alarm from the Evil One. To your steel, O, my brothers! The hour is now."

Each brother stepped swiftly back into the shadow of the wall, sword in hand, gazing towards the clock. While all the lights went out except two on each side of Betsy.

Then the master of the hammer spoke again, saying, "Cast open the hidden chamber—that we may behold an intruder and smite him with the stroke of Ing. Who seeketh unlawfully to unveil the hidden mysteries of Konar hath incurred the penalty and wrath of the brotherhood."

Whereupon, the master caused the red veil to slide down between him and the brethren.

Young Clinton and Swartwout then seized the back of a high bench, fastened to the wall by iron clamps, and dragged it over towards them. Whereupon a creaking sound came from the wall behind the great clock. The rusty mechanism began to move.

The overhead crowing of the cock ceased, and the panels of the eight-day clock opened up from the front, like the leaves of a great iron book, with a harsh grating, grinding sound, exposing, to the astonishment, anger, and dismay of the entire body of men, the pale, frightened form of Miss Betsy, fastened helplessly to the hinges of the unfolding panel by her dress in such a way that she could not move an inch to the right or to the left.

Her head hung down discomfitedly, her face was suffused with blushes, her arms and hands were stretched out at right angles (in the form of a living cross), and from her black, lustrous eyes, great bead-like tears began to roll.

The members of the lodge, sword in hand, rushed out of the darkness toward her (amazed at what they saw); then they stopped suddenly halfway, irresolute, as if recollecting something. They had all thought the intruder a man, a government secret service agent. Now this clock mechanism had been devised in a previous century for the purpose of trapping spies as well as part of the ceremonial. When the old, grey-bearded man (the outer guard) turned the crank in the wall, he had set the spring of the man-trap that now held Betsy helplessly a prisoner.

The iron hammer of the master again sounded thrice, louder than before; the outer guard knocked on the door in response. In the clang of the master's hammer, there was a note of menace and rage not to be misunderstood.

Immediately, every brother came to attention except Clinton and Swartwout, who continued of their own volition to hold on firmly to the lever mechanism that moved the clock and held Betsy captive. If they had pulled it forward another inch, Betsy would have been crushed to death in an instant.

Burr made a sign to the master with his sword, which the master replied to, by another sign without speaking. Then Burr walked over to where Betsy was fastened, moved the lever which locked the mechanism, and stood by her side as if on military parade. She saw him through her agitation and felt safe again. Meanwhile the master's mind was busy considering how he should act. After fully five minutes had elapsed, he stood up and, in slow even tones, evidently hiding a deep emotion, said:

"Brethren! This—this—is terrible, terrible. I hardly know what to do or advise. Never before have I, during twenty-five years' membership of the Order, been placed in such a predicament. Here we have discovered an intruder—a spy—my own daughter—one known to us all. If it had been a man, we would ere this have rid the world of him; for assuredly, the deepest foe of our order is ever him or her who seeks unlawfully to fathom our fates and our purpose. But can my own daughter, can the child of your chosen master, can Elizabeth Schuyler, be considered and treated as a traitor and a spy? Brethren, what shall I do? What shall we all do? My daughter must certainly have heard some of the secrets—she must have listened to the penal oath of the Third Abode, she must have seen the mystery of the great ING—she must have beheld the grips and tokens of the Ninty-and-Nine—she must have heard the Omnific Echo, which we have all sworn that no non-initiate can hear and live. She must also have hearkened to our plans for overthrowing and out maneuvering the king's authority—and in high affairs of the state, a woman's tongue is never to be trusted, even though she be a daughter, a sister, a wife, or a mother. Such, I declare, is the unalterable law. The prisoner before you, she who is my beloved daughter, has thus committed an offence against the Iron Cross, which it is impossible for us as a body, or even as individuals, to condone—on peril of our own lives—for we belong to a world-encircling society that has never yet permitted any breach of its unchangeable constitution. Therefore, should we personally be unable or unwilling to uphold its sacred constitution (in the workings of our own lodge), our lives shall surely pay the forfeit. Brethren—our lives are at stake."

Colonel Schuyler continued in cold, calm, judicial tones—there was not even a tremor in his voice. He had steeled his heart to go through with the matter. He felt that there was no one present who could act on higher grounds than himself, as master of the lodge—as the oldest initiate—and as father of Betsy. (However, he had seen in his own mind a method of escape but judiciously gave no hint of it by act or voice. Colonel Schuyler was a diplomat and an old Indian warrior. He knew how to snatch good out of things evil.)

"The constitution," he said, "clause ten, proclaims the penalty of immediate death against anyone who surreptitiously and unlawfully obtains full or partial knowledge of our mysteries.

"We have all, individually and as a body, sworn a solemn oath to protect these mysteries and uphold that constitution, as against the entire world—more especially against women and slaves, and even against our own kindred—our own mothers, fathers, sisters, wives or daughters.

"Thus, you see the very trying position we are placed in, as a lodge—and the tragic position I am placed in, as a presiding officer of this lodge and father of the imprisoned intruder.

"Even though she is my daughter, the law as it stands must be vindicated. The unwritten code I affirm shall be upheld: as long as I am wielder of the hammer, BETSY SCHUYLER MUST DIE!"

Then he repeated aloud that portion of the code which commanded absolutely the summary execution of all spies and traitors.

When Betsy heard her father's judicial words, a wave of chilling terror shot through her body. She rolled her eyes and looked around at the ghastly skulls, the snake flag, the coffin and its cabalistic letters, the shining book, and the half-hidden faces of the brethren, with their bloody swords, standing around the burning altar. Then she swooned.

When she regained consciousness afterwards, Betsy found herself fastened securely in a heavy oaken chair in the center of the lodge. Burr stood by her right hand side and a young doctor on her left.

The doctor was saying in an undertone, with his thumb on her pulse: "She is coming ground. She is both healthy and strong—stronger in her nerves than many men—which is very fortunate. Indeed, she is a veritable chip off the old block."

Lord Stirling then arose (he was an American by birth, afterwards a field general under Washington). He was a tall, robust, square-built man, slightly grizzled but of a ruddy complexion: a lineal descendant of the Lord of the Isles, famous in Scottish song and story. His mother was the widow of New York's celebrated smuggler "Ready Money Prevost."

"I can keenly feel for Colonel Schuyler," said Lord Stirling, "and I appreciate his inexorable justness in declaring his own child worthy of death. That his beautiful daughter—our beloved, bright-eyed Betsy—has committed a heinous crime against our ancient order I admit, but surely we can discover some other way of securing our secrets and keeping our obligations to the Iron Cross without slaying her. I hope so anyhow."

"If Lord Stirling can suggest any method," said Judge Livingston, "I am sure all of us shall be most happy to adopt it. We are in a sad dilemma. If we execute Miss Betsy, her blood will be on our souls, and if we do not, we ourselves shall be held guilty by an invincible organization and denounced as traitors. In due time, thereafter, we shall assuredly be destroyed by the heavy hand, while even our families shall remain under a curse for three generations. Brethren, I adjure you, do not commit yourselves in haste."

Miss Betsy, I am satisfied, has not become an eavesdropper with any malicious intent. She cannot surely be a royalist spy."

"Betsy," said her father, "what did you do this for? Why were you eavesdropping? For what foolish purpose did you hide yourself in the alcove? Did anyone else know you to be there?"

"Oh, father, I am so sorry," answered Betsy pleadingly, "I did it all just for fun. I never thought I was committing a crime. No one else knows anything about it. Oh, father, do save me. Don't let them kill me!"

"What did you see and what did you hear?" asked her father sternly.

Betsy, thoroughly frightened, explained in a severe cross-examination that she had heard everything of importance, knew all the passwords, grips, and signs—and saw the tragedy and heard the secret speeches. She also repeated the omnific word of AMEN—the word that had never previously been uttered by the lips of a woman or slave. (Many other test questions were put to her which had better remain unwritten, for the Iron Cross is by no means extinct, it is only a thousand times more exactingly select.)

Colonel Schuyler then took his seat on the dais and put the chief question to the vote of the brethren.

"Has Betsy Schuyler incurred the Penalty of ING?"

The voting was unanimously in the affirmative and was so announced, while Burr and Dr. Spring supported Betsy in the chair.

Lord Stirling again rose and said: "Brethren, let us not be too hasty. That the captive is guilty, we all know, but shall we execute her that is another question? I therefore beg to put another test question to the vote if I am in order. It is this: Should Betsy Schuyler be now executed by the members of this lodge in accordance with the ancient formula?"

This led to a prolonged and heated discussion, for every brother well knew that his own life was involved in the decision. Each man understood that in joining the Iron Cross, he carried his life in his hands.

Lord Stirling's motion was put to the vote by the master. The result was ten for and ten against; the casting vote of the master, her own father, could thus settle Betsy's fate.

Betsy's life hung on a hair. Only her father could save her. Col. Schuyler showed no sign. His face was like stone.

Then he arose and dropped his "AYE" vote into the urn, saying: "Brethren, I must vote in the affirmative. My obligation is more to me than the life of a beloved daughter. Let the penalty be carried out. The cause of the Revolution is more to me than the life of any living being—I—I—I will do my duty brethren, even as Job—'though all my kindred perish.'"

At this point, Aaron Burr arose. His fertile brain had also, in the meantime, been busy seeking for some expedient whereby Betsy's life could be saved and the lodge exonerated at the same time from blame or penalty.

"I have a suggestion to offer for the good of the Iron Cross and our own fame."

All the brethren turned inquiringly towards him.

"It is that Miss Betsy Schuyler be now initiated into this lodge, in the regular and lawful manner. By doing so, we can free our minds from the memory of her death and free ourselves (officially at least) from the penalty of the Iron Hand. Our action can thereafter be referred to the Supreme Council to pass upon. I am sure if this trouble is properly represented to them, by our executive, that they must absolve us from the severer blame."

Burr's idea seemed to meet with general approval. The brethren began to look happy again, and Betsy took courage and glanced pleasantly at Burr through her tears and blushes.

Then Robert Troup arose and said: "But if we initiate a woman to our order we break another vital law: 'NO WOMAN SHALL ON ANY ACCOUNT BE ADMITTED.'"

Hamilton then arose and said:

"I believe that Brother Burr's suggestion is a most excellent one. I think we should all feel extremely grateful to him for his very timely proposition. We have also an excellent precedent for such action as he has suggested in an event which happened 8,900 years ago in the kingdom of Surrapuk. A beautiful princess of the royal line named Zilla, being consumed with a burning curiosity to know the mysteries of the Ing, intoxicated her lover, (Crown Prince Arling) by means of a magical love-drug and wormed out of him the first token of the second amen.

"The grand commander—when this was discovered—ordered her to be first initiated into the order, then married to her lover and immured for life in one of the triple-walled harems of the High Priest.

"Thereafter, Prince Arling was kept under the perpetual surveillance of the Selectors of the Slain and finally disappeared in the midst of a great naval battle with the men of Thurar, his younger brother, a man of sterner stuff, being anointed to the throne."

Then George Clinton (afterwards Governor of New York) arose and said: "I also have an idea. It is this that Miss Betsy be initiated as if she were a man and possessed of a man's name. She can adopt her father's name, for example. Thus, we can avoid the difficulty alluded to by Brother Troup.

"Brethren, let us escape from this very awkward predicament the best way we can. Let us accept Miss Schuyler as a sworn brother of the first degree and thus free ourselves from a very grievous responsibility.

"Let her be instructed to avow herself a *man* and we need

not (officially at least) doubt her declaration. Technically also, such declaration will be true, all women are 'mankind.'"

At this, Judge Livingston arose and said, "Brethren and anointed Master, might I also make a suggestion? It is this: Why not also provide Miss Betsy with a husband before she leaves the lodge room? This would be an additional precaution and perhaps a very effective one. As the wife of a brother, her tongue would be doubly sealed. She would not surely consciously betray her husband, father, brother, and cousins to their sure destruction and the confiscation of their property."

The older men smiled grimly at this proposition, but the younger men received it with evident enthusiasm.

The beautiful, blushing Betsy had won the sympathy and love of nearly every one of them by the very brave manner with which she bore herself through an ordeal which might shake the nerve of the strongest man.

Whereupon the question was formally put to the vote:

"Shall Phillip Schuyler, Junior, be elected and initiated as a member of this lodge of the Iron Cross?" Needless to say, Betsy was elected.

She was then released from the bonds that bound her, removed to an ante-room and permitted to arrange her dress for the coming ceremony—in accordance with the preparatory regulations and rules of the order which were quickly explained by her father (who now felt as if a mountain of lead had been lifted from off his heart).

Then the lodge room was rearranged and Betsy readmitted with only her hands bound. By her side walked Burr and Dr. Spring, each armed with a naked sword. . . .

"Mr. Phillip Schuyler, I must now claim your attention to some searching questions, and I expect an honorable series of replies," said the Master to Betsy from the dais as she entered under guard.

"You have been elected as a first-degree brother of the most noble Order of the Iron Cross—an order more ancient than the Pylonites of Atalanta, the temple of Eleusis, the caverns of Kos, the pyramids of Khem.

"Are you now prepared to face every trial with a stout heart, for it is our custom to test the courage and fortitude of every one seeking to lift the Weapon?"

"I am," answered Betsy, prompted by Burr.

"Do you pledge your sacred word of honor not now to withdraw from the distinction of initiation which the Iron Cross proposes to confer upon you, both for its own safety and for yours? Remember, Mr. Phillip Schuyler, Junior, your life is absolutely forfeit, and if we spare that life, we expect you to swear unlimited obedience to the lords of the Iron Cross and be faithful till death. Are you ready to take such oath and make such sacred and solemn declaration?"

"I am," answered Betsy, again prompted by Burr.

"Art thou by inheritance a man of the blood: free-born and without blemish?"

"I am."

"In the hour of supreme dismay, in what dost thou put thy trust?"

"In the Averter of Destruction."

"In what else?"

"In mine own fortitude and the unflinching aid of all my brethren of the blood."

"Should you ever betray the mysteries and purpose of our order, what do you agree should be thy fate?"

"Annihilation," replied Betsy, still prompted by the kind gentle tones of Burr, who quietly stood beside and encouraged her from time to time.

"Art thou prepared to give up friends and family and go forth to battle at the Order's call?"

"I am so prepared," replied Betsy.

"You agree to be a companion, good and true, to strictly uphold the principles of the Iron Cross, as handed down to you, and obey at all times the summons of the Supreme Seven?"

"I do," replied Betsy.

"You agree that it is not in the power of any human being, or association of human beings, to make fundamental changes in the ritual, creed, or secrets symbolized by the Iron Sign, and the Saga of Thurar?"

"I do."

"You agree to aid any brother (companion of the Order) in all his laudable ambitions when requested by him so to do; also at all times and under all circumstances to defend his fame, and his private and public reputation to the utmost of your strength and ability, whether you believe him to be right or wrong?"

"I do."

"You agree that men are fundamentally divided by nature and from birth into the noble and the base?"

"I do."

"You agree that no power, either spiritual or temporal, can abrogate the iron law that the higher man has a just and proper right to reign and possess and, also, that it is nobler in this world to rule over others than to he ruled over?"

"I do."

"You agree that the higher and the lower among men, and throughout all animate nature, can only be discovered to us through and by the omnific Word and procedure of the Sign of Ing."

"I do," replied Betsy.

"You agree that the secret arts, parts, and philosophies of the Wonderful Legend cannot safely be entrusted to subordinate personalities, to woman or to slaves?"

"I do."

"Your answers to these leading interrogations proving satisfactory," continued the master of the hammer, we have now to request you to subscribe to the ancient obligation as a final test of your sincerity; you will therefore take this naked steel in your right hand and this fleshless skull in your left hand.

"Then raising the steel thus, you will repeat after me."

The members of the lodge surrounded Betsy and held their swords in the form of an arch over her head.

"I, Phillip Schuyler, Junior, in the name of the Iron Cross and of the Three Amens, seated upon this coffin, with emblems of mortality in each hand, and in the presence of twenty one brethren of a superior degree, do hereby and hereon, most solemnly and sincerely, pledge on my sacred word of honor to conceal the double philosophy of the Fiery Volume from all persons whatsoever outside the Ring of Fate, that I will hide the same from child or wife, from father, mother, sister, or brother, from fire and wind, from wood and stone, from paper and ink, from solid and liquid, from all things living or dead, from all things spiritual or temporal, from all things born or yet to be born upon Earth, above Earth or beneath it under no less a penalty than that of being taken out at the hour of high night and. . . . with my name and the name of my family being razed forever and ever from the everlasting records of the Lords of the Iron Ing.

"I also pledge myself to uphold and defend the chastity and honor of a brother's wife, sister, mother, and daughter and to never, on any account, reveal what passes within this lodge to priest or to physician, whether in sickness, in death, or under torture."

After further questioning and impressive symbolic ceremonial, the star-eyed Betsy was entrusted with the second sign, countersign, and simulacra of the first degree, and around her waist, Aaron Burr knotted the Mystic Girdle and the Weapon of Fate.

Then spake her father from the dais:

"Brethren, I sincerely thank you for admitting my daughter. I thank you also for my own sake, as well as hers. My position tonight, if you had voted for her rejection, would indeed have been terrible, to say the least. If you had voted for death, I can assure I would never have raised my voice against the immediate execution of the sentence, though it would have wrung my heart and probably blasted my life—or driven me insane.

"It is, I know, better that one life should he extinguished than that all of us should be destroyed. It requires no further words of mine to remind you of the omnipotence of the Iron Cross. Better that we individually and collectively had never been born than to incur its hostility.

"However, under fearful provocation, you have given me back my child. It is as if she had been born again, and in gratitude, therefore—also as an additional safeguard to us—I now adopt the suggestion of Brother Judge Livingston, for it will be admitted that we must to the utmost make ourselves absolutely secure.

"It would be well, I think, that my daughter should marry someone from among those who are present tonight. I therefore offer Betsy as a wife and £10,000 in gold to any man of you whom she herself may select. I will add an additional condition also: that he whom she selects most win himself a high and honorable position in the world within five years."

This proposition met with universal favor and enthusiastic acclaim.

Betsy looked at Burr inquiringly, then at Alexander Hamilton, then at Clinton and young Brockholst Livingston, and then again at Burr.

"Betsy," said her father. "In gratitude for the salvation of your life, are you willing to obey my wish in this matter. You have heard my proposition. Will you now promise to pick a husband exclusively from among the members of this lodge, who are now, every one of them, chancing their lives to save yours?"

Betsy replied in the affirmative—looking demurely yet furtively at Burr and Hamilton alternately—while the tears again rolled down her cheeks.

"Father," she replied. "I will do as you wish. But, O, this is dreadful. Did ever a girl have to go through such terrible things?"

Nevertheless, Betsy had already decided to marry Burr, and if not him, then Hamilton.

Then the lodge took an interval for refreshments. Biscuits, wine, and cheese were placed on a side table. They seated Betsy like a lovely queen on the center of the circle and toasted her, with clinking glasses and naked blades clashing above her wondering head.

Thus, the toastmaster Burr sang,

> "A bumper to Miss Betsy—
> Confusion to the King—
> Now fill your flowing glasses
> And let your voices ring."

Thus, the brethren enjoyed themselves for a while, drinking revolutionary toasts (as was the old custom), while many of the younger men were eagerly making love to Betsy.. After a while, Colonel Schuyler took Betsy over to the clock and explained its hidden mechanism while, at the same time, gently chiding her for her perilous breach of decorum. He showed her how the machine was intended for the entrapment of spies or eavesdroppers, how it was fitted up to crush and slay anyone who ever surreptitiously hid therein, how the turning over of a lever within the lodge room set it in motion, and how, upon the pressing of another lever, the crushed body would be cast into a sewer that connected with the Hudson.

Before the business of the gathering concluded, Colonel

Schuyler made a short address, impressing upon the brethren the increasing necessity of care and circumspection in all external affairs and lodge matters, as the times were full of danger, suspicion, underground conspiracy, threatenings of civil war, arrest, and deportation.

He also spoke of the unwritten and traditional history of the Iron Cross, pointing out that it had been in existence for ages, that, being founded on the eternal order of things it could never be crushed out, that it arose again and again (at critical periods) to vindicate the inherent identity of the individual man against the groping terrorism of insane monarchs, shrieking demagogues, and crazed serviles.

Then he turned to Betsy and, quoting from the Book of Ritual (the Book of Double Interpretations), read unto her in highly impressive tones:

"Should you ever, from any cause whatsoever, fail to remember your solemn pledge tonight, and, in consequence thereof, should injury result to any of the brethren or to the Order in general, then evil shall surely come upon thee and thine to the third and fourth generation.

"Thy days shall be shortened in the land of thy fathers and thy children made desolate. For thine iniquity and treachery, thy kindred shall suffer as well as thyself. They shall be cast down and beg their bread from door to door, for the punishment of wrong-doing cannot be absolved. Their dwellings shall be given over to the loaners of money, who shall sweep away all that they hath. No one shall aid them in the dark hour of their despair, for the penalty of sin is in the blood of the sinful breed. No one shall have mercy upon them, and both thou and they shall be blotted out forever from the memory of man and woman.

"As nature is inexorable to the backslider (and to his generations), so is the Iron Cross. It neither relents nor relaxes nor repents. Onward and ever onward it goes, over good and evil, through glacial ages and ages of flame, through joy and through sorrow, through tranquillity, decay, and hushless whirlwinds of strife."

Now, Colonel Schuyler was, in his heart, very proud of his beautiful daughter for her display of courage, and when the ceremonial and the toasts had all been concluded, he kissed and commended her tenderly and walked out of the open lodge door with her on his arm, warning her again and again to be silent and discreet.

It was the small hours of the morning before the brethren completed their labors and finally dispersed. It was agreed that the next meeting should be held in Liberty Hall, at Elizabethtown, one of the Livingston's new mansions. A few of the brethren living at a distance were cordially invited to stay all night by the hospitable Judge Livingston who afterwards became the personal friend of General Bonaparte (the grandest, boldest, and most commendable venturer of his age.)

Burr and Hamilton departed together. At that time, Burr was sojourning with some relatives of his brother-in-law, Judge Tappan Reeve.

"Well, with the exception of the trouble over Miss Betsy," remarked Hamilton inquiringly, "our first move has been an exceptionally brilliant success. What next, Burr?"

"O, don't be in a hurry," replied Burr, "let the yeast work—let it have time to work. A little leaven, you know, leaveneth the whole lump. One thing, however, I do not like is this unfortunate affair of Miss Schuyler. It fills me with a curious foreboding of evil to you and to me. There is an old saying—and, I think, a true one—that bad luck overtakes conspirators who share their plans with a woman?"

"What do you mean, Burr? Do you think Miss Betsy will denounce us to the government before our plans are completed. Betsy, our newly made 'brother', the beautiful, black-eyed Betsy."

"I don't know what to think," answered Burr. "But an inner voice tells me that the presence of a woman among us in this early stage of our venturing presages misfortune, the breaking of friendships, perhaps the spilling of blood. I think she is in love with you too, Hamilton. If so, you are a lucky dog. She is very handsome, well-born, well-bred, has a certain dowry of ten thousand pounds in gold, and her father has a splendid lumber and trading estate near Saratoga. He is, I hear, the richest man in Albany, a sort of Colonial baron."

"Look here, Burr," Hamilton's replied. "That Miss Betsy is handsome, I admit, but that she is in love with me, I doubt. She danced all the best dances with you and young Livingston. For my own part, I love another woman—a lovely creature. But I am a penniless student, and Betsy's promised dowry is an almost irresistible attraction. Is she not good, beautiful, and rich?

"In this world, a man without money is like a prisoner in chains. And to marry without money is, therefore, a hazardous undertaking, very. After all, Burr, gold is, the universal divinity. Gold, gold, how glorious is gold! And yet, love is glorious too. How happy must he be who has them both. I have no patience with those who laud the beauty of poverty. Let them be poor who want to be poor, but give me riches. Ah, it is godlike, Burr, to be wealthy and powerful and young."

"No doubt about it," answered Burr. "Your sentiments are mine. Gold is certainly the most convincing thing in the world, but the love of woman is sweet beyond compare. Why, then, not marry Miss Betsy if she loves you? Why not set yourself out to capture her? But, by the way, who is this other 'lovely creature' you rave about?"

"Her name is Prevost. You have never met her," replied Hamilton. "And the trouble of it is that she is the wife of another man and is ten years older than myself. You've heard of Colonel Sir George Prevost, who led the Royal American Regiment so gallantly at the storming of Quebec under General Wolfe. I met her about three months ago in New York, and I can assure you she stole my heart before I had spoken five words to her. Indeed, I was drawn towards her as if she were a living magnet."

"What is the new divinity's name?"

"Her maiden name is De'Visme—Theodosia De'Visme. She is of Swiss descent, has great, lustrous hazel eyes, long, brown hair, a glorious complexion, a superbly moulded ankle, walks with the step and mien of a Cleopatra, and wears a silken turban, which sets her off to great advantage."

"But," replied Burr, "as you cannot have the wife of another man, you had better marry Miss Schuyler. I am sure it would please her father, for he has, I've heard, a very high opinion of you because of those pamphlets you wrote in conjunction with Livingston."

"Burr," said Hamilton "you touch me to the quick. I really don't know how to act for the best. What would you do if you were in my shoes?"

"I would be practical. I would marry Miss Schuyler. She has the money, and with money, you can become famous.

"You have never been in love?" inquired Hamilton.

"No, I don't know what love is. I only know of love as it is in books. I have met many specimens of the superb feminine, but none of them has ever put me off my balance."

"You will meet your fate some day, Burr, and that you'll understand how I feel. I believe I could willingly lay down my life to gain Mrs. Prevost. I love her madly, Burr. I love her with a fierce, passionate, burning love, a love that can never be quenched within me, except by the clods rattling down on my coffin lid. Burr, I feel I could commit murder for that woman."

"Hamilton! With all your cold calculating phrases, you are yet as full of sentiment as any maiden. She must indeed be a glorious woman to have captivated you in that way, for you are so very fastidious."

"She is, Burr. She is a royal creature—a woman beyond compare."

"But as she is married," replied Burr, "that is an insuperable difficulty."

"Married or not married, I love her still," cried Hamilton with an emphatic gesture. "Her husband may die."

The two friends walked on conversing thus until they reached Ferry Street.

That night, as Aaron Burr blew out the light in his room before retiring, hhe muttered to himself, "Betsy loves me, not Hamilton: that I am absolutely certain. She and her ten thousand belong to Aaron Burr, if he so desire. I have a strange wish, however, to behold this lovely Mrs. Prevost of the Silken Turban. Do I care for Betsy? No. No I don't."

Hamilton, after he had bade farewell to Burr, also began (as was his wont) to inwardly reflect on all that happened during that eventful night.

Damme! he thought to himself. *What an infernal ass I was to tell the secret of my love to Burr of all men. He will never rest now till he makes her acquaintance, and then, it is all over with me. Every woman who beholds him becomes his captive.He has a wonderful influence over women. They crowd around him like moths around a candle. Even Betsy, whom I felt so sure of until to-night, is no longer sure. She has met this Puritan Lovelace. However, there are as good fish in the sea as ever came out of it.*

Chapter V.

THE ENCHANTED CLEARING

The lightning flashed in blinding sheets. The heavens were veined with flame. The rain poured down in drowning torrents. The bitter wind howled ferociously, driving icily from the iron North. It seemed as if the traditional windows of the sky had suddenly burst open. Thunder roared and rolled like the growling of some wild aerial monster. The world shivered. All nature shook in terror.

The entire army halted. It was impossible to march further in the teeth of such a snarling hurricane. It was more than human nature could do to stand up against such a tempest. The wind actually lifted men off their feet. Into the faces of soaked and hungry regiments, the shrieking blast hurled its whirling floods of sleet and water.

The troop horses turned end-for-end in the ranks and shook with cold. Their ears drooped sadly. They looked the very picture of misery. Neither by whip nor spur could they be prevailed upon to face the angry blast. No trooper moved out of the saddle, for to do so would be more unpleasant still. Horses and horsemen stood there and shivered while the storm moaned and howled and the rain splashed down. The men wrapped their overcoats and cloaks about themselves (those who had any) and waited patiently "for orders."

The ground rapidly became soaked with water. What had been dry soil a few hours before was soon a morass. The hoofs

---

1 *The Princess: The Splendour Falls on Castle Walls* by Alfred, Lord Tennyson.

of the horses, the wheels of the wagons and cannon, ploughed it up like a furrowfield. The rear regiments closed, to where the advance guard halted. It seemed as if the army was as an islet of men and horses in the midst of a yellow, muddy, gurgling sea. The creeks went rumbling down in tawny flood, and the great river swelled higher and ever higher up its sloping banks.

The infantrymen soon broke their ranks and crowded under the lee of nearby rocks and boulders, or sought shelter in hollow half-burned trees that slowly rotted black and solitary in the dreary valley. Some of the men, too tired to move, stood out in the open, huddled together, sheltering one another even as wild animals do when overtaken by a blizzard on the open prairie.

After about an hour of waiting, the rain abated, but the wind increased in violence and frigidity. From over the mountains and ice fields of Canada, it raced. Then cloaks and coats and beards froze hard and stiff. Icicles hung to moustaches and to the manes and tails of the horses, while, away in the distance, the passing thunder boomed and reverberated towards the South. Then with approach of evening, the welcome order was given to off-saddle and pitch camp for the night. Whereupon everybody felt happy. Even the horses whinnied with evident satisfaction. Soon, the tents were pitched in rows, the horses picketed, the wagons hauled up together, and tarpaulins stretched over them as shelter for the teamsters. Gradually, and with infinite patience, the wet, weary, and footsore soldiers scattered to gather damp wood, which they quickly split up with tomahawks carried in their belts. Before long, a thousand bivouac fires were burning and steaming on the muddy ground while the soldiers sat around cooking meat on the end of ramrods, building shelters, drying their clothes, or trying to keep warm and yet outside the smoke of the fires.

As darkness rolled down, the scene became extremely picturesque to those who had time or inclination to think of such an unpractical thing.

The camp was in a valley, surrounded by low hills and on the bank of a river. Here and there, forest trees stood up gaunt and bare, wintrified, ghastly, and charred black by bush fires.

For miles, the bivouac fires spread over the valley and reflected themselves on the swollen river—now level with its banks. The camp fires gleamed and glittered and sputtered in the darkness. From a distance, they looked like the lamps of some great city as seen from the sea, or as a galaxy of stars and will-o'-the-wisps dancing a wild fandango along the distant shores of some enchanted island.

Around the outside of the camp, sentries were posted at stated distances, and in the center thereof stood a square marquee tent over which flew a pennant. The tent was that of General Benedict Arnold, commander of the American army, the army that invaded Canada in 1775. The expedition having been badly managed was a failure, and the army was in slow retreat upon its base.

From the start of this expedition, everything seemed to go wrong, especially the commissariat, which is the backbone of an army, inasmuch as men cannot fight well or march well who are not well fed. The bravery of the soldiers, their endurance and fortitude, could not have been surpassed, but what use is bravery and endurance if the directing genius be missing? Verily, soldiers are plentiful, and brave men are not scarce, but great generals are rare.

Night closed down. General Arnold sat in his tent by a rough table of newly split pine slabs. He was a tall, handsome man, evidently fond of "good living." He was eating and drinking heartily, while, outside, many of his very best men were shivering without rations and without shelter of any kind. This, however, did not in any way disturb General Arnold. He was not built like a Cæsar. He cared nothing for the comfort of his men. He thought only of his own comfort, his own beef and wine

On the table before him were steaming dishes of grilled venison, roasted potatoes, and flat corn-cakes, and nearby were two casks of liquor: one of Jamaica rum and one of Spanish wine.

In the center of the tent, a brazier of charcoal burned, its purpose being to heat and dry the tent. Soldier-servants bustled about, putting things in order and making their commander as snug as possible. On the tent pole hung the general's hat, cloak, and sword. By the door of the tent lay two or three half-frozen saddles, and not far away stood a row of black field guns, from the black muzzles of which, and also from their muddy wheels, hung icicles.

In the distance behind, the campfires flashed and flamed. Now and then, the wind would take a whirl and fling high in the air millions of blazing sparks.

While in the act of gulping down a large tumbler of liquor, the general was surprised to see the slight form of Aaron Burr, his favorite aide, enter. Upon Burr's handsome but somewhat emaciated face, there was a look of some set purpose.

General Arnold gazed at him inquiringly. "General," spake Burr, "I have come to place my resignation in your hands. I am sick unto death of this business. There is no more fighting to be done here, and I have certain private affairs to attend at home."

"Mr. Burr, this is most surprising to me. What is the matter with you?" replied the general wonderingly.

"Sir," answered Burr (at this time, he was a major, having been promoted to that rank for conspicuous bravery in the field and "special service" at Montreal), "all through this unfortunate expedition, I have served both you and General Montgomery most faithfully. As long as there was any fighting to be done, I have always done my share. You know I never shirked any hardship nor any duty, however arduous, however desperate."

"I know," interrupted General Arnold, "but continue."

"Now that there is no more prospect of battle, for we are marching homeward, I am desirous of returning direct to Albany, where more exciting things than a slow and orderly retreat are happening. I would go back to where there is some hope of participating in real war. If I stay with you, I must gradually degenerate into a mere drill-instructor like the rest. That is not my ambition. I feel as if, somehow, I was made for higher things. I, therefore, officially place my resignation in your hands."

Burr handed him a paper, whereupon the general poured a glass of wine and, courteously, but unsteadily, handed it over to the young officer. Burr drank it to the last drop, for the night was one in which a glass of good strong liquor could not fail to be other than acceptable, especially to a rain-soaked, storm-battered soldier.

"Major Burr," spake the general kindly, "your words astonish me; you almost take away my breath. Why should you retire? You are one of my bravest, most vigilant, and most trusted officers. Just as you are getting seasoned to military life, and accustomed to me, you wish to resign. This seems unreasonable. Why not stay with me, and I will see that you get all the promotion you desire? You have already been highly recommended for your bravery in front of Quebec, and as to your conduct in carrying my dispatch to the late General Montgomery, it was and is beyond all praise.[1] Stay with me, Major Burr, and before you are twenty-five, I guarantee, if the war goes on, you shall be a brigadier-general. What more can any man wish for? I see you are overflowing with ambition, and I like you for it. Ambition becomes a man.

"I will even admit that your natural military talent perhaps equals my own, but then, your youth: you are not yet twenty-one, and your very boyish appearance is somewhat against you for appointment to positions of sole responsibility.

1 ≠ General James Montgomery. "The Princely Montgomery." Son of Sir Thomas Montgomery. M.P. for Londonerry.

"I have now with me very few officers of first-rate ability, foresight, and resolution. Most of them take their knowledge of strategy from antiquated drill hooks. They do not attempt to think for themselves. They rely too much on superior orders. This is the weakness, the unfortunate weakness of my force, and it is also the very reason why I particularly desire you to remain with me. You seem to know instinctively how to keep my motley command together, without any discouraging martinetism and, at the same time, without imperiling the essentials of battle. Besides that, you have a commendable talent for guerilla tactics.

"I know I can depend on you to do the right thing, at the right time, even without orders. You are a most self-reliant man, Major Burr, and, in such a war as this, men like you are invaluable. You seem to understand the tremendous possibilities that are latent in things"

"General, I thank you for your very high opinion of my military capacity. Nevertheless, I must go. I am a volunteer officer—not bound in any way—and my resolution to resign is final.

"Indeed, I have a boat waiting in readiness on the river for my departure. I have employed six discharged soldiers to row me down to Albany. I start tomorrow morning from Crow Point, near the Hanging Rock ford."

"Burr," said the general with asperity, "I have not yet accepted your resignation. I appreciate your services too highly to part with you. I wish you to sleep upon it. The physical miseries of our march are nearly at an end."

"My general's appreciation of my services is very gratifying. But it would have been more gratifying still if you and Montgomery had adopted my suggestion and captured Quebec. I still believe, if that suggestion had been acted upon, this army would have accomplished the mission it was sent by Congress to perform. Now we would have been camping as conquerors within the great Canadian citadel.

"It fills me, therefore, with bitter humiliation and wrath to think that I should be wasting my time and any talents that I possess to no practical purpose and, at the same time, exist in this state of semi-hunger and camp misery.

"If Montgomery had given me the scaling party, as I wished, and then deployed his own men in extended order instead of quarter column—with instructions to close in and charge at the critical moment—we would certainly have captured the block-house and, through it, the entire city.

"Then afterwards, General Arnold, if you also had considered my proposition, Quebec would have had to surrender through sheer starvation. You remember I advised the systematic denudation of the country around the city and the burning of all possible supplies. Is it not ever characteristic of a good general to strike at his enemies' chief source of supplies? Here again, I failed to gain your ear, though you now commend me in words—mere words.

"Consequently, your command is retreating without credit. All this I have brooded over. It makes me sore and determined to no longer serve under a commander who needlessly marches his men to failure, disaster, and defeat."

At this, Benedict Arnold arose from his seat, his face purple with anger. He made as if to reach for his sword but, on second thoughts, withdrew his hand, saying in tones of half-drunken asperity:

"Major Burr, do you wish to insult me, sir? Do you know who I am, sir? Beware, sir. You carry your self-sufficiency too far. But I will discipline you, sir. I now positively refuse to accept your resignation. Here, take it back. Go away, sir. Go to your tent, sir. Consider yourself under arrest, and do not leave the camp without my positive orders."

"General Arnold," answered Burr, "I have made every arrangement for going, and I am going."

"If you leave this camp without orders, sir, I will court martial you for mutiny and have you shot—shot, sir—shot like a mutineer. You are a brave man, sir, in action, but you do not understand discipline. Go to your tent, sir; consider yourself a prisoner," said the general, foaming at the mouth with anger.

"General Arnold," replied Burr haughtily (now thoroughly aroused and boiling with youthful indignation), "I will leave your camp when it pleases me. You talk of having me court-martialed. Do you know that there is not an officer or a man in your whole army who would lift a hand against 'Little Burr'? In this matter, you are 'general' only in name. You imagine you have the power to 'discipline' me and have me shot, but you are mistaken. You haven't the force to do it. You have my written resignation in your hands. I am free: I am leaving the camp. If this is mutiny, make the most of it. I am Aaron Burr."

The young major turned on his heel and strode out of the tent. *The drunken beast*, thought Burr to himself as he mounted his old troop horse in the darkness and straightway rode out of camp toward the Hanging Rock ford. *Does he think to imprison me in his camp like a raw recruit?*

Such incompetent commanding officers would ruin any army. They are only fit to be drill sergeants. He has no control of himself, little real self-confidence, and his strategy is that of an old apple wife. He cannot contend with our new American conditions; he hasn't the brains nor the organizing instinct; and he smiles and flatters too fulsomely to be genuine. How he praised my 'military capacity' because he wished to annex my brains and gain for himself the credit of my study and my plans. But I see through him. I know every move of his mind.

Verily, he would have made a famous politician. That's just where General Arnold would have shone: filling his paunch with beef and wine, his pockets with other peoples' money, betraying his friends, selling his country, and looking pious.

Only for me, the entire expedition would have been wiped out. I have but saved from total ruin an incompetent general. Why should I have done it? What good have I done? Would it not have been better to let him be ruined? There are better men waiting for a chance to distinguish themselves. For the future, I will not give my brains to build up the reputation of any man.

Now, Major Burr's horse was not in good condition on account of the hard marching and general insufficiency of corn and grass. Consequently, although the distance was only about fifteen miles to the spot where his boat lay waiting, Burr calculated that it would take the best part of a night to accomplish the journey.

When about halfway, one of his horse's forefeet got jammed in a tangle of roots that littered the road. In struggling to recover itself, the horse dragged off a shoe, together with a portion of the hoof attached. This caused the weary animal to go lame entirely, and Burr thereupon concluded to leave the horse at some convenient place along the road and walk the remainder of the distance on foot.

Now the road to the ford was only a narrow bridle track, cut through the dense woods and winding around and over low hills, with here and there a clearing. Burr had never traveled it before, and, therefore, it is not surprising that in the pitch-darkness, he lost his way at a point where several trails crossed one another.

After traveling along for about an hour, leading his lame horse slowly by the bridle, he came to a small natural clearing in the woods or what appeared to be such.

In the midst of the clearing shone a round, glassy, inky-looking lake, from which steam arose. Alongside the lake was a pyramidal mound shaped like a woman's breast. A grass-grown footpath wound around it to the top, where stood a square altar of unhewn stones upon which a fire flickered. Halfway up the mound, a small log cabin had been roughly erected, the chimney of which rose through the side of the mound. A big fire was burning inside, for the smoke rolled out in dense clouds that coiled up in fantastic shapes against the light of the sinking moon, across the face of which, the clouds rushed south as if in pursuit of each other.

Burr walked up the mound, leaving his horse below, and looked down the wide open slab chimney. What a strange spot for a home, *he thought*. Perhaps it is a place of robbers or a hermit's hut

Through the chimney, he could see nearly all the interior. A strange sight met his gaze.

Upon a couch of dry leaves alongside the fire lay a young and very beautiful woman. She had an Oriental appearance with long, wavy hair and brown-tinted skin. She was slumbering. The color of her hair was golden-red (the color of greatness and power). She was half-covered with a long, gauzy robe.

Over the fire hung an old-fashioned iron pot with three legs, from which arose a pungent but not disagreeable odor. All around the woman was a halo or emanation of peculiar undefinable luminance. She was dreaming and talking in her sleep. Every now and then, she kept repeating alternately in French and English, "Come unto me, O my true love, come unto me. Over waters and forests, I wait my spirit unto thy side—my wish to thy ear. My dark-eyed conqueror, I behold thee once more. Come to me, my true love, my true love. Come to me that I may clasp thee to my bosom, forever and ever, that all may be fulfilled."

At this, she wound her arms as if holding some loved one to her breast. Burr understood French perfectly, and as he heard her passionate prayer, a curious, wondering feeling of love and mesmeric fascination took possession of him. Yet he felt somehow half-doubtful of himself, half-terrified. In his heart was a fear; in his brain was a fire. *What does it mean?* he thought.

Meanwhile, the storm had rolled up again. For ten minutes, the rain plunged down in swishing torrents, Whereupon, he determined to seek temporary refuge in the little log hut.

He felt like a man enchanted, as if some unknown power had possession of his will and impelled him, as it were. to do exactly what it wished. An inner voice kept urging in his ear, "Go inside, Aaron Burr. She is calling unto thee. Be not afraid."

Thereupon, he walked around to the door and knocked, but no reply came. He knocked again louder, still no reply. Then he looked through a crevice in the door. The beautiful woman still slept; the pot still boiled; the fire still burned.

"Go inside, Aaron Burr," said the voice. Hesitating no longer, he pushed open the unfastened door and entered. As the door swung ajar, the light from the fire shone upon an unrusted horseshoe nailed on the door. It seemed somehow familiar to Burr, and he therefore examined it closer.

"Wonder of wonders," he thought to himself. "It is my own horse's shoe, lost an hour ago. I know it by its brightness, its peculiar shape, and the piece of bleeding hoof attached."

Now, Aaron Burr was neither a spiritual, moral, nor physical coward, yet at this discovery, a thrill of involuntary dread passed through him.

"There is something uncanny here," he thought. The dreaming woman lay by the fire, moaning as if in pain and repeating what appeared to be a liturgic incantation in some unknown tongue.

Burr spoke to her in English, in French, in Latin, and in several other languages he knew. She did not reply and yet seemed half awake. Then he stretched forth his band and touched her naked flesh on the shoulder; she did not move. He shook her, yet she continued, impassive. Every time his hand came in contact with her skin, however, a peculiar sensation swept over him like a galvanic shock. Wonder at "the Unknown" grew slowly upon him, and his hair began to stand on end.

This is creepy, thought he. *Perhaps she is dying or in a trance or has fainted. But why is such a woman here? Her beauty is extraordinary. Her flesh is warm and soft, and she looks so lovely, so magically bewitching. What shall I do?*

He stepped back towards the door intending to go away. Then, irresolute, he turned to her side and, stooping, picked up her hand and felt its pulse. The pulse was normal. However, as he let go of her hand, it seemed to cling to him and fill his excited brain with strange, overmastering thoughts.

"She is in perfect health," he said to himself, "and yet, I am sure there is something wrong with her. What is it, and what

shall I do? That is the point. How beautiful she looks in her thin gauzy robe. Her form and features are positively divine. She reminds me of some Oriental princess. How soft and warm and pleasing she is to me. I believe I could love her."

But even as he gazed, a curious change came over her appearance. The long, glossy, gold-colored hair became grey. The shimmering, gauzy robe became coarse linsey-woolsey. The delicately moulded features and rounded limbs were transformed, and the swelling bosom shrank. What appeared to be a young and charming maid was changed, as it were, in a moment of time, into a parchment-faced, weazened, little old woman, half-blind, halt, and lame.

It is, it must be, some occult sorcery. It surpasses all I have ever read or heard of before. Perhaps there is something in magic after all. Is not "magic" the ancient name for "science"? There may be half-hidden forces and elements in nature that certain persons, by accident or otherwise, have re-discovered and applied, The wisest of us are but as infants in knowledge. In my own being, I know there are unaccountable powers and instincts. Verily, the magic sciences of ancient tmes may have had greater modifying and cre-

*ative power over both life and death than we can now conceive of
as probable or possible.*

With such unspoken thoughts as these flashing and dancing incoherently through his bewildered brain, he again turned to leave the seemingly bewitched hut, whereupon the wrinkled old woman awoke, and looking straight at him, she said familiarly, as if she had known him all her life:

"Aaron Burr, be not alarmed at what thou hast held. But let no man know. In days that are past, thou did'st live and strive. In days yet to come, thou shalt live and strive again and again. For thou art one of the immortal ones, even as I am. I die not, and neither shalt thou die. I summoned thee to my side here and now because thou art the reincarnation of him who loved me and made me happy in centuries long gone by.

"For the tenth time my Manoa invocation for the restoration of youth and love has proved a failure; the spell of Mantra, from the *om* of Konar Thurar, still rests on me, and on thee also. Thus, our lives are still separate. The combination of ingredients that I have searched for to the ends of the world have again eluded me. The beverage of regeneration that I brewed with such confidence and skill has again proved incomplete. Thou doubtest me, O Aaron Burr, but, nevertheless, the 'herb' is that, once tasted, maketh man or woman 'eternal' in the flesh and the peer of all human loveliness.

"As thou did'st see, I failed, but, someday, I shall succeed. My wish, however, through all the ages, is for thee and only thee, but thy greatness is not yet. Remember, O Aaron Burr, thou shalt be born again to a mightier name and a mightier fame—within a century from the day of thy death.

"Then thou shalt know pure delight, and then I shall know youth and beauty and be seated at thy side while brassy legions go marching by in triumph, conquerors of the world.

"O, Aaron Burr, thou that are 'yet to be' (in the fullness of time), how blessed, how truly blessed a thing it is to be young, famous, beautiful, powerful and beloved?"

Burr looked at her long, lean features, her outstretched skeletal arm, with a feeling of mingled awe and wonder. Seeming to read his thoughts, she continued:

"Go, Aaron Burr, go. Go forth to meet a foreordained destiny. Go forth to live and love, to do and die, not once or twice or thrice, but again and again and again. Thou shalt drink deeply of the bitter and of the sweet. Thou shalt see blood and rise to power. Thou shalt lead warriors amid the acclaim of men, and thou shalt win (even as of old-time) the mad, undying, cruel love of woman.

"Thereafter shalt thou be dashed down and betrayed, and no man shall dare raise his voice on thy behalf. Nevertheless, all is well with thee—all is well. And some day we two shall meet again and wed again, even as in the golden days of silk and sendal, by the banks of, the beautiful river that flows past the seats of the strong.

"Verily, I say unto thee, O my beloved one, the conquest of age and of death cometh unto man. Life is everlasting to some. When man emerges from the womb, he is arising from the tomb.

"Go, O Aaron Burr, go. I belong to the half realm of Val, but thou art as yet in the land of men."

Then, with a piteous wailing sigh, she motioned him a second time to go, pointing towards the outer darkness with her long, gaunt, bony hand, upon which gleamed (in the fading firelight) a great flashing carbuncle with a curious device, like unto the Coiled Serpent Banner of the Iron Cross.

Chapter VI.

THE PROPHECY

Passively, as if controlled by some unseen power outside of himself, Aaron Burr turned to depart. Then again, he scrutinized closer the transfigured woman. As he did so, he observed a small wound upon her breast from which blood slowly oozed.

Suddenly, a further thought struck him, and he turned and said unto her, in his most winning way, "Madame, I perceive there is something more than human in this interview. I feel that you may, perhaps, know things hidden to mortals. I would therefore question you again."

"Two questions only will I answer. Then thou must depart. I listen."

"Madam, it is well. When first I beheld thee, I was inflamed with love and desire, but now thou art so changed, so strangely transformed, that I hardly know thee as the same person. Nevertheless, I would ask from thee (for surely thou art a seeress, a beyond woman perhaps), what is my fate? What is the fate of my country and people? I am sure, O weird woman of the woods, that in some way unknown to me, thou canst see into the immediate future."

Whereupon she stood up, looked into the boiling cauldron, stirred the fire with her lean arm, and gazed long and steadfastly into Burr's face in a searching way, saying:

---

1   Francis James Child, "Kemp Owyne" or "Kempion", Child Ballad 34, *The English and Scottish Popular Ballads* (Boston: Haughton, Mifflin and Company 1882–1896).

"Aaron Burr, learn to endure and bear with fortitude calamities no man may cure. For as thou art born, so shalt thou be, and all is well with the world.

"As for thy people, they shall become invincible for a period and half a period. For a time and half a time, the world shall sink before them. Pygmy Europe and hoary Asia shall they measure with a single glance of the eye. Their armies shall be as thunderbolts and their families as broods of young lions. Their fleets shall sweep the oceans, steer into the Pit beneath the seas, and soar on pinions of the wind over mountains of iron and of gold.

"I see mighty engines of metal and uranium. I see rushing machines of creation and destruction. I see the red victors and pale vanquished. I see haughty Babylons on the shores of embattled lakes and on banks of lordly rivers. I see the smoke and storm of flaming iron, the rumbling roar of looms, the ceaseless clang of hammers, the hissing snarl and flash of harnessed lightning.

"I see grandeur and power, glory and wealth, then decay and the fiery re-borning. I see majestic temples and altars of the gods. I see magnificent days of wrath and wood and ashes. I see earth-shaking monsters and warriors of flame, the sea boiling like a pot, the moon colored like blood, brother fighting against brother, father against son, and—confusion of confusion— wives wandering free.

"There is blood upon thee, O Aaron Burr, but fear it not. Go the way of the warrior. The man of peace is not beloved of the gods. Nobility is in thy purpose, but strong foes shall come up against thee, stronger than thy strength.

"Three things do I adore in my beloved: a proud heart, a silent tongue, and hands that fear not death.

"Farewell, my past and my future lover, thou delight of my soul. Go the way of the proud one. Let no man make thee afraid and no woman weaken thy soul."

As Burr turned to go (this time, he went), a sort of hypnotic numbness came over his brain. A phantasmagoria of his own future career galloped like Brocken wraiths thru his brain in a series of stage-like scenes. His memory refused to retain them, but all through his afterlife, he recognized them one by one as they came true (which they all did).

As he walked out of the hut into the cold damp air that night, he felt himself like a man awaking from a drug-induced stupor.

Meantime, the thunderstorm had again abated, and the angry moon shone out brightly over a dripping forest.

Burr walked back down the mound to where he had fastened his horse to a tree, at the entrance of the clearing. He began to remove the saddle and bridle with the intention of letting the lame animal go.

To his intense surprise, the horse seemed unaccountably filled with new life and vigor. Upon arrival at the clearing, the poor brute could scarcely walk, but now his lameness had entirely disappeared. He cocked his ears like a three-year-old colt and actually pranced. Looking at the hoofs, Burr observed with further astonishment that the lost shoe had been replaced.

He picked up the horse's foot and examined it by the light of the moon, and, as far as he could see, it was exactly as when he left General Arnold's camp a couple of hours ago.

Aaron Burr wondered mightily and thought to himself, *Am I dreaming? Am I losing my senses? Am I bewitched or dazed? What is the matter with me? What is the meaning of these mysterious happenings? How attractive was the sight of that young woman on the couch of leaves! Surely I have seen her before, and yet I cannot recollect where. Then she knew my name? I can never forget her. there was a something positively uncanny about her. Perhaps human life may be artificially prolonged for centuries, nay for ages, and the old tradition of rebirth—reincarnation—may have a solid basis in fact. I feel within myself wonderous throbbings of some double existence in the past—some half-unknown life of long ago wherein I sojourned, as it were, in a sort of dreamland. It is not impossible that I may have really lived and loved and fought in ages long gone by."*

With such thoughts chasing each other through his sur-charged brain, he tightened the girths of his saddle, mounted, and started to ride away. Then an impulse came to him to have one last look at the scene of his adventure. He turned round in the saddle and saw nothing. He rubbed his eyes and looked again. The very landscape had been transfigured. He was now riding along a narrow bridle track, and all around were gaunt, wet, moss-grown trees, swaying from side to side by the over-head force of the wind. The log cabin with the blazing fire, the circular mound with the burning altar on top, and the steaming lake had all disappeared.

Aaron Burr pinched his thigh to discover whether he was really alive or dead or just dreaming. As he did so, a gaunt, grey she-wolf, came slinking across the trail right ahead of him. Her eyes glittered with a supernatural light.

The horse snorted and shied in great terror. Burr reached his right hand into his holster. He grasped a pistol and attempted to withdraw it but could not. He tugged at the pistol with all his strength, but it would not move an inch out of the holster. Meanwhile, the old she-wolf limped away through the woods and disappeared with a prolonged mournful howl that sounded almost human. Then the pistol came out with ease but too late for use.

Burr's horse was now in splendid heart. He cantered down the valley towards the river in grand style. He leapt flooded creeks and wind-thrown trees as if he had wings. In less than an hour, horse and rider covered the remaining seven miles and arrived at the Hanging Rock ford.

Here the boatmen had pitched their initial camp. One of

them unsaddled the horse, whereupon the beast fell down and died. By this time, Major Burr had grown so accustomed to wonders that the sudden death of his troop horse did not further surprise him. To satisfy his curiosity, however, he examined the lead animal's hoofs and found that the shoe torn off during the first part of his journey, and then so mysteriously replaced at the clearing, had again disappeared. Indeed, seemingly, it had never really been replaced, for the horse's hoof was raw and torn and bleeding.

Burr said nothing about this weird adventure to the boatmen. *They would think me mad*, he thought, *or laugh at me. They have no conception of anything outside the common rut.*

Then, being very weary from the days' march and the long night ride, he straightway went into a bell tent (which the boatmen had prepared for him), where he lay down upon a rough couch of dry leaves, covering himself with military rugs, and soon fell sound asleep.

By daylight next morning, the boat was launched on the yellow river. Aaron Burr was rapidly steering south—steering home—between banks lined and overhung by a grand primeval forest, in which the wild beasts roamed and roared while preying upon one another with all the energy, strategy and valor of human beings.

Now although Aaron Burr was ever a man of sane and steady judgment, to the end of his days he related this curious experience with the eerie woman in the northern forest without being able to offer any rational explanation thereof.

When closely pressed, he was wont to say to his intimates, "It is beyond reason or logic, I admit, but reason and logic may not include everything. It happened. That's all I know. The meaning thereof is utterly beyond me. I cannot explain the unexplainable nor can you. I doubt not that more things exist in this world than are imagined in any philosophy. We live in the midst of perpetual mystery and miracle (or what appears as such to us). Our very existence is a miracle; it may all be explainable some day. Without question, the greater part of a man comes down to him from the past. That I am sure. As to the 'why and wherefore', I know nothing. Neither doth any one else."

After innumerable adventures on the trip down the river, including a battle royale with bushwhackers, being nearly drowned in the rapids, being chased by redskins, and nearly losing all his baggage, Aaron Burr at last arrived in Albany.

Here he received a letter from Mathias Ogden. It was written in one of the ciphers of the Iron Cross and ran as follows:

My Dear Cousin,

The Iron Cross is a tremendous success. Everywhere, young men of wealth and ambition are joining and forming private lodges. These are the kind of men we want. Our own lodge is getting along swimmingly. Clinton is colonel of the 3rd Regiment; Van Ranneslaer has got the 6th Regiment; Van Ness commands the 9th; and Livingston, brother of Nellie and cousin of Helen, is colonel of the 4th. We are pushing each other to the front in every possible way.

Swartwout is captain of the Minutemen, and Rosenkrantz has got a command on the Jersey side. Morton, Morgan, and Roosevelt have obtained good positions in the Commissary Department. Your brother-in-law, Tappan Reeve, is made a judge, and your friend-Hamilton is captain of the Hearts of Oak, the King's College artillery company.

Schuyler is a commissary general, the very thing that he is specially fit for. Truxton is to get command of Hancock's privateer brig and sail out as a commerce-destroyer. Paul Jones is also slated for a sloop of war, now nearly ready for launching.

Just as Drake and Frobisher hunted down the

treasure-laden galleons of Spain, so we propose to hunt down the wealthy fleets of England.

The Earl of Stirling is appointed a brigadier general under Washington (the new commander-in-chief), who is, by the way, Lord Fairfax's business partner; I myself am a colonel; and you, not yet twenty-one, are a major, already renowned for valor and adventure. Your military exploits in Canada are much talked of in the most influential circles. This means much to you.

Thus, our plans are working beautifully. The revolutionary sentiment seems to carry everything before it. The De'Lancey gang alone hold aloof. Fortune is favoring us in every way. That we shall rise on the crest of the coming wave I have not the slightest doubt, especially if the war lasts, and I think it will last, for kings never give up without a bloody struggle.

After all, war is the thing. I am delighted with war. Hurrah, I say, for fame and love; they go together, as you say; peace is for pawnbrokers, theologians, and professors. "The wars, for my money," as Shakespeare writes. When wars come young men have a chance to rise. If a few do get riddled, what matter? Are there not plenty more where they came from? When wars break out, then the clever old greybeards must take a rear seat and leave to youth the moulding of events. What a fine thing it is to be young, Burr. Did you ever think of it?

You write much of James Wilkinson. Is he returning with you? From what you say of him, he seems to be a splendid young fellow. He has one very grave fault, however: being rather too fond of the wine when it is red. Overmuch indulgence in the brimming glass has, I know, a somewhat relaxing effect on a man's veracity.

Betsy Schuyler is more subdued now and, I think, more beautiful than ever. She looks as if she had a weight upon her mind, some secret sorrow. Every time she meets me, she inquires about you and grows quite enthusiastic over your action in carrying off the body of General Montgomery through that fierce snow storm and hail of bullets. The whole story is related in the papers by the chaplain of your regiment, the Rev. Samuel Spring.

I am satisfied in my own mind that you hold a tender place in Miss Betsy's regard. Hamilton is evidently your strongest rival. He is first favorite with her father, you know, who is very rich, Hamilton is now quite celebrated as a political writer. He publishes pamphlets in collaboration with Judge Livingston, directed against the Loyalists.

When the papers described you with the body of the dead general on your back, amid the hail of grapeshot at Cape Diamond, I heard Miss Betsy remark to Hamilton: "O my, wasn't that just grand? I always thought Mr. Burr was a hero, and now I'm sure of it."

A look of vexation passed over Hamilton's vivacious countenance, but he replied circumspectly.

"Brave? Aaron Burr is the bravest man I ever knew and as cool as ice. He is full of energy and eager for advancement. He is of a temper that thinks no enterprise too hazardous and sanguine enough to think none too difficult. He is one of those men who would scale Olympus and carry off the thunderbolts of Jove."

Hamilton is your friend, but, if you are to be rivals in love, I would advise you to watch him closely. A man's own brother is not to be trusted when there is a woman in view. Women are the very devil, you know, for breaking up friendship between men. I am confident that Hamilton means to marry Miss Betsy and win a truly good and beautiful wife besides 10,000 pounds in gold.

Clinton is deeply in love with a certain Miss Monroe of Philadelphia, and, as for myself, I am of !ate never happy except in the neighborhood of the lovely Miss Dolly. I want a wife badly and must have one. Like Hamilton, I would like to capture one possessing those three divine attributes of a perfect woman: goodness, beauty, and wealth.

Helen Livingston desires to be remembered to you. She is General Montgomery's sister-in-law. I met her last week at the Garrison Ball, a really superior affair altogether. Helen was positively charming with her great big blue eyes and hanks of raven hair.

All our leading men were present including the stately General Washington, a big Southerner who is now Commander of the united forces in all the colonies. He is personally highly pleased with your services and activity in Canada. Though his nature is somewhat chilly and sombre he almost waxed enthusiastic over your escapade in carrying Arnold's dispatch to Montgomery, and your being hidden twenty-four hours in the convent among the French nuns at Montreal.

Washington desires me to specially inform you that he will provide for you and that he expects you to join him and stay in his family as one of his aides. "I want men like Major Burr near me," he commented, "young men of daring initiative, full of resource and self-reliance."

This will be further promotion for you. Indeed, it is quite an event in itself. To be so directly complimented by the C. I. C. is a feather in your cap. Besides developing your military ambitions, you will thus have splendid opportunity to become acquainted with all the finest belles and heiresses of the land, and there are some dashing ones, I do assure you. I envy you, Burr, I really do: you are a lucky fellow. So is Hamilton.

As the general's secretary, you will also be enabled in a thousand ways to promote the policy of the Iron Cross.

Washington, as you are probably aware, is the wealthiest and most influential man in America. He has a magnificent carriage, is over six feet tall, of a good old Cavalier family, has a fine fortune, a very extensive landed estate, and, I believe, belongs to our 5th degree. He fought for the king all through the late Indian and

French wars, has a large tobacco plantation in Virginia, owns hundreds of slaves, is a famous athlete, and, when in the city, drives about in a splendid chariot behind six handsome bay horses. It is the widely expressed opinion that he is just the right man in the right place, as all classes can unite under him with safety and perfect confidence.

Notwithstanding the current leveling theories to the contrary, I still hold to the well-tested old faith that the wealthiest men in a community are its natural leaders. Woe unto any nation that pulls down its strongest and most successful personalities to exalt those of low degree. The "failures" in life are necessarily of weak character and, therefore, wholly unfitted to be entrusted with the management of great affairs.

I went out of my way to meet you coming down the river, but, unfortunately, I missed you. I desire to talk over some private matters that cannot be safely entrusted to the cypher.

By the way, I have sold your black horse. I wanted the money badly, and you won't object, I know.

One last word before you arrive amid attractions and lures and dissipations of New York and Albany. As your best friend, I speak: Beware of the feminine, Burr. Beware of the feminine. There is weakness and destruction in their soft dalliance. You have a fatal fascination for nearly every woman you meet. I know this of old. It must eventually be your ruin if you don't watch out. Women will trip you up in the path of greatness even as they have done before to so many good men and true. Everywhere, the feminine sits by the highway, luring men off from the pursuit of power and fame.

I remain, my dear friend and brother,
Most sincerely,

Mathias Ogden
Lieut. Col.

Chapter VII.
"AN APOLLO OF REVOLUTION"

An extraordinary attractive young woman, with great masses of lustrous auburn hair clustering over a noble brow, sat reading a long letter on the balcony of No. 1 Broadway.

Thus she read:

In New York society, Major Burr is the centre of all attraction, and, truly, he is a fascinating and remarkable man.

He is a social lion of the season, and his manner and bearing is simply delightful. He is as pleasing to the wrinkled old lady of sixty as to the budding young maiden of "sweet sixteen." Indeed, wherever he goes, the women flock around him like buzzing bees. Rich and poor, it is all the same. He has only to smile upon a feminine, and she straightway falls down and worships him. To me, also, he seems the very embodiment of chivalry and knighthood: handsome, generous, patriotic, recklessly brave.

The men laugh and call him a dandy—a "ladies' man." Indeed, his reputation as a ladykiller has preceded him. This reputation seems, as it were, to prepare his way for new conquests. Most women, you know, are very much interested in the man who is reputed to be deeply admired by other women.

1   Rudyard Kipling, "Ballad of East and West," 1889.

We are never tired of listening to accounts of his romantic adventures and hair-breadth escapes during the Canadian expedition. Especially how General Montgomery, your uncle, (when riddled with grapeshot) fell dead into his arms at Wolfe's Cove.

I feel sure that if Major Burr lived in Asia, he could out-rival old King Solomon in the number of his wives. In dress, he is a fashionable beau, and when he speaks, the musical timbre of his deep, rich baritone voice penetrates one like the throb of a drum. I really believe there is something unnatural and uncanny about him, for his eyes positively sparkle and glitter like midnight stars.

All the men are highly jealous of him, some of them say very spiteful things behind his back, and a young French minx, whom he danced with last night at the Clinton ball, says positively she believes that he has the evil eye.

All my brothers, however, speak enthusiastically of Major Burr and so do the Southern officers—you know General Washington made him his aide and amanuensis—but Major Burr resigned because he desired to see more active service, having no talent for the life of a clerk, wishing to fight rather with sword than pen. I hear he is now to join General Putnam's staff in New York.

I am quite angry with Washington for not making Mr. Burr a general. So is Captain Swartwout, Mr. Burr's most intimate friend, who tells me General Washington did not like "Little Burr" because the latter is too independent by nature and not easy to control.

O, Margaret, I am in love with this bewitching young officer—I am sure I am. I am sure he is noble and great of soul and such a perfect gentleman. How handsome and winning he looks when he talks and smiles; then, my heart seems to sing with joy.

This letter was signed "Helen Livingston" and addressed to

the reader thereof "Miss Margaret Moncrieffe." It contained many more pages in a similar gossipy, girlish, impressionist style—but they had better remain unprinted for at least another 100 years! They contained the cream of New York society gossip—relating principally to love-entanglements, engagements, marriages, births, etc., etc.—the things that all women delight in.

Miss Livingston was the twenty-year-old daughter of Judge Livingston. As will be inferred from her letter, Helen Livingston was deeply in love with Aaron Burr, and, being herself of a warm trusting nature, she did not seek to disguise the fact from her female intimates.

Most of her friends pretended to joke and make light of Helen's infatuation, but as many of them—most of them perhaps—were more or less in love with Burr themselves, their joking partook somewhat of jealousy, and this Helen knew instinctively and resented.

Margaret Moncrieffe was a cousin by marriage, also a confidante and personal friend of Helen's. She was residing with General Putnam's family in New York's No. 1 Broadway: the headquarters of the army of the revolution. At this time, the British were preparing to assault and capture the city.

Margaret, though reading the letter for the tenth time, had first received it when resident in Elizabethtown at the house of Mrs. De Hart, from whence she had recently been escorted over by order of General Washington.

The officer in charge of the detail of troops that brought her to New York was named Webb. He was accompanied by Major Burr.

Margaret's father, Major (afterward Colonel) Moncrieffe was a British officer—Lord Percy's Brigade Major—then stationed on Staten Island. (This Lord Percy was a direct descendant of the hero of Chevy Chase.) Miss Moncrieffe's grandmother was a daughter of Sir John Vining, six times Lord Mayor of Portsmouth. Her grandfather, Colonel Herron, became governor of Annapolis (and died there). Her uncle was a British admiral. Colonel Herron was a relative of the Duke of Bolton and Lord Delaware.

Major Moncrieffe was married to a New York Livingston: Helen's aunt. Afterwards he was married a second time to Miss Jay, a sister of the statesman John Jay.

When hostilities first broke out, it was thought that perhaps he might be prevailed upon (like so many other English officers with American affiliations) to throw in his lot with the Colonies.

Every possible inducement was held out to him (including the offer of a generalship in the American Army) for he was known to be an engineer officer of remarkable ability, However, though married to an American heiress (and related therefore to nearly the entire revolutionary junta) and possessing more than £10,000 worth of landed property in New York (a considerable fortune in those days), he choose to cast in his fortunes with the king, from whom he held his commission.

During the secret negotiations between the leaders of the revolution in New York and Major Moncrieffe, his daughter, Margaret, was kept captive—a sort of hostage as it were—by order of Congress but against the express wish of General Putnam.

Major Moncrieffe proved intractable. In opinions, he was fanatically Royalist, and his daughter, Margaret, as might be expected, was also an impassioned Loyalist, though she was American-born. In after years, Major Moncrieffe became much talked of in connection with the siege of Savannah and Charleston.

On one occasion, it is related, when Washington proposed the toast of "the American Congress," Margaret Moncrieffe being present, refused to raise her glass, whereupon the commander in chief laughingly protested, calling her "the fiery little Tory."

Margaret then arose, her cheeks flaming, and lifted her glass defiantly, saying, "Here's to our King and to success for his Redcoats."

                                    RIVAL CÆSARS

Whereupon Washington refilled his glass with good red wine, stood up, and said, with courtier grace and amid much merriment, "Beautiful maiden, I drink to thy loveliness and spirit but not to the king."

This incident caused quite an altercation between Washington and Putnam, the latter having introduced Margaret to the assembly. Disputes arose over the affair among the other officers, and several duels were fought in consequence.

Putnam warmly defended Margaret, saying, "We keep this maiden here against her father's express wish. She is half-ward, half-prisoner of the American Congress, and her disloyal audacity should merely amuse us. Is she not, after all, only a child?"

Now, Miss Margaret, among her other accomplishments, was an amateur artist of no mean ability, and, for hours every day, she would sit on the roof of General Putnam's residence sketching birds, dogs, ships, horses, and the faces of men and women who happened to attract her attention. While thus engaged, she might often be seen gazing wistfully across the bay towards Staten Island, where she knew her father's brigade lay.

On several occasions, she had attempted to make a sketch of Burr's clear-cut, handsome face, but, somehow, she ever failed to catch the elusive expression. His was a strange, intangible expression: Sphinx-like and full of pride but very pleasing to every beholder.

Most of her time, however, was spent in painting flowers, the language of flowers being then all the rage.

Miss Margaret was, for her age (about sixteen), a splendid-looking, laughing maiden, with long, golden hair and a mole upon her chin. Her eyes were dark hazel, her features clear cut and distinct, with that peculiar expression and contour that is ever derived from good breeding and superiority of descent (proud indeed might he be who felt himself born of such a maid).

Margaret's great cluster of warm, gold-red hair was particularly noticeable. By it alone, she would be specially remarked among a thousand.

(Strange that almost all the mightiest men and most famous women of the world have had "red" hair. The great conquerors and the great conquering clans have also generally been red headed. In Aryan mythology, red hair is the luminous color of the gods and goddesses. Artists, sculptors, and saga-writers have ever delighted to depict the divinities and heroes and heroines with flaming red locks and superabundant beauty of form—and there is a meaning in all this.)

Without doubt, physical strength is the only sure foundation of lasting and real beauty in man or woman. A beautiful face and figure is no accident. It is the harmonious result of a healthy body and perfect anatomy; these excellences are, in their turn, the flower and bloom and blending from generations and generations of the brave, the handsome, the pure of blood, and the noble of spirit.

Beauty of form, beauty of mind, and beauty of figure are the outcrop of ancestral selections, the outward and visible sign of inward hereditary distinction and grace.

Truly, Margaret Moncrieffe's figure was glorious to look upon. Youth and abounding health surged through her veins. Her skin was soft and clear like that of a tender rose leaf—her glance magical, alluring, man-bewildering—her thoughts full of innocence—purity and all kindness.

She was indeed a superb specimen of young American maidenhood, possessing all those indefinable graces and charms that attract and capture men.

An air of proud yet refined aloofness and intellect rested naturally upon her face, and when she spoke, the tones of her rich soft voice seemed as the ravishing strains of some fair enchantress' magical harp.

"She was indeed a rich-souled creature in whom the first germs of womanhood had blossomed forth without a weed to check or a chill to blight her growth."

Margaret Moncrieffe (the niece General of Montgomery and Colonel Livingston) seemed as if she might well become the mother of kings and conquerors, for the mental and physical balance that denotes perfection of birth and breeding seemed to be about equally and highly developed within her (or at least in the process of development, for she was still on the tremulous borderland of womanhood).

As one gazed upon her in all the radiant brilliancy and glory of life's pulsing springtide, the men of old renown who staked their fame, power, wealth, and honor for the love clasp of a superb and beautiful woman seemed not as foolish and weak as the hysterical writers of modern Christendom have delighted to depict them.

After all is it not the first duty of a hero to leave a splendid progeny behind him, and how can he do so without the love and co-operation of a superb feminine? Therefore, why should he not go to any extreme in order to obtain possession of a thoroughbred woman, a glorious Eve, a woman who might become the mother and ancestress of valorous, mighty, and unconquerable men?

If it is heroic and commendable to invade, conquer, and possess a virgin continent, is it not equally commendable for greatness of soul to assert its own wild will in the capture of a glorious feminine to be thereafter the mother of victorious sons? (Is not the immortality of a man in his descendants?)

What is the world itself but an arena for love and conquest? Are we not here to increase and multiply and take possession? Whosoever "believeth" otherwise hath surely not been endowed with the power to either think or observe. He is but a wise man in the estimation of the foolish.

The warrior and the woman: verily, what on Earth has ever been greater than those two?

The initial passions of men and women, the ever endless hunt for food and love (that is to say, for power) are assuredly the original impulses that set everything in motion. They are the glowing fiery furnaces blazing underneath the ever-grinding Enginery of Existence, and into them must always be poured, in one unceasing stream, the living, pulsing fuel that keeps them burning: the bones and brains, the lives and souls, of countless millions.

Love the great creator of life, and war the great selector! Who that is human can gainsay them? In the fullness of their all-sufficing pride and overwhelming strength, they, now as of old time, sweep away every obstruction, no matter how well contrived.

Only individuals of weak, untempered metal can afford to smile and laugh at these "unbindable" elemental forces—forces tragic and inexorable, forces that have flamed empires into ashes and withered continents as with a breath, forces that will do it again and again—for, verily, the woman and the warrior are unsuppressible.

After reading Miss Livingston's letter, Miss Moncrieffe thought to herself, *Helen fancies that I do not know Mr. Burr. Little she thinks that I have already learnt to think of him even as she does. What splendid eyes he has! I shall never forget them, and Helen speaks truly when she calls him a "perfect gentleman."*

I only met him ten days ago, and I really believe I have also fallen in love with him. But then he is in the rebel army, and I could never think of marrying an enemy of the king. I wish he was an English officer, for I like him just a little. A curious instinct draws me towards him. He fascinates me. I tremble when he looks at me.

Then she put down the letter, gazed wistfully out over the bay toward blue Staten Island, and went on painting a half-finished lily.

The quick decisive step of a man sounded, coming up the stairs. An officer with jangling spurs and dressed in bright uniform entered. He was a young man bubbling over with life and health, his coal-black eyes tense and a-glitter, his step springy and strong and full of self-reliance. There was something about him which seemed to issue this challenge: "I am a man, and who shall dismay me?"

He bowed gracefully to Miss Moncrieffe, and she smilingly saluted him in return. Then he walked over to where she was busily at work on the easel, sat down by her side, and began to examine her painting.

"You paint divinely, Miss Moncrieffe," he said, looking deep into her sparkling eyes, eyes, like his own, all aglow with pulsing life and youth.

"I do my best, Major Burr," she answered. "I love flowers. They are my favorite subjects. I like beautiful and natural things."

"So do I," he said, pleased at her evident artistic enthusiasm. "Beautiful flowers, beautiful thoughts, beautiful actions, but first of all the beautiful things is a beautiful maiden." And he looked upon her with admiration while she blushed with evident embarrassment.

"But beauty, after all, Major Burr, may be only skin deep," she replied demurely and with a certain tinge of questioning coquettish archness.

"Luckily, it is not always so," he said. "Skin-deep beauty is not always deceiving."

"Now, look at that lily I am painting," she said. "Though beautiful to the eye, it is not real: it is but paint, a mere shadow of the real."

"Very true," was his answer. "The world is full of illusion, yet, somehow, I've always felt that outward beauty of form and figure is intended by nature to signify internal purity of heart and goodness of disposition."

"I will not gainsay you, Major, but surely there are beautiful things that are bad."

"That depends," said he, "on what we mean by bad. The matter of what is good and what is bad cannot be satisfactorily decided by one strict rule. What is one man's good is another man's poison. However, I think, Miss Moncrieffe, that the evil things of the world, the Calibans and slave souls, are generally of unpleasing exterior."

"But may not beauty of form in a man or woman be an evil, Major?" said Margaret tormentingly.

"That's what the professors taught us at Princeton, but I never really believed them," he said.

"You think beauty is a mark of goodness then?"

"Scarcely that, Miss Moncrieffe, but I do think ugliness of form has in it something fundamentally evil. I think ugliness is a sign of some inward defect or some blood-taint. Even when I go to buy a horse to carry me in war, I seek not only courage and endurance but also equine beauty and grace of form."

"O Major Burr, that reminds me of poor Selim, my Arab pony. You know, the horse I rode from Elizabethtown. He hasn't had any exercise since then. Could I not take him out for a ride? I do like riding, and Selim is such a beauty too, now isn't he, Major Burr?"

"I will ask the general, Miss Moncrieffe. I am sure he shall only be too happy to oblige you. If he consents, I invite you to come with me for a ride around the batteries. I am going today to inspect progress and report upon the new fortifications."

A smile of undisguised delight lit up Miss Moncrieffe's bright, vivacious countenance as she thanked him. Whereupon he went away to seek the general, "Old Put."

Going down the stairs, he met Alexander Hamilton and one of the Miss Putnams coming up. Miss Putnam told him her father was in the front office talking to a dispatch rider just arrived from General Washington.

Hamilton then related how he had got an appointment on Washington's staff, the position vacated by Burr a few months previously.

Burr congratulated Hamilton and, at the same time, warned him that Washington was a very hard man to get on with.

"To be secretary to the commander in chief is a good position, however," answered Hamilton gaily. "Even if I have to suppress my own personality somewhat, the experience and knowledge I must gain will be of immense service to me afterwards and to you also, for, of course, I reckon you a sharer in all my good luck."

"By the way, Hamilton," said Burr, "how is your suit progressing with Miss Betsy? I hear you are 'the man.' "

"I have not seen her lately," replied Hamilton, "but her father and I are becoming very intimate. He introduced me to Washington and is enthusiastic over my writings in the press. Indeed, he and Livingston have supplied me with some splendid points, which, as you have seen, I made good use of."

"Goodbye, Hamilton. I wish you luck. I must now go down to see Putnam."

"Goodbye, Burr. Everything goes well."

Burr went downstairs, and Hamilton went up. Burr found General Israel Putnam poring over the contents of a letter that had just arrived from the commander in chief. A look of relief appeared upon his face as his young aide entered. "just the man I want," he said. "Here, Burr, what do you make of this? I can scarcely read it."

Burr took the letter and read it aloud without difficulty.

"What is your opinion?" asked the general.

"I think now what I've always thought," replied Burr, sitting down at the desk. "New York cannot be defended successfully as long as the enemy's ships can command the harbor and sail around the island. For urging this view on Washington some months ago, he took a dislike to me, and I hope, General, you will not do the same. My opinion on the matter has in no wise altered. We are in a trap here. The British fleet may capture this city whenever it likes to try. Without ships, we are helpless. They can land behind us, cut off our supplies, and then bombard at their pleasure."

Putnam answered, evidently much pleased, "I most certainly am not, and shall not be, offended at you for stating your opinion upon this very important and much-mooted point. Have I not requested you to do so? I know you have given deep study to siege problems (for you were at Quebec), and, notwithstanding your youth, I have learnt to place confidence in your practical common sense and undoubted ability. Now, what would you suggest as a proper reply for me to send?"

"I would tell him," said Burr, "that his orders would be obeyed to the letter, that every man of the present garrison is prepared to die at his post in defence of the city, but for all that, you have not the remotest hope of being able to triumphantly defend the town because the strategic position of the enemy on the water is superior in every way to our own.

"Then I would plainly intimate to that New York should be burnt to an ash-heap rather than surrendered.

"Nevertheless, I would make the enemy expend all his strength to gain possession, then vacate ourselves and leave him a smouldering heap of blackened ruins, instead of a great city, for an offensive base.

Alen should not rush lightly into war, but when they do, then they ought to go at it with a will. Everything that can injure, weaken, or paralyze one's foe is then a good and proper weapon. And of all the weapons of war known to me, none is more terrible, none is more fearsome to an enemy than fire. If we could only burn the British fleet out of the water, for example."

"I will consider your ideas," said General Putnam much interested. "Your argument for fire is, I think, very reasonable. Fire is a tremendous weapon and has always been used in war from the earliest times, but this is now the question, Burr: Is it good policy at present? That's what Washington must consider. Might it not alienate the property holders?"

Now Aaron Burr's brain was keen and hard, hard with the hardness of hammered iron, keen with the keenness of tempered steel, and he therefore replied, "Good policy, General, is that which wins. Why make concessions to the gallery? If Washington won't sanction it, and the British land, let us burn the city ourselves."

"But that would be disobedience to orders Burr and must not be even considered," replied the old general gravely.

"Nevertheless, the greatest of generals have become famous through disobeying orders more often than by obeying them," said Burr with a smile.

"The dispatch rider returns tomorrow," answered the general, "and, in the meantime, I will sleep upon this matter. What you say I will carefully consider."

Burr arose to go, saying, "Very well, General. I am now going out for a ride 'round the new earthworks, also to see what progress is being made with the gun emplacements by the northeast bastion.

"But before going, General, I have a personal favor to ask of you. Can Miss Moncrieffe come out with me? She is eager to exercise her pony. She is one of those dashing Dianas who're never so happy as when she has a springing thoroughbred prancing beneath her."

"O certainly, Major. Take her with you, by all means, but see to it you don't lose her or lose your heart. She is really a splendid girl. When I look upon her, I only wish I was a younger man. She is a wicked little Tory, though, and you'd better beware she does not corrupt you and carry you off, bag and baggage, to the king's side. We can't afford to lose officers of your stamp." Thus said General Putnam as he, laughing pleasantly, mixed himself a whiskey punch upon the most approved principles.

Major Burr and Miss Moncrieffe rode down the Battery Road together. She was mounted on her high-mettled pony, whose glossy coat shone in the sun like polished glass. The pony pranced and pawed and arched its neck as if in conscious pride of its fair burden.

Margaret held the reins and her seat in the saddle with the confident ease and lithe abandon of the practiced horsewoman.

If she looked beautiful painting flowers under the awning on the house-top, she now looked positively ravishing in her tight-fitting riding habit with the flush of youth and health glowing in her cheeks.

Burr gazed at her rounded contour, sparkling eyes, and rosy complexion with undisguised admiration. No maiden had ever before seemed half so attractive to him.

She is the one for me, he thought. *I will marry her if I can. Helen is too plain, Catherine is too delicate, Betsy I do not care for (and Hamilton wants her), Flora is altogether too intellectual, Louise is too wild, and Rebecca is a regular little flirt, but Miss Moncrieffe—Margaret—is just the maid for me. She is kind and good, well born, well connected, and well bred.*

Now, Burr's horse was a tall raw-boned chestnut with blood-shot eyes, Roman nose, a long swish tail, deep chest, and legs like bars of banded steel: "With the mouth of a bell, the heart of Hell, and the head of a gallow's tree."

Fastened to the saddle swung a cavalry saber, and in the holsters were two long heavy horse pistols. Major Burr wore the blue-and-gold revolutionary uniform, and his seat in the saddle was that of a young centaur. He seemed, as it were, part of the steed he rode.

In the eyes of a maid, especially such a maid as Margaret Moncrieffe, he looked the very beau ideal of what a man and a lover should be: young; handsome; manly; a veritable warrior Apollo; the virile incarnation of strength, valor, pride and victory, the qualities in a man that the unsophisticated natural woman instinctively admires.

The delight which all women take in men of power and valor is elemental and undying. From the dawn of time, it has ever been the instinctive wish of a good woman to mate herself with the boldest and most heroic man of her acquaintance. And in this, there is a profound mystery and meaning. Its purpose is divine and godlike, that is to say, selective of the best and bravest.

Woe, woe unto the nation when it ceases to produce warmen. Woe, woe unto the nation wherein the Man of Battle is not regarded as the highest and holiest product of connubial love.

Burr and Margaret rode along side by side, passed through many an old wooden gate, and were everywhere met by pleasant words and glances. After inspecting the "works" that Burr had come out to see, both of them turned their horse's heads homeward by another route than that whereby they came.

When within sight of home, Margaret insisted on jumping her horse over a low fence "just for practice, you know."

She rode at the fence and leaped it most gracefully, her long, bronze hair flaming out like a golden banner, but as Sam landed on the other side, the saddle turned round (the girth having become stack during the long morning ride), and Margaret fell heavily on the ground, her foot hanging in the stirrup.

High-spirited Selim immediately began to prance and rear up in fear. Then he started off at a gallop, dragging his fair mistress over the rough road, striking her violently against the stones and stumps that littered the ground, and kicking viciously all the time.

Burr saw what had happened. "By God, she will be killed, kicked to death before thy eyes!" he gasped.

Plunging the rowels into the flanks of the big raking chestnut, he cleared the fence at a bound and galloped up alongside of Selim. Then he reached out his tight hand to grasp Selim's dragging rein, but the rein broke in his hand, and Selim rushed away again, plunging and kicking savagely at the saddle swinging under his belly, in which the legs of his mistress were hopelessly jammed and tangled.

Then another idea came into Burr's quick brain. He drew his long, heavy saber and again followed Selim at a hand gallop. Overtaking the terrified animal, he swung the saber with the accurate precision of an expert swordsman, bringing it down with a quick, shearing cut upon the tightened stirrup leather (wherein Margaret's foot was fastened), severing it clean in two.

In a moment, Margaret lay still upon the ground, her face and dress torn, stained, and covered with blood, dust, and grime, while Selim dashed away like mad, rushing this way and that, bucking, snorting, and plunging wildly with the side-saddle dangling tantalizingly between his hind legs.

As Margaret lay there, Burr looked down upon her for an instant before jumping off his horse to go to her assistance. Then in a flash, as it were, he remembered where he had seen her before.

By heavens! he thought. *She is the very image of that unknown woman I saw transfigured by the fire in the enchanted clearing.*

Chapter VIII

THE BEAUTIFUL SPY

She was good as she was fair.
None, none on earth above her!
As pure in thought as angels are,
To know her was to love her.[1]

The historic battles were being fought. The cities were being besieged, captured sometimes, relieved sometimes, burned sometimes. Great reputations were being destroyed, and great reputations were being slowly built up. There were heartburnings and jealousies and the usual troubles incidental to all war. The American people were intoxicated by the spirit of revolt, and their brains teemed with visions and dreams of high hope beyond the battle glare. Every man, as he went forth to fight, felt that he had something substantial to win, and even the heart of the English soldier was not overenthusiastic in the business of fighting against his own kindred. The war became essentially a guerrilla campaign upon an extended scale. In his woods, the American rifleman proved himself worth a dozen ordinary "shilling a day" soldiers, drilled to move like automatons in a barrack square. The nature of the fighting is gauged in a remark once made by the Marquis of Tweeddale: "I hope it will never fall to my lot again to fight the Americans. Every one of them fights his own individual battle and is, consequently, a most dangerous enemy."

The theory of battle outlined by the chiefs of the Iron Cross was being carried out to a triumphant success:

The thunder deed followed the lighting thought

---

1   "Jacqueline," Lord Byron, Samuel Rogers, *Lara, A Tale. Jacqueline, A Tale* (London: J. Murray 1814).

By daring of heart and hand.
With their face to the danger, like heroes they fought
When they stood for their own dear land.[1]

Two lovers sat on the balcony of General Putnam's New York home in the warm summer afternoon. He was a dark young man in a staff officer's uniform, and she a "midene faire with goudene haire."[2] They were talking those pleasant nothings that can never possibly be reduced to cold type and were apparently deeply absorbed in said nothings.

In fact, the world spirit at its strongest was throbbing in their souls. In each other's eyes, they saw the eternal and the light that never was on sea or land. The "song without words" was pulsing through their hearts: the song that is sung through all animate creation; the song of desire that shakes the spheres and whirls the stars in their orbits; the song that transfigures the red kingdom of the inexorable into a realm of perpetual romance.

The two lovers had sat there for a considerable time and were very happy, exceedingly happy, in each other's company.

"I love you, Margaret," he said.

"I know you do, Aaron. I am sure you do, but what will my father say? I fear and love my father. You know he is a rigid, austere Presbyterian and an uncompromising Royalist."

"Margaret, I will marry you. I will marry you as soon as the war is ended. That won't be long. Wilt you wait for me and be true to me till then?" asked the young officer coaxingly.

"I will," replied Margaret Moncrieffe, and tears glistened in her great, soft, brown eyes. "I will do anything you wish me to

---

1 "Our Fathers are Praying for Pauper Pay," *Voices of Freedom and Lyrics of Love!,* Gerald Massey (London: Watson, Queen's Head Passage. 1851).

2 The lyrics "maiden fair with golden hair" come from the song "One Morning Sweet in May" (1875, Henry David Leslie), popular in songbooks from the turn of the 20th century.

do, I love you, Aaron, as much as you love me, but why should we not get married now? Why should I not stay with you, rather than return to my father and, thereafter, live in continual trouble with that hateful stepmother of mine?" (Margaret's stepmother was a Miss Jay, sister of the famous congressman and diplomatist.)

"Margaret, that cannot be," replied Major Burr gently. And he put his arms around her and kissed her passionately. "You are only sixteen, and I am not twenty. I could therefore not get a marriage license in New York or elsewhere, without the consent of your father. You are also a ward of Congress and, therefore, the generals would never give their consent to our marriage. As you are a hostage of war, it would be a dishonorable act for me to marry you. It would be so regarded by my own commanders as well as by Lord Cornwallis, who is your father's personal friend and the foster-father of your brother. Though I love you, Margaret, beyond all things, I do not wish to blast my own career by doing anything that might be construed as dishonorable."

"But what need we care for such things, Aaron? I belong to you absolutely," she answered.

"But there are good reasons against such a course, Margaret. I am a soldier and must march wherever ordered, and it would also be bad policy for me to make enemies of my commanding officers. How can I take you with me in such a war as this is going to be? (We shall never be two nights in one camp.) Then I really believe our army must evacuate New York at an early date and march inland for some severe campaigning. If I could, I would marry you now, Margaret, but you see it is utterly out of the question. I think it would be very impolitic for both of us."

"O Aaron, I'm so sorry. I hate to go back to my stepmother."

"Nevertheless, I see no help for it. It is best for you to be near your father until I get his consent, or until the war is over. This is no place for you. Your father is furious at your detention, and Lord Howe writes, demanding your immediate surrender or exchange. He even threatens reprisals. It would cause a grave scandal if you were not surrendered."

"My brain tells me you are right, Aaron, but my heart rebels. I wish to stay where you are and go with you everywhere. I would tend you if you got wounded and weep upon your grave if you should be killed. O, how I wish this awful war was over. My father and brother fighting on one side and my lover and all my cousins fighting on the other. O, it is terrible, Aaron, terrible! Supposing you all meet in the battle and slay one another? The thought of it makes me shiver.

"O, Aaron, Aaron, I don't want to leave you. You, the lover of my heart and dreams. Something tells me we shall never meet again."

Thus spake Margaret, and she wept as if her heart would break, which made Burr very uncomfortable and vexed with himself for being so utterly unable to comfort her.

"Margaret, Margaret, dear Margaret, please don't weep so. It is all for the best, I feel sure it is. You are my first love and my only love. You know it is so, but, under the circumstances, how can I undertake the responsibility of abducting you, you, the ward of the American government, the government I have sworn to serve? It would be madness for me to do it. It would disgrace and dishonor me, and you would not like to be the wife of a disgraced and dishonored man.

"Margaret, this war is my supreme opportunity to gain fame and fortune. Once to every man comes a chance, and this is mine. I know it is, Margaret, I know it is. But if I thwart the will of Washington and Putnam, then my career is at an end. Washington's word goes a long way. I could not hope for advancement if I gained his ill will or that of his confidential advisers.

"Then again, if I do not take a prominent part in the war, I will be at a disadvantage among my fellow countrymen when peace returns. Every man among us must now fight or be shamed.

"And I dream, night and day, of magnificent deeds, deeds to make you proud and happy and shout with joy. I would do great things, Margaret, things that would be memorable and live for all time in the thoughts of men."

"But, Aaron, I would be at your side to encourage and comfort you when the strife is hardest and the hour is darkest. I am the daughter of a soldier and a race of soldiers. I have been bred amid wars and wounds, and I know how to inspire and aid those whom I love. And, as the old book says, and as my mother used to say to my father, 'Whither thou goest, I will go; and where thou lodgest, I will lodge; thy people shall be my people and thy god my god. And where thou diest, I will die, and there will I be buried.'"

"Ah, but my country calls, Margaret, and the practical must also be considered," said Burr in his kindest voice.

"Do you place patriotism before love, Aaron?" she pleaded.

"I do, but it is hard, very hard, for me to do it. I place the welfare and independence of my country before every other consideration. I may be foolish in doing so. Nevertheless, Margaret, I pledge you solemnly my sacred word of honor as a soldier and a gentleman that ere the last shot is fired in anger, I will come and claim you as my bride. All I ask of you now is to wait and be true to me until then, when I will take you to my home, the home, perhaps, of a famous man."

"But the war may last a long time, Aaron, may it not?" she urged.

"I hope it will not last more than a year, Margaret, and by that time, I may be a general and able to place a wife in a high and honorable position as befits her. O Margaret, you will be proud of me yet. Meantime, you have no conception of what it means to come campaigning with me. It is now more than many a strong man can endure."

To which Margaret answered, "I feel you are right, my love. I will do as you say. But meanwhile, I am a hostage in this city, I am a captive, and how shall I escape to my father or brother?"

"I have thought of a plan to get you away at an early date," he replied. "Indeed, you must be got away somehow, for in case of bombardment, your life would be in peril. You are neither happy nor safe in New York, and I may also have to leave it at any hour."

"What is your plan?" she inquired.

"O, a splendid one."

"Tell it to me," she insisted eagerly, as she dried her tears.

"Very well, here it is," he answered. "I have already thought it out fully and am satisfied it must succeed. Let us first make it appear that you are a British spy. As soon as the rumor gets about, strict watch will be set upon you, whereupon you are to act as it were really true. You must give those who watch you excellent reasons to think it true. And then when they give in their report to Washington, he will order you to be immediately sent out of our lines. He would never think of immuring you in prison. You have too many relatives on our side for that."

"I will do anything you desire, Aaron," she answered. "I will trust you implicitly. I live a very uncongenial life here anyhow. The Miss Putnams are very lurid to me and so is the dear old general, but all the other girls who visit us, especially the Miss Schuylers and Livingstons, are quite jealous of me because nearly all the young American officers—including yourself—are forever making love to me. Some of them have even gone so far in their jealousy as to hint already that am a 'little spy.' You see, I cannot hide my feelings when they are condemning my father and reviling my king."

"Just the very thing," said Burr enthusiastically, rubbing his hands with unmixed delight. "Now, you must act as if you were a real spy, and I will show you how."

"First, be very mysterious in your movements, and take care to be often seen writing. And when you are talking to officers, discuss the war, the guns, the number of soldiers, etc. Then, here take this. Look it over: It is a sketch of the new Richmond Hill redoubt now under construction. You must remember the place—near where you were nearly killed by Selim."

Margaret blushed and nodded assent, and the young major continued:

"Now take up your brush and paint a flower. Any flower will do. Exactly. Then under the flower, in faint outline, draw the left angle of the redoubt, and on the back of the finished picture, place the letter A. Very good.

"Now paint another flower, another and another, and under each and all of them draw a section of the map, in miniature, until finally you have copied it. Now you see my idea. It is very simple. When all these outlines are recopied, hereafter and placed in A, B, C, D rotation, they will form a complete and mathematically correct map of our new defenses. Even the half hidden and most strategic windings of the trenches are fully and proportionately delineated.

"After you have completed all this, come and tell me. Then I will see that your paintings and their ciphers are 'discovered.' That will be convincing proof that you are a spy.

"Then I prophesy that you will be packed off to your father on Staten Island before another week has passed away."

"Ha, ha, ha," laughed Margaret. "Me, a spy, a British spy! Why, it is quite romantic. A girl of sixteen sketching the forts for the great generals! O, but it is too absurd, Aaron. And then, too, they might hang me." Here a look of alarm came over her face.

"No fear of hanging you, Margaret, not the slightest. Is not judge Livingston your uncle? Everybody will take it for granted that you are a real spy, for when minds are excited by fear or treachery, any story gains credence, no matter how absurd. You follow my instructions and all will go right. You must escape from here. I have a thousand reasons why my intended bride should not remain in New York."

Burr's scheme worked like a charm. Within a week, Margaret was with her father. One morning, without warning, she was put aboard a barge belonging to the Continental Congress (with twelve rowers, a general officer, and his suite) and taken out to the British warship Eagle. The day was very tempestuous, and the heavy seas broke over the barge, threatening to swamp it and soaking everyone aboard with brine.

The officer in command carried with him a number of letters, one being from General Putnam to Major Moncrieffe that ran as follows:

"I send you a present of a fine daughter. If you don't like to keep her, send her back again, and I will guarantee to provide her with a true-blue Whig husband, whom I suspect she already admires and wants to marry."

In after years, Washington heard of the stratagem that had been played upon him by Burr (much to Burr's disadvantage).

Now, in the lining of Margaret's bodice, when she went away, a small sheet of parchment was carefully concealed. Upon it, with chemical ink, Burr had written the "key" to a secret cipher. By this method, the two lovers agreed to communicate with one another through the lines of the two hostile armies as opportunity offered.

The cipher was simply composed thus:

A	B	C	D	E	F	G	H	I	J	K	etc.
1	2	3	4	5	6	7	8	9	10	11	etc.

The letters were to be written as figures and the figures as letters. Then to vary the cipher for each communication, it was arranged that any letter might be used as number one, to be designated in a peculiar way. To vary and complicate this again, a large number of arbitrary signs and words were invented to denote certain definite persons, things, or facts.

Cipher writing for confidential correspondence was at that time commonly used. Even after the war had concluded, business men were chary of using the mails except by means of some understood cipher.

Now, Aaron Burr had an idea in his head of hereafter becoming a lawyer. When at Princeton, he was considered an exceptionally brilliant student of law and history. Even in his leisure hours on the march, he often carried his law books with him to keep up his studies. Of course, no one imagined in the early months of the war that it would last for eight years.

For months after Margaret's departure to Staten Island, Burr received many communications from her to which he replied. Sometimes, she complained of being ill, which alarmed him, as she was remarkable, when in New York, for the robust vigor of her health.

One morning, when deeply immersed in his law books, he received a missive from his betrothed that upset him not a little. The following is an extract :

My Dearest Aaron:—

...It is with mixed pain and love I address you. My tears fall fast upon the paper as I write. My hand shakes, and all my soul trembles for love of you, dearest creature. And yet, Aaron, I am ill, sick, nigh unto death. I have hinted to you of this before.... I have been hoping from month to month to recover my health, but the doctor tells me that I am getting worse and that if I persist in disobeying his advice, my very life is in peril....

O, Aaron, how can I properly explain myself? How can I make you understand that I am wasting away because of love, because of love for you, my own darling, Aaron. O, to be beside you once more, Aaron! O, to be enjoying unbroken bliss!

The doctor, who is a kind old gentleman and a friend of my father's, tells me, in his bluff, blunt way, that I must soon get married or be buried.

My father also, while stroking my head the other day, asked me why I could not find a husband among all the wealthy and titled young officers of the king's army, many of whom admired me and spoke of me as 'divinely lovely.'

Then, for the first time, I told him of you, Aaron, of the young rebel officer who saved my life when Selim ran away. I also told him how good and brave you were, how you had stolen my heart for ever, and that I would never marry anybody but you, no, not even if I died.

He asked me all about you, and who you were, and I told him all I knew. Now, this is the substance of his reply: 'Write to Major Burr, and tell him I will obtain for him a commission in His Majesty's Army if he will come over and marry you at once. I know he is a promising young officer, for I've already heard of him through the Livingstons. He was also with my brother-in-law, General Montgomery, at the siege of Quebec, but he is a rebel, and I will never marry my daughter to an enemy of the king, no, not even if she dies.'

O, Aaron, do come unto me, or surely the bells shall toll my funeral dirge. I long to clasp you to my breast. I long to be with you once again I long to live and love, not to die and be eaten by worms. Do come unto me,

Aaron, do come. Do come and serve the king, and my father will make your fortune. He has great influence, both here and in London. This offer to you is my last hope. O, do accept it, Aaron, do accept it. Is not love and life greater than anything else? Now come to me, Aaron, come, and deliver me from the grave. My life is ebbing! I know it is! My heartbeats are irregular, I often swoon for hours, my face is as white as snow, and my colored maid says I am 'in a decline. I am broken-hearted, Aaron, I am broken-hearted, and I often think over the lines of the grand old tragedy you were so fond of reading:

> Give me to drink mandragora
> That I may sleep out this gap of time,
> My Antony is away.[1]

When Major Burr read this letter through, he put it down and wiped away the salty, burning tears that welled up to his eyes. And thus he thought, *What a fool I was, after all, to let her go to her father. I should have kept her here at any cost. But could I marry her? Ah, there's the rub. What else could I have done? How could I have foreseen her sickness? O, Margaret, Margaret, how can I save you? How can I now deliver you? How can I rescue you from the midst of a hostile army? How can I carry you off from Staten Island, guarded night and day by 10,000 men? Shall I abandon my country, or shall I let my true love die? God! was ever a man placed in such a dilemma? My heart, from grief and rage, is turning to blood. My brain burns and throbs like the brain of a madman, yet what can I do? What CAN I do?*

As might be expected, there was no rest for Aaron Burr that night. Up and down the apartment he paced, thinking over

1   William Shakespeare, *Antony and Cleopatra*, Act I, Scene 5.

plan after plan to free Margaret from death and marry her.

When daylight came, he had written her a reply, outlining a well-thought-out scheme for her escape to a boat in the harbor, which he promised to have waiting at an appointed place and date.

He told her distinctly he would never fight for the king against his own countrymen but that, nevertheless, he was ready to resign his commission, abandon his promising career, marry her straightaway (consent or no consent), then retire to Albany and practice law till the end of the war.

"It shall never be said of Aaron Burr," he concluded, "that he proved himself recreant in the hour of trial. Though my heart strings be torn asunder, though my beloved should perish before my eyes, though I be burnt with fire, yet wilt I be true."

The very next night, the British landed in New York. All the following day, the battle of Long Island raged up and down the river.

Again, Major Burr distinguished himself by personal gallantry in action and astute presence of mind in the presence of difficulty. He saved an entire brigade from capture or destruction by leading it out of an untenable position. This brigade was under the direct command of General Knox, who, from that day forward, became Burr's bitterest enemy.

Throughout that wild and dismal night, with thoughts of Margaret nerving him on, Major Burr "galloped through the red, infernal powder smoke. And his broadsword was swinging, and his brazen throat was ringing trumpet-loud."[1]

---

[1] Guy Humphrey McMaster, "Carmen Bellicosum." Reprinted in many turn of the century books collecting popular nationalist American poems.

Chapter IX.

MARRIAGE BY COMPULSION

New York City was captured by the enemy (as Burr foresaw) and held by them till the conclusion of the war in 1783.

The vacating American garrison, under Generals Stirling, Putnam, and Knox, slowly retired inland. Thereafter Putnam's headquarters became the headquarters of the British garrison, and nearby to it but further down the street, Major Moncrieffe took up his residence with his partly convalescent daughter, Margaret, and her governess.

Within a month of the occupation, Margaret had made two daring attempts to escape through the lines and reach and rejoin her lover.

On each occasion, she had been brought back: once by the officer on night duty at Richmond Hill and the last time by her father and Earl Percy, both of whom had galloped after her far beyond the outer lines.

In returning, they had been pursued up to the very muskets of their own men by a party of American scouts, led on by Burr, who had been impatiently waiting for her at the appointed rendezvous.

Now, upon a couch in her father's drawing room, she lay bound a prisoner, a captive, fastened firmly by a series of military saddle straps, two around her ankles, two around her wrists, and two more around her body. Sullenly, she lay there unable to move yet dressed as if for a long journey. Her wavy, lustrous, sun-red hair was spread in a disheveled mass over the pillow.

1   See Deuteronomy 22:28-29, Exodus 22:16-17.

Her breast heaved with emotion, and her face was red with anger, vexation, and weeping.

Her father stood by her side, dressed in the blue-and-green uniform of the Royal Engineers. A look of pain, yet of inexorable resolution, overspread his face.

Major Moncrieffe was a soldierly looking man, splendidly built, over six feet in height, and about forty years old. He had a hard, steely, handsome expression, and his teeth, when he smiled, were very prominent. His nose was shaped like that of an eagle, his eyes were grey and bold, his face tanned and ruddy, and his entire general appearance that of a man of action, a masterful man, a man who knew the world and all its ways and was not to be lightly trifled with There was nerve—tempered nerve—and aggressiveness in this man. Indeed, it was written all over him: "this is a man of iron."

He leaned forward toward his daughter, stroked her hair kindly, and kissed her tenderly. Then he drew a chair nearer the couch upon which she was fastened and sat down.

Great tears stood in Margaret's big, brown eyes, and she looked at her father reproachfully but not alarmedly, saying, "O, father, father, why do you bind me like this?

"Margaret," he answered, "my wild and wayward daughter, you are becoming every day more unmanageable. If you were a son of mine, I would know better how to handle you, but you are a girl, and there is now no one here to look after you properly. Your dear mother is dead, and I can see that I must marry you to somebody. Nothing else can I do to save you from yourself."

"O father, send me to Major Burr," she answered, and a pleased look came over her face.

"Maggie," he went on, "your mother died when you were young, and with my last wife you could not agree. Your bringing up, therefore, has given me much anxiety, more than you can comprehend. Now that you are growing into womanhood, my anxiety on your account is becoming agonizing. I have, therefore, determined to marry you to some worthy man and thus save you from your own headstrong will and my family from disgrace.

"I have selected Captain Coglan, a rising officer of the navy, a man who has sailed around the world with Captain Cook and aided in the discovery of Australia and New Zealand. Captain Coglan has already asked me for your hand. I am under special obligations to him and have, therefore, promised that he shall have you.

"At any moment, I may be ordered away from here on duty. I will probably be sent down to build the defenses of Charleston and Savannah, and it would never do for me to leave you in New York without some female relative, older than yourself, to take care of you and guard you from those who would take unfair advantage of your girlish enthusiasms and want of knowledge of the world. I will not hand you over to the Livingstons, with whom I have quarreled, and to take you with me is impossible.

"The fortunes of war and every circumstance demand your immediate marriage to someone, Margaret."

"But, my father," she replied, weeping, "you know I love Major Burr. Do let me go to him. In his last letter, he says he is ready to marry me at once if I will come outside the British lines."

"Margaret," he replied, as a scowl of anger came over his countenance, "you know what I have said to you about Major Burr. Rather than see you marry a rebel, I would see you dead. However, I have told you long ago that if Major Burr will come over to the king's side, I will give you to him and also guarantee him a colonel's commission in the infantry. My family influence with Howe and Cornwallis is sufficient for that."

"He will never come over, father, not even for me. Therefore ,let me go to him. Please, please, do send me to him, through the lines, under a flag of truce."

"It can never be Margaret—never. More especially now that Coglan demands you. Coglan knows important secrets of my life, and it is in his power to absolutely ruin me. He knows that General Washington and I have been secretly in communication with regard to my New York property. Washington offered me through your uncle, Judge Livingston, the command that was given to my brother-in-law, the unfortunate General Montgomery. He has also offered to make me his engineer general if I would join him. Coglan knows all these things and more.

"Coglan can thus hang me as a rebel and traitor to the king. Do you understand? You must marry Coglan, therefore, or I must either hang or desert to the American side. Now, Margaret, do you wish to see your father swing on the Traitor's Tree at Tyburn Hill or from the yardarm of the Admiral's flagship?"

"O, no, my father, that would be too awful," she answered, and the big round tears flowed afresh. "O father, how I detest that man Coglan! I could kill him; he is so hateful to me. Let me up, father, give me one of your pistols, and I will go and shoot him—yes, I will shoot him dead! I—I hear his voice even now. He is in the parlor there, with Lady Bette Percy and Mrs. Monteith. O, father, father, please, o, please, give me a pistol and let me up."

"Now, Margaret, be a sensible girl. You are my beloved and only daughter; my love for you is without question. I wish for your welfare. You are and have ever been as the apple of my eye, and though I have tied you here, I shall do you no hurt. You know if you killed Captain Coglan, you would be executed for murder, and then the cause of the trouble would be investigated, whereupon the whole story of my intrigue with the rebels would be exposed. Margaret, do be reasonable and accept Captain Coglan, as I wish. Without question, he is a brave, handsome, and dashing officer, not to mention well connected."

"I won't, my father," she replied hysterically.

"But you *must!* I command it, and I shall be obeyed," said Major Moncrieffe sternly.

"O, father, dear father don't force me to marry this abominable man! It will break my heart, father, it will break my heart!"

"Margaret," he replied, "don't be so emotional. You will have to marry him if I have to handcuff you during the ceremony. I have said it. I have pledged my word to him, and I will keep it. So you had better make up your mind to obey me, for I've made all the arrangements. If you refuse to marry him voluntarily, or attempt to create a scene, then I will use other and harsher methods—methods I would rather not use if I can possibly avoid them. I have had you bound where you now are—not for the first time—to tame you and teach you that my will is law in this household. Nevertheless, it is my sincere wish to see the ceremony proceed quietly and without scandal. Therefore, I ask you for the last time to obey me quietly."

"If you make me that hateful man's wife by force, father, you will make my whole life miserable," she replied, sobbing wildly.

"Can't help it, my daughter. I have no other choice. You must be married to someone. I gave you a month to choose from among the other officers, and you refused to select. Now I have selected one for you. He is in his way a good strong man, a man quite capable of controlling even you. Now, Margaret, be sensible and do as I wish. You know very well I would do nothing. that I thought would injure you permanently. What I am now doing, I am doing for the best."

"Will you marry me laying bound here, father?"

"I will. I have explained all the circumstances to the Reverend Doctor Auchtmuchty. He is my best friend. The others also understand and will bear me out, for I am acting strictly within my paternal rights. Until you are twenty-one, I am your guardian. You are my flesh and blood. You are the daughter of my first love. Now I say you must be married, Margaret, this very hour. Your own condition and my future career all demand it."

Major Moncrieffe spoke with the tone and look of a man

who had steeled himself to go through anything, who also knew that perhaps he was committing a mistake but, nevertheless, had determined to "chance it." From his own point of view, there was no other way, and he firmly believed Margaret would finally become reconciled to the handsome captain.

"But, my father," answered Margaret, "why not let me go to Major Burr, the man I love, the man of my choice?"

"Margaret," said Major Moncrieffe, "you are young and foolish. He could not marry you without my consent. To marry a girl of sixteen is against the American law, also. As to love, poor girl, you think it is all in all, like many others, but you are mistaken. It is the instinct of all women to overglorify this passion, but, as they get older, they learn better. Then it is often too late to learn, for youth and good looks are fleeting. In spite of all the sentiment that is written or spoken, I assure you, my dear daughter, that there is nothing more inconstant than love, except for the weathercock on the church steeple. Love is as the wind that blows. Love is as transient as the shadow that flies when clouds sweep the moon and storms prepare. The passions of men and women are constant *never!* All is change. Today, it is love; tomorrow, hate. Someday, you will learn this, even as I have learnt it.

"I am sure this young rebel officer will quickly forget you, and you must forget him. Even if he did save your life, remember that I also claim some of your gratitude and devotion, for was it not I, Margaret, who gave you that life? Do as I wish, therefore, and save all further trouble."

A furtive tear glistened for a moment in the strong man's eye as he gazed down upon his daughter and thought of her mother and "the long ago."

"O, my father, my father, have mercy upon me. Do not be so hard. Do not break my heart entirely. Do not destroy my happiness forever."

"Maggie," he answered, "you are in bad health, though a beautiful girl. You are just entering upon womanhood, and all your best days are before you. You are a brave girl too and just as head-strong as your dear dead mother. You have all the strong tame-less spirit of her family and mine. You are a true Moncrieffe, and such as you never yet died of a broken heart because of unrealized love. Your blood is too rich and strong for that. The life within you is too mighty. By the time you are twenty, and a mother, you will learn the mockery of romantic love. As the old doctor says, mar-riage is the cure for your malady of brain and body."

"O, father, father, father" was all the answer Margaret could make. Then she wept and moaned for about ten minutes while her father (accustomed to such outbreaks in women) patiently sat and waited. After she became calmer, he again spoke, saying, "My daughter, I cannot argue with you forever. It is a waste of time to talk any more. I have made up my mind absolutely. You shall marry Captain Coglan and you shall marry him now.

"In the next room is the Rev'd. Auchtmuchty of Trinity Church, Captain Coglan, two of your maiden aunts, Earl Percy, your brother, Colonel Monteith and Mrs. Monteith, and your governess. Here is the special license, issued this morning by my friend Sir William Tryon, the Civil Governor. Now, will you rise up and go through with it in peace, or shall you remain bound?"

"O father, do have pity on me," she answered. "Doctor Auchtmuchty confirmed me, but he can only wed my hand to Captain Coglan—never my heart. That is in the keeping of Aar-on Burr."

"That is merely sentiment, Margaret, nothing more. When the ceremony is over, Captain Coglan will be your lawful hus-band. It will then depend on yourself whether your married life is happy or miserable. I would advise you to bend to the inevi-table. After all, Coglan has many good qualities, and I believe he really loves you, but he is not an expert in lovemaking. If you treat him well, you will have no reason to regret selection. After the ceremony, only him must you serve and obey, or bring your father's grey hairs in sorrow to the grave."

"I cannot marry him, father. I can never love him. I can never honor him; I can never obey him. I would rather poison him. If he compels me to marry him, he is the murderer of my soul." She said this with fierce emphasis while the fire flashed from her eyes.

"Your head is turned with those silly nurse-girl romances that you have been reading, else you would not be so obstinate. I may tell you that your passage is arranged on the packet sailing for London tomorrow. You will go with Captain Coglan to Cork as his wife; there, his brother is both an alderman and an Admiralty contractor. From thence, you will go via Killarney Lakes to Dublin, where my own brother is lord mayor. You will travel in the best of style, and it will be your own fault if you do not enjoy your honeymoon trip."

Major Moncrieffe then arose and said to her: "For the last time, I ask you, Margaret. Will you go through the ceremony of marriage where you are, or shall I unbind you?"

Finding that her father's will could not be conquered, either by words or tears, she gave in and answered sullenly:

"Yes, father, I will go through with it with hatred in my heart, yet I will wreathe my face with smiles; I will do it for your sake, father. Please, unbuckle the straps and let me up before you open the door to let them all in. O, how I hate that man, father, but I will harden my heart. I will be as marble—and as cold."

Whereupon Major Moncrieffe said, "Remember now, my daughter, that as soon as you have signed your name and finished the ceremony, Coglan is under contract to give to me the cipher letters and other documents which make my property and future standing secure."

"I understand, father," she answered. "He will give you the papers, but I will be even with him hereafter."

"You promise, Margaret, to do as I wish?" he said.

"I do," she replied.

Major Moncrieffe, much relieved, unbuckled the saddle straps that held her prisoner. As soon as she regained her feet, she stepped forward and wound her arms around her pleased father's neck and kissed him, saying:

"Captain Coglan, father, is your enemy as well as mine. I can see it; I know it; I feel it. He holds you under compulsion, and me also. He takes me by force, as it were. O, how I hate him father, how I long to slay him. O, some day I will have my revenge. I will pay him out. He shall live and die in a tideway of torment."

"My dear little fire-the-braes," he said as he kissed her kindly, "I am sorry for you, but am sure you will get over it all. Time is the physician that cures all human woes."

Then he went over and opened the door, greeting his guests with characteristic urbanity and graciousness.

Within ten days, Aaron Burr received in cipher from Margaret Moncrieffe a detailed account of her forcible marriage to Captain Coglan. He did not straightway fall down and die of a broken heart, for that was not his way. Nevertheless, he felt the stunning blow that had fallen upon him. It pierced him to the marrow. It was his first experience with defeat. While it had a sobering effect upon him, he never uttered a murmur to anyone. He smiled as usual and went his way and hid his secret sorrow and keen disappointment deep in his own heart.

Indeed, all through life, he was something of a stoic. Whenever he met the inevitable, he faced it with unvanquishable stolidity and iron fortitude. He was one of those rare, strong, leonine characters, so seldom seen in real life. If you tore out his heart with red-hot pincers, he would scarcely utter a solitary groan but die in silence, like a wolf, and mayhap gulping his blood into your face.

The forced marriage of Margaret made him suffer all the mental agonies that it is possible for a man in love to suffer and not go mad.

"O Aaron," she wrote, "forgive me, forgive me. They have given me to another. I have lost you forever. By force and threats, my father compelled me to marry Captain Coglan... The marriage took place on the 28th of February 1777... Tomorrow, I sail for Ireland in Captain Kidd's packet ship... Sorrow and anger has almost driven me off my head. I am weak and sick, and the doctor is constantly calling to see me. I hardly know what to do or how to think. All night long, continually, I cry in my agony and despair, 'O God! O God! O God!'

"But in spite of them all, dear Aaron, I love you still. I will love you forever. And if there is a world beyond death, I will also love you there. I will clasp you to my bosom forever and forever...."

Aaron Burr sat in his tent, thinking as he read. Thus thought he:

Margaret, you and I have met in some former life, of that I am convinced; I also feel we shall meet again at some future time, either in this life or in another.

I fell in love with you, Margaret, when first I saw you, and I knew not the reason, and when in your face I afterwards recognized the shadow-marks of that transfigured woman in the Northern pine forest, I knew there was a something more than human that drew us to one another. Ah, is there some hidden essence in our lives that first attracts and binds together only to thereafter hurl us malevolently apart?

If I had only 50,000 men tonight, I would storm New York—make another Troy of it—to rescue the woman I love. I would leave it a smouldering heap of ashes for Margaret's sake.

But my strength is not equal to my conception. That's my trouble: want of power, not want of will.

I feel myself as helpless as an eagle in an iron-barred cage. Why is this? Am I a man born out of time or a spirit in hell? Am I a free man or a captive soul?

Chapter X.

THE BURNING OF THE FARM

And the days and the years rolled on.

"Who goes there? Who goes there? Who goes there?"

CRACK!

In rapid succession, the three challenges rang out on the midnight air, swiftly followed by the sharp, angry report of a heavy rifle.

The sentry had suddenly seen the figure of a man cautiously emerging from out the surrounding mist. Thereupon, he shouted the regulation challenges as rapidly as his tongue could repeat them, and then, without waiting for any reply, fired point blank. *This time I will be on the safe side*, he thought.

The man approaching him had came from the direction of the British lines.

The sentry, who was soaking wet and standing under the shadow of a great oak tree, had been urged to unusual vigilance of late by his superior officers, under special instructions from General McDougall. Now the sentry, in his own mind, had determined to be "vigilant."

As soon as the report of the rifle died away, a voice, a strong, angry voice, came to him from the gloom, saying, "You infernal damned idiot: you've shot your own commanding officer!"

Now, the sentinel was a big raw-boned backwoodsman, the

---

1   William Sharp, *The Immortal Hour: A Drama in Two Acts* (Maine: Thomas B. Mosher, 1907).

veteran of quite a score of Indian wars. He had taken part in the capture of Havana ten years before and was also with Wolfe on the Heights of Abraham. His name was Holroyd. He was a strange character, a sort of military privateer, a soldier of fortune who loved war for war's sake and also for the loot (or possibilities of loot) that it brought him. If there had been no war of Independence, he would most likely have been taking part in some frontier raid or Mexican filibustering expedition. His whole life had been spent amid battle and blood and hardship, yet he was a strong, healthy, clear-headed man. His grandfather had been one of Cromwell's troopers, and the probability is that his ancestors originally came over the North Sea in a Viking cruise centuries ago, in search of booty along the coast of England.

He had strong opinions upon what is to good fighting men the all-absorbing question of "loot." On this subject, he was wont to wax quite eloquent around the bivouac fires. Thus, he would say, "Why do men go to war? Is it not, in some way, to better their condition? All these newfangled notions that men fight for other things than their own personal advantage are pure delusion. It is the solid things of life that men are ever after, though some of them haven't the courage to admit it. What is love of country but love of its good things?

"Now, what I desire to know is this: If we want to shoot a man in war and he badly wants to shoot us, why should we not take his property—if we can—as well as his life? Isn't that the way men win a 'fatherland' first? Don't they fight and conquer the original owners and then take the land? Very well then, what is the good of being a soldier—of risking your life and being a brave man in battle—if you cannot seize from your beaten enemy what your greater valor wins and what you stand badly in need of?"

Holroyd looked down ruefully upon patched boots of rawhide and torn breeches (from which his great hairy knees protruded) and continued:

"These old, womanish rules about 'no loot' are the ruin of an army, sir. If the soldier hasn't anything material to gain, he naturally enough loses his enthusiasm. Fame and glory are very nice but so is gold and silver and a new pair of breeches now and then. There is magic in war-won gold, for a man knows he has given the highest possible price for it. Hasn't he risked his life where the bullets whistle past his ears and whizzing shells explode under his horse's tail? I am for loot, my lads, beautiful loot. It's the finest thing in the world. I'd storm the gates of Hell for loot. A soldier is like any other man. He must make his business pay, else he gives it up. And if the soldier 'gives up,' who is to defend the country from the 'other fellow,' who comes along from a far country, also on the lookout for spoil?

"Now, these farmers all around this camp are mostly wealthy old Tories who don't seem to believe in 'America for the Americans!' They are either fighting against us openly, like the De Lanceys, or spying upon us secretly, like the Wombwells. And they have plenty to eat and good houses to cover them, while here we are marched about like a lot of born fools, all in rags and tatters, half starved, and sleeping in the snow. Now, why should we not loot them? Shouldn't the fighting man be more considered?"

Now, when Holroyd heard the voice through the mist, he immediately knew whom he had shot at.

Why, it's Little Burr, the colonel, he thought as he hammered home another bullet. *I hope I haven't hurt him, though. However, he brought it on himself. He is always prowling about the posts at night. Indeed, I often wonder when he sleeps. I always said he would get a bullet some night, but I never thought he would get it from me. He's a brave, gentlemanly little cuss but too much of a*

"Good God, Colonel, I hope I haven't done for you," said Holroyd as he walked hastily up to where Burr lay bleeding from a bullet wound in the foot. "I am very sorry, Colonel, that I shot at you but sorrier still I did not miss you. I would never have fired nohow if I had thought it was you or any of our own men. I really believed it was a Tory spy, sneaking around to knife me in the back. Are you much hurt, Colonel?"

"No, I am only lamed," replied Colonel Aaron Burr without a trace of anger in his tone. "You fired too low, or you would have killed me, Holroyd. Your bullet has gone through my right foot. It is bleeding profusely. Come and pull off my boot and help bandage the wound. Why in the name of heaven did you fire so quick?"

Holroyd made the best excuse be could, for he was really sorry, stating that only three nights before, he had been fired at by a British scout from the identical place where Burr lay. Then he bound up the ugly wound most skilfully.

By this time, the piquet, alarmed at the shot, arrived to see what was the matter.

Soon, four pair of strong arms lifted their colonel out of the frosty grass and carried him to the picket tent. The tent was neatly hidden from observation in a clump of pine trees.

A cheerful fire of logs burned in a hollow. Over it hung from a branch a large three-legged iron pot in which potatoes, a leg of pork, and half a sheep were stewing. The food had been procured "in the usual way" by Holroyd, who, among his other military accomplishments, was a "splendid forager."

The fire was so situated that the glare thereof could not be seen from the enemy's lines.

Burr decided that he would be taken over to the nearest farm. Led by Holroyd, the soldiers made a litter of intertwined branches to carry their Colonel upon.

In about twenty minutes, with Burr on their shoulders, they reached the vicinity of the farm. But they did not approach too close. They saw that the old homestead was in a state of tumult and confusion.

From the windows, lights shone and flitted intermittently. Evidently something unusual was happening; under the direction of Burr, the four soldiers crept towards the farm cautiously, feeling their way as it were, each man with his rifle in his hand ready for instant use.

As they got closer, they could hear the sound of angry voices, the lowing of disturbed cattle, the barking of dogs, the crying of children, and the raucous cackle of geese and barnyard fowls. Horses neighed, men shouted, and women shrieked.

"It is a British patrol looting Captain Delafield's farm; we must move very cautiously as they are probably in force," said Burr to Holroyd. "Carry me as near as you can without discovering ourselves. Then put me down and get your rifles ready. We'll give them a fight for it as soon as we get our bearings and ascertain how many they are."

So they carried him behind a tall black stump within a hundred yards of the barn. Then, under his instructions, they stretched themselves out on their bellies in the long, wet grass and waited.

The officer in command of the looting party could now be distinctly heard giving instructions to his men.

"Put your own saddle on that black stallion there, Tom: he is a fine beast. Let your own horse go: he is about played out. Then go and help Corporal McDermot drive off those cattle: they'll make first-class Christmas beef for us. Tell Sergeant Joubert to send two men for that big bay gelding and the three thoroughbred mares. You, Ebenezer, catch that iron-gray colt and put him in the spring cart. Then load up with all the more valuable stuff and move off as quickly as you can. Don't forget those two casks of whiskey and that box of books. Sergeant Dalton, send one of the big wagons up here and the other to the barn. put all the grain you can find in one and meat stuffs in the other. Get those squealing hogs killed and thrown in also. Mind you bleed them well. Hurry up now, my lads! We haven't a moment to spare. Those damned Rebels may be here at any moment. We're alongside of their lines. I'm sure they can't be far away. Hurry up, my lads, hurry up, or we'll lose everything—Christmas beef, whiskey and all—and have a fight into the bargain."

The scene before Burr and his four men was most interesting. The farm was being systematically looted by the enemy. Soldiers with guns in their hands were moving from room to room searching for valuables. Some were tearing open mattresses and pillows, seeking for hidden money. Some were digging up the floors, smashing boxes, and chests of drawers. Some were breaking open safes and cupboards in search of food. Some were chopping out the wainscots or peering up the chimney or creeping among the blackened rafters, where the smoked hams and dried beef hung.

Outside, some of the Redcoats were standing on guard, while some were chasing fowls, turkeys, geese, etc., or strapping them to their saddles. The troop horses seemed quite accustomed to all this; evidently, they were old to the business. They stood and coolly munched bundles of oaten forage while the wings of turkeys and geese flapped among their legs.

Quickly, the wagons were loaded with corn and oats, wheat and potatoes, dead calves, dead hogs, dead sheep, dried fruit, hams, bacon, etc., etc., and moved off up the road under escort.

"We'll have a jolly good feast this Christmas, anyhow," said one soldier to another as he knocked the top off a long-necked wine bottle and drank heartily.

"Yes," replied the other. "Christmas comes but once a year, and this is the way to get good cheer. Let us enjoy life, I say,

 RIVAL CÆSARS

while we can. What's the use of moping around and looking glum?"

"Aye," said the first speaker as he finished the bottle. "This is a real generous way to carry off the enemy's "good things" and feast thereon. It is a good Ian too for people can't fight if they have nothing to eat. It's the belly that fights. Hurrah, I say, for Christmas and jolly good cheer."

Meanwhile, under a guard of four men with fixed bayonets, the women and children had been removed from the house to the barn. They consisted of two noble-looking matrons, several boys, and four young girls, one of whom nursed a baby boy.

In the midst of the main body of raiders, two male prisoners stood handcuffed together.

The men on guard were busy eating cakes, which had been found in the cupboards. Some were also examining, with much curiosity, a number of newly captured American muskets, whose very ingenious "sights" were made of bone and whose stocks were elaborately lashed with strips of white horse-hide.

After everything had been loaded up and carted or carried away, after the last wagon had moved off, loaded with vegetables and fowls (dead and alive) with whip cracks and shouts from the drivers, then, again, the harsh, cold tones of the captain in command rang out (he was an American, and his name was De Lancey): "Sergeant Major, see that the house and barns and outhouses are immediately set on fire and burned down."

During all this scene, Burr lay behind the stump alongside of his four men. He saw the madness of making a direct attack with four guns against at least 200. So he and his men lay still, waiting for a favorable opening to attack the farm-burners.

"Men," said Burr, "keep silent; our chance will come directly. See that your priming is good, and when most of them have moved off, let us give battle to the rearguard. We will take them by surprise and shoot as many as we can. They will not see us in the dark, and we will be able to easily see them as soon as they set fire to the farm. They will imagine we are a large party and fly. Then we can pour it into them."

Presently, a burly Redcoat, whom the sergeant designated "Patrick O'Connel," stood up on one of the window sills of the farm house. Balancing himself carefully with his left hand, he held a blazing torch (made of wood, and paper from an old family bible) in his right hand. Reaching up, he applied the torch to a heap of dry wood and other combustibles, made of broken tables, splintered cradles, beds, chairs, etc., previously collected in the frame of an upper window.

Gradually, the little spark of red flame spread and grew bigger and bigger. The boards and flooring and ceiling hissed and crackled and roared in the hot flames.

Soon, the house and barns became a whirling, blazing furnace, sending sheets of forked flame aloft like great streaks and spears of swaying gold, which shone and reflected upon the long, cruel rows of naked bayonets with a lurid, unearthly glitter. Outhouses and haystacks were all wrapped in the crimson shroud while some of the soldiers wheeled wagons and carriages (that could not be taken away) into the fiery, roaring, all-consuming cauldron.

Everything burned. Even the iron melted in the intense heat, and chimneys and walls fell in.

"That's the way to lessen those Rebel farmers as to the meaning of rebellion," Captain De Lancey said to his lieutenant as the two British officers stood alongside the oaken draw-bucket by the well, watching the flaming farmstead in admiring wonder. "They seem somehow to imagine," continued the captain, "that a civil war can be conducted according to the rules of an old maids' card game, but such things as this ought to teach them different. All is fair in love and war, and the heaviest blow that can be dealt to an enemy by land or by sea is, next to taking his life, the utter destruction of his property."

Captain De Lancey was the son of Chief Justice De Lancey and a relative by blood and marriage of the Clintons and Livingstons. The De Lanceys were of Norman and (bar-sinister) royal descent and, like the Livingstons and Clintons, were semi-nobles of the "realm." Indeed, De Lancey's brother, the Earl of Abingdon, was in the English House of Lords, as were also certain of the Clintons and Livingstons. Baron Livingston of Columbia County, N.Y., was a direct descendant of one of Mary, Queen of Scots' famous "Five Marys."

When the war ended, the immense landed estates of the De Lanceys were confiscated by Act of Congress. These lands were valued at more than a million dollars.

"But how about the womenfolk? I feel sorry for the poor things. Look at them, weeping over there as if their very hearts would break, while the children clap their hands to see the home that they were perhaps born in flame up," said Lieutenant Morris to his captain.

"Yes, I admit it is very pathetic," replied the captain, "but war is war, not a garden pleasure party. When men go to war, they must expect this sort of thing, or else they are very stupid. War cannot be carried on as if we were all holy saints on a church window. War is the iron game, the game of the great inexorable, and our womenfolk must also take their chances with us. There is no absolute protection for women and children in war, except convention and agreement. Neither women nor men can escape the consequences of victory or defeat. Man must fight, and women must weep forever and ever. In private life, it is the same: the fortunes of women are bound up with their menfolk.

"The business of a householder is to fight in defense of his home and family, and if he is defeated, or if through the fortune of battle he is driven off, then his entire household remains at the absolute mercy of the victor.

"Now, the victor may be kind and generous to the household of a defeated mortal foe, or he may not, according to his disposition or other circumstances. Unlimited victory places the victor under no obligations to obey any one else's opinion than his own. Who can dictate right and wrong to Cæsar?

"These are elemental and unvanquishable facts that cannot be got over by tears, protests, sympathizing philosophy, or eloquent hysteria."

"But our own women and children and property-holders may be treated in the same way tomorrow," replied the more tender-hearted young lieutenant

"And they will, if we are defeated," answered the hard-headed captain of the farm-burners. "My remarks apply all round. If a conquered people receive any consideration at all, it is only by the grace of the conquerors. For example, I have great possessions in this state. I have wife, children, and relatives by the score, and if the Royalist side loses, what mercy can any of us reasonably expect? For my own part, I don't expect any.

"If the king's forces are defeated, a new government must be established by the victors, and, assuredly, they will—if they are not crazy—confiscate our lands and perhaps also exile us.[1] If they take pity on us, that is their business, but I, for my part, claim no "rights" of any kind if my side is worsted. The stakes are for those only who win the game. Let us then be sensible and do unto the enemy even as the enemy would do unto us."

"But the Rebels have not burned farms nor carried off the property of our people, have they?" inquired the young lieutenant, still unconvinced.

"Why, of course they have, and I don't in any way blame them for it either. Their grievances," said the captain as the light

---

1 ⧧   From 40,000 to 100,000 Royalist exiles—men, women and children—sailed away to Canada and other British colonies at the end of the war. Their property was seized by the conquerors under the Confiscation Act of 1783. Isaac Roosevelt, an ancestor of President Theodore Roosevelt,
obtained some of the De Lancey lands situated on the Bowery.

from the burning barn illuminated his strong, dark Norman face, "are not unreasonable. I myself think the king has been badly advised. I sympathized also with them at the beginning of the outbreak but could not well join them, because my people and all my material interests are bound up with the king's government.

"Surely, you must also know that the war actually began in the open destruction of property in Boston Harbor and elsewhere, including the burning of the Peggy Stewart and the king's revenue cruiser Gaspee. Many of the arms of the Loyalists have also been bunted and looted. Only last week, Lieut-Colonel Dayton of the Rebel army burned and totally destroyed the private homestead of Governor Johnston and carried off all the cattle, horses, negroes, forage, food, and livestock, exactly as we are doing now."

"It's a pity, Captain, that war could not be conducted on more humane methods," answered the lieutenant. "War is hell. My own people also own property in New York and are widely connected with the Livingstons, Clintons, and Schuylers. Like you, yourself, Captain, I have much at stake."

"Humane methods in war are, in my opinion, out of place," replied the captain. "They are a weakness and always end in disappointment. When men go to war, they should fight on till one side or the other is thoroughly thrashed. That saves further disputes.

"You say truly that 'war is Hell,' but your quotation is incomplete. 'War is Hell to the vanquished,' that is the correct Latin of it. It is heaven to the victors. If there is any Heaven on Earth, or possibility thereof, it is for the great victor nations, certainly not for weak and cowardly and unvictorious peoples. The vanquished peoples are really the transgressor peoples, and you know the way of the transgressor is somewhat hard."

"I never thought of it in that way before, Captain," answered the lieutenants. "You almost convince me that war is a blessing in disguise."

"Exactly what I believe," said the captain. "Good always results from a great war. The main point is not to be on the wrong side.

"You must also know that outside the coastal cities, all the ground between the two armies is now a continual scene of rapine and murder. On this debatable land, every kind of outrage and brigandage prevails. Ambushes and petty battles are the regular order. No man goes to his bed, whether Tory or Whig, without being under the apprehension of having his house broken into, plundered, or burnt, or of having his cattle driven off before morning.

"The Tories burn and plunder the farms of the Whigs, and the Whigs burn and plunder the farms of the Tories. There are nights when the whole countyside, as far as eye can see, is lit up with burning hayricks, homesteads, flour-mills, and barns.

"Then there are professional marauders—assuming to belong to either side as suits their purpose—looting both Whig and Tory.

"Indeed, many of the bushwhackers care naught for either cause but fight only for their own hand and are making fortunes in the business. Only last week, we hanged seven of these gentry in Orange County and three in Westchester. The cattle they 'lift' from the Rebels, they sell in our camp; the cattle they 'lift' from our people, they sell in the Rebel camp."

"But all the same, Captain," said the lieutenant, 'I don't like this business of farm-burning, and I think I will resign my commission. It seems to me too much like warring on women and children. Of course, I know the fate of women and children is inseparably bound up with the fate of their male relatives. War, as you say, is a grim business, and more than all such petty things as rules and regulations, it is a network of almighty musts. But

I also am an American, and my heart revolts against the horrors I see.

"If you had seen as much of war as I have," said the captain, "you would have had all such sentiment knocked out of your head. I have been with Clive in India and have seen the populations of entire towns and villages wiped out; I have also seen whole regiments of my comrades, including their womenfolk and little children, annihilated in a night. My heart is just as tender as yours, but I have learnt that feelings and opinions are as powerless to avert the calamities of war as to avert the stroke of a thunderbolt or to bridle the stars in their courses.

"At this very moment, for example, the enemy may be creeping upon us to destroy us. Even as we talk here in the glare of the flames, a bullet from the rifle of that handsome, dark-eyed woman's husband may come crashing through your skull or through mine. I tell you, war is no joke, and there shall be grief and mourning, tragedies and blood, to the end of the world."

Scarcely had these words left his mouth before four rifle-shots rang out on the night. Four redcoats fell, including Captain De Lancey. The captain's gushing lifeblood hissed and spouted in a hot, crimson stream from a hole in his throat. The heavy hunter's bullet of Holroyd had completely severed his jugular vein, and he was bleeding to death.

The lieutenant leaned tenderly over his dying captain and attempted to staunch the wound and bind it up, but a bullet came and smashed his own arm and made his efforts clumsy and slow.

Again, the four rifles "talked" at the whisper of Burr.

"I told you so," said the dying captain as he coolly plugged the hole in his neck with his own thumb.

"I am done for. I have got it this time. But you get out of range as quickly as you can, order the rear guard to retire immediately beyond the glare of the flames, then take cover and return fire.

"Tell them they must fight the death and retire slowly, or they will lose the whole convoy and the Christmas cheer to boot. Go, Mr. Morris. Attend to your duty. All depends on you now if the Rebels are in force. I will be dead in ten minutes. But, but, stay a moment. Put your hand in my breast. Take the packet of letters. Yes, that is it. They are for my wife, mother, and daughter in New York and one for my banker, Mr. Angerstein. Take them with you. Go, go, go, goodbye for ever. God bless you, Morris... God save the king."

Then the Royalist Captain's hand fell limp by his side. His eyes glazed in the flame's glare and the red blood spurted afresh from his wound. It gurgled out like liquid escaping from an inverted bottle. It splashed against the broken grindstone and a wrecked baby carriage. Hot and warm it spurted, and sparks from the fire, blown by the rising wind, fell into it and hissed themselves out.

The captain rolled on his side, his head hung down limply, then he pitched backward convulsively, bled white, and died.

And underneath his neck, the blood coagulated in a pool.

Again, Colonel Burr's four rifles rang out from the surrounding gloom; four more Redcoats tumbled in their tracks and

lay there dead or crept away wounded into the bushes.

"Holroyd," spake Burr, "you are the best shot. Now try and bring down that officer before he gets out of range."

"I'm doing my level best, Colonel," replied Holroyd as he lifted the hammer of his musket. "I've got my eye on him. He has blazed his last trail. I have already hit him once, I think. If the light from the fire keeps up, knock him over for certain this shot." -

Holroyd held his bronze-barrelled hunting rifle against the side of a fence post, took long, careful aim, and fired.

Lieutenant Morris was running for cover; Holroyd's heavy bullet smote him on the spine above the kidneys, glanced upwards, and went through his heart. He jumped high in the air and fell heavily forward upon the top of a small sapling stump. The stump, being as sharp as a knife, penetrated through his bowels, coming out at his back. There he died, groaning in extreme agony, with Captain De Lancey's papers grasped tightly in his left hand and his sword in the right.

(Those papers were brought to Colonel Burr next morning by Holroyd and proved of great value to him in after years. One was signed "Charles Lee" and another related to the title of an estate called "Richmond Hill.")

Again, the four rifles "spoke." Three more of the running enemy fell or were badly wounded. Before the four Americans could load again, the Redcoats were safe in the distance outside the illuminated circle. But Burr's troopers pursued them cautiously, firing into them at random, until, finally, the pursuit had to be abandoned owing to the proximity of a squadron of Lancers, sent out as reserve and reinforcement from the enemy's camp.

When the four soldiers returned to where Burr lay helpless, they bore him on the litter to a sheltered nook in a corner of the garden wall. There, wrapped in his cloak, tired out and worn, he soon fell sound asleep, his lullaby being the sad soughing of the wind and the dull roaring of the sinking flames.

When morning dawned, not the sign of an enemy could be seen. The blackened walls of the buildings stood up gaunt and bare. Inside, heaps of debris smoked and smouldered, and every now and then, portions of the walls fell with a crash.

Some wounded horses were limping about, their legs hanging by ligaments of flesh and sinew to broken bones. They whinnied piteously in their pain and seemed to say, "Come and help us! Come and help us!"

Bleak and cold and raw was the morning. The wind whistled and moaned through the trees disconsolately. Grey rushing clouds gathered in the North, and a slight penetrating rain began to fall. The wind bore up the ashes of the fire, re-scattering them far and near in sooty whirls as if in stormy, sardonic derision.

One of the soldiers walked smartly up and down in order to keep himself warm and, at the same time, act as sentinel. The other three cooked a rough breakfast. One was busy boiling a kettle of coffee on the prong of a hayfork over the embers of the house. Another was roasting a fat turkey on the end of a long pole thrust through the parlor window.

When the kettle boiled, Holroyd walked across to where the women of the farm were shivering, alongside of the barn walls, and offered each of them a cup of strong coffee with some corn cakes, made in the ashes of their own home.

In their precipitate retreat from the sudden onslaught of Burr's troopers, the Redcoats had forgotten the women and children, who thus escaped being carried off as hostages.

The women smiled graciously through their tears on the soldier-trapper and, while gratefully drinking the coffee, inquired how many men had been killed on the previous night.

Holroyd told how the four Americans, because of their superior shooting and strategy, had killed and wounded fifteen Britishers. He also told them how his own colonel had been wounded in the foot and now lay asleep behind the garden wall.

"Is that your colonel over there?" said one of the ladies, a very handsome woman with black eyes, a silken turban, and a flowing gown. Her long, loose hair hung down in dishevelled hanks over splendidly poised shoulders and bust. She had all the appearance of a distinguished and high-bred matron.

"Yes, that is he," replied Holroyd. "He is the bravest and coolest little gamecock you ever saw. And he knows how to plan things as well as how to do them too. It was his wits last night that made four of us hunt 200 men over the hills and far away.

The destroyed farmstead belonged to Captain Delafield, an

American officer away with Washington. The women were his wife, her two younger sisters, and Mrs. Prevost, a near neighbor, together with the latter's two children, two boys overflowing with animal spirits.

The black-eyed woman with the turban of silk was Mrs. Prevost, at that time, the wife of a brilliant British officer.

It was she with whom Alexander Hamilton had became infatuated, as described in a previous chapter.

Mrs. Prevost resided with her younger sister in most beautiful home at Paramus. She drove over on the day before to Mrs. Delafield's; Mrs. Delafield was her husband's first cousin.

She witnessed the burning and looting of her friends' home as already described. Even her own buggy and her favorite trotting pony, Jessie, had been carried off in the foray.

Presently, she wrapped a heavy cloak around her shoulders and walked over to where Col. Burr lay asleep in the dawn.

She looked down intently upon his clean-cut features and thought to herself, *He looks quite a boy. Yet the soldier who gave me the coffee says he is a very bold and brave man. How handsome he is too. He lies there in the mist and smoke like the picture of an old-time Roman warrior. I like him. I like his looks, but how pale he is! Perhaps he is badly wounded. I must do something for him; it's a woman's place to succor the wounded.*

Whereupon she stooped down and, without disturbing him, attempted to examine his wounded foot, the bandage of which was saturated with blood.

Then a sudden idea struck her, and she returned to where Mrs. Delafield and the children were. Mrs. Delafield was weeping bitterly as she looked upon the blackened ruins of her home.

"Don't give way to your feelings, Mrs. Delafield. Be strong and do not weep," said Mrs. Prevost to her. "We have no house or shelter, and there is a snow storm gathering. We cannot stay here. Let us ask one of the soldiers to go over to the next farm and get assistance. The roads are too muddy, and the creeks are all in flood, or we could walk across ourselves. Now, try and be calm, Mrs. Delafield. Our lives and the children are safe, and the house can be rebuilt again. There are many worse off than we."

"I don't see what else we can do," replied Mrs. Delafield, sobbing violently. "All our things are gone, our home is in ruins, and the poor, young officer who fought for us and saved us from being carried off may die. Where is he wounded?"

"The bullet is in his ankle. It must be a very painful wound," said Mrs. Prevost.

"War is terrible," sobbed Mrs. Delafield. "Perhaps my own husband and son may be wounded like that. O, I wish this cruel war was over. Why did God make men to fight anyhow? O, how I pity the wounded and sick."

Whereupon she seated herself on the hub of a smashed wagon wheel and burst into that universal feminine argument of protesting powerlessness: a torrent of tears.

Mrs. Prevost, who had seen many wars, attempted to console her but could not.

Meanwhile, the children were very busy with long sticks, raking up the smouldering embers of their father's house in order to see the sparks fly upon the wind. From time to time, as they succeeded in tossing a big heap of sparks up in the air, they would clap their hands and shout in uproarious glee. They were happy because they knew not and did not understand.

The four soldiers were busy eating breakfast, having first shared what they had with the women and children; Burr was leaning against the garden wall, drinking a cup of hot coffee and, nearby, three slightly wounded prisoners were digging a trench for the dead.

Far off down the road, some moving object approached through the mist and haze and smoke. It came rapidly round a curve over a low rise near the river.

"To your arms, my men," said Burr as he watched it come nearer and nearer. He thought it might be some ruse of the enemy. The prisoners were ordered to lay down on their faces. Each soldier reached for his loaded rifle, took up a commanding position behind the wall, and raised the hammers to half cock.

The alarm was unnecessary, however, for the moving object proved to be a carriage, driven at a wild gallop by a tall and very beautiful red-headed girl, whose luxuriant locks streamed on the chilly morning blast like some semi-divine Valkyrie, out searching for the dead.

"It is my sister, Miss De Visme, with Dr. McDougall's carriage. She has seen the smoke of the burning and is coming to our assistance. She knows I am here," spoke Mrs. Prevost, at whom Burr was looking with much interest.

The night of terror was over, a memorable night to Aaron Burr, to Alexander Hamilton, to Mrs. Prevost, and to all concerned. The soldiers, instructed by Burr, took their prisoners back to camp, but Burr himself rode away with the ladies to the neighboring farm.

There he lay for a month, unable to move, while Mrs. Prevost attended his wound. Thus, the future vice president of the United States became first acquainted with Mrs. Prevost, "the charming Widow Prevost" of ballad and story. She fell madly in love with him, and thereby hangs a tale—nay, half a dozen tales—and a tragedy.

As they drove away the sound of artillery could be heard in the distance.

BOOM!   BOOM!   BOOM!

The roar of heavy guns came rumbling down the wind. The battle was on again somewhere.

BOOM!   BOOM!   BOOM!

The future conquerors of the world were busy training each other. It was the snarling of the lions.

boom! boom! boom!

The proper price of freedom was being fairly paid—BLOOD! In blood is the salvation of man. The despot and the revolutionist were in mortal grips—and why shouldn't they be?

boom! boom! boom!

The struggle for existence was proceeding tumultuously, just as it proceeded a million years ago, even as it shall proceed a million years hence!

BOOM! BOOM! BOOM!

May the best man and the bravest man ever win, and may fortune and fame and love ever smile upon the strongest.

BOOM! BOOM! BOOM!

Weapon against weapon, brain against brain, to the pitiless end. "Love and women and war." The lion in man, the tiger in man: verily they are in him forevermore. A monster would he be if made otherwise.

BOOM! BOOM! BOOM!

The battle thundered. The cold rain drizzled down. The wind snarled. The men of the hammer and anvil were beating out red-hot hearts. And all was well.

BOOM! BOOM! BOOM!

The whinging of the bullets, the whizzing of the shells, the flash and whorl of the red conflagrations; are they not directed by the same impulse that spins the spheres? Is it not all for the best?

BOOM! BOOM! BOOM!

Is not the sword of conquest the scythe of selection? Is not the leaping forks of fiery light the signal of the true? And, is not the crash of cannon the actual voice of the gods?

Chapter XI.

"IT WAS NOT TO BE"

> *And louder still and louder*
> > *Rose from the darkened field,*
> *The braying of the war-horns,*
> > *The clang of sword and shield,*
> *The rush of squadrons sweeping*
> > *Like whirlwinds o'er the plain,*
> *The shouting of the slayers,*
> > *And screeching of the slain.*[1]

And the days and the years rolled on. And other things befel.

The revolution was working out its mighty destiny. The Iron Cross was busy. Battles and sieges were being fought all along the Atlantic coast and throughout the Thirteen States. There were few pitched battles but innumerable engagements.

England gradually tired of the war—Parliament even refused to vote supplies—whereas the Continentals everywhere gained heart and courage by their successes. A French army, a French fleet, and a French loan came to their aid in the nick of time. Also, loans from Spain and Holland.

The heroines and heroes of our tale were all bearing their due part in the eventful conflict, each one with a different mind and a different purpose yet all unconsciously evolving one great destiny. They were building better than they knew, even amid jealousies, heartburnings and some disillusionments.

The brethren of the Iron Cross had (on scores of bloody fields) proved their patriotism and their valor. Hamilton, Burr, and General Schuyler were specially conspicuous, for, as all men

---

1   Thomas Babington Macaulay, *The Lays of Ancient Rome* (Philadelphia: E.H. Butler & Co., 1864). This book was also quoted in *Might is Right*, see AMiR 4.3:10.

should, they had an indomitable faith in their own proposition.

Washington, Putnam, Gates, Greene, etc., all had their difficulties and dangers, their ups and their downs, their struggles, failures, triumphs and successes, "even as you and I."

Margaret Moncrieffe, after her marriage (by compulsion) to Captain Coglan, went to Ireland. On the trip over, Coglan was forced to fight a duel with the commander of the packet about her, in which the captain of the ship was badly wounded. The captain of the ship, named Kidd (nephew of the famous buccaneer), had threatened to confine Coglan as a lunatic. At Cook Haven, Ireland, they fought a second duel with pistols, and Coglan was laid up for fourteen days.

Mrs. Coglan was studiously insulting to her husband in front of the other passengers. She neglected him systematically and never wearied of relating the tale of her forced marriage and her hatred of him.

Nearly everyone on the ship took her part, and, thus, Captain Coglan was ostracized. Being a splendid shot, however, and a first-rate fighting man, he was not insulted.

At last, the vessel arrived in the Cove of Cork, and, there, Margaret was taken to her relatives residence in the suburbs. She journeyed from thence, by way of Killerney, to Dublin in a closed carriage and was there hospitably entertained by her rich uncle, who was lord mayor.

Here the quarreling between Mrs. Coglan and her hated husband became intense and almost scandalous. She attempted to run away but failed. She was forcibly brought back (handcuffed) to her husband's house and kept in a state of domestic imprisonment and espionage.

Then Capt. Coglan bought an old castle in Wales (it once belonged to Owen Glendower) and proposed taking her there to live, threatening that he would break her spirit or break her heart.

However, she escaped from him at Bristol and went to reside with relatives, named Agnew, on the Isle of Man.

Afterwards, she journeyed to London and became a fashionable actress. Here she gave birth to a daughter, who became, in after years, the mother of a renowned Confederate general.

Pursued by the law and the hired myrmidons of her husband, she eluded them again and again, for wherever this remarkable woman went, her splendid beauty and the pathetic story of her sufferings and unnatural marriage ever won to her side most ardent and powerful friends.

She had lost in Aaron Burr the only man she could ever admire or look up to, the man who was by nature designated to be the lodestar of her life and the father of her children.

Whoever says that love is not the chief of the gods either lacks of experience or perception. He knoweth not that which is real from that which is illusive.

Verily of all instincts and passions of the human heart, love is the strongest and most overmastering. For it, men slay their own brothers, women abandon their children, and kings desert their thrones.

The old romances repeat themselves ceaselessly. Love and ambition are always and ever the same. And better is a dinner of herbs where love is than a stalled ox and hatred therewith. So they say.

Burr lost in Mrs. Coglan the woman of all women, the only one that could have made his future happier and perhaps more successful.

Their forcible separation had a lasting embittering and evil effect upon both their lives. It made him cynical. It made her reckless.

He had lost the only woman who could ever have bound him down, and she lost in him the man alone in whom she could absolutely place all her faith and trust, the only man her powerfully passionate nature could ever love.

Gradually, she broke loose from all conventions; she spurned her husband openly and laughed at her own relatives who vainly protested at her course.

In despair and shame, Capt. Coglan fled from England and went to Russia. There he fought and died bravely as a soldier of fortune. To the end of his days, however, he never regretted his action in marrying Margaret. "I would do it again," he said on his deathbed. "I loved her beyond all things. I would have sold my very soul to possess her. I only regret my want of power to coerce her. Alone, I could not control her. My strength was not equal to my will. Would that I had been an absolute monarch, then, ah, then she should not have defied and escaped me."

During his life he fought seven duels in defense of her reputation, including one with Lord Thomas Clinton of London, a relative of Sir Henry Clinton, the general, and of George Clinton, Governor of New York.

FFrom 1780 to 1795, Mrs. Coglan made no inconsiderable stir in the court and fashionable circles of London and Paris, but, all the time, her heart was over the seas.

She became the reigning beauty: her name was on every lip. Painters vied with each other for the privilege of transferring her beautiful face and voluptuous figure to their canvas.

Lords, dukes, princes, kings, great emperors, ambassadors, and veteran generals were among her innumerable "conquests." George IV bestowed on her a necklace of pearls, and, thereafter, everybody who counted for anything in society, politics, or diplomacy was happy to do her honor.

She was known to dictate the fate of statesmen with a nod; she drove high ladies and queens to despair and suicide; she even ruled the destinies of nations, made treaties, and broke ambassadors with the glances of her glorious eyes.

She was on intimate terms with such men as Fox, Pitt, Napoleon, Talleyrand, etc.

But sorrow and anger—deep, bitter implacable resentment against "the world and all its works"—was in her heart. She inwardly cursed the kings and the queens, the presidents and the statesmen, the glitter and the show, for all these things were as mockery to her, since she had failed to become the wife of the dashing, black-eyed American colonel.

In the midst of all her ups and downs, his memory and his words were never once forgotten.

"O," she would say to herself in the privacy of her chamber, "O, that I could be as I was before. O, that my Aaron could be mine."

Numberless duels were fought on account of her, and the banks of the Seine and Thames were oft reddened with the hearts' blood of competing noblemen and great soldiers because of her smile, her word, or her frown. The dagger of the assassin, the lie of the editor, and the cup of the poisoner, performed their deadly mission upon nobles and kings, upon admirals and generals, upon women and menials because of her.

Alternately, Mrs. Coglan was reveling in wealth as the mistress of a nobleman, a prince, or a king. Again, she would be sunk in poverty, homeless and forlorn.

She bore children and raised them to manhood and womanhood but gave them not her name; she wrote books and published them with the money of men she loathed and despised; and with her love-songs of passion and tragedy, she delighted and charmed the most fastidious audiences in the world.

Thirty years passed away before she again saw Aaron Burr: he, a widower and a refugee from "justice"; she, the wife of another. Again, the wand of romance waved above them; again, "the old, old story" was re-enacted. Again the wand of romance waved above them—again "the old old story" was re-enacted.

In 1793—ten years after Colonel Burr had been married,

when he was still in the height of his fame and power, when his house at Richmond Hill, N.Y., was the center of fashion and politics, intrigue and hospitality—Mrs. Coglan published her "Memoirs," to the astonishment and rage of governments, princes, and presidents.

Now, Aaron Burr was at all periods of his life a voracious reader. The thoughts of the world's best writers were familiar to him. He kept himself thoroughly informed of all the latest and rarest publications. He never was a mere provincial.

As soon, then, as the "Memoirs of Mrs. Coglan" appeared, a copy was immediately mailed to him by his London bookseller. Sitting at breakfast one day, with Theodosia, his twelve year old daughter, by his side, he received the book, and, opening its pages thus he read:

"The writer of the following sheets, nursed in the lap of tenderest indulgence, sprung from a father whose attachment to a king even surpassed the duties he owed to his country; she who once basked in the sunshine of fortune has lately herself struggled with all the miseries she has here endeavored to describe.

"Affliction cuts deeper than the recollection of former enjoyments; the memory of past joys sharpens the sense of her present sufferings; she once little dreamed of those scenes of horror through which she has passed; she little anticipated that whenever she should have occasion for the world's assistance, the world would withhold it from her. She had fondly imagined that every one was her friend. Nor was the veil of deception withdrawn till, alas, she had occasion for its friendship. Then the very persons who had been most anxious to court her smiles, who had beguiled her with their delusive flatteries, who had encouraged her errors and soothed her vices, were the first to keep aloof and shun the wretchedness they had helped to accomplish. They who had been the bosom friends of her father refused even to hear the hapless tale of his ill-fated child. Nor did his unshaken zeal in the cause of his sovereign ever produce to his daughter the recompence of a shilling from the English government. (Major Moncrieffe lost all his poses sessions in the American war.) These are the reflections of a woman, chastened in affliction's school, restored to reason by the wholesome lessons she has received from the most instructive of all monitors: adversity.

> Want, wordly want, that hungry meagre fiend,
> Is at her heels......[1]

"To drive off this fiend, alas, she has no other hope than the problematic advantage she may derive from the faint productions of her pen.

"The perspective that the world now presents to view is gloomy indeed; nevertheless, it would be greatly brightened if she conceived that her example might serve as a beacon to others of her sex.

> O, what is friendship but a name,
> A charm that lulls to sleep,
> A shade that follows wealth and fame
> And leaves the wretch to weep?[2]

"In America, the land of my birth, my heart received its first impression, that amidst the subsequent shocks which it received, and which has rendered me very unfit to admit the embraces of an unfeeling, brutish husband.

"Oh, may these pages one day meet the eyes of he who subdued my virgin heart, whom the immutable, unerring laws of

---

1   Thomas Otway, *Venice Preserv'd or A Plot Discover'd* (London: 1682). The original has "my" instead of "her".
2   Oliver Goldsmith, "Wooing and Winning The Hermit," *The Vicar of Wakefield* (London: R.Collins, 1766)

nature had pointed out for my husband but whose sacred decree the barbarous customs of society fatally violated. To him, I plighted my virgin vow, and I shall never cease to lament that obedience to a father left it incomplete.

"When I reflect on my past sufferings, now that, alas, my present sorrows press heavily upon me, I cannot refrain from expatiating a little on the inevitable horrors that ever attend the frustration of natural affections. I myself, who, unpitied by the world, have endured every calamity that human nature knows, am a melancholy example of the truth, for if I know my own heart, it is better calculated for the purer joys of domestic life than for that hurricane of extravagance and dissipation on which I have been wrecked.

"Why is the will of nature so often perverted? Why is social happiness forever sacrificed at the altar of prejudice? Avarice has usurped the throne of reason, and the affections of the heart are not consulted.

"We cannot command our desires, and when the object of our being is unattained, misery must necessarily be our doom. Let this truth, therefore, be forever remembered: once an affection has rooted itself in a tender, constant heart, no time, no circumstance can eradicate it.

"Unfortunate, then, are they who are joined if their hearts are not matched.

"With this conqueror of my soul, how happy should I now have been, what storms and tempests should I have avoided (at least I am pleased to think so), if I had been allowed to follow the bent of my inclinations; happier, oh, ten thousand times happier should I have been with him in the wildest deserts of our native country—the woods affording us our only shelter and their fruits our only repast—than under the canopy of a costly state, with all the refinements and embellishments of courts, with the royal warrior who would fain have proved himself the conqueror of France.

"My conqueror was engaged in another cause, ambitious to obtain other laurels: he fought to liberate, not to enslave, nations. He was a colonel in the American army, and high in the estimation of his country. His victories were never accomplished with one gloomy, relenting thought: they shone as bright as the cause which inspired them.

"I had communicated, by letter, to General Putnam the purposes of this gentleman, and I was embarrassed by the answer that the general returned; he entreated me to remember, that the person named, from his political principles, was extremely obnoxious to my father and concluded by observing, 'That I surely would not unite myself with a man who, in his zeal for the independence of his country, would not hesitate to drench his sword in the blood of my nearest, should he be opposed to him in battle.'

"Saying this, he lamented the necessity of giving advice contrary to his own sentiments, since in every other respect he considered the engagement, as unexceptional. Nevertheless, General Putnam, after this discovery, appeared extremely reserved; nor did he ever cease to make me the object of his concern to Congress; and after various applications, he succeeded in obtaining leave for my departure."

Next she described her arrival at Lord Howe's with a letter to her father.

Then she told of the marriage in these pathetic words:

"Captain Coglan, my present husband, saw me at an assembly, when, without either consulting my heart, or deigning to ask my permission, he instantly demanded me in marriage and won my father to his purpose.

"In a savage mind which only considered sensual enjoyment, affection was not an object, for I told him at the time he had not my affection and conjured him, in the most persuasive terms, to act as a man of honor and humanity; his reply was congenial to his character; he valued not any refusal on my part so long as he had the Major's consent, and, with a dreadful oath, he swore, 'that my obstinacy should not avail me.' Indeed, my refusal signified nothing; he insinuated himself so far in my father's confidence as to draw upon me the anger of a parent to whose displeasure I had never been accustomed and whose rebukes I had not the resolution to resist.

"Confined to my own apartments, I was forbid his presence unless prepared to receive the husband he had provided for me. Wretched in mind, smarting under the sad reverse—I who had only known the heart-cheering smiles of parental fondness becoming the object of parental anger—the idea overcame me; besieged, I unhappily yielded, and, here, fate dashed me on a rock that has destroyed my peace of mind in this world and may, perhaps, have paved any way to eternal torments in another.

"Unable, as I have said, to withstand, etc., I took to my bed a viper who has stung me even unto death, who has hurled me from the rank to which I was born and forever banished me from all the amiable enjoyments of society, without which life is a vacuum not to be endured.

"My union with Mr. Coglan I never considered in any other light than an honorable prostitution, as I really hated the man whom they had compelled me to marry.

"When Dr. Auchtmuchty joined our hands (I cannot say our hearts), he wedded me to a series of wretchedness from which Heaven alone holds forth a prospect of relief.

"Educated in the school of virtue, and, I trust, naturally averse to those scenes of vice in which my unhappy stars have since involved me, let my example serve as a salutary caution to other parents who attempt to influence the choice, or to force the inclinations, of inexperienced female youth on a point where everything sacred is concerned.

"Let the compulsion practiced on me apologize with the liberal mind for the transgressions of youth doomed to the chains of a detested marriage.

"Had it been my lot to have been united in wedlock with the man of my affections, my soul and body might have been now all purity and the world not then have lost a being naturally social, generous, and humane."

Tears arose in his eyes as he put down the volume. The cold, calculating man of the world, the hard lawyer, the iron-willed Revolutionary colonel, actually wept.

Memories of Margaret in her youthful charm, maiden beauty, and innocence arose before his mental eye.

One thing, however, thought he, *I did all in my power to marry her. Nature intended that we should wed but destiny has fought against us. by is this?* Then other thoughts arose and poured through his brain: his strifes, hopes, loves, successes, ambitions.

Next day, Burr walked over to his bankers (Angerstein & Co.) where he arranged for a draft to their London office for $1,000 to be straightaway mailed to Margaret without intimating from whom it came.

As he dropped the registered package into the post office he murmured to himself, again and again (this was in 1793), "Ah, if Margaret had been my wife, I would ere this have been a general, perhaps a president. Beloved among women was my dead wife—my kind, my faithful, my darling Theodosia—but thrice beloved art thou, O Margaret Moncrieffe. Margaret, Margaret, my heart has ever been thine. Over the gray waters, I waft thee my prayer. Ah, would that my life could be lived anew, and that thou wert a maid once more. But it was not to be."

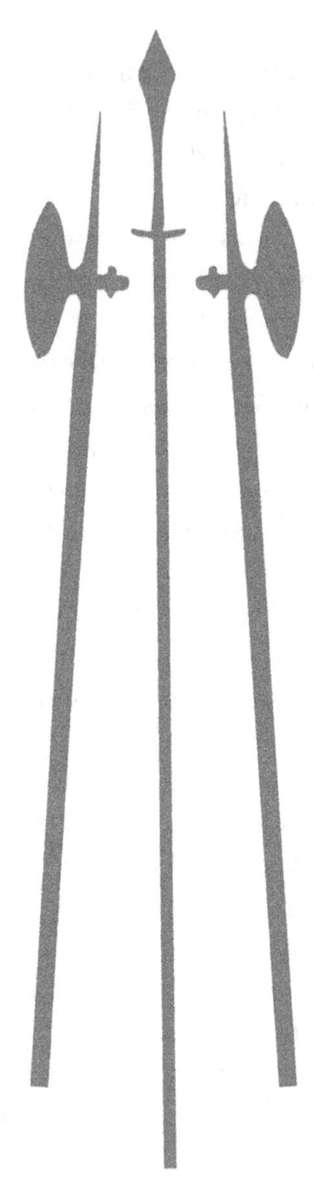

Chapter XII.

THE WIDOW PROPOSES

"She with decorum all things carried
Frowned—blushed—wept, and then was
married."[1]

And the days and the years rolled on.

Now Alexander Hamilton, though frantically in love with the dashing young widow Prevost, had avowed himself a suitor for the hand and heart of the much richer, much more beautiful, and much younger Betsy Schuyler.

He had all along been first favorite with her father, though Betsy held coquettishly aloof and refused to accept him straightway. But she did not reject him. She was diplomatic. She liked him very much and considered him a possible life partner (in certain eventualities), but her soul was centered on Burr. She secretly hoped to gain Burr and in order to do so, dallied with his friend Hamilton. Her idea was to make Burr jealous, and therefore, more eager. She thought, *If Colonel Burr likes me, he will show jealousy, and then I will know how to regard Colonel Hamilton.*

But Burr proved indifferent to her wiles, though he liked her and also saw her stratagem. He thought to himself, *If it had not been for Margaret, I might have taken more interest in Betsy. As it is, I clearly do not love her. Therefore, I will stand aside and give Hamilton a chance. It will be a good match for him, and gain him promotion, to marry a general's daughter. Also, he is my friend: I am bound to do all I can to promote his interests.*

---

1   Oliver Goldsmith, "The Double Transformation: A Tale", found in *The Traveller, The Deserted Village, and Other Poems* (Goodrich, by Lincoln and Stone, 1819). The original has "So" instead of "She", the original second line is "Miss frown'd, and blush'd, and then was—married."

Helen Livingston was also a-dreaming of the famous young colonel about whose exploits everyone was talking. Wherever he went, in Albany or elsewhere, she was bound to be there. Indeed, she was as deeply in love with him, as was her rival Betsy. Needless to say, there was no love lost between Betsy and Helen, although they met with great apparent cordiality from time to time and even kissed each other's cheeks with ardour and soft, purring words of feminine conventional delight.

Now upon the scene comes the widow Prevost still further to complicate matters, for she also loved Burr and had determined to marry him. Her knowledge of the ways of men gave her a certain advantage in the contest over the younger women.

Burr delighted in the company of the more mature widow, for she studied his ways and tried to flatter and please him.

Mrs. Prevost was of Swiss descent. She could speak several languages and talk entertainingly on the very things that interested him. Nevertheless, his heart remained untouched while his judgment was charmed.

However, be finally came to the conclusion to marry someone. "I must have a wife," he said, "and it might as well be the interesting and accomplished widow as anyone else."

From the practical point of view, both Betsy and Helen would have made a better match, for both were very beautiful and wealthy and young, and both would have been glad to say "yes" to the handsome colonel.

Mrs. Prevost, on the other hand, was neither very rich nor very beautiful. She, however, made up for her other deficiencies in being extremely fascinating and ladylike, and a natural air of graceful poise made her very attractive, especially to such a man as Burr, who had at all times a somewhat unusual admiration for the outer graces of style and manner.

Mrs. Prevost was physically a fully developed woman of the vivacious brunette type, with large lustrous eyes, coal-black hair, a glorious complexion, about five feet, five inches tall.

Though not more than 30 years of age, she was still playful and romantic and, unlike the average woman of the period, was a great reader and somewhat intellectual.

It was her very evident mental ability that first impressed Burr with the idea of marrying her.

"The very woman I want," he thought. "My carer must be a public one, and a woman such as this, brainy as well as graceful, will be of great strength to me. As the mistress of a public man's household, she will be unsurpassable."

Now by the time he was twenty-five, Aaron Burr had become somewhat tired of feminine admiration. As already pointed out, nearly all the women whom he met were eager for his attentions. The gleam of Colonel Burr's eye struck women into trouble as the gleam of his sword struck men to death.

Now "the Widow Prevost" was, to all men who approached her, exactly what Burr was to most women, that is to say, a sort of human magnet. Men worshipped at her shrine in dozens, and numberless romantic tales are still handed down at Paramus relating to jealousies and intrigues originating in love for this delightful and fascinating widow.

When, therefore, two such remarkable male and female personalities met (after the burning of the farm, as previously related), it is not to be wondered that they soon began to regard each other with mutual favor. She became enamoured of him long before his wound had healed, and he, even while still unable to walk, looked at her often in an inquiring way as perhaps a possible substitute for Margaret Moncrieffe.

She is now introduced to the reader as an honored guest at General Schuyler's old Dutch mansion in Albany; on the anniversary of the battle of Bunker Hill a grand ball was being held there, at which nearly all the celebrities of the time were present in full force.

The old rambling house was lit up from basement to roof. In every window, a light shone. Lanterns hung in the shrubberies and bowers of the trim and formal old-time garden, and all was gay and bright and happy. Eyes looked into eyes, and the "old story" (the story that is never old) was told again and again with the usual consequences.

Ye olde time chariots of the best Colonial families stood around the gateways or upon the broad, winding avenue that led up to the entrance of the great hallway and overhanging portico.

In a sheltered, half-hidden nook, upon a rustic bench, facing the house, sat two old friends: Aaron Burr and Alexander Hamilton. They had been conversing earnestly for some time upon the course of the war and the rival merits of Gates and Washington.

They were upon the point of parting when Hamilton said, "I hear you are engaged to Mrs. Prevost. Is it true?"

"It is not true, Hamilton. Why do you ask?"

"Because she is the only woman I have ever strongly loved, as I told you before; if you win her from me, it will be an unfriendly act," said Hamilton significantly yet in a half-jocular way.

"I admire her very much," replied Burr in his most confidential tones, "but recently only have I considered the possibility of marrying her. If she prefers you, however, I will not stand in your way. You are welcome to her, Hamilton. She is not the woman I love. That I do assure you on my troth."

"I love her passionately," answered Hamilton, "and believe I could have had her long ere this if you had not came between us. Of course, I do not in any way blame you. I merely state the fact as it appears to me."

"What about Betsy Schuyler?" suggested Burr, smiling

blandly at his old friend. "I have always thought you were moving in that direction. Once you told me, if my memory serves me correct, that you intended to marry the superb Miss Betsy. You cannot surely want both. But proceed, win them both if you can. I won't consciously balk you. Perhaps you want to start a harem and go into the King Solomon business."

Thereupon, Burr broke into a fit of amused laughter in which Hamilton also somewhat ruefully joined. Just then they were interrupted. A messenger came to call Hamilton upon official business connected with his position as chief secretary to the Commander in Chief.

Upon another seat, within sight of the two friends but unseen by them, sat Mrs. Prevost. She was thinking of Burr and thus thought she:

I have done him no harm, and though I love him well and even take pains to let him see it, somehow, of late, he avoids me. I am sure he does. If he bates me, O, I shall die of grief. Until I have speech with him, I am in unrest. Oh, that I could read his heart and know if he really loves me or not. I cannot sit at ease or do anything because of him. Love for him constraineth me, overmasters me. I felt great love for my first husband, but for this man I feel a love thrice as passionate. It crowds my soul; it renders me useless for anything but thoughts of him. I must talk with him. I must unburden myself. He is going away to the wars again tonight. He might get killed. Who knows how long it shall be before we meet again? Perhaps never.

Then she arose and walked over to where Burr sat musing and seated herself coquettishly, without ceremony, by his side. Then be said unto her, "I hope you are enjoying yourself, Mrs. Provost. You danced most divinely with the French admiral."

"I never enjoy myself so well as when I am talking to you," she replied with an appealing look that meant volumes. "All the other men seem so stiff and formal or over complimentary or insipid. I like men to be natural and straightforward and speak to me as a reasonable being, like you do. Because of the stiffness and formalism, I don't enjoy these grand functions anymore. They seem so like play-acting to me now, so hollow, false, pretentious, and insincere. I like the small home assemblies, where everybody knows one another and where one feels he or she is not playing a part. But why have you avoided me so much of late? I have scarcely seen you."

"I have not avoided you, Mrs. Prevost," he answered, "but some important despatches from the front kept Colonel Hamilton and myself busily engaged for upwards of two hours. Indeed, he has only just now gone inside to confer with General Greene regarding the news from Savannah,"

"I don't like your friend Colonel Hamilton," she said with decision.

"Why?" answered Burr much interested. He likes you. I am sure he does."

"He has twice attempted to propose marriage to me, but each time I have laughed him off or evaded the subject. How can you and he be friends? He is so unlike you in his ways, and I believe he really hates you." Thus said the widow in very suggestive tones.

"Hamilton has always been my friend. We hunt together, as it were. But why would you reject him? He is a fine fellow at bottom and sure to rise in the world." Thus said Burr diplomatically in order to draw her out, as he thought. Meanwhile, she had resolved to carry out her own plan of campaign and bring Burr to the point.

She therefore arose from the rustic bench under the laurels as if to look around for intruders, and, sitting down again, she took care to seat herself closer to Colonel Burr, saying in her most seductive tones, "My heart has been stolen by another man, Colonel Burr, and therefore I don't like Colonel Hamilton."

"If you loved him, would you marry him, Mrs. Prevost?" he asked.

"Indeed, I would," she answered. "I would marry the man I loved, no matter what happened." And looked at Burr in a way that no mortal of flesh and blood could fail to understand.

"If I, for instance, dared to love you Madame," Burr replied, "what would you say?" He then leaned towards her and took her unresisting hand in his own.

Womanlike, she made no direct reply to this question but did not withdraw her hand. He felt it tremble in his own. A strange elemental feeling came over him, and he drew still nearer to her and she to him. The force that rules the universe was attracting the one to the other with an impulse irresistible and uncontrollable. Then her fingers closed impulsively around his, and she looked up into his eyes, saying, "O Aaron, dear Aaron, it would fill my heart with delight."

"Do you love me?" he said to her in that strong manly, vibrant voice, the voice that had so charmed the soul of Margaret Moncrieffe, Helen Livingston, the lovely Miss Betsy, and scores of other famous belles of "ye goode olde time."

"I do," she replied as tears of joy and triumph welled up in her eyes and she rested her head upon his shoulder.

Burr was now in quite a dilemma. The widow had completely out-generalled him, bringing on the crisis before he was prepared. By no means was he fiercely in love with her, though under certain circumstances, he saw no objections to making her his wife. He also kept thinking of Hamilton and said unto himself thus: "I must do the right thing here. Hamilton and I are brethren of the blood. I cannot interfere with his suit."

But Mrs. Prevost had also to be reckoned with. She had seen her opportunity and did not intend to let it slip past. She was a widow and knew men. She also knew women and made up her mind to triumph over the two great beauties and heiresses, viz., Miss Helen and Miss Betsy. She was perfectly well aware that both of them were dying for a proposal from the famous young colonel. So, eencouraged by Burr's attentions, she unhesitatingly replied, "My heart is yours, Aaron, for ever and ever. So truly do I love you that I would lay down my life for you, aye, even though we were never wed. O Aaron, Aaron, how I love you. When I first saw you stretched out wounded at the burning farm, I loved you. I have loved you ever since. You are my knight, my beloved, my peerless one."

Burr was now in a most desperate predicament. *What shall I do and say*, he thought. The cold sweat stood on his brow, but in his veins, a tumultuous passion burned (as would be natural enough in any man under such circumstances.) Then, unable any longer to stand the strain, he gave way and, clipping his arm unresistingly around her soft, splendid, pulsating form, said, "Madam, I am overjoyed that you should think so highly of me, a Rebel against your king. You have paid to me the highest compliment that woman can pay to man. I would be less than a man not to reciprocate."

"You being a Rebel is nothing to me," she replied. "My love for you oversteps all things. And it is noble sometimes to be a bold, young lion of revolt. I would give up all the kings and queens of Heaven or Earth to go with the man I loved. I would, I would, I would!" And she nestled still closer.

"But I have no private fortune," said Burr, "and cannot wed until I have at least made one or become a general or till the end of the war."

"O," she answered, and her breast rose and fell most tantalizingly. "You can have my fortune. It is not much, but it will keep us both as long as I live. It is an annuity. O Aaron, the end of the war may be afar off, and you may be killed therein. Then I should die: my heart would break, longing for him who could never return. Let us live and love while we may, Aaron. Tomor-

                                              RIVAL CÆSARS

row may be dark and cold and stormy. When the shadows fall upon our powers, then where are we? Let us enjoy life while we are in possession of it."

Now, Aaron Burr did not wish to marry just then, so he said to her deprecatingly, "Nevertheless, I am a soldier, and as long as my country requires me, I must fight her battles. I have resolved to win both wealth and position before I wed. I love you dearly, Theodosia (this was not untrue), but I must return to my command, for some great move is in preparation. I will come back, however, and marry you. Will you wait for me awhile? I truly love you, Theodosia, and will wed you. I pledge you my word as a soldier and a gentleman."

Then she answered hysterically and said unto him (and she looked rapturous and ravishing in her white ball-room gown, with the jewels of her last husband flashing on her soft, bare arms and in her glossy silken hair), "I feel, my beloved, that you are as wise as you are brave and courteous, and so much do I love you that, even though it pains my heart to part again, I agree to everything you say. But you are already famous. How nobly you fought at Quebec, Rhode Island and Hackensack."

Whereupon he drew her gently to him and kissed her on the lips again and again. She now felt herself in a seventh heaven and so did he. To each other, they were, all in all, the center of the world, at least for the time being. From one to the other streamed the great creative impulse. The shadow of the eternal rested upon them there in the laurel grove, while, outside, the world rolled on in its grim old tragic way.

Alexander Hamilton and the blood compact were forgotten.

"When the time is ripe, I will marry you my beloved," he whispered in her ear. "Even though my fortune remains unmade. Meanwhile, I am still ambitious, and the place of ambition is not in the bowers of ease and security but in the forespent line of action. I will not betray my dreams of greatness. I will still go forward and be strong. Destiny calls me to "boot and saddle" not for nothing. It is now, not next year, nor the year after and after, that is the time to do things. Now is the day of judgment for me, my Theodosia, and you know I want to be a general."

Then she wound her arms about him and kissed him over and over, and, with tears of burning passion running down her full, soft cheeks, she said, "May God protect you, my Aaron, where the angry bullets fly. May He lead you in safety and send you back unhurt and as bonnie as ever. Go Aaron, go. I will never selfishly prevent the man of my choice from realizing his ambitions. For I also am ambitious. I would that be whom I love should be mighty and great, not weak and mean. How grand and beautiful it is to be the wife of one who is noble and strong and held in high honor?

"Go, my Aaron, go! Night and day my prayers shall be with you where the rifles rattle, where the bugles blow, where the red angels of death hover near."

Then, enraptured with love, they parted. Stooping down for the last time, he lifted her head between his two hands, kissing her passionately and bidding her goodbye. (And the jewels of her last husband sparkled like stars.)

"Goodbye, my love, goodbye." She cried as if her heart would break in the wild welter of triumph and love and sorrow that strove and raged within her.

He went out under the shade of a giant spruce tree where an orderly held his horse, a tall roan with pricked ears. (The chestnut he rode around the battlements of New York with Margaret Moncrieffe had long been killed in action, with "little Burr" on his back. A shell fragment went plunging through his ribs near Ramapo Pass.)

Mounting the big roan, he rode off at a slow walk, his head whirling with illimitable thoughts of love, war, and ambition. Gradually, the music from the ballroom windows died away behind him. On he went and on through the darkness. And as he rode, he soliloquized thus (To soliloquize is a habit common to all men who ride and think much.):

"She is a superb creature and will make me an excellent wife. I think no less of her because she made the first advances to me. It aids a man for a woman to show her preference. As for Hamilton, I still leave him an opening. If he can, he is welcome to win her while I am away. He has every opportunity, and I really don't care much if he does win her. I do not love her in any overpowering way. Never have I stood in Hamilton's light, nor do I intend to do so now; yet a secret something tells me that he hates me deep down in his heart, chiefly because of this woman, whom I couldn't escape if I had tried to. The more I know of Hamilton, the more I see he has a very ungenerous and jealous disposition. He positively hates to see excellence in any one but himself. I have a strong suspicion against him of late. He has Washington's ear, yet I do not obtain promotion. I must watch Hamilton. Nevertheless, I will keep my oath to him in all things. He knew the widow first and is therefore entitled to every consideration. She is bent on marrying me, however, but I have made up my mind not to wed until she has unmistakably rejected Hamilton. How I wish she was Margaret. Then it would be all so different. I wouldn't give Margaret up for any man. If a thousand oaths stood in the way, and I had power, she should be mine. What an infernal fool I was to let her leave New York. Ah, there I made a mistake. But, was it 'mistake' or was it destiny?"

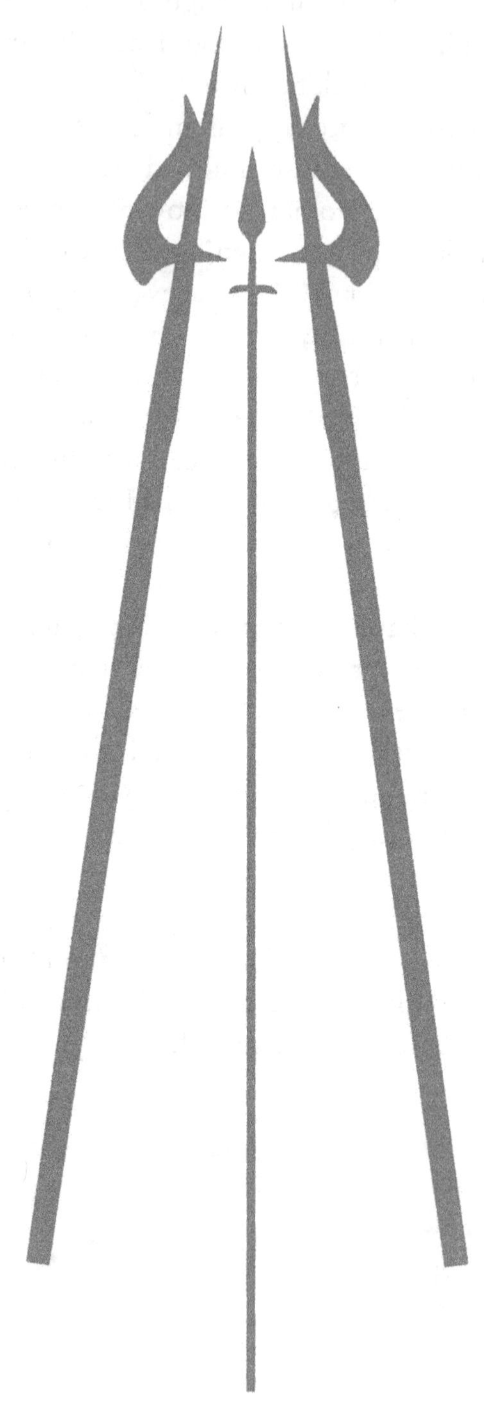

Chapter XIII

THE BATTLE IN THE DARK

"Sigmund turned him back and fro;
At every turn a man he slew."[1]

"O, Mrs. Prevost, I have found you at last. I have been searching for you everywhere and could not find you. I thought you were lost or gone home."

The speaker was a young and distinguished-looking officer in the bright-green-and-gold artillery uniform of the Continental Army.

It was Alexander Hamilton.

Now, the widow Prevost (after Aaron Burr left her) remained in deep thought for some considerable time. After a while, the moon arose over the tree tops, flooding the place where she sat with a mellow white light. It was the rising of the moon that discovered her to Hamilton. As he approached, she was pensively leaning with her head between her hands and murmuring to herself, "O God, how I love my Aaron."

When Hamilton spoke, however, she raised her eyes without evidence of surprise and answered smiling courteously, at the same time comparing him unfavorably in her mind to Burr.

"Indeed, Mr. Hamilton," she said, "what is the matter, pray? I have been here for over an hour. The night air is so balmy and enchanting that the time slipped by on wings. It is delightful to be here amid the green laurels and yet within sound of the music."

"I agree with you as to the beauty of the night and its entrancing charm, and with your permission, madam," said Colo-

---

1   *The Tale of Thrond of Gate: Commonly Called Faereyinga Saga* (Frederick York Powell, translator) (D. Nutt, 1896).

nel Hamilton gallantly, "I will seat myself by your side and also enjoy, for a brief period, the cooling air and the sweet strains of the music, the music that as you know has an occult effect in soothing heated minds. It is none too often I have the monopoly of your company. I would also ask your advice upon a matter of great moment to me."

"O, I shall only be too happy to be of any service to you, Mr. Hamilton. Now, tell me your trouble, Colonel, and I will be your father confessor."

Mrs. Prevost instinctively knew what was coming, and in order also to know exactly how to treat Hamilton, she had brought the somewhat dilatory Burr to the point beforehand. So she now spoke to Hamilton in a most coquettish and encouraging way, much to Hamilton's surprise, for on other occasions, she had not been so gracious. He was all aflame with passion and hope as he again spoke.

"My mind is stirred with many things, my dear madam, but that which absolutely wrecks my happiness and makes my days a continual misery is this: I love a good and noble woman, and I know not if she loveth me in return. What, then, shall I do. What would you advise me to do, Mrs. Prevost?"

"It is a very odd predicament for a gentleman to be in, Mr. Hamilton," she answered, still smiling in her most alluring way. "Your trouble is commonplace, and I think you exaggerate its importance. Why not go straight to the 'fake damozel' and tell her of your ardent love and then hear what your inamorata says. If she is a good and true woman, she will treat you with all due respect and take your avowal as the greatest honor that a man can pay a woman. I am sure Colonel Hamilton's love is not very likely to be scorned by any sensible woman."

"Yes, I've been considering that for some time," said Hamilton, "but am afraid she might possibly humiliate me by refusing and then talking of it afterwards to my ridicule, for she is very attractive, very witty, and has many worthy and high-placed admirers."

"Nevertheless," answered the astute widow, "I still advise you to be straightforward and chance results. Be bold and to the point, Mr. Hamilton. Faint heart, you know, never won an empire or a fair lady. Faint heart wins nothing. You are a soldier and ought to be courageous. Courage in the heart covers a multitude of sins. I've heard General Washington affirm that he once saw you at Harlem Heights, or Monmouth (I forget which) ride up to the cannon's mouth. Indeed, every one says you are a very brave man in battle, and women like the men they love to be brave in war and in love, reckless of all consequences. All women despise men who are too cautious. Boldness, I tell you, is the high road to a woman's heart, but not over-boldness. It is the same in love as in war, Colonel. Want of courage is the great inefficiency. A man without the manly qualities is never acceptable to even the tamest-spirited woman. A timid man is utterly abhorrent to them. A woman likes to be besieged, beleaguered, and stormed like a fortified city set on a hill."

"But when I have plucked up resolution on previous occasions," said Hamilton, "it all evaporated when I drew near her. She is so cold. As soon as I approach her side, my being is filled with an unaccountable dread, as if I were walking over an open grave. Something tells me she intends to reject me, and if she does, I see my fate. My life is henceforth an arid waste."

"You alarm me, Mr. Hamilton," replied the winsome widow. "I never believed you took women so very seriously. I always thought you were a student of Lord Chesterfield. Nevertheless, I do understand you. Perhaps you have some presentiment of evil as a result of your love. Perhaps you have a rival who would kill you for jealousy. Nevertheless, take heart and be bold. What is to be will be. If the open grave is there, you can't escape it. You can't evade destiny. Don't be intimidated by a foreboding of future trouble. Be bold, I say, be bold. This is my advice to every man in love. The universe bends in homage before him who loves and wars and is strong. You are already a successful soldier, and success in the field of Mars presages success in the groves of Cupid."

"But in this matter," said Hamilton. "I feel a nameless, instinctive cowardice, a mysterious, involuntary timidity, and when I talk to her, she speaks to me in such a business tone, so icily, so philosophically, and I see not the lovelight in her eyes. I fancy she may love another man. I fancy that I must have a rival in her affections."

"Be not discouraged at that, Colonel. A woman in love often disguises her love effectively. She waits in ambush, as it were, to try her lover's spirit and ardor, or she pretends admiration for another in order to arouse his jealousy and stir his pride and thus hasten a declaration. She appears outwardly cold as ice, but deep down in her bosom mayhap a volcano bolls. Perhaps she loves you all the time. Be bold, Colonel Hamilton; take my advice and fear not," said Mrs. Prevost, laughing pleasantly, all the time calculating in her mind what words she would use to reject him without offending him.

Encouraged by her demeanor and luring, laughing manner, Hamilton replied, "I will take your advice, madame. I will do as you say." Laying his hand gently on her shoulder, he spake impressively and with evident passion: "Thou art the woman, Theodosia."

"O, Mr. Hamilton," she replied demurely, pretending to be very much surprised. "This is so bewildering, so unforeseen," she continued, striking his hand coquettishly with her fan.

"But it is true," he said ardently, drawing closer to her while she moved away a little from him. "It is God's truth. I love you, dearest Theodosia. I love you with all my being. I have loved you ever since you first landed in New York and brought me those letters from my darling mother in Nevis. My happiness is absolutely in your keeping. Day and night, I think of nothing but you. I love you passionately, devotedly, beyond any other woman I have ever known. My soul and body are yours to do with as you like."

Now, Mrs. Prevost had not been married for twelve years without thoroughly understanding the male sex and all their ways. She was a well-informed woman (also the mother of two sons), and the affairs of the heart were to her as an open volume, one she had read and re-read from end to end. For years, she had known that Hamilton loved her.

On several occasions, she had serious thoughts of giving him active encouragement and of ultimately accepting him. She admired him somewhat and thought he would make a good husband in certain eventualities.

But Burr, Aaron Burr, the idol of women, with his Satanic black eyes and cavalier style, had come upon the scene, with disastrous results to the wily widow's heart, to Hamilton's passion, and perhaps to his own entire career.

Burr's fascinating glance, mysterious Odic force,[1] enchanting grace of person and voice, and cultivated intellect carried the widow by storm. She was dazzled, fascinated, lifted off her feet, as it were.

The shrewd, calculating, but kind-hearted Mrs. Prevost became Burr's hopeless captive. And she had fully resolved (as we have already seen) to marry him.

As before related, Madame Prevost could not be called beautiful, and yet her face, though homely, possessed a nameless, indescribable charm. She had rosy-red lips, a dazzling pink and white complexion, glorious shoulders, superbly moulded arms, a large but gently swelling bosom, the nobly curved hips of a Venus Medici, and a pose like unto that of a born queen. If

---

1   The "Odic force" is the name, given by Baron Carl von Reichenbach (1788–1869), to a vital life force that permeates all things. The Odic force is used to explain hypnotism.

ever the saying "female form divine" could be truthfully applied to any woman's figure, it could be applied to hers. It is not to be wondered at, therefore, that men of the stamp of Burr and Hamilton were held in her thrall.

Now, she felt sorry for Hamilton. She saw he spoke honestly, and no feminine is ever deeply offended at the man who dares to love sincerely and energetically. With the instinctive sagacity of a true woman of the world, she therefore thought, He is the bosom friend of my beloved Aaron, and he is also a power in the councils of General Washington. I must reject him, therefore, very diplomatically, or else he may become, through me, an enemy to my betrothed."

Whereupon she replied, "You astonish me, Mr. Hamilton. You take away my breath. You in love with me, a plain old widow with two children, neither rich nor good-looking nor young." She pointed to the livid scar that marred the beauty of her cliff-like brow.

"Nevertheless, I love you with all my heart and soul," replied Hamilton, endeavoring to draw still closer to her. "I am your slave." And he placed his hand on top of hers and drew nearer.

"However," answered she somewhat icily, "if I do not love you, what then?"

"O, pray do not say that," spoke Hamilton tremulously. "But even so, I will marry you just the same if you but say the word. Surely you can see that my love for you is beyond all question: it shakes my very being. My prospects are also, in every sense, bright. My future is assured. The Commander-in-Chief is my personal friend. I want a wife, and you are the woman I have chosen. Will you marry me, Theodosia, and make me happy forever?"

The widow looked down, tried to blush, and half-succeeded. Then, with emphasis, she replied, "Mr. Hamilton, I cannot love you as you deserve to be loved, and I therefore can never marry you, but I respect you as a gentleman and a friend."

"You love another man," answered Hamilton inquiringly, and his brow clouded while the gleam of jealousy (natural to him) fairly shot from his eyes.

"To be frank with you, Mr. Hamilton, I do. It is my dearest hope to be the wife of another man. Your love for me, therefore, must go no farther, but you are still, I hope, my kind friend, as well as the son of my dearest cousin in the Isle of Nevis. O Mr. Hamilton, let us continue our friendship, but let us no longer talk of love." Gently, she removed his hand from her own.

Hamilton's brow contracted savagely, and he replied with half-suppressed but very evident bitterness. "I had suspected this, madame. Colonel Burr has taken you from me. I know his deft handiwork. Something tells me it is he who has crossed me. He thwarts me at every turn. You have never been the same to me since you met him."

"Colonel Burr," she replied smoothly, "is a man whom I love and honor. He is my dear friend also, and you must not be offended at him. It is my wish to be his wife. Don't look so terribly at me, Colonel Hamilton, don't, pray don't. Let not my confession prey upon your mind in that way. Are there not numbers of splendid young women in Albany, only waiting to be wooed and won? All of them want husbands. Now, come, let me introduce you to the lovely Leah Roosevelt, daughter of the wealthy banker, and also to the latest arrivals, those two vivacious Oglethorpe girls from Georgia. Then there is my own sister Miss De Visme, the four rich Livingston girls, Miss Van Wyck, Miss Naomi Hann, and, also, the delightful and famous Betsy Schuyler. Now, Mr. Hamilton, after all, is not dear Miss Betsy your ideal?"

Here the widow looked archly at him and continued. "Now Mr. Hamilton, don't be so dreadfully gloomy. Is there not as good fish in the sea as ever came out. Come, let us go inside, or they'll wonder where I've gone to. I have four dances promised, one to General Washington and one to Marquis De Lafayette, and I am sure you must also want to have another dance with the dear Betsy?"

And so they arose and walked away, side by side, through the avenue of lamp-lit trees, up a flight of oaken steps, into the vestibule of the old time ballroom. Here a string band played dance tunes and patriotic music, and more than 50 couples, representing the wealthiest Revolutionary families, promenaded the flag-festooned hall.

On the walls hung shot-torn banners stained with the blood of men, and at the inner end of the hall were two small guns whose trunnions had been smashed off in battle.

The men were in bright uniforms with light dress swords and wore silver buckles brightly sparkling on their shoes. In the hair and around the necks of the well-dressed women costly jewels shone. All was going as pleasantly as the proverbial marriage bell. Men and women were busy making love to each other (or planning war) even as in "the beginning."

As Mrs. Prevost entered the ball room with Hamilton she said unto him jocosely,"You think I don't know, Mr. Hamilton, of your proposal for the hand of Betsy Schuyler, but I do." This was her parting shot; he did not reply, for others were listening.

Then Hamilton relinquished the diplomatic young widow and straightway returned to the seat in the shrubbery. Sitting down, he rested his head on his hands and went into deep and sullen thought. He was bitterly vexed with himself and all the world, for this was his first serious reverse.

After a while, he started up suddenly and walked away in the moonlight, saying unto himself between his clenched teeth, "Curse him, the crafty traitor. He is the ruin of all my plains. His apparent honesty and sweetness of disposition is only an ambush. He is my evil shadow. All I take in hand prospers until he appears on the scene. Then everything goes wrong, He alienated the heart of Betsy, whom I must marry, and he is going to wed the very woman I really love.

"Then again, his martial reputation exceeds mine. He is widely advertised as a capable and daring regimental officer. Curse him! I'll have to shoot him yet. Shoot him! No, that won't do either. Have we not sworn eternal friendship? Ah, there, again, he entrapped me. He disarmed me with that oath of brotherhood. But my turn will come yet. I must lay myself out, from this day onward, to take revenge. He never was my friend. He and I are foes, born foes. I am mad to believe in the possibility of human integrity anyhow. Every man I meet is capable of treachery and falsehood.

"I've already put my knife into him, though. That last confidential report to Washington will end his military advancement, that is if Washington remains at the head of the army, which seems certain.

"It shall never be said that Alexander Hamilton was humiliated and surpassed by the son of a Puritan pedagogue from the wooly wilds of Connecticut. Damn him!"

Meanwhile, Burr had been riding steadily towards his destination, a military camp where his command lay. As he passed a clump of trees by the roadside, he fancied he detected something move therein.

Spies, thought he, for the whole country had been denuded of inhabitants. Every man found therein, therefore, was most probably a foe.

Quick as a flash, he turned his horse driving in his left spur and almost dragging the plunging animal around by the left rein while reaching into the right holster for one of his heavy horse pistols.

CRACK!

A pistol shot from among the trees. The bullet whistled

spitefully past Burr's left ear.

CRACK!

Another shot. Again, the bullet missed him but embedded itself with a thud in the pummel of his military saddle.

"Damned narrow shaves," thought he coolly. Then grasping his sword in his left hand with the reins (and gripping a pistol in his right hand), he dashed into the underbrush from whence the shots came. *The best way to meet sudden danger*, be thought, *is to go straight at it.*

A tall man seated on a heavily set bay horse leaped out of the foliage, a smoking weapon in each hand.

Burr fired point blank. The stranger's horse rocked in the midst of its stride, fell over convulsively, and died. The bullet had entered the animal's brain, and the blood spurted out of its nostrils like water gushing from the nozzle of a fire engine.

The rider disengaged himself smartly from the stirrups as the horse tumbled. He was an active man and full of grit. Then he jumped to his feet, and, sword at point, waited Burr's attack in the semi-darkness.

Burr now drove both his spurs into the raw roan. The roan shied at the quivering body of the dying horse but leaped forward gallantly. As he did so, Burr lifted his saber and made a shearing cut at his antagonist but missed.

Before Burr could wheel his horse again, the stranger's sword penetrated the animal's intestines. Blood and water gushed forth. The roan, maddened with pain, gave a mighty bound to the right. Burr's body struck against the overhead limb of a dead tree. It swept him off the saddle. He fell backward upon the ground, half-stunned. Only for a second, however; swiftly, he scrambled to his feet and rushed upon the stranger.

Neither man spoke a word. They were now fighting for their lives. Their teeth closed savagely. Their eyes flashed. The world spirit was raging within them. (The best man was to be selected).

They lunged at each other, they smote at each other, they involuntarily hissed at each other between clenched teeth, but they did not speak. There was no time to speak. (Talk is superfluous when blades are drawn). Each believed the other a mortal foe.

The stranger stood his ground manfully. He did not give way an inch. Decidedly, he was a man of valor.

Burr now fought more guardedly, feeling he had this time met his match. He received a wound on the hand. It nearly severed a forefinger. The stranger was deeply gashed over the left eye. Blood streamed down half blinding him.

Overhead, the trees swayed in the rising wind. A storm gathered. The heavens became black and threatening. The darkness grew denser. The half-moon shone out fitfully from behind the rushing clouds. The owls whooped. The bitterns boomed in the sedges by the swamp along the river.

Still, the two men fought on, both standing in a pool of blood: blood from the two dead horses mingled on the soil with their own. Their swords were red. Steel clashed against steel and sparks flashed out. Ten minutes passed. A quarter of an hour. Both were plainly becoming exhausted.

I must kill him, thought Burr, *or he will kill me.*

I must kill him, thought the stranger, *or be killed.*

The two swords writhed and twisted and clashed. Burr made a false twist of his wrist. In a second, the stranger felt his chance. His sword penetrated between Burr's left arm and body. The hilt thumped viciously against the future vice president's ribs with a resounding thump. Burr staggered. The blow nearly knocked him down. The breath of the stranger blew hot in his face.

Ha, now I've got him! thought Burr, recovering himself, and, as a sheet of lightning flamed across the sky, he made a rapid backward twirl with the sharp, crimsoned blade that literally slashed the stranger's throat from ear to ear.

The body of the vanquished man sank limply backwards across a log, and his blood gushed and hissed, in two curved streams, from the severed veins of the neck.

Burr stood still and rested, panting for breath. Then he slowly wiped his weapon on a moss-grown stump and looked at it intently—oh, how intently!—while the perspiration of combat dripped from his bare brow and wet hair.

The joy of absolute and unlimited victory, the grandest and most godlike of all joys, swelled up fiercely within him. Lifting the now clean, shiny blade to his lips (his eyes with triumph red), he kissed the naked steel softly, saying, as a clap of thunder burst directly overhead, "Good blade! Mighty overcomer! Trusty friend! I salute thee! Verily, thou art my saviour, my deliverer, my iron redeemer! Glorious steel, ruler of earth and ocean, thou wast never a backbiter yet! In the hour of need thou didst not desert me!"

He reached for his scabbard, inserted the point of the sword carefully, sent the blade home with a smart click, and lovingly patted the hilt.

Thereupon, he coolly and methodically bound up his own wounded hand with some linen taken from the saddlebags of the dead stranger.

Then leaning over the upturned body of the vanquished one, with its open staring eyes, red gaping throat, and distended jaws, he gazed down closely at the features.

Great Cæsar, thought he to himself, *as sure as I'm alive and he is dead, it's the same naval officer who, in '75, pinked Hamilton in the arm at Weehawken. There must be something in this. He is a blood relation of the De Lanceys. Before 1775, he was in the king's secret service. I must search him and search him thoroughly. This may be an event for you, Aaron Burr.*

Then Burr turned the body over, systematically searched it, and found sufficient evidence to show that his dead antagonist was a spy, disguised in the Continental uniform.

Pulling off the saddle from his foeman's dead horse, he rapidly ripped open the lining, removed the hair stuffing, and found just what he instinctively expected to find: a packet of letters written in cipher on very thin paper. Among the letters were a series of confidential dispatches addressed to General Washington, General Knox, General Arnold, and General Lee.

By this time, daylight began to break. Burr tore open the enclosure, sat down on the rump of one of the dead horses, his feet in a pool of blood, and began to read. There were four packets of letters, one within the other, along with a partial key to the British cipher.

(Now, it seemed that an American dispatch rider had been captured by a British patrol sometime before and his papers taken. Thus, British and American secret dispatches were both found in the same package.)

One of the documents was signed by a certain "Major Andre" and one by the fashionable wife of General Arnold. There were also a number of other documents, the reading of which opened Burr's eyes to many things—and made him doubt the integrity of officers and congressmen of the highest repute.

One cipher document was a private and confidential letter from Colonel Alexander Hamilton, addressed to General George Washington at Philadelphia. Thus it ran:

> You ask me confidentially what I think of Colonel Aaron Burr, with regard to a higher military appointment. In reply, I desire to state that I believe him to be an unworthy, sinister, and dangerous man. That he is an able and brave soldier I do not deny, but his views are those of a Roman Cæsar or, rather, of an impecunious Catiline. He has an ill opinion of Republican principles and forms and laughs sardonically at the philosophy of Jefferson and Franklin. His ideals are, indeed, those of a

Stafford or Bolingbroke.

If vested with high military command, he is therefore very likely to use it (upon occasion) for purposes that you can better imagine than I can prophetically describe. He is also, I understand, constantly visiting, surreptitiously, the home of a certain widow at Paramus, within the British lines. He rides there. I am told, from his own camp at midnight, crossing the Hudson, with his horse fastened in the boat. Then he rides rapidly to her home and returns to camp before morning.

She is or was the wife of the English officer and baronet who defended Savannah. By our intelligence department, she is suspected of being a secret agent or "go-between." Burr's loyalty to the revolution is therefore seriously in doubt. I myself have reason to suspect it, but can prove nothing. I therefore advise strongly against the further advancement of this very suave and ambitious man.

Alexander Hamilton

P. S.—Written in Cypher No. 4 D.

"Et tu, Brute? I thought so," said Burr to himself. "I half-suspected it. My intuition was right: there is no integrity in men. Hamilton is my foe secretly, while openly professing friendship. Now I understand why Congress refused to give me the generalship after I saved Knox's brigade. I must circumspectly continue to watch this West Indian Machiavelli who writes like a Jesuit and thinks like an Iscariot. Someday, I will ram this infernal libel down his accursed throat. Yes! Some day I must shoot that man. I must by God! I must! But not yet, not yet. Don't be in a hurry, Aaron Burr. Select your own time to smite. Don't be in haste. Less haste, more speed."

Then Colonel Burr refolded the letter and put it carefully away in his pocket with the others. Two of these others were secret cipher dispatches of a nature that we dare not even mention. One concerned negotiations between Chief Justice De Lancey, Judge Livingston, General Burgoyne, John Laurens, and the firm of Roderique Hortalez & Co., of Paris.

Now Burr, as one-time staff officer and secretary to Washington, to Putnam, and to Arnold, and also as initial organizer of the Iron Cross, knew and had himself devised many of the secret ciphers used at headquarters.

"I must shoot him for this," again said Burr, emphatically half-aloud, as he drew a long breath and strode away through the long, wet grass. "By God, I must. This letter is Hamilton's death warrant. Now I understand him, the crafty, double-faced underminer. His words are smoother than butter, but war is in his heart. Now, indeed, it is 'Mortuum Bellum,' and woe to the vanquished."

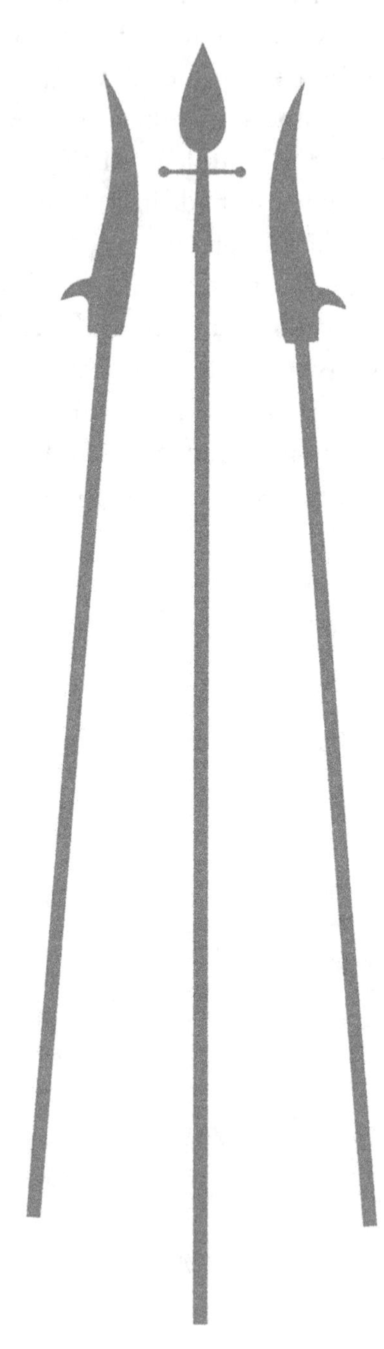

Chapter XIV

MR. WARWICK HAMILTON

"Up the rocky mountain.
Down the wooded glen:
The man whose thought is iron,
Is worth 10,000 men."[1]

And the days and the years rolled on, and other things befel, enough for a dozen romances.

February 1801. The mercury stood at zero. The sullen darkness of the wintry evening was falling over the great, growing city. From out the strong and wrathful north, the cold, piercing blast howled down. It winnowed the leaves and stripped the branches bare. Frost and snow lay everywhere. It covered the housetops and hung on the trees. Even the pumps were frozen. The streets were iron hard, as were the streams and gutters.

The wind moaned and whined and blustered around the dreary buildings or whistled shriekingly between the tall, ghostly, leafless trees by the roadways.

The city seemed almost deserted. The homes and shops were closed. It was a Sunday afternoon. Nothing could be heard but the north wind (the wind that makes conquerors) soughing its sullen growl, like the growl of a wild beast. Savagely, it shrieked and roared and rose and fell, even as the notes of some daemoniac Aeolian trumpet.

BOOM!

---

1   William Allingham's (1824–1889) poem "The Fairies" begins in a similar way: "Up the airy mountain,/Down the rushy glen..." In a 1910 essay by Eugene W. Debs, he used the phrase "But others, whom defeat inspires with fresh courage, whose bugle-blast is worth 10,000 men, born leaders, inspire new hopes by setting forth the fact, though one organization was defeated, if all the organizations having interests at stake had federated for the fight, victory would have flashed along the lines of the workingmen and perched upon their banners."

A clock from the Church of the Holy Redeemer sounded forth the hour. Away, through the hard, cold air, the clang rolled for miles.

BOOM!

Once, twice, three times it sounded. Four times.

BOOM!   BOOM!

Driven from opposite directions, two coaches met as if by prearrangement. They stopped under the shelter of a half-finished building, over the main entrance of which had been newly chiseled the motto "*Ab uno disce omnes.*" The scaffolding stood around the unfinished wails like the basket work of giants.

Two men wrapped in furry great coats reaching down to their heels, and high collars raised up around their ears, stepped out of the carriages and at Paramus, within the British lines.

Their footsteps sounded weirdly, crackling on the frozen snow drift. Of these two men, one was over six foot tall but loosely built, the other stout and of medium height.

Judging by their dress, they appeared mere ordinary citizens, but their general tone and style betokened men accustomed to command, men of the ruling classes, propertied men, men of assured position.

The tall man was Thomas Jefferson, a Virginian political philosopher and tobacco planter, who was then the Republican—that is to say, the radical—candidate for the presidential chair.

Mr. Jefferson was generally recognized as the literary inspiration of his party and its most highly respected political chief.

Like nearly all the leading men of his time, be was comparatively wealthy, owning a large estate and 150 negro slaves.

The other man was General Alexander Hamilton (Director of the Bank of New York), political chief of the federal, or conservative, element in the nascent nation.

He had been Washington's favorite secretary of state and

minister of finance and met with considerable success in establishing the Interstate Constitution and the public credit.

Without doubt, he was the brains of his party. As an orator, writer, constitutional lawyer, thinker, and organizer along his own particular lines, he was without a peer or an equal in his own party.

So true is this that after his death, the party he formed and led went absolutely to pieces.

"Hamilton," once said the irascible but honest John Adams, "was practically commander-in-chief of the House of Representatives of the Senate, of the heads of departments, and—last of all, if you will—of myself, the president of the United States (1796 to 1800.)

The original Federal Party was a one-man power, and that one man was Alexander Hamilton.

Now, Hamilton and Jefferson were strongly opposed to each other, not only as politicians but also as philosophers and by temperament.

They represented two great rival schools of thought, two schools that have existed and contended from the beginning of time and must exist and contend to the end of time.

As the rich and poor are with us forever, so are their respective mouthpieces and philosophies.

Hamilton represented the aristocratic element in the young republic, the Cincinnati and the old landed gentry; Jefferson, the democratic, or republican, element. Hamilton believed that the masses of men must be ruled over absolutely for their own good (and in this he was somewhat logical). Jefferson believed that they should rule themselves by electing representatives on a majority basis, and in this he was very enthusiastic. Jefferson's chief propositions were based upon the affirmation that three men have a "natural right" to rule and reign over two men, or over one man. Hamilton's fundamental thought was that the best men (always few and troublesome to select) should make law for the worst and weakest.

Jefferson was ceaselessly denouncing Hamilton as an advance agent of despotic government in "this new world," and Hamilton forever pointed to Jefferson as demagogue, a menace to security, a disturber of the public tranquility, a Robespierre type of wild revolutionist, and therefore an enemy of the best people, who wished to live peacefully and prosper within the country.

Upon this bitter winter afternoon, these two rival politicians met, the appointment having been carefully and privately arranged. The preliminaries had been as carefully thought out, as if the two great leaders had been kings or opposing generals arranging for a truce between their armed and bannered hosts. Jefferson was, at this period, about 60 years of age and Hamilton 45.

"It is a fearful night," remarked Jefferson. "I cannot stand this frightful Northern climate in winter time. The frost and cold winds pierce into my marrow bones. I must get back into Old Virginia. 'God's Country' is good enough for me. I wouldn't live here for every acre of land in the whole state.

"Besides, I am not, as you know, supposed to be here. I had great difficulties to contend with in arranging so that this interview should be kept in every way sub rosa."

"We might have met at an inn," remarked Hamilton in reply. "Only, I thought it more judicious to discuss this matter where we could be neither seen nor heard. I am sorry, however, the afternoon has turned out to be so bleak and cold. I myself was born in the genial climate of the Carribean Sea and feel these New England winters very severely. However, as we are here, we might as well proceed with the business in hand. The sooner we get through, the sooner we get home."

"I have come according to your invitation sent to me

through General Smith. I meet you in all good faith and am now prepared," said the Sage of Monticello, "to hear what your 'weighty proposition' may be. Meanwhile, Mr. Hamilton, please remember, that I—as a Southern gentleman and candidate for the presidency—cannot consider any 'proposition' whatsoever that has the slightest tinge of 'doubtful or unfair' methods. Nor can I consider anything that conflicts with my basic principles."

"As to that, my dear Mr. Jefferson," replied Hamilton, "you need not be the least alarmed. I am a soldier and a gentleman, and, rest assured, nothing in any way subversive of the highest honor and fair play between man and man shall proceed from me. My position and reputation must in no way be jeopardised. I pledge you my word of honor that I have now no suggestion to offer you that is not strictly fair and above board. Indeed, there is no other way to settle the matter, and necessity is above all law. Yet my proposition is not by any means of a nature that either you or I would like to hear shrieked from the housetops or shouted by the town crier. There are many things, Mr. Jefferson, that are perfectly proper and legitimate yet nevertheless would be injudicious, very injudicious, to publicly proclaim."

Here a rustling noise was heard overhead, and a heavy piece of plaster fell with a crash at their feet. Both men looked up at the scaffolding overhead but mutually concluded that the plaster fell by accident or was blown down by a gust of wind. However, this was not so.

Upon the scaffolding, wrapped in a great fur cloak, lay a man, stretched out, listening intently to every word. It was John Swartwout. He had arrived about ten minutes before and taken this method of concealing himself. Both Hamilton and Jefferson had been for many years closely watched by the agents of Burr. Thus, the conference became known to Burr. Hence many things.

"Very well, Mr. Hamilton. Proceed," spake Jefferson. "I am

all ears. I wish to get through with it, for the cold is dreadful."

"You wish to be president of the United States, Mr. Jefferson?" inquired Hamilton,

"I do."

"Well, I can decide the election in your favor," said General Hamilton, the chief of the federal caucus, "but I have conditions, Mr. Jefferson."

"Explain, Mr. Hamilton."

"I will do so," said Hamilton, "but, beforehand, I wish to know if you are prepared to pledge me your word of honor never to divulge what I say to any living soul under any circumstances, now or hereafter.

"I pledge you my word of honor to that effect," replied the inventor of the rotary office stool. "What is spoken to me in private shall remain private forever, even though it be to my injury. I am not a man to betray confidences."

"Then I will proceed," replied General Hamilton. "I will make you president on certain conditions, private conditions between you and me, you and me alone."

"Name your conditions, but first explain to me your power to cause my election."

"In the first place then," said Hamilton, "there are sixteen states in the union, that is to say, there are sixteen state votes to be cast for president. Eight of these votes are cast for you and six for Burr. Two are doubtful, for the votes of two states have been absolutely delegated to two individuals, and these two individuals are very friendly disposed towards me and not wholly unfriendly towards Burr. Nevertheless, they may possibly be induced to cast the votes of their respective states, Vermont and Maryland, for you.

"You know what that means. Without gaining over one of those two states, you cannot win the presidency. Now, Mr. Jefferson, I can control them both. Whatever side I desire them to take, they will go to that side. I also possess means of influencing two other states. You are doubtless well aware of all this, as well aware of it as I am.

"Thus, I cast make your votes nine by simply sending the signal to either Bayard of Delaware, or General Morris of Vermont. Or by going the right way to work, I can make Burr's votes, and then it is possible for my friends to win over one of your votes and thus make Burr's nine and elect him president.

"Two of the states that have gone Federal are prepared to vote for Burr at any time I think it judicious. Indeed the Federals are not unfavorable to Burr, because, unlike you, he sees nothing to object to in the consolidation of authority, i.e., in a more binding union.

"At heart, he is also well known to be of aristocratic instincts, whereas you are feared as being a hopeless Leveller, a sort of philosophic Marat, ready to set up a guillotine in Union Square. The fact is, Jefferson, that while I personally am convinced of your sterling honesty and unyielding patriotism, you must be aware that men of property and position are alarmed at your preachments and, therefore, very unwilling that the control of the army and government should pass into the hands of such a Leveller and revolutionist as they believe you to be.[1]

"Except in your own Southern states (and among the non-propertied class), you are regarded as an unsafe man to be entrusted with the reins of power, more especially in view of the wild mob terror recently let loose in France and believed to be indirectly inspired by your own principles and writings. There is little doubt that when La Fayette and his army returned to France, they carried with them the germs of the Reign of Terror.

"These things are undeniable, Mr. Jefferson, and therefore if

---

1 ≠   In 1800, there was a strong reaction against "democratic" principles on account of the recent French revolution. A few years before, Louis the XVI had been guillotined, Mirabeau poisoned, and Danton, Robespierre, Marat, Tinville & co. raged in Paris. Fear of similar events was strong in 1801 on this side of the Atlantic and lent a very bitter feeling to all political conflicts.

you are to be president it is essential that you should at least give some assurance (it may be private and confidential assurance) that you will not carry your principles too far, discountenance dangerous agitations, guard the status quo, protect property, and uphold the national credit."

To this Jefferson replied calmly, though internally much agitated: "I think I perceive what you mean, General Hamilton. I know that within your own party lines, your power is that of a dictator, but I had no conception until now that you could also manipulate the votes of my party."

"I can do it," said Hamilton with emphasis. "I can do it and without doubt."

"What pledge can you give me, General Hamilton, of your ability to perform what you say you can?"

Hamilton thereupon drew forth a packet of legal and other documents from out the inner pocket of his coat. He opened them up in the gathering dusk and handed them one by one to Jefferson, who, as he read, handed them back again. After Jefferson had concluded the reading of all the papers, Hamilton refolded them and carefully put them back in his pocket.

Between the planks of the scaffolding above, the dark, eager face of John Swartwout peered down, listening with absorbing attention to every word of the two great statesmen.

Hamilton, after a pause and scrutinizing glance at Jefferson, again spoke, saying, "You now see, Mr. Jefferson, that I can make my word good. Two of these men are ready to do my bidding willingly, and one, if needed, I can gain over. Then there is that fourth man, whose own casting vote decides the vote of his state. He would not dare to vote against my wish. He is in no position to defy me, and you know it, Mr. Jefferson.

"There are no witnesses here to repeat this conversation, and, therefore, both you and I are safe in speaking frankly to one's another, face to face.

"I am unable to elect Adams or Pinckney, (the nominees of my own party), but I can and will decide whether the presidency of the United States goes to Colonel Aaron Burr or to Thomas Jefferson.

"In the voting within the Electoral College, you and he are 'equal.' Strange, is it not?" said Hamilton smilingly, laying considerable and somewhat ironic stress on the word "equal."

"After twenty-seven ballots, you and he are still absolutely even."

"From your own point of view, Mr. Hamilton, I see no fault to find with your logic. I have other reasons besides your documentary proofs to satisfy and convince me that you say is true. The knowledge of this made me willing to meet you tonight. I acknowledge your arguments and I accept your proofs while deploring the weakness and duplicity of men. But sorrow and anger on my part cannot now alter the actual circumstances. Without doubt, Mr. Hamilton, you are the Warwick of the situation. But what are your conditions? I am curious to hear your demands. Name them."

As Jefferson talked, there was a perceptible tremor in his voice. Though a very tall, rawboned man, his voice was not equal to the expectations aroused by his stature: it was weak and somewhat like that of a woman. On this account, he was an impossible orator, though as a writer of beautiful and sentimental sentences, he excelled.

He continued, saying, "It would mortify me to have it said in after years that I owed my elevation to Major General Hamilton, leader of the opposition, the man whom I have so strongly denounced on every possible occasion.

"Politics is a curious game, Hamilton, a cutthroat game. Like misfortune, it makes men acquainted with strange bedfellows. Truly, it is no business for a gentleman. It would corrupt the principles of a saint."

"Perfectly true, Mr. Jefferson. Politics is not a game for saints. It is a hard business, and those who enter upon it must be hard. We must accept conditions even as we find them, no matter how unpleasant they may be to us personally. We are not as gods that we can purify the world by raging against the heathen with the breath from our mouths. We are not mad enough to believe that we can overturn the methods of nature or change the minds of men in the course of our little lifetime.

"Let us, therefore, do the best we can with the things that are and waste not strength on quixotic efforts to transmute men into angels.

"Even if a man does set himself out to redeem the millions, born and unborn, he must first secure his own position. And by the time he has accomplished that iron task, his enthusiasm for humanity will be somewhat damped down.

"Burr is right when he says, 'democratic institutions must be worked out logically,' and you perceive, Mr. Jefferson, the obvious logic of the present crisis in your fortunes. This is the opportunity of your lifetime. Now you can realize your ambition and give your 'principles' a practical test in an environment of extraordinary favorableness.

"You ask my conditions. They are as follows:

"I desire a written guarantee, to be deposited in the Bank of _______, that during your term of office as president, you will not—if elected by my favoring intervention—remove from office any of our Federal appointees to the number, etc., here scheduled." Hamilton handed a blue document to Jefferson.

"Next, that the English treaties as they now stand shall remain unaltered," he continued, "and that no aid be given by your administration whatsoever to this Corsican Cæsar Napoleon Bonaparte, whom I know you are somewhat inclined to favor.

"Next, that no effort be countenanced that trends in the direction of changing the Constitution or of further weakening the federal union.

"Next, that you will preserve our present financial system intact and uphold the decisions and operation of the Supreme Court.

"Next, that you will uphold the public credit at home and abroad, cease all talk of repudiation, aid in maintaining the efficiency of the Navy, and make every possible effort for the acquisition of New Orleans."

"Such terms would bind me hand and foot," replied Jefferson, evidently much perturbed. "If I acceded to your demands I would be utterly powerless, and in the eyes of my friends and supporters, I would also be disgraced. They would say I am a man of straw, that I do not carry out my election pledges; that I am but a man of words, and that I have no backbone. Indeed, if I agreed to such terms, I would be merely a make-believe president, a sort of impotent grand llama, giving voice and authority to the policy of others. No, Mr. Hamilton, I will not become president by capitulation; I will not be humiliated and made a dummy ruler over a free people."

"You are over-punctilious, Mr. Jefferson," said Hamilton. "There is no king or ruler in any civilized nation who can, strictly speaking, carry out his own will. All are hedged around by conditions and precedents that to overstep would bring ruin upon them. The days of the absolute monarch—who is not a conquering general like Napoleon—are numbered. All American presidents are intended to be conditional rulers. It will be no humiliation for you to be numbered among them.

"Your best friend, indeed, may never know of the proposed compact. Except you inform them, they shall never be informed by me. And as for your last argument, it is merely sentiment. You will have an immense patronage and considerable power even after complying with my not unreasonable requirements. Surely, if I help you, it would only be fair for you to help me.

One good turn deserves another.

"Again, is it not better for you to be president under conditions than not to be president at all. This may be your last chance, Mr. Jefferson."

"I will not accept your conditions, Mr. Hamilton," said the author of the Declaration of Independence.

"Then you cannot be elected, Mr. Jefferson," spake General Hamilton. "I am absolute master of the position. The election is in my hands. I hold, beyond question, the balance of power. I can raise the scale in which you stand, or I can lower it and elevate your rival, whom I know you mortally detest, though he is the ablest of your lieutenants.

"Now, I invited you here, Mr. Jefferson, in order that we might come to some mutual *modus vivendi* that might possibly eliminate Burr forever. You know enough of diplomacy and practical statecraft to be aware that such compacts as I have proposed to you are made in every country on Earth. Wherever the material interests of men clash, there must be war or diplomacy: men must come to blows or make an agreement. You are not able to conquer me, nor am I able to conquer you; therefore, let us come to an understanding and make concessions."

"But if I refuse," replied Jefferson, "what then?"

"Then the armistice is at an end, we must fight it out, and you, being the older man, are more likely to weary of the conflict than I am.

"Should you persist in this refusal, I will straightaway make Burr's votes eight. This will cause a tie. My friends in the Electoral College are obstinate. They will stand by me to the last, each man for his own good reason. You have read what Bayard wrote to me by the last carrier pigeon.

"Now, in the event of a tie that cannot be in any way arranged, then the election is thrown into the House of Representatives, and there again, my friends hold the balance.

"Thus, I can elect Burr as easily as I can elect you. Further, Burr is a mere matter-of-fact man, without previous theories, and cares not a jot for the Constitution or what is written therein. Without doubt, he stands ready to accept any compact I may propose to, him."

"Well then, suppose I agree," replied Jefferson, who now thought to find out more as to the master manipulator's real power.

"If you agree, I shall be truly glad. I have one more condition, however. It is this: If I appoint you to the presidency and make Burr vice president, then Burr is shelved for four years but is not entirely overthrown. At the end of his term, he may again become a formidable foe to me and an entrenched rival to you. He has a strange faculty for bringing things to pass.

"Now, you will be Burr's colleague for four years, and, during that period, I shall expect you to aid me in discrediting him before the public. Like you yourself, I also regard him as a very able, very ambitious, but very dangerous man. He is, by nature, of strong aristocratic instincts, and you know that a bankrupt aristocrat is a very dangerous personality in any state, especially if he is at the same time a good soldier, a good lawyer, and an eloquent politician.

"In a republic, such a man is as much of a menace to the status quo as a crownless king in a monarchy. Around him ever gather all the elements of discontent and rebellion.

"If you and I, therefore—you as leader of one great party and I of the other—conjointly endeavor to destroy his fame and influence, especially in the North, where his strength lies, we must, of course, succeed. No mortal power could prevent us. Public opinion is, for all practical purposes, confined to the ranks of the two great parties, whose policy is controlled almost absolutely by you and me.

"No one man dare stand up against both of us at once. He

would be snuffed out like a candle. Except he had an army at his back, he could not withstand us. Our editors, correspondents, and agents would quickly dispose of him. Burr, I say, must be removed from our path.

"But in addition, Mr. Jefferson, there is a threat involved. If you fail to come to terms, I will, without hesitation, elect Burr upon the same condition.

"Remember that the public has learnt to regard you not as a man of action but rather as a philosopher, who philosophizes in such a way as to please the mob.

"You must thus perceive, my dear Mr. Jefferson, that whether you agree or do not agree, I am prepared for either alternative."

Now, Hamilton had no real intention whatever of electing Burr. He merely used the threat of doing so to terrify Jefferson into a more tractable frame of mind. During the whole of the interview, he was congratulating himself on the success of his manoeuvre, thinking, *I've got him exactly where I want him.*

Jefferson answered:

"Mr. Hamilton, you are clearly the uncrowned king of this situation. I do not deny it. But are you prepared to accept the responsibility of electing Colonel Burr, a man whose highest ambition is to be a Western Bonaparte? He would conquer Louisiana and Mexico and then establish a military monarchy on the ruins of all our theories. Is he not one of those elemental beings who has no reverence for anything but his own will and who would, if the occasion suited, burn my Declaration and your Constitution in the same bonfire?"

"Yes, I've thought of all that and am willing to risk the results. I know Burr. I've known him ever since we were young men in Washington's family. He is perfectly safe if properly handled, but how to handle him is the difficulty. He is a man of pleasure as well as daring, but want of money and increase of years will assuredly act as a brake upon his energies. No man can accomplish much without gold and youth.

"Of course, I condemn him all I can, because in New York, he is my chief foe; nevertheless, his instincts as a politician are with the party I belong to rather than with yours.

"He is a patrician by nature, one of the haughtiest of men, though a spendthrift, and, in his heart, I know he abhors your principles as much as I do. I am sure he thinks you more fit for a pope than a president.

"I assure you Colonel Burr is a Jeffersonian from circumstances rather than convictions. I've often heard him speak ironically of your Declaration as 'a string of of poetic fancies,' 'a superb campaign document,' and so forth.

"You, I know, believe most absolutely in your own philosophy, Mr. Jefferson; for that I admire and respect you, while being constitutionally unable to become your convert. My brain positively refuses to think as yours does, and, therefore, I openly oppose you.

"Burr, on the other hand, believes neither in your theories nor in mine and dares to assert that the chief duty of man is to affirm his own being irrespective of all theories whatsoever. He accepts your politics only as a means to his end. In private, he has always sneered at them as only fit for unhistorical minds and simple souls. He is an astute and shrewd man who believes in 'liberty and straight hair' for the votes that are in it. He has none of the disinterested patriotism that you, I, and the poets so much admire.

"Furthermore, I have already sounded Burr upon this matter through his friend John Swartwout and am satisfied I can make good terms with him."

(*You infernal liar!* thought Swartwout overhead.)

"But could you rely on Burr's pledge?" said Jefferson. "If he first gained fame by annexing French or Spanish territory, he would assuredly snap his fingers at you and do as he liked. With an army behind him, what could you do about it? He is one of those kind of men who would order out a platoon of men before breakfast and have you shot.

"He has often urged upon me a project for the seizure of Texas from Spain. When I protested against the self-evident immorality of seizing other people's territory, he answered me by saying that if our forefathers had thought that way, the United States would never have existed and that 'petty morals are not for men of grand aims.'"

"If it came to that, then I should not hesitate to have him removed by other methods," replied General Hamilton. "Nothing is impossible to a willing mind. Cæsar had his Brutus, Charles the First his Cromwell, and a good cavalier never lacks a lance.

"But I do not think it would come to that. Burr would take care never to overstep the limits of possibility, and there are other means of compelling him to give hostages for good behaviour. But we need not start building a bridge until we reach the river to be crossed. I know also that everything he possesses is under mortgage to Messrs. Angerstein & Co., and '*absque argento omnia vana*,'[1] you know."

"I perfectly comprehend the points you make, Mr. Hamilton," answered the future president, "and appreciate them. Nevertheless, Burr is a man of the Homeric type, a man whose shot you can never make sure of. He is as shifty as Ulysses and his resource is phenomenal. When you think you understand him you know him not. He will smile upon you and smite. He bums with desire to rule. His fingers can play on every keyboard, and, like the wise men of old, he neither forgives nor forgets."

"Nevertheless, I am ready to chance my ability to control him," interjected the Major General.

When Jefferson perceived that Hamilton was inexorable and that it was perfectly feasible for Burr to supplant him, his heart

---

1   "Without money all efforts are useless."

weakened and he became more tractable. His tone of haughty refusal changed, and he said, "Mr. Hamilton, I am well aware of the tremendous hidden meaning, import, and trend of this interview. I see the immense significance of a majority-ruled Commonwealth as I never saw it before. I have had a glimpse of the real, and it has astonished me. I perceive that circumstances are more powerful than institutions and that I, if ever I am to obtain executive power, must bend to those circumstances.

"The conditions you offer, Mr. Hamilton, I cannot however, conscientiously decide off hand. It requires time for consideration. I am really in a predicament, a mortal predicament.

"I do sincerely desire to be president for the good that I know I can do and also because it is my highest ambition. Nevertheless, as chief executive, I would be free—free in the fullest sense, without hampering conditions—not tied down like a prisoner on parole, and yet, and yet, I am growing old."

Hamilton replied, and there was a hard, cold, unsympathetic ring in his voice, saying, "The event is absolutely in your own power. You have only to pledge yourself to do justice to public creditors, maintain and increase the navy, not to disturb those holding high office, and unite with the Federals in a campaign against Burr, and, straightway, the reins of government are placed in your hands."

"I would have time to consider," answered Jefferson, who was not the sort of man to decide things rapidly.

"You can have forty-eight hours, Mr. Jefferson," was the answer. "In that time, surely you can think it over and decide. Meanwhile, the balloting can go on indecisively. Fifteen or twenty ballots have already been taken. I will attend to that, and if I do not hear from you by the end of 48 hours, I shall consider my proposition rejected and immediately proceed with the election of Colonel Burr. Then farewell to all your hopes."

"You can send your reply—'yes' or 'no'—in the cabinet cipher No. 3, L7. It is the same cipher employed by you in official correspondence when ambassador in Paris. We are both well acquainted with it, and it is unquestionably safe."

(*Is it?* thought John Swartwout as he grinned to himself. *Every cipher you know is known to Burr.*)

"Within forty-eight hours, you shall hear my decision," replied Jefferson as he wrapped a big red muffler around his throat and chin.

"It will give me much pleasure to hear from you in the affirmative, Mr. Jefferson. I must frankly confess that I would rather see you in the presidential chair than Burr.

"Burr is one of those aggressive and absolutely self-centered men who make things somewhat unpleasant now and again. He cherishes vast aims, has a subtle imagination, possesses immense energy, and is as true a pagan as ever wore the toga of a senator and strode the Roman Forum."

As Hamilton ceased speaking, the bell in the clock tower of the Church of the Holy Redeemer rang out again: once, twice, three times, four times, five.

It was five o'clock. The conference had lasted an hour. Both men had walked back and forward during the talk in order to keep themselves warm. Overhead, Swartwout was nearly frozen to the planks. He dared not move for fear of discovery. Every now and then, his fingers, buried deep in the pocket of his greatcoat, nervously grasped the butts of a pair of heavy pistols. Being essentially a man of action, he was busily revolving, in his mind, a plan for getting possession of "those infernal papers."

Hamilton and Jefferson looked out. The silent snow had been steadily falling. The wind had gone down somewhat, and the sky became grey and black. It was night.

Both men stepped into the snow. Their coaches waited.

"Good night, Jefferson."

"Good night, Hamilton."

Then, in opposite directions as they had arrived, the two famous history-makers rolled off.

As soon as the carriages had disappeared, John Swartwout climbed slowly down from his perch, shivering and stiff with the cold but hot with indignation.

To the door of the building, he walked and gave a low, peculiar whistle. In a few minutes, a slave youth trotted up out of the darkness, delivered to Swartwout a saddle horse, then trotted away again, as if previously instructed how to act.

Swartwout put his arm through the reins of the horse, rammed his hands deep into his coat pockets, and commenced to walk rapidly after Hamilton's carriage in order to warm himself. As soon as the blood began to circulate, he jumped into the saddle and started off at a swinging canter, the stinging north wind hissing against his face and ears.

Fastened to his saddle was a heavy military rifle. Presently, as he rode on, following the wheel marks in the snow, he heard two pistol shots in rapid succession. Cautiously slowing his pace, he came round a bend in the road noislessly.

General Hamilton was climbing back into his coach, and the dead body of a man lay by the roadside. The carriage drove off again.

Swartwout rode on. He looked down on the body. It was that of a young man with fair white face. There were red spots on the snow.

It is murder perhaps, thought Swartwout as, without alighting, he rode on.

He was stalking General Hamilton. He unfastened the heavy rifle and laid it carefully across his knees.

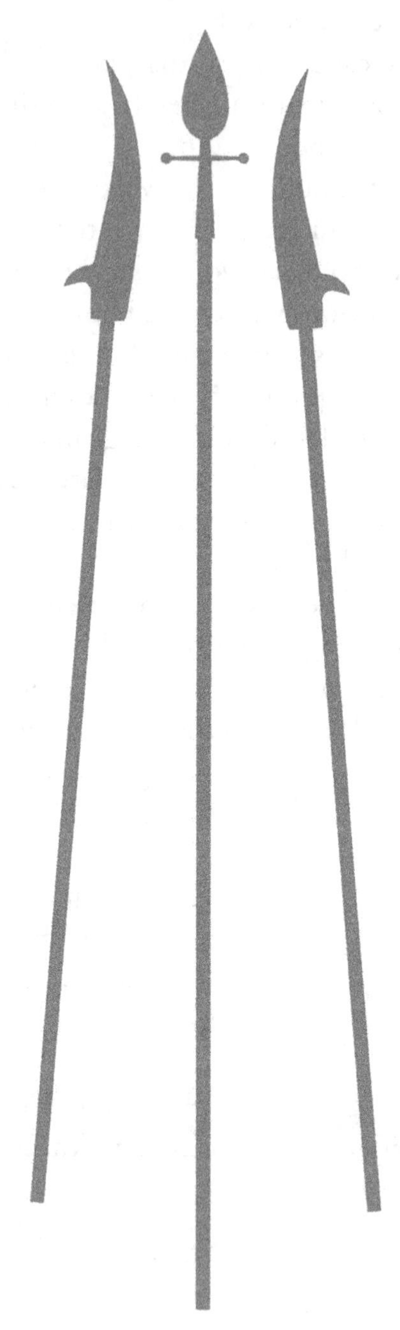

Chapter XV.

ROBBER ROB ROBBER

> *"To rob and ride*
> *Is not a shame*
> *The noblest born*
> *Have done the same."*
> *—Old Saxon Ballad.*[1]

Jefferson gave explicit instructions to his black slave to drive as rapidly as possible. Then he drew some bearskin rugs carefully around his legs, turned up the collar of his coat, buttoned it tightly, and, shivering with cold and vexation, leaned back to think. Thus thought he:

A curse on my bad fortune. This Hamilton is my evil genius. I always had an instinctive dread of that man. Just as I am on the point of triumph, in he steps to mock at me, nay more, to make me his helpless captive. Clearly, he has the power to elect me. I hate the man. He is so cold blooded and hard skulled, but behind him, there is an immense, positive power. How neatly he engineered this "equality" plot to upset my purpose, to put me on the rack, as it were.

He could not defeat me with Adams and Pinkney as his nominees. Adams is deficient in tact, and Pinkney is not popular. Now he defeats me by intrigue—legitimate intrigue, of course—and I am as helpless as a newborn babe to resent it or even to expose it. I have given my word of honor to keep this interview secret, I cannot openly denounce his cool demands. Besides, the fact that I met him at all would condemn me.

Even if I did attempt to expose the scheme, I would only be

---

1   In is 1478 work *Fasciculus Temporum*, Werner Rolevinck details a song attributed to Westphalian nobles that tried to become freebooters: "Ruten, roven, det en is gheyn schande, / Dat doynt die besten van dem lande." This is conveyed in *History of the German People at the Close of the Middle Ages, Volume 1* by Johannes Janssen, A. M. Christie, M. A. Mitchell (K. Paul, Trench, Trübner, & Company, Limited, 1896).

laughed at: nobody would believe me. Nobody would believe I was even here tonight. And to be laughed at is death to a politician. It is the ridicule that kills. Then again, how can I prove it? But it is all the same. Many things exist that cannot be proved. But even if it could be proved, such proof would not take away Hamilton's power to decide the election.

No doubt about it, he has got me 'on the hip'! Me! Thomas Jefferson, author of the Declaration of Independence, that glorious avatar of human liberty, that immortal document, that written word which made this government a possibility—and gave Washington, Hamilton, Adams & Co., aye all of them, the chance of their lifetime—that majestic decree whose Edenic Ideal is already toppling down the moth-eaten thrones of decadent Europe and whirling forth the all-conquering legions of this Corsican Napoleon.

And now, alas, I am voted 'equal' to lawyer Burr and 'Warwicked' by lawyer Hamilton. Next they'll vote me 'equal' to my own darkeys!

Ha! Ha! Ha! It's positively sardonic. Mine own "independence" is gone already. I must be Hamilton's tame mouse, or the country is at the mercy of that little devil Burr. Truly, Mr. Thomas Jefferson of Monticello, you are between "the devils" and "the deep sea"—a very deep sea and very deep devils.

Verily, politics is a heartbreaking business. This makes me doubt the practicability of unlimited democracy. Is it really possible when men are so false and fearful of personal ruin? That is the crux. Are "the majority" capable of acting a disinterested, a noble part? Do they really love their country? Do they? I really begin to doubt it. But we may 'educate' them, just so; but in that also, there is a possible flaw. Cannot delusions be taught in public schools as well as arithmetic? Who is to write the school books and mark time?

However, I am face to face with a crisis in my fortunes. I cannot afford to let the presidency slip through my fingers. I am an old

 Rival Cæsars

man now: I am grey, and my strength is waning day by day. Now is my chance or never. "Aut Cæsar, aut nullus."[1]

Upon my soul, upon my honor, I abhor and detest and abjure this proposition, but, but, but let me see, let me see, shall I permit this government, the child and creature of mine own brain, to fall into the hands of these Rival Cæsars—this soulless gang of New York Catilines—or, or, or shall I take upon myself the possible odium of the compact and, by doing so, save and deliver unborn millions from a fearful, a positively fearful, fate?

Truly, this Hamilton is another subtle Cardinal Richelieu. He has his hands in everything, his secret agents are everywhere. Must I bend before him—must I crouch to... to... to Washington's word-furnisher? Must I accept his terms? No, there is no escape. That is absolute. If I refuse, Burr is straightway president. If so, he will assuredly upset everything. He would use the entire machinery of government to destroy me and make his own re-election sure.

No. No. Burr shall not be president. Not if I can help it. Let him be vice president. There he is safe. He can't do much harm there. It is a high, ornamental office without real power.

Only should I die—Ah! There, a new train of thought arises. Who would be in the line of succession if someone slew me—and there are many quite capable of it—what then? Why, Burr is straightway president! He is heir apparent. It almost makes me break out in a cold sweat to think of it. It reminds me of Livy and Tacitus. Verily, I am like unto a somnambulist suddenly awakening on the verge of a yawning abysm.

Then I must play the courtier to Mr. Warwick Hamilton. It is a choice of alternatives. I must capitulate. It is enough to unbalance a man's brain. I have a mind to go home to Monticello and burn all my books. Republican institutions! Bah!

Was ever a man before in such a pitiless predicament? I have read and read till my mind has grown weary of reading. I thought

---

1   "Either a Cæsar or a nobody."

I had acquired the wisdom of the wisest. I had honestly purposed to eradicate from the land of my birth the last fibre of ancient or future aristocracy, and here I am, on the point of being appointed a mighty ruler not by the great common people but by a subtle Manhattan caucus boss.

He! He! He! How would it look 'Thomas Jefferson, president of the United States by the grace of God and Major General Hamilton'? Am I opposed to a stronger practical intellect than my own? It must be so, for I am beaten. A conqueror's hoof is on my neck. I have not proved myself 'equal' even to Hamilton, let alone that little devil Burr. That is 'a self-evident truth.' It is positively heartbreaking, astounding, but it's a fact nevertheless.

I thought myself an Occidental Moses, a Republican Luther, a Virginian Rienzi, a Mohammed of democracy, and here I am, riding through the snow on a bleak, wild, wintry night, trapped like a lamb, vanquished, laughed at, dictated to, 'Warwicked'!

Then the third president of the United States leaned forward on his seat, his head between his hands, and wept with vexation and impotence, aye, wept passionately. His long, gaunt frame shook with emotion, and bitter, bitter tears ran down through his lean fingers. His tears were the tears of an honest ambition, of disillusionment and thwarted hopes.

"I thought myself a valiant hero, a mighty overcomer, but, after this, I shall never more believe there are any perfect heroes outside of fairyland or the two covers of a story book."

Thus soliloquized the shivering Mr. Jefferson. For two solid hours, his mind wandered from subject to subject but always came back to the one supreme question: *Shall I accept Hamilton's terms?* He turned the matter over and over, again and again.

He studied it from every point of view without perceiving the slightest loophole of escape. He hesitated.

     RIVAL CÆSARS

Meanwhile, "Mr. Warwick Hamilton" or "Washington's word-spinner," as Thomas Jefferson described him, was being driven as rapidly as the snow and bad roads would permit to his suburban destination.

He sat in the coach smiling complacently and thinking of Jefferson's amusing nervousness and evident bewilderment.

Jefferson, he thought, *is as likely as any man I know to accept terms, and, at present, he will be much safer than Burr. He is full of strange notions and philanthropic ambitions, but he has never been a soldier, and thus there is no hardness in him. He is not the stamp of man that would have grit to use an army in order to maintain himself in power. The very thought of such a thing would fill him with hysteria.*

If I am not mistaken, Jefferson will calculate and trim and always consider what will promote his own reputation and advantage, and the probable result of such a temper is the preservation of established systems. Thus, should he be elected, my 'crazy hulk of a constitution' may, after all, get a fair trial.

With all his subverting theories, Jefferson is not a real iconoclast. He hesitates and thinks too much. Thinking always kills action. Savants are seldom deed-doers and never soldiers. They are always in the rear of action. They build up their 'principles' and 'philosophies' to harmonize with accomplished facts.

Even Jefferson's sublime faith in the rule of numbers is wholly inherited and traditional. Majorities are nothing except they have arms in their hands. Indeed, intelligent persistence is capable of making one man a majority. Jefferson ought to have been inducted into the Iron Cross. Then he would have known better.

The horses in Hamilton's carriage trotted noiselessly over the snow. Suddenly, the dead silence was broken by the sharp, menacing crack of a pistol.

Immediately, the carriage stopped, and a pleasant, musical voice from a man on horseback came through the gathering gloom, saying, "Hold the horses in, coachman. Ah! Now step down, fasten the reins to the wheel. Very good. Stand there against the Ivan and hold up your hands. If you lower them during my interview with your master, you will receive a bullet through your thick, black skull. Hold up your hands! That's it."

The coachman, being a negro and a slave, obeyed with alacrity.

Meantime, Hamilton, out of the pockets of his overcoat, drew a pair of beautiful mounted pistols that had seen much service in his hands. He guessed what was coming, and not being a dreamer or a mere philosopher but a very practical man of action, he looked to the priming of his weapons and cocked them carefully. *Whoso maketh himself a dove is eaten by the hawk*, he thought grimly as his hands closed over the butts of the pistols.

Presently, the door of the carriage was violently flung open.

"Come out!" said the musical voice of the highwayman, for such he was. (In those days, suburban roads were infested by bold riders inclined to think it much more honorable to take money than to make it.)

Hamilton did not move.

"Come out!" said the melodious voice again, in a tone of impatience. The road agent clicked the hammers of his pistols ominously.

Hamilton sat still, his fingers toying gently with the triggers and his mind made up.

"Ho! my defiant gentleman, I'll have to bring you out," spoke the road agent angrily, riding up to the carriage door. Thrusting into the carriage the muzzle of a heavy horse pistol, he said to the silent Hamilton, "Come out immediately, or I'll blow your brains out."

Hamilton did not move. Being in the darkness, he knew he could not be seen with certainty and therefore calculated the robber would not waste his shot by firing at random.

After waiting a little while, Hamilton answered in a feigned weak voice, "I cannot come out: I am a crippled old man. What do you want?"

"I want," replied the highwayman, somewhat mollified, "your money or your life," and he brought his pistol up on a level with that portion of the carriage's interior where he imagined the voice of the supposed cripple came from, tightening the reins of his horse on his left hand.

Now the entire body of the highwayman covered the carriage door. This was the opportunity Hamilton had been strategically waiting for.

"But I don't propose to let you have either, sir," replied Hamilton coolly as he raised both his pistols and fired point blank through the open carriage door.

Both bullets took immediate effect. The bandit, taken completely off his guard, was slain almost before he knew where he was. One ball went in at his right eye and out through the crown of his head (taking some of the brain with it), and the other passed through his intestines, lodging in the spinal column.

Hamilton drew his sword and stepped out. The black coachman was bending over the prostrate body that lay in the snow.

The blood trickled from the wounds of the highwayman while his horse trotted away with the reins hanging between its forelegs.

Hamilton leaned down and examined the unconscious, dying man. He looked into his face. It was the face of a youth under twenty with bold, clear-cut features. His clothing was that of a gentleman. He appeared to be of good lineage.

Ah, thought Hamilton. *Youth for daring, he is quite a boy. He had pluck, however, and pluck covers a multitude of sins, it takes courage to be either a highwayman or a statesman. I have spoilt your career however, my lad. There was a serious flaw in your philosophy, Mr. Deadman. You failed, and to fail is crime, as you and*

I have so eloquently demonstrated unto each other. Perhaps if you had been more expert, you might have had my purse.

Then Hamilton quietly reloaded his pistols, returned to the carriage, and resumed his journey.

Ah, he thought again, *the saintly Jefferson is wrong. His sublime confidence in the inherent goodness of all mankind is misguided. Men are the wolves of men. It has always been so. This simple incident is typical. It typifies the opposing interests of men, those who have and those who have not. If I had not defended my property, would I not have lost it? Certainly, I would.*

My pistols and my own strength delivered me. So is it everywhere. Men of property must always stand ready to defend their possessions.

There is more solid philosophy in that poor boy's horse pistol than in all the dreary tomes that have ever been written, from Jefferson to Jeremiah, from Plato to Paine and Rousseau.

Theoretically, Jefferson is a bold and dashing destroyer of systems but is as timid as a hare when it comes to doing anything. I foretell that if he becomes president, he will alter naught.

He has an instinctive constitutional horror of war and is therefore not likely to build up an army; indeed, if he had an army, he would not know how to use it. Therefore, he is a safe man and will allay discontent. Is he not the leader and supposed 'Moses' of the discontented? All this country now wants is internal peace and quietness. Jefferson will give it that. Like a man afraid of his horse, he will not attempt to go beyond a pleasant amble for fear he might get shook out of the saddle.

Burr has been a soldier and is, therefore, an entirely different man. War burns up the mental cobwebs that are liable to gather in a man's mind from overmuch contemplation of ordered tranquillity. War is the grim realist. It places a note of interrogation opposite every belief and every opinion, however hoary, however sanctified. War makes men iron, hence fit to be rulers. Luckily for us, Jefferson is not a warrior.

About a mile further on, Hamilton was again disturbed in his cogitations by the crack of a rifle from behind a tree on the roadside.

More robbers, he thought, again preparing his pistols for eventualities.

Presently, the coach rolled over on its side into a deep gully, crossed by a narrow wooden bridge. One of the horses had been shot when crossing the bridge, and the other, frightened, plunged through the railing into the half frozen creek below, dragging the coach on top of himself. The fall broke the ice on the stream, and the horse's head went through into the water. Unable to withdraw his head, he drowned there.

Meanwhile, Hamilton, stunned and bleeding, pushed his head and shoulders through the uppermost panel of the coach door, grasping one of his pistols.

The moment his head showed up, the black muzzle of a heavy military rifle was pushed coldly against his eye. He looked undauntedly along the bronze barrel and at the other end thereof perceived, in the intermittent moonlight, the head of a black-bearded man with a white handkerchief over his face, in which had been cut two holes for the eyes.

Hamilton felt instinctively he was in a dilemma this time. The blood trickled profusely from a wound in the temple, and one of his hands seemed numb or broken.

"Drop that pistol, hold up your hands, and surrender instantly, or you are a dead man," said the masked man behind the ugly rifle. "If you do not drop it, I will lift the top of your head off. I will shoot to kill."

Hamilton saw no means of escape. He felt himself at the mercy of superior strategy. He understood in a flash that he had to deal this time not with a boy highwayman but with an old and experienced hand, 'an inexorable one.' Therefore he smiled his most affable smile and said, in his most musical and insinuating tones, "What do you want with me, sir? Do you know who I am, sir?"

"Yes, I know who you are. I know you too well, damn you. I want those papers in your breast pocket. Hand them over."

Hamilton's heart sank within him. *This is more than highway robbery,* he thought. *Burr is behind it. I am sure he is. This is his fine Roman hand. But I am trapped. The man behind the gun means business. I can read it in his eyes. I must submit or be shot.*

Hamilton turned over in his mind several plans of throwing the robber off his guard and then attacking him. The robber was also calculating on this and considering how he should get the papers without committing murder.

"Come out of the carriage, Mr. Hamilton," said the bandit coaxingly, "then remove your overcoat and hand it to me."

The highwayman never removed the rifle from before Hamilton's eyes.

Hamilton, rapidly revolving a plan to suddenly push the rifle aside and leap at the throat of his adversary, did as he was told.

As he drew off his overcoat, however, the robber jumped upon him and overthrew him. A short, sharp struggle on the snow ensued. Hamilton's arms being entangled in the sleeves of the coat, he was quickly overpowered and reduced to order.

"Be quiet or I'll kill you," hissed the victor (who weighed about 200 pounds, while Hamilton weighed about 180), as he brought a short, broad-bladed knife in front of Hamilton's right eye. At this the major general lay quiet, now thoroughly vanquished. *Realism in excelsis,* he thought.

Hamilton having submitted, his captor bound his two hands firmly together with one end of a rope and threw the other end of the rope over the top rail of the bridge and made it fast.

Thus Washington's famous secretary stood, his toes in the snow and his hands lashed firmly overhead to the broken bridge.

In the creek lay the two dead horses, their blood splashed on the ice. The coachman was helplessly entangled in the harness, or pretended that he was to escape coming in contact with a very possible bullet.

The masked man thereupon leisurely searched all Hamilton's pockets. Then he searched the inside of the coach. He found more than he thought to find. He got not only all the papers shown to Jefferson but also another packet, of even greater importance, together with a Spanish sketch map defining the location of a long-forgotten safe deposit vault in the City of Mexico that had been covered up and hidden by the priests before the Great Temple was burned by the Spaniards. This map had originally belonged to Burr, who got it from Holroyd, and thereby hangs another story that cannot now be related.

"Why don't you take my money, my watch, and other valuables instead of those papers?" said Hamilton in a tone of appeal. "Of what value are mere legal papers to you? And I have a diamond ring on my finger worth $500. Why not take it, also my purse, and leave me those papers?"

The robber put the papers carefully away in the pocket of his overcoat and then replied in a gruff voice, "Keep your infernal money. I am after higher game. The eagle does not stoop to catch flies." Then the burly robber in the white mask climbed up the bank of the creek where his horse was tied, mounted, and rode away. Before doing so, however, he threw his captive's pistols far into the snowdrift, and, as he rode off across the bridge, he cut the rope that bound Hamilton, saying as he did so, "You can now release your own hands at your leisure and walk the remainder of the way. And I would advise you to say nothing of this little affair to anyone. You would not like to see those papers published, would you? Therefore, hold your tongue, I advise you."

The highwayman, who was none other than John Swartwout (disguised), then rode off.

Now, Burr and Hamilton kept each his own private corps of detectives to watch the other's movements. Knowledge thus obtained was often used to win elections. Burr employed many women for this purpose as he found them very clever in worming out hidden secrets. Through the agency of one of these lady "friends" in Hamilton's own household, the whereabouts of Burr's "last papers" had been discovered. Also the facts relating to Hamilton's proposed expedition on this particular night. The information first came to Swartwout, who immediately determined to attempt the recovery of the papers, with what results we have seen.

He had not only obtained one series of very important documents but also another set that, previously to this, Burr had known nothing about and, in addition, had discovered Hamilton's intrigue (or, rather, proposed intrigue) with Jefferson.

John Swartwout was a wealthy New York merchant and general of militia who had served in the Revolutionary War alongside of Burr.0 He was Burr's most intimate personal friend and trusted lieutenant. By disposition, he was very loyal to his friends and possessed the valor and Pythian fidelity of ancient Greece and Rome.

He was both daring and resourceful and would go through fire and water to serve Burr, whom he idolized. He also hated Hamilton for an injury that he believed Hamilton had once done him over a law case concerning confiscated property.

On this eventful night, however, all his risks and exertions proved utterly in vain, for as he rode on (about two miles further), he himself was set upon and robbed by a band of seven masked footpads. They first shot his horse, then seized and bound him as he fell.

Then they took from him all his money, his watch, pistols, rifles, overcoat, and (greatest loss of all) the secret papers and cipher letters wherewith Hamilton had been negotiating Burr's ruin.

Being a man of resource, however, he made a treaty with them for the ransoming of the documents, He promised them a thousand dollars, which they duly received, but the papers were not all returned to him afterwards, although he thought they were.

Afterwards, the seven robbers quarreled over the sharing of their booty and fought a pitched battle in the woods when inflamed with liquor. Four were killed outright, and wolves and ants ate the flesh from off their bones. The survivors "went West" to aid in the great work of territorial expansion. One of them joined Burr afterwards in an attempt to capture Texas too soon (thirty years too soon). Strange how the wildest characters, the "criminals" of civilization, have ever taken the most pronounced and strenuous part in the heroic work of colonization.

If Burr had received those papers in time, Jefferson could never have been elected, but he did not receive them until two days after Jefferson had won by the aid of the Federals. Bayard, of Delaware, and General Morris, of Vermont, voted for Jefferson, and both of them were intimate personal friends of "Mr. Warwick Hamilton."

Bayard, on the 8th of March, wrote to Hamilton as follows: "The means existed of electing Burr, but this required his cooperation. By deceiving one man (a great blockhead) and tempting two (not incorruptible), he, Burr, might have secured a majority of the states and became president. He will never have another chance."[1]

Judge Cooper, a delegate from New York (father of J. Fennimore Cooper), wrote to Thomas Morris, on the 12th of February 1801 "We are running Burr perseveringly. Had Burr done anything for himself, he would long ere this have been president.

1 ≠   By the old method, all the candidates were nominated for the presidency, and he who received the second largest number of votes became vice president.

If a majority vote of the individuals would answer, he would have it on every vote."

Burr thoroughly understood the why and wherefore of Jefferson's (the Southern man's) election. He knew he had been robbed of the presidency but said nothing. He was too proud to complain. He was too haughty and self-contained to repine. But down deep in his heart, he registered a vow of vengeance. (And Hamilton and Jefferson knew and feared.)

Defeat never broke his spirit. It made him more determined than ever to get even with his enemies, open and hidden.

He was wont to say, confidentially, to the grim and fiery John Swartwout, "Swartwout, you know well I am president of the United States by the will of the people, although the honor I did not solicit. If Hamilton had kept his hands off, the Electoral College would have given it to me. The Feds, in their hearts, were for me to a man. Jefferson is unlawfully in possession of the seat of power. He is an usurper, equally as much so as Bonaparte or Cromwell. He is in control of the government by coup d'etat, the coup d'etat of Major General Hamilton. But what is the use of talking now? It is too late, too late. I am beaten, and when a battle is lost, words are vain.

"If I had an army to back up my words with hard knocks, it would be so different. Then they wouldn't count me out. No! By my troth, no. I'd fling the whole damned administration into the Potomac first.

"Am I not the rightful president?"

Swartwout, much chagrined and brooding angrily at his evil luck, walked on smartly towards the city lights that gleamed in the distance like a galaxy of stars. Presently, he heard rapid footfalls on the crisp snow immediately behind him. He turned round and looked to see who or what it was.

It was Hamilton.

Now, Swartwout and Hamilton were personally well acquainted, so of course they were very courteous to each other. Soon they began to mutually relate their experiences of the night with the wicked highway robbers. Hamilton had not the slightest conception that he was talking to the very man who had robbed him. John Swartwout had removed his disguise, had lost his overcoat, musket, and horse, and was a widely known and highly respected member of New York's best society whom no one could possibly suspect of turning highwayman.

And so, they walked along side by side until they came to a little roadside inn known as The Angel of Glory.

There was a large heap of broken bottles outside and a number of large ale casks inside. Behind the bar were rows of black bottles on shelves.

On the walls hung antlers of deer, trophies of the chase, pictures of racehorses and cockfights and bullfights and man fights. In the place of honor hung a smoky painting of "Washington at Yorktown." The principal room of the hostelry was odorous of tobacco smoke and whiskey fumes. Upon a wide stone hearth, a bright log fire burned merrily, and over the mantel, an old Brown Bess musket hung on a nail by a sling sewn of Indian scalps.

Weary of their unaccustomed long walk, the two men entered the tavern and ordered a bottle of wine, some cheese, and biscuits, which Hamilton paid for.

Two recent newspapers lay on the tavern table. One was the *American Citizen*, edited by Cheat'em; the other, the *Richmond Register*, edited by Carender.

Sitting down wearily, Hamilton picked up the *Citizen*, and leaning back in his chair, he commenced to glance curiously through its contents and study the flaring headlines. Suddenly, his attention became riveted.

Swartwout, meanwhile, opened up the *Register* and looked over it with languid curiosity, then also with intense interest.

Several minutes passed away, both men deeply absorbed in what they read. Suddenly, Hamilton burst out into a loud guffaw, and, about the same instant, Swartwout did the same.

Both were seemingly highly amused at what they saw printed in the two hostile opposition journals, and yet neither man knew exactly what the other was laughing at.

What Hamilton read was a stinging editorial against himself as "The Machiavelli of New York politics," etc. The first headline being

MAJOR GENERAL HAMILTON: THE SAWDUST HERO

Underneath were sub headlines and such sentences as follows:

A WOULD-BE NAPOLEON.

...who spills more ink than blood...turned the Treasury Department into a Seraglio...Has never accounted for that "Lost Million." ...In a suburban cabbage garden, he now plays at being Cincinnatus, with a hoe in one hand and "Cicero-on-Catiline" in the other. . . His drunken editor in N. Y. assails the sunny and genial disposition of the Hero of Hackensack...madly jealous of Colonel Burr's talents and popularity...Describes the great Republican Party as "Robespierre Jefferson's red-rag rabble." Insinuates that the home life of the Man of Monticello is not idyllic... Reynolds, "the husband" of his paramour, disappears... Said to have been knocked on the head (to close his mouth), and then flung into the North River at midnight. John Adams, president of the United States, describes this half-Britisher—this crafty West Indian who calls the great common people "a beast",this

                                    RIVAL CÆSARS

would-be Man-on-Horseback who aspires to the seat of Washington—as "the bastard brat of a Scotch peddler."[1]

So the article ran on and on for a column and a half. Presently Hamilton threw the paper down and laughed heartily till the tears came to his eyes.

(Here it must be clearly understood that men like Hamilton, Jefferson, Burr, and Swartwout were "old" at the game of politics. They knew exactly what ink-slinging was worth and what it cost and what it was intended for. Indeed, they were so accustomed to newspaper vilification that they seldom lost their temper, even in face of the most venomous allegations.)

Now, Swartwout was as much amused as Hamilton at what he also had been perusing. As soon, therefore, as he concluded the article that interested him, he handed his paper across the glasses to Hamilton, pointing out at the same time the following editorial:

THE RED-RAG ROBESPIERRE AND HIS CONGO HAREM.—THE DIVINE AND DUSKY SALLY FIENNESY.—MONTICELLO SWARMING WITH BLACK-AND-TAN JEFFERSONS.—THE VIRGINIAN VOLTAIRE AND HIS PHILOSOPHIC FOGS...

A chat with Tom Jefferson's overseer, Grady, and Captain Bacon. The philosopher of human equality does not permit his slaves to be flogged except for very heinous offenses. Then he sells them in Richmond at a sacrifice. He orders a beautiful octoroon girl to be freed, nearly white as anybody and very beautiful, said to be his own daughter; she has tawny red hair and is inclined to philosophy. Sends her north by post chaise to be educated in the City of Brotherly Love....Sarah Hennesy,

---

1 ≠   See *Life of John Adams*—See also *The Conqueror* by Mrs. Atherton.

from Senegambia....Young Randolph....The Angelic Fiddler and his Cotton Factory. How his cotton mill is driven: child slaves.

Now, Thomas Jefferson had never been very popular at the North. He was (in spite of all his protestations) considered as favoring the great Southern tobacco and cotton growers rather than the commercial and manufacturing interests of the North Atlantic states.

John Swartwout, as a firm follower of Burr, never liked Jefferson but supported him for policy's sake.

"Hamilton," he said, sipping his wine, "that damned editor fellow of yours is a brilliant genius. He must be worth his weight in gold to the Feds. There seems no limit to his riotous imagination. But you've put him up to this, haven't you? Last month, he was shrieking against your old friend Burr as a cross between Blue Beard, Old Nick, and Judas Iscariot."

"Ah, Swartwout, all is fair in love and war, and to that may be added politics. Was it not Jefferson's vitriolic editor, Callender, who ferreted out my harmless little intrigue with Mrs. Reynolds?[1] You've read the pamphlet I had to publish in rebuttal. The affair was unfortunate for me, on account of the strong Puritan sentiment in the North. My mistake was in appointing "the husband" to a clerkship in the Treasury Department. That's where your people had the advantage over me."

"Ah, I know all about it," answered Swartwout, smiling suggestively. "However, it destroyed you as a presidential possibility. Of course, it is all politics. Everybody knows that, but, as your opponent, I'm not supposed to say so."

When Hamilton finished the article that represented his own side of the argument, both men looked across with a smiling but inquiring glance at each other.

---

1 ≠   See Parton and other *Lives of Jefferson.* Also *Jefferson in Monticello,* by the Revd. H. W. Pierson, D. D, Scribner, New York, 1862. Page 110, etc. Also the newspapers of the time.

"All these charges and counter charges are buncombe," said Hamilton impressively. "Upon my honor, they are."

"Certainly," replied Swartwout, refilling both glasses from the bottle. "It's all politics right through, intended for effect to fool the free and independent."

"Men of sense don't believe such insane diatribes," remarked Hamilton.

"Men of sense are somewhat scarce and far between," answered Swartwout. "The vast majority of men, being futile and hopelessly weak, always delight in having the successful men among them taken down a peg; hence the plebeian appetite for journalistic scandal-mongering."

"It's a great evil," said Hamilton.

"That is so," answered Swartwout, "but we must put up with it. It seems to be human nature. If a man is bold enough to seize the greatest game, he must expect to face the petty jealousy of those who haven't the heart to dare anything."

"Yes," replied Hamilton. "That's the devil of it. No man's private life is held sacred any more. His goings forth and his comings home are watched and chronicled. The mob wants to pry into everything. A man's lightest peccadilloes are magnified a hundredfold and blazoned abroad, with a view to catch the votes of the vulgar. If he happens to wink at a beautiful woman, he is held up as a monster of iniquity to the dear old grannies of both sexes. If he does not, in all things, conform to the standards of the herd, he is straightway trampled underfoot. O, politics, politics, what a hideous thing thou art!"

"Truly," answered Swartwout. "Politics would soil the Prince of All Evil himself. But as we've taken the plunge, we may as well make the most of it. A man who leaps into an ocean of slime must swim in it or drown in it."

"By the way," said Hamilton, "have you read Callender's book on Gen. Washington?"

"No. Have you? I've never heard of it"

"You ought to read it, Swartwout. It's equal to Junius for style and subtlety of insinuation. Jefferson prompted it, I feel sure. He always cherished a secret hatred and jealousy of Washington. He keeps Callender going with money too. Callender is one of those strange men of talent who, like Edmund Burke, can write on any side of a question if properly inspired."

Swartwout to this answered, "Yes, I know, 'if properly inspired,' and Callender and Cheat'em are convivial bosom friends, aren't they?"

"Yes, I believe so. But who would ever suspect it to read the lurid diatribes they every now and then hurl at one another?" said Hamilton.

"Nobody! These newspaper men are a curious set. Like the priests of antiquity, they know the whole gamut: friends in private, foes in public. Always burning with divine patriotism, you know."

"Many of them are men of striking genius. Yes, 'striking': that's the very word. They can strike a man to death with a grey goose quill. The pen is mightier than the sword, you know, Swartwout."

"It is 'in the copy books,' as Burr would say in his searching, sardonic way," replied Swartwout with a laugh. "But I don't believe it."

"Do you think Burr will be elected?"

"I do. He has an even number of Republican votes, and the Federals are all for him to a man, so he cannot help winning."

"I hope he may win," said Hamilton impressively. "He deserves it. He is my dear old friend, and his abilities are transcendently great. While I disagree with him politically, I admire him deeply. He will make an excellent and patriotic Chief Magistrate, every way superior to that wearisome old demagogue, Jefferson."

"If that be so, Mr. Hamilton, why not throw all your weight

for Burr and thus give the presidency to New York? Pinckney and Adams have no chance whatever, and the tie between Jefferson and Burr still stands unbroken."

"It would delight me very much, Mr. Swartwout, I assure you, if I could be of any present service to my dear, brave old friend Colonel Burr. But don't you think it is too late now?"

"As you say, I think it is too late, General Hamilton. I've always known you had a very high personal regard for Colonel Burr, and I know he sincerely reciprocates your kindly sentiments. If he wins the presidency, he may probably retain you as his secretary of the treasury. You have already made a record in that department."

"I wish he had assured me of that before, Swartwout," said Hamilton impressively and with a strange twitching around the corners of his mouth.

"So do I," answered Swartwout, reaching for his hat and rising to go.

Thereupon, the two men stood up, refilled their old-fashioned, long-shanked glasses, smiled sweetly across the table, drank the old toast—"Here's to true friendship!"—and departed by different roads.

Little he knows, thought Hamilton, *that I have just given Burr the deadliest thrust and knockdown blow he ever received in his life.*

Little he thinks, thought John Swartwout, *that I know the whole of his devilish game.*

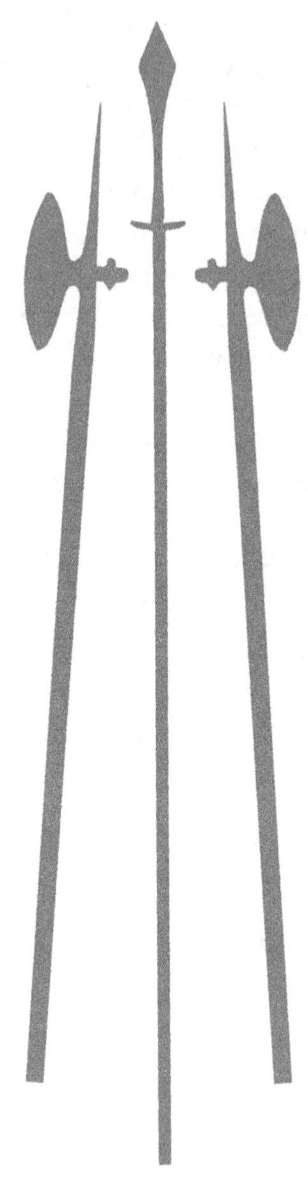

Chapter XVI.

THE SECRET TRIBUNAL

"At every step solemn and slow,
The shadows blacker fall."[1]

The marriage of Senator Burr's beautiful daughter, Theo, to Joseph Alston took place in Albany and was a memorable society event. The marriage party rode to the old church in sleighs jangling with bells, three feet of snow laying on the ground.

Nearly all the legislators, their wives, and their daughters, were at the wedding, which passed off with great éclat, for Colonel Burr was at all periods of his life a superb joy-master. Indeed, he delighted in hospitality: first, because it was his nature; second, because he found it to be "good politics."

Being a thorough judge of human nature, he clearly saw that the vast majority of men and women were always more inclined to be swayed by such means than by dry arguments or mere logic addressed to their understanding.

Early in his career, he discovered that the "understanding" of average persons was very limited.

Now, Joseph Alston, the happy bridegroom, was a dilltante young millionaire planter of South Carolina. Like the young millionaires of the present time, he was utterly without high ambition. Until be came in contact with Aaron Burr, he had no higher idea of life than to be a fashionable man-about-town. Sated with "good things," the desire to grandly excel had little scope to develop within him. (He had very little notion of the power and glory that lies hidden in the aggressive use of money.)

Afterwards, however, he entered public life (at Burr's sug-

---

1   James Thomson, "Summer," *Jahrszeiten* (Severin, 1798).

273

gestion) and became governor of his native state, but possessing little real ability, he never rose higher. He owned too much money at the commencement of his career.

At the time of his marriage, he had 500 slaves, numerous relatives in high positions, and nearly 100,000 acres of land inherited from early English settlers.

Theodosia upon her wedding was presented by her father with a necklace of pearls. The money that purchased the necklace came from the Manhattan bank; that is to say, Burr made his enemies pay for his daughter's dowry.

The method employed by him to do this was most astute.

The Manhattan Bank had been founded by Burr in the teeth of relentless opposition. Afterwards, his shares were bought up by political enemies, whereupon they straightway began to freeze him out. They refused him accommodation and threatened him with bankruptcy. But he turned the tables and made them beg for mercy. One morning, he drove down to the managing director and pointed out that he could, if he so willed, wreck the credit of the bank because of a flaw in the original charter, a charter which he himself had drawn up. The bank, understanding the gravity of the threat, surrendered, and not only surrendered but promised to financially carry Burr for many years thereafter. Nothing showed the preternatural foresight of this man more than the extraordinary fact that he thus actually compelled his most relentless enemies to provide him with ready money and unlimited credit wherewith to fight themselves. But that also is another tale—for another time.

During the seven days of secret balloting and negotiating for the presidency—when the entire community was distraught with excitement and in a turmoil of expectancy, while civil war, revolution, anarchy, were wildly predicted by the Federal editors (because of their defeat) while Hamilton, Jefferson and Bayard were quietly planning his political and financial extinction—Burr was busily engaged at Albany, where he was a legislator, in arrangements for the nuptials of his idolized daughter.

All Theodosia's former suitors had been invited to the wedding. Many of them came and did their best to appear joyful, while their hearts were bursting with disappointment and anger.

Now, at the time of the inauguration of Jefferson, Major General Hamilton and Colonel Aaron Burr met in one of the corridors of the Supreme Court. Hamilton was accompanied by Bayard of Baltimore, Burr by Judge Van Ness of New York. Hamilton saluted courteously, saying, "How-de-do, Mr. Vice President?" Hamilton laid particular stress on the word "vice," and there was an ironic ring in his voice, which did not escape the affable colonel."

Hamilton smiled blandly, and Burr bowed benignly, saying in a condescending and patronizing tone, "Good morning, Mr. Major General."

Then both men shook hands effusively, and Hamilton again spoke, saying, "Permit me to congratulate you, my dear old friend and comrade-in-arms, upon your elevation to the second-highest position of honor and emolument in the gift of your admiring fellow citizens."

Whereupon Burr answered blithely in his most seductive tones, at the same time laying his right hand upon his left breast and bowing profoundly:

"Thanks, dear brother and kind old comrade. I reciprocate your friendly interest in my present advancement. I know it wells from the bottom of your heart. In answer, allow me to say that, as one good turn deserves another, I treasure the earnest hope of someday aiding in your elevation to an even higher position.

"I assure you that when my opportunity comes, and of course it must, nothing shall give me keener rapture than to repay, with interest, your disinterested and very fraternal kindnesses."

"You must be well aware, my dear Major General, that I have always sincerely believed in the Golden Rule of doing unto others as they do unto me."

Then the four men smiled delightedly, waved their adieus to one another, and, arm in arm, went their respective ways.

Soon, Hamilton spake to his companion in soothing congratulatory tones saying, "Ah, Bayard, this is my innings."

Whereupon Bayard replied, saying, "Don't be so sure, Hamilton. Burr is a hard man to down. His smile makes me shudder. When he spake just now, his words had in them the hiss of a snake."

Burr walked on erectly, clenching his hands self-repressingly until his fingernails sank into the flesh. Then he turned to Van Ness and said, "Ah! Van Ness, he would jeer at me! But someday, I will 'elevate' him. He laughs best who laughs last. My turn cometh. I know how to wait."

Van Ness replied with venom in his voice: "Yes, damn him, the cunning old fox. We'll hang his scalp in our wigwam yet."

"Ah," replied the vice president. "Fox! Truly a Sir Reynard! Mark me, Van Ness, you and I will be 'in at the death.'"

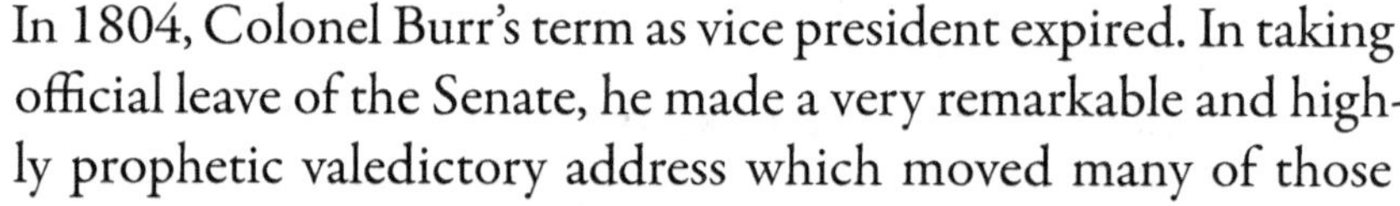

In 1804, Colonel Burr's term as vice president expired. In taking official leave of the Senate, he made a very remarkable and highly prophetic valedictory address which moved many of those hardened sinners to tears. Singularly enough, his concluding words have been preserved:

"This house is a sanctuary and a citadel of law, of order, of liberty, and it is here, here in this exalted refuge, here if anywhere, that resistance will be made to the storms of popular phrenzy and the silent arts of corruption. And if the Constitution is ever destined to perish by the sacrilegious hand of demagogue or usurper, which may God avert, its expiring agonies shall be witnessed upon this floor."

But we anticipate.

By the time 1804 had arrived, the vice president's fame had so sank in public estimation that it would have been fatuous for him to again become a presidential candidate.

The two great political parties had done their very utmost to systematically blacken the vice president's reputation, as per prearrangement between their respective leaders.

Everything that he did was misrepresented by the organs of both parties and ladled out in windy, leading articles to the great common people. Editors "properly inspired" vied with one another in raking up every old scandal or gossip against his name and distorting beyond recognition all his words and actions.

They cast doubts on his loyalty to his own country, upon his bravery in battle, upon his fidelity to his wife (dead ten years), and even went so far as to say his mother was mad and that he kept a harem of Indian and French houris at Richmond Hill.

All his financial troubles were exposed in the newspapers, his creditors pressed him and crushed him in every possible way, and they were compelled to do it by an insidious but steady pressure upon themselves.

If he had been twice over a millionaire, he could never have successfully stood up against such odds. Being a comparatively poor man and without any interstate organization, he was wholly unable to reply effectively to his pitiless assailants. He was impotent to retaliate, which is the most effective way to answer political denunciations. The dead weight of entrenched power was steadily, remorselessly grinding him down.

Now, it ever seemed to be the motto of his life to express his real opinions by actions rather than by words. He liked to do things in a dignified and dramatic manner, trusting the public to judge (a very foolish trust).

Throughout all his life, he was never known to apologize

or express regret or penitence for anything he had ever said or done, and he scorned all underhand methods of vengeance, for he prided himself on being, in all his dealings, a soldier and a gentleman of the old school. "They call me a pirate," he was wont to say, "but may not a pirate be a gentleman?"

In 1803, the vice president requested from Jefferson a foreign ambassadorship, thinking this might possibly be granted to him in recognition of his present position and of his past services to the Republican Party, also as an old soldier of the Revolution.

His request was sullenly refused, and the refusal blazoned forth insultingly. Then in fair desperation, the vice president became an "independent" candidate for the governorship of New York. Immediately, both the old parties, led on by Jefferson and Hamilton, entered the lists against him, with all the resources and skill that money and power and government prestige could give them. The vice president was defeated by a nonentity named Morgan Lewis, 35,000 votes against 28,000.

Burr attributed his defeat primarily to a set of very malevolent letters written by Alexander Hamilton and extensively but privately circulated. Many of these letters came into Burr's possession afterwards, but he himself never made any public use of them.

Thus step by step, with the precision of a classic tragedy, the animosity between those two powerful personalities fanned itself to a white heat, and the thought of immediate mortal combat took possession of not only their own minds but also the minds of their personal followers. "These two men must fight before long" was in nearly everybody's mouth.

Burr had overthrown Hamilton in 1800, and Hamilton overthrew Burr in 1804. The one had wrecked the other, and Jefferson was winning all along the line.

Thus, they stood, as it were, like two glowering gladiators

weakened by loss of blood but still valiantly returning blow for blow with indomitable hatred.

As the material prizes of office glided out of their grasp to Jefferson (whom both despised), the conflict grew fiercer and more rancorous and more unscrupulous.

Their friends despaired of any other solution than the total subjugation of one or the other.

Like two crouching tigers, they glared into each other's bloodshot eyes and waited for an excuse or a chance to spring.

The Northern states were much alarmed at this state of mutual hatred between their two greatest leaders, for it meant the passing of all administrative power into the hands of Southern men through the continued triumph of Jefferson.

The quarrel deepened. Men even talked of secession. The commercial interests of the North were systematically neglected by Jefferson, and bad blood existed between the small farmers of the North and the baronial planters of the South.

Then the Iron Cross interfered. It's all-hearing ear had not been deaf. Its all-seeing eye had not been blind. It saw the national danger. It heard the undergrowl of universal discontent, and its ukase[1] went forth.

It determined to reconcile Hamilton and Burr or destroy them both as traitors to the Order.

Already, it had acted in a perfunctory way. It had summoned both "brothers" before its tribunal. It had officially and unofficially admonished them more than once. It had even gone so far as to threaten Hamilton with its heavy hand.

All to no purpose, however. The feud would not hush. It was too deep seated, too fundamental.

No open evidence was forthcoming to prove "unbrotherly conduct" against either one or the other, although the fact of said conduct was apparent to everyone. A man blind, deaf and

---

1   In Imperial Russia, a "ukase" was a proclamation of the tsar, government, or a religious leader that had the force of law.

dumb, could not help knowing it. And so, the Supreme Council had allowed the matter to drop from time to time for both men were strongly represented on the Council.

Finally, the Supreme Seven took a decisive stand with results far-reaching.

Now, the Iron Cross had always favored and even commanded the advancement of Burr and Hamilton, and largely through its power, the influence and fame of both men grew and grew.

But the personal animosity between them tended to nullify the society's deeper efforts towards grander things. This was very exasperating, and, finally, the Supreme Council took decisive action.

Burr had never said or done anything that could bring him officially under the cognizance of the Order. On the other hand, Hamilton's hatred overmastered his discretion. It carried him off his feet. It made him act and write like a crazy person. Hatred of Burr became a brooding mania with him. He wrote letters that he would never have written if he had been in his proper senses. These letters by devious channels fell into the possession of the Supreme Council and proved, beyond doubt, that Hamilton had deliberately broken his solemn oath and obligation to the most powerful secret society in the world.

This was a heinous offense under the constitution of the Great Iron Order. It was the crime against the spirit of the Ing that is punishable with death. It was a flagrant breach of the fundamental mandates as written on the iron leaves of the Fiery Scroll.

Upon a day appointed, Major General Hamilton and Vice President Aaron Burr were summoned before the Supreme Seven in the darkened council hall then situated in Murray Street. The Seven sat on the raised dais, their faces hidden by red veils and a red robe of thin silk hanging from their shoulders. Each one held a naked sword in his right hand and a burning taper in the left.

After some preliminary ceremonial, the spokesman of the Seven said, "Brothers Aaron Burr and Alexander Hamilton, you have been haled before us that we may officially inquire into the growing scandal of your mutual hostility. But in order that we may do so legitimately, it is essential that one or both of you make a formal complaint. This will put the matter in order before us as High Inquisitors, and then we will proceed to adjudicate according to the ancient laws and customs of the brotherhood.

"Brother Aaron Burr, I command you: upon the sign of Zoam, have you any complaint to make against Brother Alexander Hamilton?"

"I have none," replied Burr with decision, at the same time making the Sign of Zoam.

Now, as he opened his lips to speak, a scarlet light shone mysteriously on his face from above so that all present could see him distinctly while being themselves unseen.

"Brother Alexander Hamilton," said the chief of the Seven, "I command you, upon the Sign of Zoam: have you any complaint to make against Brother Aaron Burr?"

"I have none," replied Hamilton, making the Sign while the red light played upon his pale, drawn features.

"Then I call upon Brother William P. Van Ness to approach the altar," said the red-robed chief.

Judge Van Ness stepped forward, and the light shone upon him, leaving Burr and Hamilton in the shadow.

Van Ness was a tall, burly man, about 40, with a broad, determined chin, high cheek bones, cold, hard grey eyes, an eagle nose and light-colored hair. He was a well-to-do land owner of an old Knickerbocker family.

"Brother Van Ness," said the hidden one, "you are in possession of certain important documents relative to the unfraternal conflict between these two brethren, a conflict that tends to weaken the power and bring scandal and permanent injury upon the fair name and fame of our ancient order. We are now in session to judge between Alexander Hamilton and Aaron Burr, and we call upon you, nay, we command you to now make the accusation. This has already been intimated to you, and you must obey in terms of your obligation to the Order."

To this Van Ness answered, "I comply with the command of the Supreme Council. I formally accuse Brother Alexander Hamilton of maliciously defaming the fair fame and private reputation of a brother.

"I also accuse him of betraying the interests of the Iron Cross in preventing the election of Brother Aaron Burr to the presidency of the United States; and in aiding the elevation of an enemy of the Order to the said presidency.

"And in proof of these, my accusations, I now produce documents undeniably in the handwriting of the accused brother, some of them formally signed by him.

"I also make this accusation purely on my own volition, for the good of the Order and in direct antagonism to the wish of my dearest friend and brother, the vice president, Colonel Aaron Burr, whose desire is to be let alone to fight out his own fight in his own way."

Thereupon, Judge Van Ness handed over to the chief of the Seven a packet of sealed and numbered papers, containing letters and drafts of letters, also legal and financial documents, some of them taken by force from Hamilton's possession by General John Swartwout as previously related. One of these papers contained a fully thought-out and detailed plan for assailing Burr's personal reputation along the scandal lines laid down by Cicero in his defamatory attack on Catiline (the precursor of Cæsar). Another was a letter relating to Burr's private amours and his marriage to Madame Prevost. Another was a circular sent out to distant members of the Cincinnati, of which Hamilton was president general. Another was the copy of a secret treaty between the administration and a foreign ambassador, concerning the policy and activity of the Iron Cross. Twenty-three documents relating to the secret negotiations between Bayard, Morris, Hamilton, and others in connection with the election of Jefferson.

It would now be impolitic to reprint any of these documents and papers in full. The following extracts from one of them (a political letter of Hamilton's) shows the animus sufficiently for the present.

I admit that Jefferson's politics are tinctured by Gallic fanaticism, swelling with fanciful ideas and mind-inebriated dreams, very pleasing, no doubt, to the thoughtless and impecunious. I also acknowledge that he is crafty and persevering in his objects and the founder of the only cult we have any reason to fear....

Neither is he very scrupulous about the means of success nor over mindful of the truth, and though he is a contemptible hypocrite, the populace does not think, so and in this is his strength.

Like a Roman despot of old, the mob delights to be flattered. No praise is too fulsome for it to swallow. Thus, it is deified by its cunning courtiers, who know all the time (in their hearts) that it is a foul and half-insane monster. Thus, its favorites are only those who can complacently sink their own individuality and orate before it the acceptable things that its madness craves for....

Also (like the despots of antiquity), the mob is ever at bottom a murderous beast when its power is equal to its reasonless hate or dread.... Burr, on the other hand (who is Jefferson's only possible rival), is in every way a stronger personality and an abler man, but unlike Jefferson,

his brain is more inclined to action than to philosophiz-
ing. While Jefferson would be slowly evolving a thing in
his mind, Burr would go and do it. Burr is essentially a
man of deeds and therefore the most formidable of the
two radical chiefs. We must therefore "down" him first.

He understands our objects intuitively and has similar but rival objects in his own unbridled brain.... Jefferson, in office, would only exclude us for a period, but if
Burr once obtained authority, it would require an army
to oust him again. With all the perfected enginery of
a centralized government absolutely under his control,
he would be a monarch *de facto* and could give himself whatever majority of votes he required. Although
Washington refused to accept a third term, Burr is one
of those men who would laugh at such a precedent. "I
will make my own precedent," he would say. "Is not
Washington dead?"

Jefferson would perhaps prune our power, but Burr
would tear it up by the roots. In Jefferson, therefore, we
have, I think, an harmless foeman, a stingless creature,
but in Burr we have a pitiless privateer, a merciless man,
who would probably sink us for ever and do it with a
courteous smile and a polite bow and honied words of
commiseration. I assure you, Colonel Burr is a dangerous, a very dangerous, man.

His mind is of the Napoleonic type. He has no reverence for institutions, or musty covenants, and I verily
believe he would not hesitate to wring the necks of our
senators and legislators if they dared to seriously cross
his path when in power.

In private life, he is also as great a libertine and vo-
luptuary as Cataline. The numbers of his amours and
natural children is past belief. But with the conception

of a Cæsar, the brain of a Machiavel, and the resolution of a Cromwell, he is nevertheless always in debt. He is lavish in money, and this is his weak point. He is mortgaged up to his neck. And thus, I believe, it would be easy, by a concerted move, for us to bankrupt him entirely and thus render him comparatively innocuous. A public man, you know without money or credit is like a ship without sails and masts: a mere drifting hulk at the mercy of every storm that blows....

It is imperative, therefore, that Colonel Burr should be defeated. I adjure you to do your utmost in this matter, and I advise the use of every method consistent with success. Promise anything reasonable. If you want money to carry on the campaign more efficiently, you can draw upon Nathan Morris & Co. They will be instructed to honor your drafts on sight.

Burr has not the financial backing that we have, and, therefore, we possess a distinct advantage over him. Money talks. Money talks most eloquently. Money in the right hand gives absolute power. If Burr fails in winning this time, he is insolvent beyond redemption. His sole hope is to get into power and rob the country.

Indeed, far-rolling consequences, including disgrace abroad and ruin at home, are probable fruits of a victory over us by this indefatigable intriguer. He knows altogether too much for our safety. I shrewdly suspect that he has in his possession a certain foreign treaty secret, and, as you know, he is quite capable of using it to obtain both yours and mine. He also knows the true story of the Arnold affair and has always been a partisan of Gates, the Northern general.

Burr is capable of anything. I also suspect that he has somehow got possession of other papers, very important private documents, that were taken from me by a bandit in the winter of 1800, at the muzzle of a gun.

You suggest the formation with him of a secret alliance to offset the growing influence of Jefferson, the Southern cotton planter. That cannot be, however. I am his relentless foe, and I know he is mine, though, openly, we are ever courteous to one another. Indeed, so much do I detest the man that if they cut me up into a thousand pieces, every piece would rise up to war against him. Compromise between us is out of the question. It is war to the end. He must sink me, or I will sink him. And yet, for reasons I cannot well uncover to you, I must not battle against him directly. I must shoot from behind the hedge until an opportunity comes to shoot in the open.

No engagements whatever that could be made with him could be relied upon anyhow. Pretending faithfulness, he would only use us and play with us for the accomplishment of his own vast designs of military conquest and personal aggrandizement....

We can thus neither deceive him nor wheedle him nor obtain him as an ally. He sees all that we see and much more than most of us see. He is a deep student of history and, at the same time, an acute man of affairs with preternatural powers of penetration into motives. His brain is not swayed by any of the current arguments or beliefs. In his heart, he despises all our opinions and ideals and imagines himself looking down upon us from a higher mental viewpoint. And he is too cold-blooded and determined a conspirator to ever change his plan in accordance with any inducement that we could hold out to him. Thus, treaties and compacts with him are impossible.

Such a man is above and beyond all human restraint.

He speaks of public opinion with scorn, sarcasm, and gentle laughter and compares the common people to a herd of cattle or a flock of bleating sheep. You might as well try to bind back the Hudson's rolling tide with a rope of twisted sand as to harness his ambition by paper promises or mere signatures. I assure you, nothing to that man is either sacred or indestructible. I verily believe that if his power was equal to his purpose, he would wreck the world itself rather than submit his own will to the will of another. He will not admit the idea of a superior.

Don't be deluded by his glib popular phrases and his fulsome protestations of purest patriotism. The shibboleths of politics and popular oratory are but words and breath to him. They are a well-practiced part of his procedure of mystification and wizardism, like the incantations of an Indian snake-charmer.

As an illustration of this, I once heard him make use of the following argument at his own table:

"Why should the chief of an invincible army, or other force, when things become grave, hesitate to do his duty? Should it ever be necessary to preserve the sacred rights of property by force of arms, why should I, for example, hesitate if at the head of an army?

"As far as I can see, there is nothing essentially discreditable in being the 'man on horseback' if one has the will and power. I am scarcely vain enough to hope that such shall ever be my destiny; nevertheless, should events come my way and circumstances justify the action, it shall not be said of Aaron Burr that 'he was a weak man, unequal to his opportunity.'"

In short, all Burr's conduct and career indicates that he has in view nothing less than the establishment of supreme power in his own person. He would reform the government *a la* Bonaparte.

And yet it may be well to throw out a lure to him. It might be judicious policy, perhaps, to tempt him to start for the plate and thus lay the foundation for acute dissensions between the two Republican chiefs (Jefferson and himself.)... Then if the worst should happen, arrangements could perhaps be made to shelve him for a period by permitting him to win the consolation prize: the expensive vice presidency....

You speak very enthusiastically about what you call 'the dawning of a new era in human government,' but I think you are mistaken. The 'progress' you speak of is only an illusion, created by our wondrous arrival on a vast new continent of illimitable possibilities and the consequent relief of human pressure within the old. The nature of things is in no way changed. When the world again fills up with its hungry multitudes, the same old drama shall be acted over and over again, line by line, scene by scene, tragedy by tragedy, to the bitter end. The discovery and colonization of America is but an intermezzo....

ALEXANDER HAMILTON

When this packet of papers was given to the chief of the Seven, he opened them on the altar of the Iron Ing, first commanding Burr and Hamilton to retire to an adjoining room, in the nominal custody of the sergeant-at-arms, Judge Pendleton. It was intimated that they would be called in again to hear the judgment.

In the ante room, they bowed haughtily to one another but remained silent, Judge Pendleton sitting between them with the weapon of his office laying across his knees.

As Hamilton sat there and looked across at Burr, he thought to himself:

Again, I am out-generaled. The crisis has come before I expected it. I had thought to have warred him down without being directly implicated. Accursed be my evil luck. How did Van Ness get those infernal papers? They prove my animus beyond doubt. I have written too much, far too much.

But what is worse for me, those documents prove that Burr was truly elected president and that Bayard and I caused Jefferson to be selected. That will surely damn me with the Seven. According to the laws of the Order, I am now a convicted traitor and an enemy of the Iron Cross, punishable with death.

What had I better do? What shall I plead? Shall I be humble and crave for mercy, or shall I be defiant and brazen it out?

They dare not kill me! Me! Alexander Hamilton! Major general! Creator of the Constitution! Washington's favorite secretary! Son-in-law of General Schuyler! President general of the Cincinnati! No! They dare not do it!

Still, again, they might, for this is a very serious thing, a very serious thing. There is more in it than appears on the surface. The election of Jefferson has made me bitter enemies where least expected.

And Burr! O, the cunning one! I have no evidence against him, though he has poisoned my life and baulked my whole career. How I hate him!

In the center of the lodge-hall, a fire burned like unto the fire of a blacksmith.

By its side, blowing a bellows, there stood a man, half naked, with great hairy arms; and he was lame of one foot and grimed with soot, and on his left hand were six fingers.

To the right of him there was an iron anvil, and in his hand, he held an iron hammer.

Outside the glow of the fire, all was gloom. In the darkness, the brethren were chanting an anthem from the Book of the Fiery Scroll, and the refrain of the anthem was

"Forging! Forging! Forging!
And what are you forging there?"

And from time to time, the smith withdrew from the fire a blade of glowing metal and smote it joyfully on the anvil with his hammer.

And the hammer rang:

KLING—KLANG—KLING!
KLING—KLANG—KLING!

With rhythmic swing, the hammer rose and fell, and the sparks hissed and flew, and the unseen brothers sang in the darkness:

"Forging. Forging. Forging.
And what are you forging there?"

Then, from out the circle of gloom, a young man glided into the circle of light. He was beautiful and strong to behold. Power and pride shone from his eyes, and his locks and beard were red like gold. He trod with the step and mien of a conqueror, and looked even like unto a god, and he was robed in stars. And he held out his hand towards the smith, saying, "Give it me."

And the smith again withdrew the hissing blade from the fire and beat it on the iron anvil with the iron hammer. And he sang as he forged:

　　　　　　　　　　　　　　　　　　RIVAL CÆSARS

"Not yet! Not yet! Not yet!"
KLING, KLANG! KLING, KLANG! KLING, KLANG!
"NOT YET!"

Now, around the waist of the young man, there was a broad girdle with a buckle of beryl, and fastened to the girdle, there was a sword-ring (but no sword), and upon the girdle, the word "Biamokul," was written. And again, he stepped forward to the smith, saying, "Give it me."

And the smith went on forging.

And still, from the outer darkness, the unseen brothers sang their anthem chorus:

"Forging! Forging! Forging!
And what are you forging there?"

And the fire glowed; and the bellows creaked; and the sparks leaped; and the hammer rose and fell; and the smith raised his voice and sang as he forged, his hammer beating tune. And the tones of his great voice were very sonorous, like unto the beauty and booming of wrath and thunder.

"My anvil clangs its challenge song;
I shape the scepter of the strong."
KLANG! KLING! KLANG!

"Within my star-born flare and flame,
I weld the blade of power and fame."
KLANG! KLING! KLANG!

"From steel without a blain or flaw,
I hammer out the higher law."
KLANG! KLING! KLANG!

"In white-hot heat I burn the dross.
I forge, I forge, the Iron Cross."
KLANG! KLING! KLANG!

Then for the third time, the young man with the locks of gold stepped forward, saying, "GIVE IT ME." And the smith went on forging.

In about half an hour, the signal came to the sergeant-at-arms. Whereupon he conducted his two "captives" into the council chamber, which was now illuminated by three great lights in the center of the hall, but the Supreme Seven were invisible, hidden behind the dark curtain that hung dawn in folds before the dais.

With the sergeant-at-arms between them, Hamilton and Burr walked silent to the altar, whereon lay the somewhat significant emblems of mortality, and the Cross of Iron.

Then a solemn voice came from beyond the curtain, saying, "Brother Alexander Hamilton. A grievous allegation stands against thee. Thou art charged with doing injury and wrong to a brother and doing it with intent and forethought.

"Thou art also charged with a deliberate breach of your sacred obligation, by aiding and abetting an avowed enemy of the Iron Cross, and its unchangeable principles, into a position of power and authority at the expense of a trustworthy and reliable brother of the blood, in direct contravention of Clause 9A in the Fiery Scroll.

"If convicted upon one or both of those counts, the penalty is extinction, the when, where, and how to be decided after. All this thou already knowest. If, therefore, thou hast anything to say, either in extenuation or rebuttal, now is the time to say it, and we are here to listen. What dost thou plead? Art thou guilty or not guilty?"

"*Guilty*," Hamilton replied with deliberation, thinking to himself, *If I am to die I will die game. The proofs against me are overwhelming. There is no defense. I wrote the letters. I am hopelessly entangled.*

"Have you, or any of your friends, any countercharge to make against Brother Aaron Burr? Every opportunity will be given to clear yourself from this indictment,' said the judge.

"None whatever," answered Hamilton. "He is my foe, but I cannot prove it."

"Brother Burr," said the voice from behind the veil, "are you an enemy of Brother Alexander Hamilton?"

"I am!" answered the vice president.

"Brother Hamilton, are you an enemy of Brother Aaron Burr's?" said the voice.

"I am!" answered the major general.

"The Iron Cross would reconcile ye brethren, if that be possible," spake another voice kindly.

"Vengeance is mine," said the major general.

"And I will repay," said the vice president.

Here a pause occurred in the proceedings while the Seven consulted together behind the veil. Meanwhile, the brethren of the lodge talked to each other in ominous whispers concerning the thrilling climax of the drama, a drama extending over more than a quarter of a century (and with which most of them were more or less familiar).

After a while, the voice again spake, saying, "Brother Alexander Hamilton, hear thy doom."

"I hearken," replied Hamilton quietly. "I am submissive but unafraid."

Then the voice spoke slowly and solemnly while an unseen hammer clanged dolefully on an unseen anvil.

"Alexander Hamilton, extinction is thy portion." *KLANG!*

"Die thou or justice must." *KLANG!* "We proclaim against thee the Heavy Hand." *KLANG!* "We pronounce thy doom." *KLANG!* "Thus, it is willed." *KLANG!* "At high noon within twenty days and twenty-one hours, the Iron Cross demands thy soul. *KLANG!* "Depart on the Sign of Zoam." *KLANG!*

Then another voice came from behind the curtain, saying, with most evident emotion, "To love and be wise is scarcely granted, even to the highest.

A brother then ceremoniously removed the Three Amens and reversed the Iron Sign. Gradually, the lights began to wane, and semi-darkness prevailed. The brethren arose to disperse. Then Hamilton drew himself together and spake in a dazed voice, saying, as he lifted the iron hammer on the altar by his side and smote one blow, "I appeal!"

"To what dost thou appeal?" answered the hidden voice impatiently.

"To trial by combat," said Hamilton in a tone of defiance and challenge.

Then, again, a conference was held behind the veil, while the Three Amens and the Iron Cross were returned to their original position, and the brethren resumed their seats in silence and expectancy. After an interval, the voice spake once more, saying, "Brother Aaron Burr, thou hast heard the appeal made by Brother Alexander Hamilton."

"I have heard."

"Art thou willing to accept the wager of battle?"

"I am," replied the vice president, and he drew himself up haughtily. "Chief does not decline encounter with chief."

"The appeal is granted, but one man must die, and 'may God defend the right,'" spake the voice, and the hammer clanged again on the hidden anvil, three times three.

"His blood be upon his own head," said the major general.

"To fall by the hand of a vice president is not an ignoble

death," retorted Burr.

Again, the lights slowly darkened, except where the vice president stood. Around him played an intense and concentrated ray of luminance from above. Then a man with a scarlet mask hiding his face and his right arm bare to the shoulder came out from behind the veil. In his hand, he bore a belt, and fastened to the belt with an iron ring was a heavy sword blade with a square hilt, about one arm long.

Then a voice came from behind the veil, saying, "Vidi!." Whereupon the man of the naked arm stooped down and buckled the belt and sword around the waist of Aaron Burr while the hammer clanged three, and the voice came from behind the veil, saying, "Gladio Cincturavimus."

Then the brethren arose to disperse, but before doing so, they formed the Iron Ring, singing (hand clasped in hand) these words:

> "The law of laws shall reign—
> Thus it is willed—
> And brother by brother slain
> Till all be fulfilled."

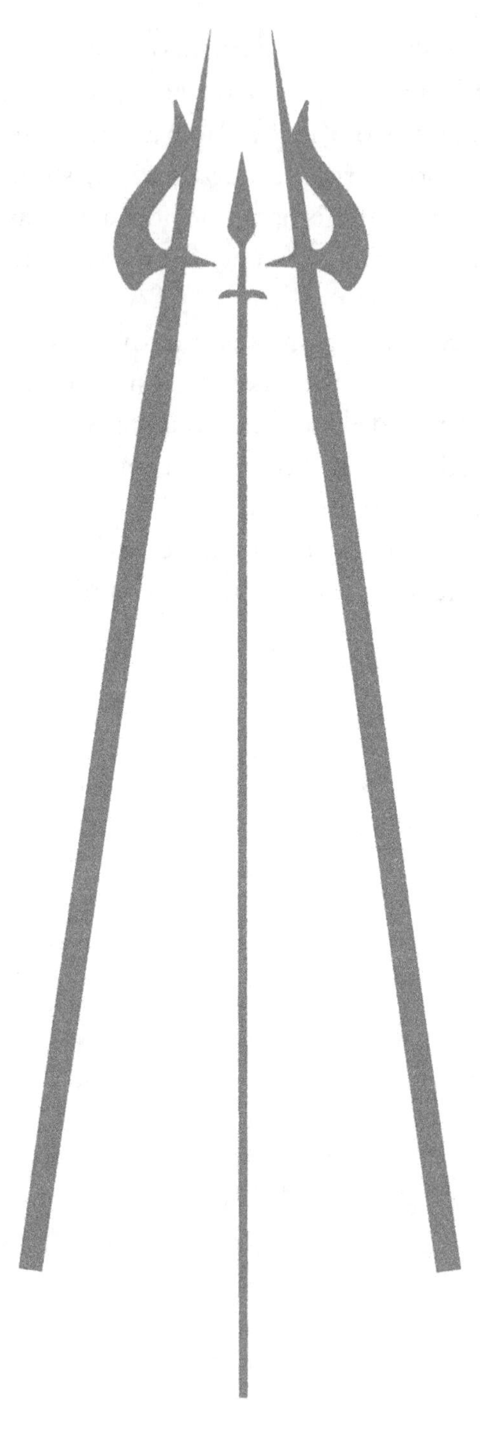

RIVAL CÆSARS

Chapter XVII.

MORTUUM BELLUM

Midnight. The shores of Manhattan Island. Two well-dressed men walked rapidly towards one another through the shimmering summer moonlight. From the south, a soft wind blew.

Between them as they approached lay the moss-covered oaken ribs of an old privateer barque that in other days had been the property of Sir Walter Raleigh, the celebrated Elizabethan buccaneer who founded the first English colony in America. The bones of this tough old ship protruded from the sand, and the dents of Spanish cannonballs were still plainly visible thereon.

The tide was low and everything still, except the dull creak of anchored ships in the harbor, straining at their cables.

The two men were Alexander Hamilton and Aaron Burr, the vice president and the major general.

Once more, those two warring spirits met, the two subtlest lawyers, the two craftiest politicians, the two bravest soldiers, and the two most accomplished gentlemen of the age.

Their names were as familiar in the furthest outlying log hut of the backwoodsman and the pioneer as in the mansions of the rich or in the historic villages and towns along the Atlantic seaboards.

It was the night of the 10th of July 1804.

When within ten feet of one another, each man made a sign with his left hand—the hailing sign of the Iron Cross. Then

297

placing their left hands on their respective breasts, they bowed profoundly.

"E la moot," said Hamilton as he saluted. "Ave morituri."

"E la moot," replied Burr, "Hail, ALL HAIL."

The cold moon shone through the rigging of the great ships lying at anchor, flooding the beach and piers with a soft mellow light that cast long, wavy, ghostly shadows.

The dark, sullen waters of the bay glanced and sparkled as if set with a million dancing stars; and away in the eastward darkness could be heard (every now and then) the sullen thunder and growl of ocean billows crashing against the outer cliffs, while near at hand, the low swish and swirl of the retreating tide sounded musically and mournfully to listening ears, like the menacing hiss of some crouching water dragon waiting for its prey.

It was a strange, weird sight, those two daring, proud, and subtle personalities meeting by the bones of the old pirate ship, on the sands over which the tides have ebbed and flowed for ages "twice every twenty-four hours." How they smiled at one another while the quenchless, accumulated hatred, the brewing of over twenty-five years, was surging within their veins.

"For the last time, we meet face to face, and on the Sign, before I shoot you," said Hamilton in slow, modulated tones, intended to be intimidating.

"For the last time, we meet on the Sign," answered Burr, without a tremor of doubt or hesitation in his voice. "Tomorrow, I 'elevate' your soul."

"We understand," said Hamilton.

"Perfectly," replied Burr.

"The Supreme Seven have commanded this meeting," spake Hamilton inquiringly. "I understand that we are to arrange preliminaries in such way as they decide, so that there may be no hitch and no possibility of anything leaking out."

Burr replied, "As far as I am concerned, all is so arranged. I am commanded that the real cause of your death must never by me be made public, for you are to die, Hamilton. The Iron Cross has decided it, and I have decided it. I have challenged you on that understanding and have so instructed Van Ness. Nevertheless, you shall have all fair play, although you rest under a sentence of death. I am not, nor do I intend to be, an executioner. I meet you in battle, where you may still have a fighting chance for your life. If you kill me, you go free."

To this Hamilton replied, "On my side, all is arranged on the same understanding. This is thoroughly understood by Judge Pendleton, my second. In the eyes of the world, it must remain a political quarrel only. The correspondence leading up to the meeting is absolutely perfect. Both Pendleton and Van Ness are as silent as the stars, and Cheetham has his instructions."

Then after a pause, Burr said, "I would now take this opportunity to ask you, Hamilton, the true genesis of your bitter animosity to me and my career. Why did you go out of your way to dash the cup of success from my lips? What induced you to break the alliance of our youth? Look what both of us have lost by it. I would have an explanation of this mystery from your own lips before death seals them forever."

"Before answering your interrogation," answered Hamilton, as he drew himself up with an assumption of cold hauteur that he did not feel (for the shadow of death was upon him, and he knew it), "I also wish to ask you the very same question. Why did you first become my rival and then my most relentless foe? Did you induce me for a sinister purpose to swear allegiance to you."

"Hamilton! Hamilton! Your mind is seething with suspicions. This is your weakness. You look to the evil side of everything, In this case, I assure you, on my word of honor, that your suspicion is wholly unfounded. I intended to be true to you and was your best friend until you interfered with my military promotion, the very thing I had set my heart upon. Then you insinuated that my wife was a British spy in order to ruin me with Washington. Here is one of the letters you wrote to blast my career. It is marked 'private and confidential' and is addressed to General Washington."

Here Burr handed to Hamilton a copy of the letter printed in Chapter 13, page 227.

Hamilton glanced at the letter in the moonlight, and his face turned green, while Burr continued:

"Now, Hamilton, I am not an angel by any means, nor do I pretend to angel virtues. I am a mortal and possess all an average mortals failings and defects. Therefore, when many years ago I read that infamous letter, I swore in my heart, and by all the gods that have ever lived and died, that I would wash out the stigma thereof in your very heart's blood, and I will do it as sure as my name is Aaron Burr.

"It is over twenty years since that missive was written by your hand and thought out in your brain. During that time, I have vindicated my patriotism, and tomorrow morning, I will revindicate my honor and the memory of my beloved wife, whom you slandered, the best woman and the finest lady I have ever known."

Now, Hamilton was thoroughly astounded at this. It took him completely off his guard, and he actually trembled before the cruel gaze of his foe. He hadn't the slightest suspicion that Burr possessed this long-lost letter. Nevertheless, he put on a bold front, and while his heart thumped against his ribs, he coolly replied, "Very well, sir. Let tomorrow morning decide between us. Weehawken Ledge is a fit place for men to die.

"You ask me the reason of my hatred. If you do not already know, I will tell you. Over a quarter of a century ago, we pledged our honor to each other to aid each other in all things. For years, we kept that sacred pledge, and in consequence thereof, we prospered mightily.

"Over the heads of older and perhaps wiser men, we pushed our way. We sought for fame, and it was ours. We wished for fortune, and money poured upon us. We desired love, and the most beautiful women in the land smiled upon us. Before twenty-one, we were holding high commands in the most remarkable army on Earth. Aye, and successes greater than is ever again possible were within our reach. A nation, an empire, nay, a continent, was ours, absolutely ours.

"Who could have stood against us if we had kept the covenant of our youth? Who? Not Jefferson! He is the weakest man that ever occupied a seat of power in this or in any other land. He is president because of our quarrel, that and that alone. As for the others, they are but men of straw, mere mouthing parrots and mimickers of greatness.

"I might have now been president; you, commander in chief; and Livingston, Clinton, or Roosevelt in the Treasury. All these splendid prospects have been actually thrown away and nullified. Why?"

"Why?"

"A woman came between us. Thus, I learned to hate you, Burr. You took from me the woman I loved, the woman I would have married if you had been true to me. You turned my blood to gall. 'His friendship,' I said, 'is proven by his deeds; words are as the mist of the morning.'

"Thereafter, in addition, you entered into public life as the only dangerous organizer of my antagonists and became the chief conspirator of all those who hate, thwart, and accuse me. The secret work of you and your myrmidons made Jefferson's election a possibility in the Northern states.

"Are you not, therefore, the man who has ruined my prospects as no one else could do? Have you not made life a burden

to me and slew my ambitions? What do I care now for anything?

"Therefore, I long for this meeting between you and me at
the dawn. I have planned for it. I have hoped for it. I wish for it.
One of us must die, even though the Seven had never spake the
word of doom. When defeat comes upon a man, he should die;
then, I say, is the time to die."

"So be it," answered Burr coolly, putting the letter carefully
away in his pocket. "Adam swapped paradise for a sour apple.
Thy will be done.

"Nevertheless, Hamilton, I deny having ever consciously
and deliberately betrayed you. The question of women was never included in the oath of friendship. I am powerless to pro-
hibit women from falling in love with me. They pursue me as a
prey. They tear out my life, as it were. Fate will have it so. Indeed,
women have been both the boon and the bane of my life, and
I have never, positively never, had an amour in which they did
not meet me half way. Under such circumstances he would be
more or less than man who did not sin.

"And you very well know I did not marry until two years
after your own marriage. In fact, even then, it was my wife who
besieged and married me."

"All very plausible, a pretty saying of an evil one," replied
Hamilton with a look of settled malevolence on his broad,
handsome brow. "If you had not been her lover, I could have
had her. You took her from me, I say—you took her from me.
For long years, I have dissimulated my animus to you, but I am
no longer under any necessity to do so. Hear me then: I hate
you, Burr, I hate you with a merciless hatred, and, tomorrow, I
will kill you if I can.

"My mission is ended. Every day proves that this American
world was not made for me. My usefulness is past. My work is
done. My spirit is aweary. My soul is full of bitterness against

men. I feel baffled. I am condemned by the Seven, and I do not care whether I live or die.

"Death! What is death to such as I? How can man die better than in open conflict with a mortal foe?"

To this, the vice president of the United States replied, "Your heartfelt desire shall be granted, Hamilton. It well befits the antagonist of Aaron Burr to die the death of a gentleman. You know what is written on the Brazen Column: 'In blood, man is born. By blood, he lives. Salvation is by blood. Blood bideth men unto one another, so doth it unbind them.' Not for nothing have these words been handed down to us. No, not for nothing."

"The fact is," replied Hamilton, "there is not room enough on this continent to hold you and me. We are too much alike in mental equipment to ever live peacefully together. Brothers though they be, two of a kind can never agree."

"Exactly," answered Burr, "the feuds of brothers are ever the bitterest. If two brothers are determined to ride the same horse, one must ride behind."

Whereupon Hamilton interjected, "I am not the man to ride behind Colonel Burr."

"Nor am I the man to ride in the rear of General Hamilton," replied the vice president.

Both men were silent for a time. Then Burr spoke: "You were made for an ecclesiastic, Hamilton: you are so full of venom."

"You are, I know, a good shot, Colonel Burr, but remember, so am I," answered Hamilton stiffly, as much as to intimate that the interview was ended.

"Now, before we part, Hamilton," said Burr, "there is one more matter I wish to suggest. It is this.

"One of us must die. That is settled. The fight must be *mortuum bellum*. I will do my best to kill you, and you, I know, will do your best to kill me. Perhaps both of us may die.

"Now, it is said man has a soul that lives forever in another life, a life beyond the grave, a life in the stars. The existence of this beyond land is disputed. Some say it is, and some say it is not. Others say that only the souls of some men live and that the great majority of men have no souls, or souls that perish after a brief period.

"The real facts on this matter will be demonstrated to you or me soon. If the legend of the soul is true, one of us shall know it before twenty-four hours. Permit me, therefore, to make this suggestion: Let him who tomorrow dies promise to return, if that be possible, and inform the survivor as to what is beyond and the meaning thereof, if there is any beyond. I propose that we try to solve this mystery, Hamilton."

"To this proposition, Hamilton replied, "I see no objections to your suggestion, Colonel Burr. If I die tomorrow and can return, I pledge you my word to do so. But whether in this world or in the next, my spirit shall eternally war against thine. You and I are adversaries by nature and mayhap for some beyond purpose, some purpose that we cannot now clearly see. We may, at it were, be the incarnation of two necessary and elemental forces, ordained to strive against one another from everlasting to everlasting. Conflict is the highest law of being, as far as can see. It is in everything, from the mote in the sunbeam to the stars in space."

To this, Burr courteously answered, "And should I die and you live, I will return and inform you whether there is or is not an abode of the departed, I am convinced that the imaginations of men cannot leap beyond the real. There may, however, be a basis of substantial truth in this ancient legend. Prehistoric ages may have known more than we do. This the Iron Cross teaches, even in its lower symbolism, and neither you nor I have reached its higher mystery. Perhaps, far off beyond where planets wheel, the starlit ages reel."

"I agree," said Hamilton.

"I agree," said Burr.

"Let us then finish the business we were commanded by the Seven and part of the Sign," said Hamilton.

From behind the shadow of the old pirate hulk, the two men stepped out into the moonlight, facing one another.

Each held his naked sword in his left hand and a paper in the right.

"E la moot," spake Hamilton.

"E la moot," replied Burr.

Each man pushed his sword point through the paper in his right hand. Then both reached out their swords, making the Sign of Zaom and handing over the papers to one another, exactly as they had mutually received them twenty-nine years before. Thus, their oath of friendship was formally annulled.

Thereupon, they bowed profoundly, saying to one another, "It is ended," and, turning about, they walked away in opposite directions, through the lights and shadows along the sands of the shore.

As General Hamilton walked to his handsome town residence at 52 Cedar Street, many and terrible were the thoughts that surged and wheeled through his troubled, far-seeing, and ambitious brain. He thought of his gentle and loving mother in that far off Carribbean isle; of his father; of his half-hidden ancestry; of his youthful years by the flashing Spanish Main; of his arrival in Boston, friendless and alone; of his early struggles and dreams and studies; of his meeting with Burr; of the formation of the secret lodge in Judge Livingston's house; of the war and its deeds of fame and hardship; of the beautiful women who had loved him and the intriguing men who went down before him; of the baseness of politics and law; of his wife and family; of Miss Betsy at her initiation; of the weakness and corruption of man and of mobs; of the fickleness of the feminine; of the Widow Prevost; of the treachery and jealousy of his friends; of the greatness of his hopes and the meagerness of his rewards and achievements. But, ever, his mind returned to that supreme subject: his dreaded foe, the vice president.

If he lives, thought Hamilton, *I might as well shoot myself anyhow. He has vanquished me in politics, and he has conquered me in love. He is a vice president, and I am a discredited politician, curse on that Reynolds business.[1] God forgive me, but shoot him I must. Nevertheless, I will slay him to his face. If he is to die, he shall die looking at me, at me whom he has baffled and broken. And if I kill him, I have nothing to fear. They will not dare indict me for murder, for all the officials in New York are in my grip.*

Wouldn't Jefferson be proud to hear of his death? Ha! If Burr dies, it will be the making of me again. Then I shall only have Jefferson to deal with. Jefferson is easy, but Burr is a hard proposition. Burr is the devil. He knows altogether too much.

Musing thus, he arrived at his home. There he met his wife in the hallway waiting. She was evidently very much agitated. At this period, Mrs. Hamilton was a kindly, matronly woman, the noble mother of a large family of sons and daughters.

"What is the matter?" he said kindly to her as he stroked her hair and kissed her tenderly, soothingly.

"I am filled with a foreboding of evil," she answered. Then she placed in his hand a square piece of planed pine board, upon which strange characters had been scrawled with charcoal in a strong, perfect hand.

He looked at it in astonishment, saying, "It is in the cryptogram of the Iron Cross. Whence came it?"

---

1 ≠ Mrs. Reynolds was a very charming young woman whose husband had been given lucrative employment in the Treasury Department by its then chief, General Hamilton. The "affair" was discovered by Callander (Jefferson's editor) and trumpeted abroad as a sensational scandal, the object being to destroy Hamilton's probable candidature for the presidency in 1800. In explanation, Hamilton published a pamphlet confessing his "wickedness" in humble tones. This very remarkable brochure may be read in any of Hamilton's collected writings. In it, he says, on page 3, "The charge against me is a connection with one James Reynolds, for purposes of improper pecuniary speculation in military pensions. . . . My real crime is an amourous connection with his wife for a considerable time, with his privity and connivance. . . . Reynolds is an obscure and profligate man."

Mrs. Hamilton answered, "Tonight after dark, when sitting by the window in the darkness waiting for you, I saw a strange, veiled woman drive up in a splendid coach with two white horses. She alighted from the carriage, which had muffled wheels, and walked up to our door. Then, with one stroke of the hammer she carried, she nailed this board on the right door post."

Hamilton took the board and walked out into the moonlight. He read the cryptogram line by line, then he read it over again. "It is my own death warrant," he said to himself, "and Burr's too. Are both of us to die? I wonder what it means."

Being interpreted into plain English, thus the message ran:

Thus saith the wise one,
Knowing all things:
Go forth and slay
Slay or be slain.

Violent the world is
All fame is fey:
The slain man shall
The slayer slay.

Hamilton went back into the house and attempted to comfort his wife as best he could, stating that the strange writing only meant a political trick by some of his opponents.

He did not go to bed that night. He felt no desire for sleep. He sat up burning papers and writing letters, and Alexander Hamilton ever wrote with a view to ulterior publicity.

He had a strong and not unreasonable presentment that he was about to die, and this nerved him to write and rewrite much cleverly thought-out, self-vindicatory matter.

Ha! he thought. *If I do die, I will die fighting hard. I will leave written words behind to pursue him with my vengeance and make his future career a waste. I will war against him even in the grave. Aye, "the slain man shall the slayer slay."*

And so, through the small hours, he wrote on and on, ever with a view to prove in after years how he had fought

> ...not because
> Of rancour, spite, or passion
> But only to obey the laws
> Of custom and of fashion.[1]

After concluding his apology for the vote-howling multitude to read in after years, he went out into the morning air and walked up and down (to quieten his nerves) until six o'clock, when he ordered an early cup of coffee and set off to the appointed battle ground, accompanied by his second, Judge Pendelton, and, part of the way, by Bayard of Delaware.

When the vice president parted from Hamilton, he walked rapidly to Water Street, where his coach was waiting for him, and drove home to Richmond Hill. There he found every one in bed but his negro butler (who had once been the property of Carroll, he who signed the Declaration of Independence, the Carroll upon whose property the city and capitol of Washington now stands). The black slave handed to him a piece of board that had been affixed during the afternoon to one of the Avenue trees by a veiled woman who drove up in a carriage drawn by two white stallions.

Burr took the board and carefully deciphered the writing traced upon it. He saw at a glance that it was in the secret cypher

---

1   Maj. John André, "Affair of Honor," originally published in *Rivington's Gazette*, found in Frank Moore, *Songs and Ballads of the American Revolutions* (New York: D. Appleton & Company, 1856) pp. 226–230.

of the Iron Cross. After considerable trouble, he translated it, and thus it read:

> Be thou a proud one
> A strong one faring—
> Naught is ungodlike
> To power and daring.
>
> By the Sign of Iron
> Slay, or be slain:
> It giveth dominion—
> It taketh again.

Burr put it down and began to think. *This is the final command of the Seven,* he thought, *but it is more than that: it is an omen to me, an omen of evil. The Iron Cross is going to cast me aside because of my failure to win the presidency for it. That is what's the matter. And who have I to thank for that? Hamilton. But tomorrow, I will be even with him. Tomorrow, I will kill him, as sure as the sun shines in Heaven. Nothing can deliver that man from my vengeance. Good shot though he be, his hand shall tremble when he looks into my eye. He is not a man of nerve.*

Then he leaned back in his cushioned library chair and half closed his eyes. As a moving panorama, his whole life seemed to pass before him in review, scene by scene.

He saw himself at Princeton, confuting, with a word, the profoundest professors. He saw Margaret Moncrieffe, the never forgotten one; Betsy in all her youthful vivacity and charm; his wife, Theodosia, in the silken turban; Kate; Leonora; Clara; Charlotte; Helen; and dozens more.

He saw the princely Montgomery (Margaret Moncrieffe's uncle) riddled by grapeshot at Quebec, falling back dead into his arms.

He saw himself trudging through the snows, hidden in the Convent of the Three Rivers, or leading his ragged regiment in a hundred fights for home and fatherland, his heart and body full of youthful strength, enthusiasm, and pride, an "Apollo of revolution."

He saw himself hailed and acclaimed by his countrymen as a conquering hero, a chief among many, and a patriot of the noblest resolve.

He saw his beloved wife die in his arms. He saw his little daughter born and saw her married. He saw himself a legislator, a senator, an attorney general, aand, finally, elected to the presidency. Then he himself hurled down, down, down, into almost irretrievable defeat and bankruptcy by the wiliness, craft, and morbid jealousy of the "man and brother" who had once sworn eternal friendship to him who thereafter had stabbed him in the back on every opportunity: the "smiler with the knife beneath his cloak."

Ah, thought Burr. *It is too much for human nature to endure. It is more than an angel of glory could stand. I would be eternally dishonored if I did not lay him out stiff and cold. Doesn't his own editor taunt me with cowardice? Me, Aaron Burr, who has ridden a hundred times into the bloody teeth of death. I must, I will, vindicate my honor at any cost. Blood alone can wash away the stains and slurs he has cast on me and mine. Is not a man's private fame and personal honor his holiest possession? Has Hamilton not assailed me as being everything vile, hoping to gain by my downfall?*

The vice president stood up and looked at himself in the great mirror. He clinched his hands, and he shook them on high, and his eyes shone like burning coals as he spake, or rather hissed, half-aloud, "Hamilton, Hamilton, I shall kill you, aye, even though it ruins me for ever to do it, aye, though I lose all my property, all my popularity, all my fame. This time, it is a fight to a finish. If mine eyes fail me not on the morrow, I will "elevate" your soul to glory—if you have got one.

"Ah, I know it is written in the books 'thou shalt not kill,' but should I obey that unwarrior-like injunction, I am eternally disgraced, and should I not obey it and kill him, I am a ruined man. Either way, it is fatal to me.

"Ruin.

"What is ruin to me? I fear not ruin. I fear nothing. I will dare and do till the last gasp comes When the death gurgle is in the throat of Aaron Burr, then it is time enough for him to surrender. Meantime, the world is wide, I am strong, and Mexico invites. Ah, that's the idea! Let conquest follow the line of least resistance. I will do to Mexico what Wolfe did to Canada.

"Ruin.

"Let ruin come. Let the lightning from on high blast and burn my marrow; let wolves gnaw my entrails and Hell yawn and gape beneath my feet; let the stars hurl themselves from Heaven and engulf me in swirling vortexes of roaring flame, yet will I neither surrender nor retreat.

"No, I will not surrender. I will smite him down. I will slay him as sure as my name is Aaron Burr. I will put the hoarded vengeance of a lifetime into a single pistol shot.

"'Here's a smile for those who love me
And a scowl for those that hate
And whatever sky's above me
Here's a heart for any fate.'"[1]

Then he sat down to the table in his lonely room and wrote to his daughter in South Carolina what he imagined might possibly be his last letter:

My Darling Daughter,
    ...have lately written my will, and in it, I have be-

1   M.V. Dulin (attrib.) "Farewell But Not Forever," found in James Thomson's *The Poems of John Francis Myers* (Bloomington: Press of Frank I. Miller Co., 1911)

queathed all my letters and papers to you. You will take special care of them and see that none of those in the three iron boxes are allowed to be published for three generations. If I die before you then it will devolve upon you to make the necessary arrangements as to this matter. I have no other directions to give you with regard to the contents of the other blue boxes except to burn everything that might by accident injure any person, especially if the person is a woman.

If your husband should think it worthwhile to write a sketch of my life, he will find abundant material in the six blue boxes. My biographer (whomsoever he may be) should endeavor to be impartial and not spare me. I have done good things and bad in my life, as all men have. I do not wish to be painted as an angel but as a man who did the best he could with the material at hand. My enemies will probably paint me as a devil, and, on that account I leave sufficient information to confound them, but I do not wish this information to be used until the time specified has elapsed.

I calculate that by that time, this republic will be firmly established, and no danger can come to it by any revelations left by me. New men will then have arisen, capable, I hope, of viewing the happenings of today in a non-partisan spirit.

Tell my dear Natalie that I have not left her anything for the very good reason that I had nothing to leave. My estate after paying the mortgage due the Manhattan Bank (next year) will just pay my current debts and no more. I mean, if I should die this year.

If live a few years more, it is probable things may be brighter, for land all around New York is rapidly increasing in value.... Give Natalie one of my pictures. There

        Rival Cæsars

are three at Richmond Hill: one by Stewart and two by my protege Vanderlyn. Give her any other little tokens she may desire. One of those paintings I also pray you give to Dr. Eustis; to Bartow, something, whatever you please....

I pray you also—you and your husband—to convey to Peggy, my old slave and housekeeper, the small lot (numbered) which is fourth article mentioned in my list of property. It is worth about $250. Give her also $50 cash as a reward for her fidelity. Dispose of Nancy (a black slave) as you may please. She is honest, robust, good tempered and worth at least $400. Peter, my coachman, is the most intelligent and best-disposed black I have ever known (I mean the darkey boy I bought last fall from Mr. Jefferson). I advise you, by all means, to keep him as a valet to your son. Persuade Peggy to live with you if you can.

I have desired that my wearing apparel be given to Frederick. Give him also a sword or a pair of pistols, but on no account must you part with my military sword, the one I wore when I first met your mother.

You will find a small bundle tied with a red string in the little flat writing case, the one we used with the curricle.[1] It is marked "Putnam." Burn it immediately.

The letters of Charlotte are tied up in a white silk handkerchief. Those of Helen and M. you will find in the blue box numbered "5". You may hand them to Marie yourself or keep them. My letters to Clara and those to Leonora Sansay are in box no. 4. You, and someday your son, may laugh at me as you look over this nonsense, but please remember that all these things were very real to me....

---

1 A "curricle" is a two-wheeled horse drawn carriage.

The papers marked "Presidential Election 1800" are of great importance, and if I die, efforts will undoubtedly be made to get possession of them by my foes, some of whom have the government at their back. Guard these papers with extraordinary care, and beware of all attempts to get them out of your possession. In them are important state secrets and ample vindication of A. B.'s entire career.

The seal of the late General Washington (which you will find in blue box no. 5) was given me by Mr. and Mrs. John Law. You may keep it as a family heirloom.

It just now occurs to me to give poor, dear Frederick Prevost (a stepson) my watch. When you come here, you must send for Frederick and open your whole heart to him....

I leave my "Blackstone" to Judge Van Ness, and "Aristophanes" you will send to Washington Irving.

Mind you, box no. 5 is the important one. No one must open it at any time but you. There are six of those blue boxes which contain my letters and writings and private and public correspondence. The keys of all the other boxes and writing cases are in the till of box no. 5.

The library, maps, pictures, and wines are all articles your husband will need. There is one bundle of papers marked "Mexico" which I specially commend to his careful perusal. Mexico must someday be conquered, and your husband should study those papers. Van Ness and Swartwout, along with you and Alston, are joint executors in my will.

...I have called out General Hamilton and we meet tomorrow morning across on the Jersey shore at seven. Van Ness will give you the result. You know the cause long ago....

The preceding has been written in contemplation of death.... If I should fall, I shall live on in you and your son. I commit to you, and to your husband, all that is most dear to me.

I am indebted to you, my dear Theo, for a very great portion of the happiness which I have enjoyed in this life. You have completely satisfied all that my heart and affections had hoped or even wished. With a little more perseverance, determination, and industry, you will obtain all that my ambition or vanity had fondly imagined might be yours.

Let your son be proud (and have occasion to be proud) that he had such a mother.

Adieu! Adieu! Adieu! Perhaps adieu for evermore.

Aaron Burr
Vice Pres., U. S.

P. S. Your idea of dressing up pieces of ancient mythology in the form of amusing and instructive tales for children is very good. You yourself must write them. You have an excellent talent for writing.

A. B.

Now when Burr finished the above letter, he picked up a parcel of new books just arrived from London. He opened them one by one and curiously glanced through them. One was written by an unknown new author who has since became famous. He opened this book at random and thus read:

It... the duel is a direct appeal to Heaven to uphold the truth and punish falsehood... As great wars test great nations, so duels prove to individual men what they really are... It is part of an ancient Saxon religious rite... According to the oldest Teutonic law, if any man shall say unto another man, "You have not the heart of a man", the other shall reply, "I am a man and as good as you."

Then the two shall meet on the highway and fight with equal weapons till one or the other be beaten or slain; he who saves his life by surrendering shall be deemed the worser man; he who wins the battle shall be deemed the best man and in the right....

The duel is an inheritance of chivalry, and an institution for the preservation of high honor and fair dealing among gentlemen; and should it ever decline, then the honor and respect which one gentleman owes to another, must also decline in proportion.

Abusiveness in words then usurp the place of hard blows and chicken-hearted races count equal with men of the warrior and victorious races....

Thus the man who uses insulting or defamatory language towards another, whether in public or in private, whether written, or printed, or spoken, should be made to fight or withdraw from the society of gentlemen and equals; otherwise a torrent of feminine vituperation and vilification of character and motive must be poured forth on the head of every man who is nobler by nature, or who attempts to be greater in the state than his neighbors. Every man who dares to excel will be assailed with the foulest abuse against which he will have no remedy, except such as would degrade him to the level of his assailant....

The abolition of the duel, therefore, would tend not to elevate but further to corrupt and degrade human intercourse and character... It would make prestige arid power and authority possible to a lower and weaker type of man, and persons whose instincts and natures are entirely base and cowardly would hide their baseness under forms and terms of superior morality without fear of being found out by the supreme test, personal combat—a test that only the best- and bravest-bred men can face with equanimity....

It (the duel) entirely effaces a blow which an insult imprints on the honor or reputation of a man....

Besides being accepted by law and custom for immemorial ages, it is also tacitly approved by scripture, as in the case of the rival champions of opposing tribes, David and Goliath, one of whom slew and decapitated the other with the approval of the Almighty.

The duel is also uncondemned by Luke XI, 21-22, and is upheld and implied in a permanent Fact of the Universe—the unending conflict between Good and Evil, between Darkness and Light, between God and Satan. The decision of battle is unmistakably the decree of heaven.

Furthermore, all through animate nature, in air or land or sea, the battle and the duel are immovable and inexorable institutions. Not for nothing has the instinct towards combat been implanted in the souls of all the superior races of men....

Even St. Thomas Aquinas, the "angelic doctor," approves of the duel in these words:

"It is lawful to kill a man to save one's honor, and a gentleman ought rather to kill than take to flight or receive a blow from a stick."

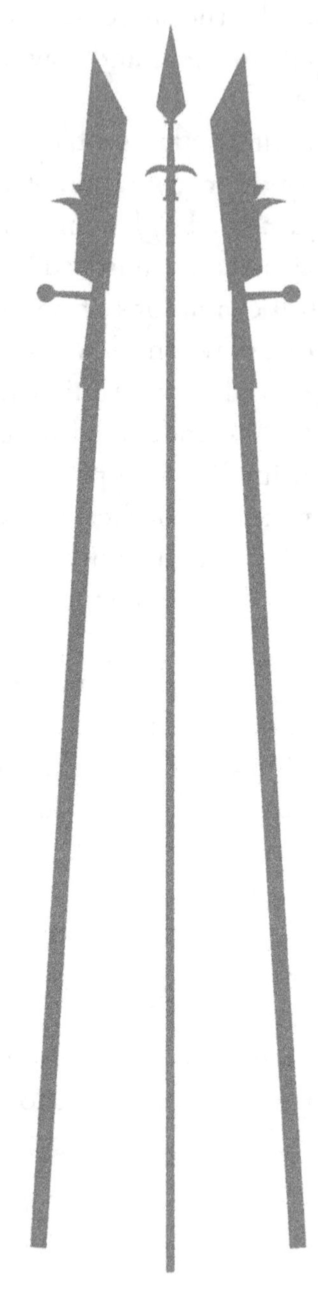

Chapter XVIII.

THE TRIAL BY COMBAT

> *"Verily, verily, it was no child's play*
> *When Sigmund and Ossur met that day."*[1]

"Tell me the story of the fight, Doctor? You were there and must know all about it. You were Hamilton's surgeon."

These words were spoken to Dr. Hosack by John Adams as the two men (old friends) rode away in a closed coach from the burial of Alexander Hamilton.

"If you will give me your word of honor, Adams, never to make any public use of my story, I am willing to tell to you what I saw. You belong to the Iron Cross and so do I. Both of us are, therefore, well aware how Hamilton was sentenced and how the duel was partly in the nature of an execution." Thus spake Dr. Hosack, an old gentleman with grey hair and a pink and white complexion.

"I give you my word," answered John Adams, making a sign. "You saw the duel, Doctor?"

"I did. It took place at Weehawken, over on the Jersey side. We crossed in one of Davis' boats and found Colonel Burr and Van Ness there before us, as per previous arrangement, I believe. With their coats off, they were busy clearing away the thistles and underbrush beneath the cliff on the dueling ground by the overhanging cedar tree.

"Every doctor in town knows the place, with its rough flight of stone steps, its brier and rose bushes, its great mass of thistles, the grey cliff behind, and the rainwashed skull of a dead horse lying in the center. Hundreds of encounters have taken place

---

1 "The Tale of Thrond of Gate: Commonly Called Faereyinga Saga" (Frederick York Powell, translator) (D. Nutt, 1896).

319

there. I have been there in my professional capacity at least a dozen times.

"Hamilton's own son, his first born, was killed on the same spot three years ago in an affair with young Ecker. Curiously enough, he was wounded in exactly the same way as his father, and under very similar circumstances. Ecker was a Burrite to the backbone. He and young Hamilton quarreled over Burr's daughter, the beautiful Theodosia."

"Strange, is it not?" replied the ex-president. "The blood of father and son mingled together in death upon the selfsame spot and over a similar quarrel, for, I believe, women have been at the bottom of all the trouble. Indeed, it is like the climax of some terrible primeval drama."

"Aye, Adams, the Cain and Abel tragedy is an eternal quantity."

"It would seem so, Hosack. The bloodiest tragedies are the wars of brothers."

"The Hamiltons do not seem to be favorites on the field of honor, do they?"

"No. Who won the toss for position, doctor?"

"Hamilton won it."

"Who won the selection of the pistols?"

"Hamilton also."

"Who gave the word?"

"Judge Pendelton. Hamilton's second."

"Who fired first?"

"That is really more than I could honestly affirm."

"It is rumored about town that Burr fired first."

"The rumor is untrue."

"You actually looked on the fight?"

"I did. I climbed up the rocks from the water side and watched it through the bushes."

"How were they placed?"

"Hamilton stood up hill with his back to the cliff and his

RIVAL CÆSARS

face to the city. Burr stood with his back to the river, his right foot poised on the bent-over stump of a huge Scotch thistle, for the rocky ledge is by no means level. Alongside of him was a wild rose bush in bloom. His own cheeks were red as the roses."

"What happened when the word was given?"

"Both shots rang out together, and before the powder smoke cleared away, Hamilton rose convulsively on his toes and sank down in a heap, the blood gushing from his side."

"What then?"

"Burr threw down his pistol, stepped towards Hamilton, and said, 'E la moot!'"

"It was dramatic!"

"Very. Hamilton turned on his elbow in the long grass and hissed back at Burr the penal word but only got as far as 'E La—
—' when he fell back in a dead swoon. I was by his side almost immediately, while Judge Van Ness hurried Burr down to the boat behind an umbrella to prevent any possibility of legal identification as to the shooting."

"Pendleton asserts that Burr fired first, and Van Ness swears that Hamilton fired first," queried John Adams. "Now, who do you think is really right?"

"Neither," replied the doctor decisively. "It's all politics with them. No mortal man could ever tell who fired first. The pistols cracked together, I tell you, and were smoking at the same instant of time. It does not really matter anyhow, as no shot was fired until the word was given. When the word is given, each man must then use his own judgment, 'whether he fires quick or slow."

"Did they have any advantage over each other in other ways?"

"If anything, Hamilton had the advantage. He selected the position where he stood, and his second had the choice of weapons and the giving of the signal. Broadly speaking, they were placed on an absolutely equal footing."

"Where was Hamilton hit?"

"Just under the heart. The bullet lodged in his backbone. An inch higher and it would have been instant death for him, but he lingered thirty-six hours."

"The vice president is said to be a crack shot?"

"So, also, is Hamilton."

"True. Both are old military men, well accustomed to the taking and giving of blows."

"Yes. To my knowledge, they have slain many men in their time. Both have been well accustomed to the use of firearms."

"Aye, that is so, now that I remember. Hamilton challenged Monroe, and he also acted as second in the duel between Laurens and General Charles Lee."

"Yes, and Burr has fought repeatedly on the same spot. In the war, he is said to have made a reputation as a man who never pulled a trigger without bringing down his man. He has splendid nerve."

"I've heard he and Hamilton were early friends and often acted as seconds to each other."

"That is perfectly true. Four years ago, Burr was wounded in the shoulder by Hamilton's brother-in-law, John Church, he who married the other Miss Schuyler. Indeed, there is scarcely a famous public man on either side of the Atlantic who has not killed his man."

"Now, Doctor, do you think, on your word of honor, that it was a fair fight? I particularly want to know that."

"I do. If I am any judge, and I have seen dozens of duels, there never was a fairer fight. Duels are in my line, you see," replied the man of probe and lancet, smiling grimly. "I've dug chunks of lead out of many famous statesmen, but, of course, I must hold my tongue."

"When they met, what was their demeanor?"

"It was that of perfect gentlemen. All the arrangements were fair and above board. The two seconds are men of unimpeachable integrity. The combat was conducted in all good faith. No doubt of that."

"How did they face one another?"

"Splendidly. Each man drew himself up to his full height, pistol in hand, and the half-suppressed fires of long-pent-up hate shone from their eyes. Yet they were cool. Ah, it was really a superb drama! I shall never forget it."

"They were ceremonious?"

"Very, but as hard as iron. One could see they meant business. There was death in their glances. They saluted, but their salutes were that of men about to slay. My breath came and went with excitement. I felt it was to be a tragedy,"

"Aye," said the ex-president. "It was the final act in a long-adjourned suit."

"You are right, Adams. Now begin to perceive the true meaning of this battle and its significance. It was a real trial by combat, and who dares to say for certainty that the verdict was wrong? The fates may know more than we. Anyhow, against their decision, no appeal can hold. Men may come and men may go, but the commands of fate are final"

"You are right, Doctor. There is more in it than our petty present-day moralists can conceive. But aside from that, it will go down to posterity as one of the most picturesque and romantic events in our history, a history positively bristling with battles and bloody encounters. The epic of those two, properly told some day, will crown our age with a halo of eternal grandeur. It is a theme worthy of the highest Homeric genius."

"You say rightly, Mr. Adams. The story, if truthfully related, outshines the wildest Arthurian romance. Two chiefs warring for a kingdom on the banks of that lordly river; two kings of men in mortal combat, fighting for a republic; one destroying the other while half the people rage and the other half weep. It is a tragic, beautiful tale, full of human nature, yet so true, so profoundly terrible, and so full of merciless meaning."

"But," replied the doctor, "I am afraid that the inburning motives of the two combatants can never become properly known. There are too many interested in suppressing the hidden story. I assure you, Adams, there was a Helen in this as well as in the tale of Troy, nay, perhaps half a dozen Helens. It was the 'eternal feminine' that embittered the strife. Verily, the flash of a woman's eye is deadlier than the flash of steel."

"I am assured of that, Doctor. What great thing ever happens without a woman being mixed up therein?"

> "'While man possesses heart and eyes
> Woman's empire never dies.'"[1]

"The struggle for the possession of women is the initial impulse that shakes the world. The truth of history is hidden in romance. I've not lived all these exciting years without perceiving that," replied the ex-president meditatively.

"I see you guess what I mean, Adams. One woman can weave more tangles in an hour than seven men can untangle in seven and seventy years."

"Yes, the web that women weave is woven with a bloody shuttle. They have slain more men with a flirting smile than all the swords and cannons ever forged. What wars have been waged, what duels fought for love of women?"

"You have heard how the hatred between Hamilton and Burr first began."

"Yes, the story of their early estrangement is known to a few of us in the higher degree of the Iron Cross. Their political disputes but disguise a fierce personal animus originating in love-jealousies. Both men, however, have been somewhat re-

---

1   Thomas Moore, "Aspasia," *Thomas Moore's Complete Poetical Works* (New York: T. Y. Crowell & Company, 1895).

served on that point. I suspect they know more of each other's private history than the public is ever likely to hear. They were both famous for their gallantries, and Burr was, without doubt, the more handsome and dashing and successful of the two. Men feared him and women idolized him; aye, many a beauty he turned to poison in the denial."

"You know Charlotte?" said Doctor Hosack.

"She of the tigress beauty, she who nearly drove little Madison off his head. I understand she brought the vice president some of those compromising letters that once belonged to Andre. She is now all the rage; a destructive type of beauty; a superb animal; a veritable Circe; a clasping sorceress."

"Yes, I've often seen her. She is said to be in the employ of Bonaparte. Without doubt, she is a lovely, a superb, creature."

"Well, she set her nets to catch Burr and worm secrets of state out of him, and instead of that, he wormed them out of her. Then Hamilton fell frantically in love with her, and she fell as desperately in love with the vice president. That tells the whole story. But that is only one "affair," the latest, in which they have crossed each other. The fact is, their loves and hates and ambitions are inextricably woven together into a subtle web of destiny and intrigue of the most marvellous complications."

"What do you think will be the upshot, Doctor?"

"I should rather ask that from you. You know the moves and men on the political chessboard better than I do. What do you think?"

"It will ruin Burr and the Burrites; it will disintegrate the Hamiltonians and give Jefferson a free hand. Burr's bullet has made Jefferson dictator. Our two greatest men in the North have destroyed each other. That is really what it amounts to," answered John Adams in a tone of sorrow and regret. "Burr must fly while the worms eat Hamilton."

"Which of them do you think the greatest man?'

"Both were great, each in his own way. In my opinion, however, they obtained success too early and too easy. It is bad for young men to win great power without a hard, a very hard struggle. Early strife and early defeat is the grindstone against which the perfect blade is ground to a lasting edge."

"But you have not answered my question, Mr. Adams."

"Their greatness is purely a matter of opinion. It depends on the point of view. Sometimes, I think Burr is the greatest mind of the two; sometimes, Hamilton. Hamilton did not have the wide grasp of things that Burr had. Burr believed in the man, Hamilton in the state. However, we live too near to the scene of action to be good judges. A century or two hence, these two men will be better understood. In my own mind, I've compared Hamilton to Cicero and Burr to Cæsar without the legions. Hamilton was the greatest organist that ever played upon a caucus, and Burr is one of those strange, all-penetrative beings who, without effort, see into the minds and real motives of men at a glance.

"Both men were somehow born out of their time. You know, Doctor, we are still but a swarm of colonists settled on the shore of a boundless continent. There is little opportunity here as yet for the display of such genius as both Hamilton and Burr possessed in a superlative degree. By and by, however, when this land seethes and roars with an ocean of humanity, the spirits of those combatants shall return to renew their conflict in thought and in deed. Certainly, neither of them shall ever be forgotten. It is always the unfortunate heroes whose memory brands itself indelibly on the popular mind."

"You believe in the resurrection of the dead?'"

"I do. I believe in the resurrection of some of the dead. The great-of-thought shall be born again."

"You are a prophet?"

"But if the great are to be born again, their opponents must also he born again. Else, without struggle, the world would be very tame and dreary. A nation of perfect saints would be a sad thing. My prophetic instinct cannot presume to enter into details."

"How about the republic?"

"The republic is an experiment but will serve its purpose. It fills up an interlude in the world drama. Much remains to be solved. When its usefulness and necessity is past, it will perish, to be resurrected again in some other age. No human institution is eternal. Even the very gods die."

"That is Burr's idea."

"I was not aware of it."

"What do you think Burr wilt now do?"

"I think he will go West. For years, I know he has secretly been maturing a scheme for the conquest of Mexico, or at least of that part of it known as Texas or the Red River Valley."

"That reminds me of what I heard him say when leaving the dueling grounds with his second. The words were, 'I'm a ruined man, Van Ness. Now for Mexico and a new start.'"

"Now that you speak of it, I also remember a remark he made once at Richmond Hill. There was a grand dinner party. Talleyrand and Volney were there.

"'If I were president,' said Burr, 'I would, without hesitation, annex Mexico, Florida, Cuba, and Louisiana by force of arms. Those territories are veritable gold mines, and sooner or later, we must have them anyhow. It is unreasonable to permit such valuable properties to remain uselessly in the possession of unproductive half-breeds.'"

"Ha! Ha! What did the famous French visitors say to that?"

"Talleyrand smiled approval in a complacent, Mephistophelian way, while his small fiery eyes burned with suppressed animation, but Volney, who is, as you know, a great humanitarian, seemed to be utterly shocked at Burr's open avowal of high-handed designs."

"Tell me what Volney said. That conversation must have been highly diverting. You must have enjoyed it"

"So I did. Volney shrugged his shoulders and entered into a voluble argument, which just amounted to this: that wars of conquest were 'wrong in nature,' against the 'principles of the rights of man,' the 'consent of the governed,' etc., etc. Also that every people were entitled to hold a share in the land of their birth without fear of invasion or molestation."[1]

"What did Burr say to that?"

"He answered, smilingly, that the strongest people, simply because of their strength, were naturally entitled to act as they thought proper for their own advantage, establishing, as a matter of course, their own conception of right and wrong, wholly without reference to the desires of feeble and inferior human tribes. He also urged that wars were not wrong in nature but right, necessary, and proper and that the 'consent of the governed' was only a rhetorical fancy, a figure of speech. He finished by stating that the American nation existed today as the result of successful invasion and conquest.

"Then Talleyrand broke into the conversation, saying, in his most seductive tones, 'I agree with the vice president. All nations at all times are open to conquest and reconquest. There is no possible limit to the action of powerful living men and nothing absolutely eternal in territorial title. You know what has been written:

"'The land is the land of the strongest hand
That can lead its legions through.'"[2]

"'This world is tilting ground for mighty individuals and mighty races of men to strive and triumph, reign and possess— if they can. The "consent of the governed" theory of Rousseau and Locke and Franklin is naught but a myth of the mind, and

---

1 ≠   Count Volney. Celebrated author of *The Ruins of Empires*.
2   John Renton Denning "A Rime of the Nations", *Indian Echoes* (London: Blackie, 1905).

there is no finality in anything.'"

"How did Burr take that? Prince Talleyrand was surpassing him in boldness of thought and clearly hinting at Napoleon's ability to protect Mexico and New Orleans."

"Burr replied thus: 'Monsieur. What you say, though somewhat unpopular, is perfectly correct. The world, and all that's in it, is still to the bravest and best. The fate of society is not in any theory or document but in the spirit and deeds of its kingliest members. In lack of strength to do things is the whole of evil. Institutions perish on the advent of a man, and that man passes in his turn when a stranger comes up against him, as you say, my dear prince, there is no finality.'"

"Ah," said Dr. Hosack, rubbing his hands together in evident enjoyment. "Talleyrand received a deadly thrust there."

"But do you know, doctor, I sometimes think Burr's philosophy true."

"It is true, Adams. There is no doubt that it is true. Who can look around upon the world as it is and deny it? The conqueror and the conquered are literally terms of natural history. Conquest goes on today by brain and sword, even as it did when Joshua rode into Carman and Cortez seized Mexico. It makes me weep to think so, but the fact itself is undeniable. Vae Victus is God's law."

"Burr is a most extraordinary man," said John Adams with decision. "He is not appreciated at his true worth. Such men seldom are. It requires greatness of mind to appreciate greatness of mind. In an Homeric age, he would have been in his element. His amours, in my opinion, have been his ruination. It is truly surprising how any individual could become so eminent as a soldier, as a statesman, as a professional man, who devoted so much time to the other sex as is devoted by Colonel Burr. They seem to absorb his whole thoughts. He is far too fond of the 'eternal feminine' to become a truly great man."

"I doubt your conclusion." replied Dr. Hosack. "My experience as a physician is that a great man must possess powerful physical motive force. It requires a powerful constitution to nourish a really powerful mind, and a powerful constitution is ever strongly excited by the female.

"Renowned personalities have always been remarkable for their somewhat unconventional love romances. Their overpowering amative instincts find vent somehow. The motor and combative spirit are generally united. Henry the VIII and King Solomon are eternal types."

"Perhaps you are right, Doctor. I had not thought of it in that light before. Certainly, the scandals now being hurled against Burr have been hurled at nearly all the mightiest personalities of ancient and modern times. When a public man cannot be 'downed' in any other manner, it is usual for his opponents to frantically proclaim his sexual weaknesses, if he has any, or invent them if he has them not. All men who would rise to prominence must expect to be thus assailed. None of us are entirely free from the power of the passions, none, but when a man attains high position, then a million eyes are forever on the watch to detect his slightest failing. None of us are 'perfect saints,' and the least saintlike of all may be the very man intended to become the leader in tremendous events, like unto David or Peter the Great or Julius Cæsar or Martin Luther or Mahomet."

"Has Burr ever expressed his religious views in your hearing?"

"Never. But hold! I heard him once say, 'Honor is the religion of a gentleman.' Do you know what he believes?"

"No. He is always very reserved on that point However, he has a profound contempt for the common ruck of mankind and their half-informed opinions. Nevertheless, I once heard him say incidentally, 'To make Government effectual, there must be a religion.' The remark struck me very forcibly, and I've never forgotten it. It contains volumes."

Chapter XIX

"O TRAGIC SHORES OF WEEHAWKEN"

"The clouds. The dark clouds round him sweep.
The dim waves o'er him roll.
His bones are dropped into red earth:
Is that his final goal?"

"But see! the well-plumed hearse comes nodding on,
Stately and slow and properly attended."[1]

Ninety degrees in the shade. In the suffocating heat, the Great City, sweltered. Solid banks of bare-headed men, women, and children lined the torrid streets. Perspiration oozed from the pores of eager multitudes. Dust storms whirled. The wind moaned and blew as from the belly of a furnace. A muggy, oppressive haze hung over the island city, the city of Manhattan.[2]

BOOM!

It was the roar of a solitary cannon shot.

A minute passed.

BOOM!

Another report rolled and reverberated and echoed over the housetops and over the bay.

Another minute elapsed.

BOOM!

The minute guns were sounding.

It was a funeral, the artillery salute for a dead general, a founder of government. A great soldier, a great statesman, lay stiff and cold. The breath of life (that mysterious thing) had passed from him, and the nation wrung its hands and wept.

---

1   Robert Blair *The Grave: A Poem* (New York: A.L. Dick, 1847).

2 ≠   The Indian name for New York. It means "the place-of-the-getting-drunk." Its original native owners have all been killed off and rooted out.

Temple bells tolled plaintively. Bugles sounded dolefully. Fifes and muffled drums played the long, slow, sad wail, the wail of the warrior, the soldier's last tattoo.

BOOM!

The mortal remains of a nation-builder, a mighty chieftain, was passing to the sacred enclosure, the place of the dead. Grief burned into every soul. Sorrow and inconsolable desolation was in every heart. A republic sorrowed for its kingliest citizen. Sadly, they bore to the sepulchre the bones of the valiant doer of things: a hero, a warrior, a conqueror, a man among men, who had fallen.

BOOM!

Half-mast high, above the city and above the ships, the draped flags, the flags of soldier and sea king, drooped and flapped and fluttered. From frigates (streaked with the shot of Aboukir), the cannon of Napoleon saluted. The war ships of the Pirate Islanders, joined in the yell of sorrow. The battleships of the young republic added their angry growl. Across the bay from Jersey and Brooklyn answered the snarling guns.

BOOM!

Cavalry! Squadron after squadron swept by, the horses curvetting proudly under the tightened rein, impatient. Artillery! The regiment of the dead commander followed in uniform of green and gold, on their caps the "skull and crossbones" over that immortal and suggestive motto "Victory or death." The guns of the regiment, covered with black velvet and hidden by flowers, are driven by grizzled men in slouch hats, veterans of battle, well ploughed with scars. Slowly, slowly, slowly, the engines of power and death rumbled over the cobble stories.

BOOM!

Then came the citizens, the merchants, the bankers, the great importers, the officials and aldermen of the city. On foot and on horseback, they came, interminable, solemn, all dressed in black, crape on their hat bands, heads bowed in the dust, sympathetic, fearful in the presence of death, the grim shadow they had been taught to dread. Their hearts shook. *In the midst of life, we are in death*, they were thinking. Over all, the burning sun glared down like a ball of blazing brass.

BOOM!

On they came, the mourners, thousands and thousands of them. Members of the state legislature, members of Congress, senators, governors of states, ambassadors from afar, ward politicians, patriots of the press, Cæsars of the caucus, judges, priests, ministers, rabbis, barristers, surgeons, sailors from the fleet, men of great renown, men of no renown, brethren of the Iron Cross, the Supreme Seven: all were there to pay their last respects to the distinguished fighting man, the dead warrior.

BOOM!

Then came the powerful secret societies: the Order of the Cincinnati; the Knights of the Wild Rose; the Order of St. Tamanend from Columbia Hall; the Society of Mechanics; the Ancient Free and Accepted Masons; the Brotherhood of Saint Andrew; the Brothers of the Black Chapter; the Knights of the Red Cross; and the students of Columbia college (where the dead man began his career).

BOOM!

Six sable horses (with nodding black plumes) drew the hearse, a gun carriage from Monmouth; the coffin was wrapped in a shot-ripped battle banner, the banner of azure blue and scarlet red gemmed by silver stars. Then moved by the dead general's favorite charger, saddled and bridled, led by two slaves dressed in white.

BOOM!

The casket! Ah! In there lay all that was left of Colonel Aaron Burr's mortal foe. From off that small, shiny, silver plate, let us, for one moment, draw back the folds of the enwrapping starry standard. What do we read thereon? (Ah! What secrets in that coffin lie hid?)

ALEXANDER HAMILTON.
Major General, United States Army,
Born: Danish Island of Nevis, West Indies, Jan. 11,1757
Died: New York City, July 12, 1804.

BOOM!

Open coaches crowded with personal friends of the great constitution-builder pass by. Then a closed carriage from which, ever and anon, ebbed and flowed the sobs and laments of women. The widow of the stricken one, the warm-hearted heroine of the Iron Cross, sat in there, her head (streaked with grey) buried in her hands in a state of nervous collapse and mental desolation. Her heart swelled with tribulation, and with mingled memories, her soul was overflowing. Ah, the tears of women are water, but the tears of men are clots of blood, for man must fight and women must weep till Earth has ceased its rolling.

BOOM!

More carriages. More horsemen. More soldiers. (Burr's old regiment is there.) More clubs and societies. More bands and drums and trumpets. More glittering uniforms and reversed muskets. Behind closed doors and windows stood the wives and daughters of the city, their tears falling in sympathetic rain. "What could he hope in other years, if longest life had crowned him, than thus to die, with a nation's tears and a world's applause around him?"

BOOM!

It was an elegant mansion! It stood at the intersection of Broadway and a lesser street. In the front parlor, gazing out upon the funeral, sat the gay and fashionable young widow, jewels gleamed around her neck. By her side sat the slayer of the

                                    RIVAL CÆSARS

major general. She was a glorious woman to behold, with great, orb-like brown eyes and a lithe, undulating, voluptuous form. It was she of the "tigress beauty."

BOOM!

"Aaron," she said bewitchingly, caressingly laying her jeweled hand upon his arm and looking tenderly into his great black eyes, "aren't you sorry for him? Poor, dear Hamilton. And he loved me so."

"Charlotte," replied the middle-aged widower, stroking her head with its wavy mass of bright auburn hair that gleamed like showers of newly minted gold in a stray sunbeam that came through the shutters, "in life, he was my mortal foe. All the injury, public and private, man could do unto man, he did unto me. Why, then, should I be sorry?"

BOOM!

"O, Aaron dear, how hard you are and yet how kind to me!" and a tear arose in the corner of her big oriental eyes. Then she wound her arms around his neck and kissed him passionately as the wail of the dead march sounded faint in the distance.

"Charlotte, you mistake me," he replied. "You do not understand that men are made to strive and must not hope to live forever. I am not hard; I am only frank. My worst enemy I have slain, but I've slain him like a gentleman. I met him on the level. I smote him on the square. I gave blow for blow. I did not seek to stab him in the back. No! I fought him without subterfuge and without fear. He was in all things my match. I fought him fairly, face to face, weapon to weapon, and I am neither sorry nor repentant."

Thereupon he put his left arm around her yielding waist, wiped the tears from her eye, and kissed her again and again behind the closed blinds as the dirge of the piercing flutes and muffled drums went wailing by.

BOOM!

Two superb warriors were they, two hurtling egos, two great elemental powers personified, two rival theories of empire. Armed, they stood and calmly gazed into one another's souls at ten paces. How grand, how splendid they looked, those two bold, strong men, each with weapon in hand, haughty, terrible, world-defiant, appealing to eternal nature's iron code. "Where the white skull bone of the dead horse lay, two brothers fought at dawn of day, 'neath the cedar tree that swayed above, they strove and bled for power and love."

BOOM!

Before the draped porch of the gray, old, ivied temple—the temple of the Prince of Peace—the hearse halted. From the square tower (wherein a bell tolls) of the temple floated and flapped fitfully a banner of the lord of war. Upon the shoulders of the living, the coffin of the dead was slowly, reverently raised and borne into the holy hall. By the altar of the crucified Jew, on the great black catafalque in the center aisle, it was rested between two columns and under a shilling arch of sabers, the sabers of the Cincinnati and the Iron Cross. ("Blessed are the departed who in the Lord are sleeping, henceforth and forevermore.")

BOOM!

Over aisle and altar flowed the soft, magic luminosity, the mystic, hypnotic light, the light that comes through painted saints. Into the farthest corner of the vast temple (like a black tide) flows the human multitude, feeling itself as it were, on enchanted ground. Not every day did they entomb one who lived grandly, who loved grandly, who fought grandly, and who *died* grandly. Verily, few and full of wonder are the deaths and births of the great of soul.

BOOM!

All heads were bowed low. By the altar of the god stood the high priest, that mystic book, the ritual of the dead, in his two hands. A venerable, a benign, a sanctified-looking man was he, a good, benevolent man. With the white robe of his office hanging gracefully from his shoulders he bended silently and invoked his god. Then he stepped slowly towards the black box that contained the bones of the mighty dead.

"I am the resurrection and the life: he that believeth in me, though he were dead, yet shall he live."

BOOM!

The high priest intoned the ancient ritual and retired to the holy altar. He straightened himself up; he spoke; he orated; the spirit of the higher law was upon him. He was an orator of

surpassing power over the minds of men. Words flowed from his mouth in an enchanting stream. His voice was solemn, deep, doleful, even as the voice of some magic organ moaning over mountain tops. It was the voice of the masterful preacher, searching into every listening heart. It rolled and echoed through pillar and dome. He was an eloquent man, a binder of the mighty spell, a divine harper; a harper of the soul. Gradually, his beautiful voice grew louder; it was a hypnotic voice, resonant and beautiful, like the funeral bells that tolled aloft in the steeple.

BOOM!

One hand rested on the holy volume that lay on the altar before him, the volume bound in purple and gold. With the other hand, he pointed to the coffin then away through the walls, towards the Hoboken shore. (To memory another scene arises: "Friends, Romans, countrymen, I come to bury Cæsar; not to praise him.")

BOOM!

Hark! Hear the words of the famous preacher, he of the silver tongue: "Oh, tragic shores of Weehawken! Crimsoned art thou with the heart's blood of our most lustrous citizen. How can I gaze upon thy woody heights without tears and pain?"

Then raising his eyes to the ceiling and lifting up his voice, he continued: "O, strife, strife, why dost thou persist in this world? Why, O God, cometh not the time when wars shall cease and sadness and slavery be no more?"

BOOM!

"O, God of mercy, love, and peace, why dost thou permit the ferocity of man? Why, O Lord, doth the bloody man triumph and the godly perish upon thine altars? Can it be true, O Power Eternal and Immortal, that thou art neither merciful nor just?"

Then turning to the multitude of mourners, he said (while, minute by minute, the rhythmic roar of the death guns continued to punctuate his oration), "We must calm our agitation before the throne of the Most High, while we weep over the bier of our unequalled citizen, who is no more, him whom the remorseless, ungodly duel has suddenly removed from our midst.

"Words cannot express the hatred with which I regard that word, 'duel,' that infamous, that unholy word, that ungodly word. Yet cruel and absurd as the practice of dueling is, it has, strange to say, its advocates among the highest in the land. "Had not a preponderance of opinion been in favor of it, never, O lamentable Hamilton, wou'd thou hadst fallen in the midst of thy days before thou hadst reached the zenith of thy fame, thy glory, and thy power.

"Oh, that possessed the talent of eulogy, that I might be permitted to indulge the tenderness of friendship in paying the last tribute to thy majestic, thy immaculate memory.

"Oh, that I were capable of placing this magnanimous, this noble, this heroic, this disinterested man before you! Could I do this, I would furnish you with an argument, the most practical, the most plain, the most convincing—except that drawn from the mandate of God, 'Thou shalt not'—that was ever furnished against dueling, that horrid practice which, in an awful moment, has robbed our country and the sorrowing world of such exalted worth.

"I know he had failings. I see in the picture of his life—a picture rendered awful by greatness and luminous by virtue and honor—some dark shades. On these, let the pity of Heaven, the pity that shelters human weakness, fall; on these, let the veil that covers human frailty rest.

"As a hero, as a patriot, as a warrior, as a statesman, he lived nobly. Would to God he as nobly fell....

"It was a moment in which his great wisdom forsook him, a moment in which Hamilton was not himself. He yielded to the force of imperial custom, and, yielding, he sacrificed a life in which all had an interest, and he lost.... In all coming years, I shall seek to fathom the enormity and the wickedness of that crime.... For this act, because he was penitent, I forgive him. But there are those whom I cannot forgive. I mean not his antagonist, over whose erring steps, if there be tears in Heaven, a pious mother looks down and weeps....

"Far from attempting to excite your emotions, I must here repress my own; yet I fear, instead of the language of a public orator, you will hear only the lamentations of a bewailing friend. But I will struggle with my bursting heart to portray the heroic spirit that has flown to the mansions of bliss, while admonishing the bloody custom and the vengeful spirit that sent him there....

"If the vice president of the United States is capable of feeling, he suffers already all that humanity can suffer, and wherever he may fly, he will suffer with the poignant recollection of having taken the life of one whose unsullied integrity is known to the world, of one who was too magnanimous in return to attempt his own. Had he but known this, it might have paralyzed his arm while it pointed at so incorruptible a bosom the instrument of death.

"Does the vice president know this now? ... If his heart be

not adamant, it must soften; if it be not ice, it must melt.... Ah, my brethren, my brethren, was that shot fired at he who sleeps in that cold coffin or at our war-born republican institution? ... Stained with blood as the vice president is, if he be penitent, I forgive him; if he be not penitential and humble before those altars (before which all of us are suppliants), then I wish not to excite your vengeance but rather, on behalf of an object rendered wretched and pitiable by crime, to awaken your prayers when flames of the pit engulf and roll over his soul forever and the world vanishes from his sight."

BOOM!

Meanwhile from out the North, a thundercloud swept down. The sky became obscured, and great drops of rain (like unto tears) began to fall, though the stifling heat remained.

Then (while the drums and trumpets and guns and bells still sounded) four brethren of the Iron Cross lifted the black coffin and solemnly bore it out into the old churchyard. There they towered it reverently—with sobs and weeping, with prayer and chant, and with three musket volleys—into an open grave.

And as the clods rattled down on the coffin lid of the hero, bugles and kettledrums sounded the "last call."

Then they filled up the grave, saying thus: "Earth to earth, dust to dust, ashes to ashes" and "Blessed are the dead who die in the Lord."

And over the grave, thereafter, men built a monument of stones that standeth until this day.

Then from out the murky cloud that threateningly swung aloft, broad, blinding sheets of clear red lightning streamed, followed swiftly by the terrific roar and crash of a thunderclap that seemed to shake the world.

The artillery of Heaven and Earth boomed forth their dirge in mutual concert. Men looked up in affright, hurried off home, or sought shelter in their carriages.

Grandly, the music of gods and men mingled in one last rolling requiem above the half-filled grave of the nation's ideal—the mighty man of power—the lofty and ambitious warrior who fittingly died in war.

Reverberating far and near, wild waves of music surged, while overhead, a radiant rainbow arched the sky, lending applause and splendor to the burial and the storm.

And the days and the years rolled on, and other things befel.

"Sound, sound the trumpet, blow the fife!
To all the listening world proclaim:
One crowded hour of glorious strife
Is worth an age without a name."[1]

1   Thomas Osbert Mordaunt, "The Call," *The Bee* (Edinburgh: October 12th, 1791).

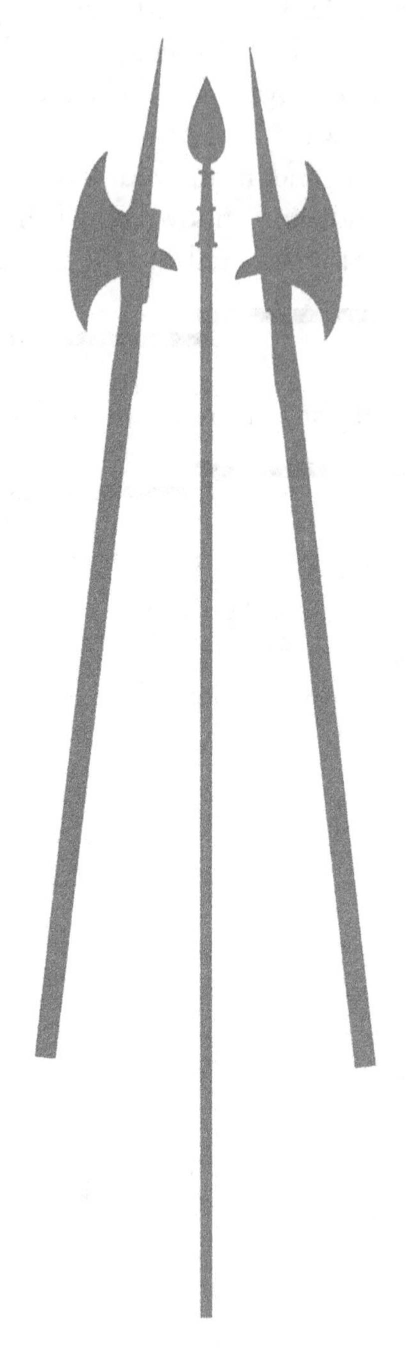

Chapter XX

THE PLAINS OF MEXICO

Come, all ye men of valor,
    Who wish to change your lot,
Who've pluck enough to venture
    Beyond your native spot.

And come, ye dashing gallants:
    With Colonel Burr we'll go
To fight for gold and glory
    On the plains of Mexico.

There're mines of gold and silver
    And lands and flocks to share
And maids with swelling bosoms,
    And health blows always there.

Leave your dull tasks unfinished;
    Put fortune to the test—
Wealth waits for men to win it
    Out on the Boundless West.

And leave behind the village,
    Where things are going slow.
Join Colonel Burr, and conquer
    The Plains of Mexico.

—Old Song, 1806[1]

1   This is a reworking of a poem titled "The Michigan Emigrant's Song." The first stanza reads "Come all ye Yankee Farmers, Who'd like to change your lot, / Who've spunk enough to travel Beyond your native spot, / And leave behind the village Where Pa and Ma do stay, / Come follow me, and settle in Michigania." The earliest found example of the poem is in the Dec. 14, 1831 issue of *New England Farmer* (Boston: Thomas W. Shepard, 1822-1835). Even *there* it states the song is reprinted from the *Detroit Courier*, which *itself* reprinted it from earlier time.

Illustration from the cover of the original edition, unattributed.